I0632343

John M. Harlan

Opinions of Mr. Justice Harlan at the Conference in Paris

of the Bering Sea Tribunal of Arbitration constituted by the Treaty of February 29,

1892, between her Britannic Majesty and the United States of America, and

composed of the following members

John M. Harlan

Opinions of Mr. Justice Harlan at the Conference in Paris
of the Bering Sea Tribunal of Arbitration constituted by the Treaty of February 29, 1892,
between her Britannic Majesty and the United States of America, and composed of the
following members

ISBN/EAN: 9783337387853

Printed in Europe, USA, Canada, Australia, Japan

Cover: Foto ©Andreas Hilbeck / pixelio.de

More available books at **www.hansebooks.com**

BERING SEA TRIBUNAL OF ARBITRATION.

OPINIONS

OF

MR. JUSTICE HARL~~AN~~

AT THE

CONFERENCE IN PARIS

OF THE

BERING SEA TRIBUNAL OF ARBITRATION, CONSTIT~~UTED~~
TREATY OF FEBRUARY 29, 1892, BETWEEN HER
MAJESTY AND THE UNITED STATES OF AMERI~~CA~~
COMPOSED OF THE FOLLOWING MEMB~~ERS~~

BARON DE COURCEL,
Senator and Ambassador of France, President of the Tri~~bunal~~

THE RIGHT HONORABLE LORD HANNE~~N~~
Of Great Britain;

THE HONORABLE SIR JOHN THOMPSO~~N~~
Minister of Justice and Attorney-General of Canada~~;~~

MR. JUSTICE HARLAN,
A Justice of the Supreme Court of the United States~~;~~

SENATOR MORGAN,
A Senator of the United States;

MARQUIS EMILIO VISCONTI VENOSTA,
Former Minister of Foreign Affairs, and Senator of the Kingdo~~m~~

And HIS EXCELLENCY GREGERS GRA~~M~~,
Minister of State of Norway.

WASHINGTON, D. C.:
GOVERNMENT PRINTING OFFICE.
1893.

TABLE OF CONTENTS.

3

[After the arguments of counsel were concluded, the Tribunal of Arbitration went into Conference to consider and determine the various matters submitted to it. All the questions discussed were examined and fully considered by the Arbitrators, and in order that they might have an opportunity to put upon record in the form of written opinions (if they so desired), the views expressed by them in conference, the Tribunal, at the close of its deliberations, adopted and embodied in the Protocol of August 14, 1893, the following resolution:

"The right is reserved to each Arbitrator to file with the secretary of this Tribunal, at any time after the adjournment, and before the first day of January, 1894, an opinion or opinions upon the questions or any of them submitted for determination, and such opinion or opinions shall be regarded as an annex to this Protocol."

The opinions below embody, substantially, what was said orally in conference by Mr. Justice Harlan upon the questions or matters alluded to in those opinions.]

PART I.

THE JURISDICTION OF THE TRIBUNAL OF ARBITRATION.

1.

REMARKS IN SUPPORT OF MOTION THAT THE TRIBUNAL FIRST DETERMINE ITS COMPETENCY OR POWERS, UNDER THE TREATY, IN RESPECT TO CERTAIN MATTERS.

(These remarks were made at the first meeting of the Arbitrators after counsel had concluded their arguments.)

Mr. PRESIDENT: It has been suggested that the Arbitrators have a full interchange of views touching the questions submitted by the treaty for determination before any formal vote is taken. I entirely approve this suggestion. We ought to have the benefit of such an interchange of views before placing upon record the conclusions we have respectively reached.

But, in my judgment, our first duty is to determine the competency of this Tribunal, under the treaty, to deal with the various matters submitted to us by the two governments. I move, therefore, that the Tribunal, before entering upon the consideration of these matters upon their merits, determine its competency, so far as it may be involved in the following questions:

1. Is it competent, under the treaty, for this Tribunal to prescribe regulations applicable to such parts of the North Pacific Ocean, outside

5

of the jurisdictional limits of the two governments, as are traversed by the seals frequenting the Pribilof Islands, if, upon the facts, regulations of that character are necessary for the proper protection and preservation of the fur seal in, or habitually resorting to, Bering Sea?

2. Is it competent, under the treaty, for this Tribunal to prescribe regulations for a closed season covering such waters of both Bering Sea and the North Pacific Ocean, outside the jurisdictional limits of the two countries, as are habitually traversed by these fur seals, and embracing the months during which fur seal may be taken in the open seas, and during which closed season all hunting of said seals in such waters shall be forbidden, provided the facts show that regulations of that character are necessary for the proper protection and preservation of the fur seal in, or habitually resorting to, Bering Sea?

We find that counsel differ widely as to the powers of the Tribunal touching the matters referred to in this motion.

The British Government, in its Counter Case, and its counsel in their printed argument, question the authority of the Tribunal, under the treaty, to prescribe regulations applicable to the North Pacific Ocean, even if it be found that regulations covering a part of that ocean are absolutely essential to the proper protection and preservation of these fur seals. And that Government and its learned counsel, at whose head is the Attorney-General of Great Britain, while not expressly disputing our power to establish a zone around the Pribilof Islands within which pelagic sealing may be entirely prohibited at all seasons, also deny that this Tribunal has any authority to prescribe regulations which, by their necessary operation, will put an end altogether to the business of hunting these seals in the open waters of Bering Sea outside of such zone or in the North Pacific Ocean.

The United States contends that the treaty requires at our hands whatever regulations are *necessary* for the proper protection and preservation of these fur seals when found outside the jurisdictional limits of the respective Governments, either in Bering Sea or in the North Pacific Ocean; that the power to prescribe such regulations is expressly conferred; and that a refusal to exert such power, if its exercise be found, under the evidence, necessary to the preservation of this race, will be a refusal to execute the treaty, and, therefore, would defeat one of its principal objects.

For one, I wish to know, before any interchange of views occurs between Arbitrators in respect to the merits of the several matters submitted, what the Tribunal deems its powers to be in regard to the subjects we are here to consider. No Arbitrator should be put in such position that it can be said that his views as to the competency of the Tribunal were withheld until the majority had expressed opinions in respect as well to the merits of the several questions of right arising under the treaty, as to the necessity of regulations for the proper protection and preservation of these seals.

If, however, it be the pleasure of Arbitrators to interchange views upon the merits of all the questions before us, not involving the jurisdiction of the Tribunal, before any vote is taken, and if they order my motion to lie upon the table for the present, I will acquiesce, if it be understood that the first recorded vote shall be upon the points embodied in that motion.

Let me say in this connection that, the arguments having been concluded, I am prepared to indicate to any Arbitrator, whenever desired by him, the conclusion reached by me touching any question before us, whether relating to the merits of the case or to the competency of the tribunal. Any such expression of views must, of course, be subject to the possibility of their being changed or modified as the result of our discussions in conference. If there are other questions of the jurisdiction of this Tribunal besides those named by me in respect to which any Arbitrator desires action by the Tribunal before coming to matters that must be covered by the award, I will coöperate with him in having such action, and this without reference to the nature of the question. If any Arbitrator wishes to know, in advance, what the Tribunal thinks as to its competency or powers, I shall deem it my duty, so far as my action can have effect, to put his mind at rest in respect to that matter.

But, Mr. President, I can not stop here without running the risk of being charged with concealing some things that are on my mind and which Arbitrators are entitled to know before acting upon this motion. My conviction is absolute that the treaty as interpreted by the British Government and its counsel, in respect to the powers of the Tribunal, is not the treaty I was asked to aid in executing. It is not the treaty Great Britain would have asked the United States to sign. It is not the treaty which the President of the United States would have approved. It is not the treaty which a single member of the Senate of the United States would have sustained by his vote. So strong is my conviction upon this subject that if this Tribunal does not conceive itself to have the power, under the treaty, to preserve this race of useful animals so far as that end may be attained by regulations applicable to the waters of both Bering Sea and the North Pacific Ocean traversed by these seals; if it decides that it can not,.for want of power, make regulations of that character, I would deem myself wanting in duty to both of the countries here represented, if I did not insist upon an adjournment of this Conference for such reasonable time as would give the respective Governments an opportunity to negotiate for a supplementary convention investing the Tribunal with full power to accomplish the object which, in every form of language, they have expressed an earnest desire to accomplish, namely, the preservation of this race of fur seals, without reference to considerations of profit or advantage to any nation or to the individuals of any nation.

I beg you to understand that I do not ask the Tribunal to say at this time what regulations are necessary to secure the preservation of these animals. If, upon examination of the evidence, it be found that regulations which in terms or by necessary operation prohibit or put an end altogether to pelagic sealing both in Bering Sea and in the North Pacific Ocean are not necessary for the proper protection and preservation of this race of animals, both countries must, in good faith, abide by that determination. I only ask that you declare in some form and in advance whether you have the power under the treaty to prescribe regulations of the character indicated by me, if the facts show them to be necessary in order to save this race from extermination. I am unwilling to remain silent upon this question of the competency of the Tribunal until I shall have ascertained what your views are on the several matters submitted for determination, and then bring up, or forbear to bring up, this question of jurisdiction, as I may agree or disagree with the views you express on the merits.

2.

UPON THE QUESTION OF THE COMPETENCY OF THE TRIBUNAL TO PRESCRIBE REGULATIONS COVERING THE WATERS OF THE NORTH PACIFIC OCEAN, AND WHICH WOULD PROHIBIT PELAGIC SEALING ENTIRELY.

(The Tribunal having on a subsequent day of its sessions voted to consider the above motion, the remarks below were made in its support.)

This Tribunal has been constituted in order that there may be an amicable settlement, by arbitration, of certain questions between the

Government of the United States of America and the Government of
Her Britannic Majesty, which are described, generally, in Article I of
the treaty of February 29, 1892,* as questions " concerning the jurisdic-

* TREATY BETWEEN THE UNITED STATES OF AMERICA AND GREAT BRITAIN CON-
CLUDED FEBRUARY 29, 1892.

The United States of America and Her Majesty the Queen of the United Kingdom
of Great Britain and Ireland, being desirous to provide for an amicable settlement of
the questions which have arisen between their respective Governments concerning
the jurisdictional rights of the United States in the waters of Bering's Sea, and concerning also the preservation of the fur-seal in, or habitually resorting to, the said
sea, and the rights of the citizens and subjects of either country as regards the
taking the fur-seal in, or habitually resorting to, the said waters, have resolved to
submit to arbitration the questions involved, and to the end of concluding a convention for that purpose have appointed as their respective Plenipotentiaries:

The President of the United States of America, James G. Blaine, Secretary of State
of the United States; and

Her Majesty the Queen of the United Kingdom of Great Britain and Ireland, Sir
Julian Pauncefote, G. C. M. G., K. C. B., Her Majesty's Envoy Extraordinary and
Minister Plenipotentiary to the United States;

Who, after having communicated to each other their respective full powers which
were found to be in due and proper form, have agreed to and concluded the following articles:

ARTICLE I. The questions which have arisen between the Government of the
United States and the Government of Her Britannic Majesty concerning the jurisdictional rights of the United States in the waters of Bering Sea, and concerning
also the preservation of the fur-seal in, or habitually resorting to, the said sea, and
the rights of the citizens and subjects of either country as regards the taking of fur-
seal in, or habitually resorting to, the said waters, shall be submitted to a tribunal
of arbitration, to be composed of seven arbitrators, who shall be appointed in the
following manner, that is to say: Two shall be named by the President of the
United States; two shall be named by her Britannic Majesty; His Excellency the
President of the French Republic shall be jointly requested by the high contracting
parties to name one; His Majesty, the King of Italy, shall be so requested to name
one; and His Majesty, the King of Sweden and Norway, shall be requested to name
one. The seven arbitrators to be so named shall be jurists of distinguished reputa-
tion in their respective countries; and the selecting powers shall be requested to
choose, if possible, jurists who are acquainted with the English language.

In case of death, absence, or incapacity to serve of any or either of the said
arbitrators, or in the event of any or either of the said arbitrators omitting or
declining or ceasing to act as such, the President of the United States, or Her Britannic Majesty, or His Excellency, the President of the French Republic, or His Majesty
the King of Italy, or His Majesty, the King of Sweden and Norway, as the case may
be, shall name, or shall be requested to name forthwith another person to act as

tional rights of the United States in the waters of Bering Sea, and concerning also the preservation of the fur seal in, or habitually resorting to, the said Sea, and the rights of the citizens and subjects of either country as regards the taking of fur seal in, or habitually resorting to, the said waters."

Article VI provides that, "in deciding the matters submitted to the arbitrators," certain points, five in number, shall be submitted to them, in order that their award may embrace a distinct decision upon each point. One of those points is embodied in the following question:

---

arbitrator in the place and stead of the arbitrator originally named by such head of a State.

And in the event of a refusal or omission for two months after receipt of the joint request from the High Contracting Parties of His Excellency, the President of the French Republic, or His Majesty, the King of Italy, or His Majesty, the King of Sweden and Norway, to name an arbitrator, either to fill the original appointment or to fill a vacancy as above provided, then in such case the appointment shall be made or the vacancy shall be filled in such manner as the High Contracting Parties shall agree.

ART. II. The arbitrators shall meet at Paris within twenty days after the delivery of the counter cases mentioned in Article IV, and shall proceed impartially and carefully to examine and decide the questions that have been or shall be laid before them as herein provided on the part of the Governments of the United States and Her Britannic Majesty, respectively. All questions considered by the tribunal, including the final decision, shall be determined by a majority of all the arbitrators.

Each of the High Contracting Parties shall also name one person to attend the tribunal as its agent to represent it generally in all matters connected with the arbitration.

ART. III. The printed case of each of the two parties, accompanied by the documents, the official correspondence, and other evidence on which each relies, shall be delivered in duplicate to each of the arbitrators and to the agent of the other party as soon as may be after the appointment of the members of the tribunal, but within a period not exceeding four months from the date of the exchange of the ratifications of this treaty.

ART. IV. Within three months after the delivery on both sides of the printed case, either party may, in like manner deliver in duplicate to each of the said arbitrators, and to the agent of the other party, a counter case, and additional documents, correspondence, and evidence so presented by the other party.

If, however, in consequence of the distance of the place from which the evidence to be presented is to be procured, either party shall, within thirty days after the receipt by its agent of the case of the other party, give notice to the other party that it requires additional time for the delivery of such counter case, documents, correspondence, and evidence, such additional time so indicated, but not exceeding sixty days beyond the three months in this article provided, shall be allowed.

If, in the case submitted to the arbitrators, either party shall have specified or alluded to any report or document in its own exclusive possession, without annexing

"5. Has the United States any right, and if so, what right, of protection or property in the fur seals frequenting the islands of the United States in Bering Sea when such seals are found outside the ordinary three-mile limit?"

Article VII is in these words:

"If the determination of the foregoing questions as to the exclusive jurisdiction of the United States shall leave the subject in such position that the concurrence of Great Britain is necessary to the establishment of Regulations for the proper protection and preservation of the

a copy, such party shall be bound, if the other party thinks proper to apply for it, to furnish that party with a copy thereof; and either party may call upon the other, through the arbitrators, to produce the originals or certified copies of any papers adduced as evidence, giving in each instance notice thereof within thirty days after delivery of the case; and the original or copy so requested shall be delivered as soon as may be, and within a period not exceeding forty days after receipt of notice.

ART. V. It shall be the duty of the agent of each party, within one month after the expiration of the time limited for the delivery of the counter case on both sides, to deliver in duplicate to each of the said arbitrators and to the agent of the other party a printed argument showing the points and referring to the evidence upon which his Government relies, and either party may also support the same before the arbitrators by oral argument of counsel; and the arbitrators may, if they desire further elucidation with regard to any point, require a written or printed statement or argument, or oral argument of counsel, upon it; but in such case the other party shall be entitled to reply, either orally or in writing, as the case may be.

ART. VI. In deciding the matters submitted to the arbitrators, it is agreed that the following five points shall be submitted to them, in order that their award shall embrace a distinct decision upon each of said five points, to wit:

1. What exclusive jurisdiction in the sea now known as the Bering Sea, and what exclusive rights in the seal fisheries therein, did Russia assert and exercise prior and up to the time of the cession of Alaska to the United States?

2. How far were these claims of jurisdiction as to the seal fisheries recognized and conceded by Great Britain?

3. Was the body of water now known as the Bering Sea included in the phrase "Pacific Ocean," as used in the treaty of 1825 between Great Britain and Russia; and what rights, if any, in the Bering Sea were held and exclusively exercised by Russia after said treaty?

4. Did all the rights of Russia as to jurisdiction, and as to the seal fisheries in Bering Sea east of the water boundary, in the treaty between the United States and Russia of the 30th March, 1867, pass unimpaired to the United States under that treaty?

5. Has the United States any right, and if so, what right of protection or property in the fur-seals frequenting the islands of the United States in Bering Sea, when such seals are found outside the ordinary 3-mile limit?

ART. VII. If the determination of the foregoing questions as to the exclusive jurisdiction of the United States shall leave the subject in such position that the

12

fur seal in, or habitually resorting to, the Bering Sea, the Arbitrators shall then determine what concurrent Regulations outside the jurisdictional limits of the respective Governments are necessary and over what waters such Regulations should extend, and to aid them in that determination the report of a Joint Commission to be appointed by the respective Governments shall be laid before them, with such other evidence as either Government may submit. The High Contracting Parties furthermore agree to coöperate in securing the adhesion of other powers to such Regulations."

Article XIV declares that "the High Contracting Parties engage to consider the result of the proceedings of the Tribunal of Arbitration,

concurrence of Great Britain is necessary to the establishment of regulations for the proper protection and preservation of the fur-seal in, or habitually resorting to, the Bering Sea, the arbitrators shall then determine what concurrent regulations outside the jurisdictional limits of the respective Governments are necessary, and over what waters such regulations should extend, and to aid them in that determination, the report of a Joint Commission to be appointed by the respective Governments shall be laid before them, with such other evidence as either Government may submit.

The High Contracting Parties furthermore agree to coöperate in securing the adhesion of other Powers to such regulations.

ART. VIII. The High Contracting Parties having found themselves unable to agree upon a reference which shall include the question of the liability of each for the injuries alleged to have been sustained by the other, or by its citizens, in connection with the claims presented and urged by it; and being solicitous that this subordinate question should not interrupt or longer delay the submission and determination of the main questions, do agree that either party may submit to the arbitrators any question of fact involved in said claims and ask for a finding thereon, the question of the liability of either Government upon the facts found to be the subject of further negotiation.

ART. IX. The High Contracting Parties have agreed to appoint two commissioners on the part of each Government to make the joint investigation and report contemplated in the preceding Article VII, and to include the terms of the said agreement in the convention, to the end that the joint and several reports and recommendations of said commissioners may be in due form submitted to the arbitrators, should the contingency therefor arise, the said agreement is accordingly herein included as follows:

Each Government shall appoint two commissioners to investigate conjointly with the commissioners of the other Government all the facts having relation to seal life in Bering Sea, and the measures necessary for its proper protection and preservation.

The four commissioners shall, so far as they may be able to agree, make a joint report to each of the two Governments, and they shall also report, either jointly or

as a full, perfect, and final settlement of all the questions referred to the Arbitrators."

Throughout the whole of the negotiations resulting in the treaty, the two Governments, by their accredited representatives, expressed an earnest desire for the proper protection and preservation of the fur seals which had their breeding grounds on Pribilof Islands in Bering Sea, as well as their willingness to unite in the enforcement against their respective citizens or subjects of all measures found necessary to prevent the extermination of that race of animals. The record before us furnishes conclusive evidence of these facts.

As early as November 12, 1887, Mr. Phelps, United States Minister

---

severally, to each Government on any points upon which they may be unable to agree.

These reports shall not be made public until they shall be submitted to the arbitrators, or it shall appear that the contingency of their being used by the arbitrators can not arise.

ART. X. Each Government shall pay the expenses of its members of the joint commission in the investigation referred to in the preceding article.

ART. XI. The decisions of the tribunal shall, if possible, be made within three months from the close of the argument on both sides.

It shall be made in writing and dated, and shall be signed by the arbitrators who may assent to it.

The decision shall be in duplicate, one copy whereof shall be delivered to the agent of the United States for his Government, and the other copy shall be delivered to the agent of Great Britain for his Government.

ART. XII. Each Government shall pay its own agents and provide for the proper remuneration of the counsel employed by it, and of the arbitrators appointed by it, and for the expense of preparing and submitting its case to the tribunal. All other expenses connected with the arbitration shall be defrayed by the two Government in equal moieties.

ART. XIII. The arbitrators shall keep an accurate record of their proceedings, and may appoint and employ the necessary officers to assist them.

ART. XIV. The High Contracting Parties engaged to consider the result of the proceedings of the tribunal of arbitration, as a full, perfect, and final settlement of all the questions referred to the arbitrators.

ART. XV. The present treaty shall be duly ratified by the President of the United States of America, by and with the advice and consent of the Senate thereof, and by Her Britannic Majesty; and the ratification shall be exchanged either at Washington or at London within six months from the date hereof, or earlier if possible.

In faith whereof we, the respective Plenipotentiaries, have signed this treaty and have hereunto affixed our seals.

Done in duplicate at Washington the twenty-ninth day of February, one thousand eight hundred and ninety-two.　　　　JAMES G. BLAINE.　[SEAL.]

　　　　JULIAN PAUNCEFOTE.　[SEAL.]

at London, had an interview with the Marquis of Salisbury, British Secretary of State for Foreign Affairs, in which the former proposed, on the part of the Government of the United States, that by mutual agreement of the two Governments a code of regulations be adopted for the preservation of the seals in Bering Sea from destruction at improper times and by improper means by the citizens of either country— such agreement to be entirely irrespective of any questions of conflicting jurisdiction in those waters. In this view his lordship promptly acquiesced, and suggested that the American minister obtain from his Government and submit a sketch of a system of regulations that would be adequate for that purpose. *U. S. Case, App. Vol. I, p. 171.*

The American Secretary of State, Mr. Bayard, being informed of this interview, wrote to Mr. Phelps, under date of February 7, 1888, suggesting that the only way to prevent the destruction of the seals appeared to be for the United States, Great Britain, and other interested powers to take concerted action restraining their citizens or subjects from killing them with firearms, or other destructive weapons, "north of 50° of north latitude, and between 160° of longitude west and 170° of longitude east from Greenwich, during the period intervening between April 15 and November 1. To prevent the killing within a marine belt of 40 or 50 miles from the islands during that period would be ineffectual as a preservative measure. This would clearly be so during the approach of the seals to the islands. And after their arrival there such a limit of protection would also be insufficient, since the rapid progress of the seals through the water enables them to go great distances from the islands in so short a time that it has been calculated that an ordinary seal could go to the Aleutian Islands and back, in all a distance of 300 or 400 miles, in less than two days."

In the same letter Mr. Bayard, referring to the threatened extermination of these seals by pelagic sealers, using firearms, nets, and other destructive implements, said : "That the extermination of the fur seals must soon take place unless they are protected from destruction in Bering Sea is shown by the fate of the animal in other parts of the world in the absence of concerted action among the nations interested for its preservation. * * * It is manifestly for the interests of all nations that so deplorable a thing should not be allowed to occur. As has already been stated, on the Pribilof Islands this Government strictly limits the number of seals that may be killed under its own lease to an American company, and citizens of the United States have, during the past year, been arrested and ten American vessels seized for killing fur seals in Bering Sea. England, however, has an especially great interest in this matter in addition to that which she must feel in preventing the extermination of an animal which contributed so much to the gain and comfort of her people. Nearly all undressed fur seal skins are sent to London, where they are dressed and dyed for the market and where many of them are sold." *U. S. Case, App. Vol. I, pp. 173, 174.*

This proposal was communicated to the Marquis of Salisbury and became the subject of conference between the representatives of Great Britain, the United States, and Russia. U. S. Case, App., Vol. I, p. 175. A counter proposition was made by the Marquis of Salisbury to the effect that " with a view to meeting the Russian Goverment's wishes respecting the waters surrounding Robben Island," the " whole of Bering Sea, those portions of the Sea of Okhotsk, and of the Pacific Ocean north of north latitude 47° should be included in the proposed arrangement." He further said " that the period proposed by the United States for a closed time—April 15 to November 1—might interfere with the trade longer than absolutely necessary for the protection of the seals, and he suggested October 1, instead of a month later, as the termination of the period of seal protection." *U. S. Case, Vol. I, App., p. 179.*

The result of the above conference is thus stated in a letter from the Marquis of Salisbury to the British Minister at Washington: "At this preliminary discussion it was *decided, provisionally, in order to furnish a basis for negotiation,* and without definitely pledging our Governments, that the space to be covered by the proposed convention should be *the sea between America and Russia north of the forty-seventh degree of latitude;* that the close time should extend from the 15th April to the 1st November; that during that time the slaughter of all seals should be forbidden, and vessels engaged in it should be liable to seizure by the cruisers of any of the three powers, and should be taken to the port of their own nationality for condemnation; that the traffic in arms, alcohol, and powder should be prohibited in all the islands of those seas; and that, as soon as the three powers had concluded a convention, they should join in submitting it for the assent of the other maritime powers of the northern seas. The United States Chargé d'Affaires was exceedingly earnest in pressing on us the importance of dispatch, on account of the inconceivable slaughter that had been and still was going on in these seas. He stated that, in addition to the vast quantity brought to market, it was a common practice for those engaged in the trade to shoot all seals they might meet in the open sea, and that of these a great number sank so that their skins could not be recovered." A similar letter was sent to Sir R. Morier, British Ambassador at St. Petersburg. *British Case, App., Vol. III, p. 196; U. S. Case, App., Vol. I, p. 238.*

The close time, thus provisionally decided upon, covered, as will be seen, not only Bering Sea, but the entire North Pacific Ocean between America and Russia, north of the forty-seventh degree of latitude.

Mr. Bayard, writing to Mr. White, the United States Chargé d'Affaires at London, under date of May 1, 1888, said: "As you have already been instructed, the Department does not object to the inclusion of the Sea of Okhotsk, or so much of it as may be necessary, in the arrangement for the protection of the seals. Nor is it thought absolutely necessary to insist on the extension of the close season till the 1st of November. Only such a period is desired as may be requisite for the end in view. But in order that success may be assured in the efforts of the various governments interested in the protection of the seals, it seems advisable to take the 15th of October instead of the 1st as the date of the close season, although, as I am now advised, the 1st of November would be safer. *U. S. Case, App., Vol. I, p. 180.*

In the course of a friendly discussion, in November, 1889, between Mr. Blaine, the American Secretary of State, and Sir Julian Pauncefote, British Minister accredited to the United States, the former (according to the report of that discussion made by the latter to the Marquis of Salisbury) said: "The fur seal was a species most valuable to mankind, and the Bering's Sea was its last stronghold. The United States had bought the islands in that sea to which these creatures periodically resort to lay their young, and now Canadian fishermen step in and slaughter the seals on their passage to the islands, without taking heed of the warnings given by Canadian officials themselves, that the result must inevitably be the extermination of the species. This was an abuse, not only reprehensible in itself and opposed to the interests of mankind, but an infraction of the rights of the United States. It inflicted, moreover, a serious injury on a neighboring and friendly State, by depriving it of the fruits of an industry on which vast sums of money had been expended, and which had long been pursued exclusively, and for the general benefit. The case was so strong as to necessitate measures of self-defense for the vindication of the rights of the United States and the protection of this valuable fishery from destruction."

Mr. Blaine's tone during this discussion (Sir Julian Pauncefote also reported) was most friendly throughout, manifesting "a strong desire to let all questions of legal right and international law disappear in an agreement for a close season, which he believes to be urgently called for in the common interest." In reply to his observations, the British Minister, among other things, said: " As regarded the question of fact, namely, the danger of extermination of the fur-seal species, and the necessity for a 'close season,'there was, unfortunately, a conflict of opinion. But if, upon a further and more complete examination of the evidence, Her Majesty's Government should come to the conclusion that a 'close season' is really necessary, and if an agreement should be arrived at on the subject, all differences on questions of legal rights would *ipso facto* disappear." *British Case, App., Vol. III, pp. 350, 351.*

In a subsequent letter, written in April, 1890 by Sir Julian Pauncefote to Mr. Blaine, the former said: " It has been admitted, from the commencement, that the sole object of the negotiation is *the preservation of the fur seal species for the benefit of mankind,* and that no considerations of advantage to any particular nation, or of benefit to any private interest, should enter into the question." *U. S. Case, App., Vol. I, p. 201, 205.* Under date of June 3, 1890, Sir Julian, writing to Mr. Blaine, observed: " Her Majesty's Government have always been willing, without pledging themselves to details on the questions of area and date, to carry on negotiations, hoping thereby to come to some arrangement for such a close season *as is necessary in order to preserve the seal species from extinction,* but the provisions of such an arrangement would always require legislative sanction so that the measures thereby determined may be enforced." *U. S. Case, App., Vol. I, p. 220.*

The Marquis of Salisbury, in a letter to Sir Julian Pauncefote of June 20, 1890, inclosing, among other documents, a copy of the above letter of April 16, 1888, addressed to the British representatives at Washington and St. Petersburg: "Her Majesty's Government always have been, and are still, anxious for the arrangement of a convention which shall provide *whatever close time in whatever localities is necessary for the preservation of the fur seal species." British Case, App., Vol. III, p. 192; U. S. Case, App., Vol. I, p. 237.*

11492——2

In his letter to Sir Julian Pauncefote of December 17, 1890, Mr. Blaine said:

"The United States, in protecting the seal fisheries, will not interfere with a single sail of commerce on any sea of the globe.

"It will mean something tangible, in the President's opinion, if Great Britain will consent to arbitrate the real questions which have been under discussion between the two Governments for the last four years. I shall endeavor to state what, in the judgment of the President, those issues are:

"First. What exclusive jurisdiction in the sea now known as the Bering Sea, and what exclusive rights in the seal fisheries therein did Russia assert and exercise prior and up to the time of the cession of Alaska to the United States?

"Second. How far were these claims of jurisdiction as to the seal fisheries recognized and conceded by Great Britain?

"Third. Was the body of water now known as the Bering Sea included in the phrase 'Pacific Ocean' as used in the treaty of 1825 between Great Britain and Russia; and what rights, if any, in the Bering Sea were given or conceded to Great Britain by the said treaty?

"Fourth. Did not all the rights of Russia as to jurisdiction, and as to the seal fisheries in Bering Sea east of the water boundary, in the treaty between the United States and Russia of March 30, 1867, pass unimpaired to the United States under that treaty?

"Fifth. What are now the rights of the United States as to the fur seal fisheries in the waters of the Bering Sea outside of the ordinary territorial limits, whether such rights grow out of the cession by Russia of any special rights or jurisdiction held by her in such fisheries or in the waters of Bering Sea, or out of the ownership of the breeding islands and the habits of the seal in resorting thither and rearing their young thereon and going out from the islands for food, or out of any other fact or incident connected with the relation of those seal fisheries to the territorial possessions of the United States?

"Sixth. If the determination of the foregoing questions shall leave the subject in such position that the concurrence of Great Britain is necessary in prescribing regulations for the killing of the fur seal in any part of the waters of Bering Sea then it shall be further determined: First, how far, if at all, outside the ordinary territorial limits, it is necessary that the United States should exercise an exclusive jurisdiction in order to protect the seal for the time living upon the islands of the United States and feeding therefrom. Second, whether a closed season (during which the killing of seals in the waters of Bering Sea outside the ordinary territorial limits shall be prohibited) is necessary to save the seal-fishing industry, so valuable and important to mankind, from deterioration or destruction. And if so, third, what months or parts of months should be included in such season, and over what waters it should extend." *U. S. Case, App., Vol. I, p. 285, 286.*

The Marquis of Salisbury, in a letter of February 21, 1891, to Sir Julian Pauncefote, expressed his assent to the first, second, and fourth questions propounded by Mr. Blaine, and, after criticising the third and fifth, proceeded: "The sixth question, which deals with the issues that will arise in case the controversy should be decided in favor of Great Britain, would perhaps more fitly form the subject of a separate reference. Her Majesty's Government have no objection to refer the general question of a close time to arbitration, or to ascertain by that means how far the enactment of such a provision is necessary for the preservation of the seal species; but any such reference ought not to contain words appearing to attribute special and abnormal rights in the matter to the United States." *British Case, App., Vol. III, pt. 2, p. 89; U. S. Case, App., Vol. I, p. 294.*

Replying, under date of April 14, 1891, Mr. Blaine observed that although Lord Salisbury suggested a different mode of procedure from that embodied in the sixth question, the President did not understand him as objecting to the question. He restated all the questions, leaving the first, second, fourth, and sixth as originally proposed, and reforming the third and fifth questions so as to read:

"Third. Was the body of water now known as the Bering Sea included in the phrase 'Pacific Ocean' as used in the treaty of 1825 between Great Britain and Russia, and what rights, if any, in the Bering Sea were held and exclusively exercised by Russia after said Treaty?

"Fifth. Has the United States any right, and if so what right, of protection or property in the fur seals frequenting the islands of the United States in Bering Sea when such seals are found outside the ordinary three-mile limit?" *U. S. Case, App., Vol. I, p. 295.*

At this period of the negotiations a correspondence intervened with respect to a *modus vivendi* between the two Governments, regulating the taking of fur seals in Bering Sea during the sealing season of

1891. While that matter was being discussed Sir Julian Pauncefote, under date of June 3, 1891, notified the Government of the United States that Her Majesty's Government were prepared to assent to the first five questions proposed to be submitted to arbitration in Mr. Blaine's note of April 14, 1891. But he added: "Her Majesty's Government can not give their assent to the sixth question formulated in that note. In lieu thereof they propose the appointment of a commission to consist of four experts, of whom two shall be nominated by each Government, and a chairman who shall be nominated by the Arbitrators. The Commission shall examine and report on the question which follows: 'For the purpose of preserving the fur seal race in Bering Sea from extermination, what international arrangements, if any, are necessary between Great Britain and the United States and Russia or any other power?'" *U. S. Case, App., Vol. I, p. 305.*

Then followed some correspondence between Mr. Wharton, Acting Secretary of State for the United States, and Sir Julian Pauncefote, in reference to the proposed *modus vivendi* for 1891. The terms of that *modus vivendi*, as proposed by the United States, were communicated to Lord Salisbury. They were returned by the latter with certain modifications and additions. The fifth paragraph of the agreement proposed by Lord Salisbury was as follows: "(5) A commission of four experts, two nominated by each Government, and a chairman nominated by the Arbitrators, if appointed, and if not, by the aforesaid commission, shall examine and report on the following question: 'What international arrangements, if any, between Great Britain and the United States and Russia or any other power are necessary for the purpose of preserving the fur seal race in the Northern Pacific Ocean from extermination?'" *U. S. Case, App., Vol. I, p. 311.*

It thus appears that the British Government proposed, in connection with the *modus vivendi* for 1891, to ascertain, by means of experts representing the two Governments, what international arrangements were necessary "for the purpose of preserving the fur seal race in the *Northern Pacific Ocean* from extermination."

President Harrison, however, insisted upon an agreement (such as he had proposed) relating only to matters that were appropriate in a *modus vivendi*.

Sir Julian Pauncefote wrote to Mr. Wharton, expressing the regret of the Marquis of Salisbury that his proposed modifications had not been accepted. But he observed: "Nevertheless, in view of the urgency of the case, his lordship is disposed to authorize me to sign the agreement in the precise terms formulated in your note of June 9, provided the question of a joint commission be not left in doubt, and that your Government will give an assurance in some form that they will concur in a reference to a joint commission to ascertain what permanent measures are necessary for the preservation of the fur seal species *in the Northern Pacific Ocean.*" *U. S. Case, App., Vol. I, p. 315.*

To this letter Mr. Wharton replied on the same day, as follows: "Sir: I have the honor to acknowledge the receipt of your note of to-day's date, and in reply I am directed by the President to say that the Government of the United States, recognizing the fact that full and adequate measures for the protection of seal life should embrace the *whole* of Bering Sea *and portions of the North Pacific Ocean*, will have no hesitancy in agreeing, in connection with Her Majesty's Government, to the appointment of a joint commission to ascertain what permanent measures are necessary *for the preservation of the seal species in the waters referred to*, such an agreement to be signed simultaneously with the convention for arbitration, and to be without prejudice to the questions to be submitted to the arbitrators. A full reply to your note of June 3 relating to the terms of arbitration will not be long delayed." *U. S. Case, App., Vol. I, pp. 315,316.*

Under date of June 13, 1891, Sir Julian Pauncefote wrote to Mr. Wharton: "I lost no time in telegraphing to the Marquis of Salisbury the contents of your note of June 11 conveying the assent of your Government to the appointment, in connection with Her Majesty's Government, of a joint commission for the purpose mentioned in my note to you of the same date, such agreement to be signed simultaneously with the convention for arbitration and to be without prejudice to the questions to be submitted to the arbitrators. I informed his lordship at the same time that, in handing me the note under reply, you had assured me that the President was anxious that the commission should be appointed in time to commence its work this season, and that your Government would, on that account, use their utmost efforts to expedite the signature of the arbitration convention. I now have the honor to inform you that I have this day received a telegraphic reply from Lord Salisbury in which, while conveying to me authority to sign the proposed agreement for a *modus vivendi* contained in your note of June 9, his lordship desires me to place on record that it is signed by me on the clear understanding that the joint commission will be appointed without delay. On th it understanding, therefore. I shall be prepared to attend at the State Department for the purpose of signing the agreement at such time as you may be good enough to appoint." *U. S. Case, Vol. 1, App., p. 316.*

On the same day Mr. Wharton wrote to Sir Julian Pauncefote: "The President directs me to say, in response to your note of this date, that his assent to the proposition for a joint commission, as expressed in my note of June 9, was given in the expectation that both Governments would use every proper effort to adjust the remaining points of difference in the general correspondence relating to arbitration, and to agree upon the definite terms of a submission and of the appointment of a joint commission without unnecessary delay. He is glad that an agreement has finally been reached for the pending season; and I beg to say that if you will call at the Department at 10 o'clock Monday next, I will be glad to put into writing and give formal attestation to the *modus vivendi* which has been agreed upon." *U. S. Case, App., Vol. 1, p. 316.*

Under the assurance thus exacted by and given to the British Government the *modus vivendi* for 1891 was signed and the negotiations in respect to the matters to be submitted to arbitration were resumed.

Mr. Wharton, under date of June 25, 1891, addressed a communication to Sir Julian Pauncefote, in which, after referring to the agreement of the parties in respect to the first five questions and to the objection that Lord Salisbury had made to the sixth question, as formulated by Mr. Blaine, said:

"I am now directed by the President to submit the following, which he thinks avoids the objection urged by Lord Salisbury:

(6) If the determination of the foregoing questions as to the exclusive jurisdiction of the United States shall leave the subject in such position that the concurrence of Great Britain is necessary to the establishment of regulations for the proper protection and preservation of the fur seal in, *or habitually resorting to,* the Bering Sea, the arbitrators shall then determine what concurrent regulations outside the jurisdictional limits of the respective Governments are necessary, *and over what waters such regulations should extend;* and to aid them in that determination the report of the Joint Commission to be appointed by the respective Governments shall be laid before them, with such other evidence as either Government may submit. The contracting parties furthermore agree to coöperate in securing the adhesion of other powers to such regulations."

In the same letter Mr. Wharton submitted a proposal for the appointment of a Joint Commission by the two Governments, in accordance with the assurance given by the President in the letter of June 11, 1891, from Mr. Wharton to Sir Julian Pauncefote. The terms of this proposal were accepted by Lord Salisbury, and they appear in Article IX of the treaty. *U. S. Case, App., Vol. I, pp. 319, 320.*

The British Government accepted the sixth question as thus formulated, and that question constitutes Article VII of the treaty. I do not find in any part of the diplomatic correspondence any criticism by representatives of the British Government of that question as last formulated.

Other evidence throws light upon the inquiry whether it was not well understood by the British Government, after the signing of the *modus vivendi* for 1891, if not before, that the inquiry as to what was necessary to protect the fur seal race embraced both Bering Sea and the North Pacific Ocean.

The commission issued June 15, 1891, by Her Majesty to the two commissioners appointed to investigate seal life recited that they were appointed "for the purpose of inquiry into the conditions of seal life and the precautions necessary for preventing the extermination of the *fur seal species* in Bering Sea and *other parts of the North Pacific Ocean.*" Substantially the same recitals were made in the letter of instructions issued to those commissioners by the Marquis of Salisbury under date of June 24, 1891. Subsequently, on the 15th January, 1892, after the two Governments had agreed in writing upon the terms embodied in and constituting Articles VI, VII, VIII, and IX of the treaty, the Marquis of Salisbury issued another letter of instructions to the British Commissioners, in which he said: "There are, however, a few points to which Her Majesty's Government consider it desirable that your special attention should be directed. You will observe that it is intended that the report of the Joint Commissioners shall embrace recommendations as to all measures that should be adopted *for the preservation of seal life.* For this purpose it will be necessary to consider what Regulations may seem advisable, whether within the jurisdictional limits of the United States and Canada, or outside those limits. The Regulations which the Commissioners may recommend for adoption within the respective jurisdictions of the two countries will, of course, be matter for the consideration of the respective Governments, while the regulations affecting waters outside the territorial limits will have to be considered under clause 6 of the Arbitration Agreement* [Art. 7 of the Treaty] in the event of a decision being given by the Arbitrators against the claim of exclusive jurisdiction put forward on behalf of the United States. The Report is to be presented in the first instance to the two Governments for their consideration, and is subsequently to be laid by those Governments before the Arbitrators to assist them in determining the more restricted question as to what, if any, Regulations are essential for the protection of the *fur-bearing seals outside the territorial jurisdiction of the two countries.*" *British Comm. Report,* p. VII.

And the report of these commissioners, presented to the British Government June 21, 1892, recites that they were appointed to inquire "into the conditions of seal life and the precautions necessary for preventing the extermination of the *fur seal species* in Bering Sea *and other parts of the North Pacific Ocean.*" In the same report will be found "a general view of the conclusions at which we [the British Commissioners] have arrived as to the condition of seal life *in the North Pacific Ocean,* and as to the measures necessary for the preservation of *the fur seal industry.*" It may be stated, in addition, that the American Commissioners, Profs. Mendenhall and Merriam, were appointed by the President "to proceed to the Pribilof Islands and to make certain investigations of the facts relative to seal life, with a view to ascertain what permanent measures are necessary for the preservation of the fur seal in Bering Sea *and the North Pacific Ocean.*" *U. S. Case, 311.*

It thus appears from the diplomatic correspondence before us and by the action of the two Governments—

1. That each Government, from the beginning to the end of the negotiations resulting in the treaty, expressed not only an earnest desire that the fur seals be protected against extermination, but their willingness to adopt such measures as were necessary to prevent the destruction of these animals by its citizens or subjects, and that their action should be concurrent;

2. That the British Government, in the early period of these negotiations, agreed, provisionally and as a basis of negotiations, that a closed time be established, from April 1 to November 1, during which the slaughter of all seals be forbidden "*in the sea between America and Russia north of the forty-seventh degree of latitude;*"

*This agreement was signed December 18, 1891. The treaty was not signed until February 29, 1892.

3. That while the original proposition of Lord Salisbury was for a joint commission to ascertain what international arrangements were necessary " for the purpose of preserving the fur seal race in Bering Sea from extermination," he subsequently modified that position, so as to require that commission to ascertain what international arrangements were necessary " for the purpose of preserving the fur seal in *the Northern Pacific Ocean* from extermination;"

4. That the British Government made a condition of its agreeing to the proposed *modus vivendi* for 1891, relating to Bering Sea, that the President of the United States would give an assurance in some form that his Government would concur in a reference to a joint commission " to ascertain what permanent measures are necessary for the preservation of the fur seal species in *the Northern Pacific Ocean*," which assurance the President formally gave to the British Government, explicitly stating at the time that the Government of the United States recognized "the fact that full and adequate measures for the protection of seal life should embrace the whole of Bering Sea and *parts of the North Pacific Ocean;*" and,

5. That the Government of the United States, having in view the explicit declaration of Sir Julian Pauncefote, that "the sole object of the negotiation is the preservation of the fur seal species for the benefit of mankind," and the equally explicit declarations of Lord Salisbury that her Majesty's Government was anxious for the arrangement of a convention which "shall provide whatever close time *in whatever localities is necessary for the preservation of the fur seal species,*" and ascertain, by arbitration, how far such a close time was necessary " for the preservation of the fur seal species," and in order that the Arbitrators, if appointed, might consider measures for the protection of seal life "throughout the whole of Bering Sea *and portions of the Northern Pacific Ocean*," modified the sixth question, as originally formulated, and, instead of concurrent regulations "for the killing of the fur seals in any part of the Bering Sea," outside of ordinary territorial limits, as was first proposed, provided for concurrent regulations (if the concurrence of Great Britain was found to be necessary) "for the proper protection and preservation of the fur seal in, *or habitually resorting to,* the Bering Sea."

It could not have escaped the attention of Lord Salisbury that the effect of this modification of the sixth question was, beyond all question, to enable this Tribunal to prescribe concurrent regulations to protect and preserve all fur seals that habitually resorted to the islands of the United States in Bering Sea, although they might not remain during the whole of each year in that sea. And the modification which the United States made of the sixth question brought it into harmony with the fifth question, previously assented to, which involved an inquiry as to whether the United States has "any right, and if so what right, of protection or property in the fur seal *frequenting the islands of the United States in Bering Sea* when such seals are found outside the ordinary three-mile limit?" These seals do not the less frequent those islands, nor the less habitually resort to Bering Sea, because their habit—as both Governments well knew—was, in the fall of every year, at about the same time, to leave their breeding grounds at the Pribilof Islands and go to the south of the Aleutian Islands into the North Pacific Ocean, from which ocean, each year and at the same time, they returned to Bering Sea and to their established breeding grounds on the islands of St. Paul and St. George.

But this is not all that is suggested by the modification made of the sixth question. Recurring to the words of that question, in its original form, it will be seen that one of the matters to be determined in the event the concurrence of Great Britain was necessary in prescribing regulations for the "killing" of fur seals in the waters of Bering Sea was whether a "closed season (during which the killing of fur-seals in the waters of Bering Sea outside the ordinary territorial limits shall be prohibited) is necessary to save the seal-fishing industry, so valuable and important to mankind, from deterioration or destruction." Here we have the suggestion by the United States of a closed season, during which the taking of those seals might be entirely prohibited. What was the reply of the Marquis of Salisbury to this suggestion? It was that if the reference to arbitration did not contain "words which attribute special and abnormal rights to the United States." Her Majesty's Government had "no objection to refer the general question of a closed time to arbitration, or to ascertain by that means how far the enactment of such a provision is necessary *for the preservation of the seal species.*" In other words, he did not object to a prohibition of pelagic sealing during such closed time as was found to be necessary for the preservation of the species. And it is a fact of much significance that while the sixth question referred to the concurrence of Great Britain in prescribing regulations for the "killing" of the fur seals in the waters of Bering-Sea that question, as finally propounded, omitted any words concerning regulations for the killing of seals in any particular waters, but made the establishment of regulations by the Arbitrators depend alone upon their determination in respect "to the exclusive jurisdiction of the United States," and the necessity, resulting from that determination, of prescribing concurrent regulations, not for the killing of fur seal, but "for the proper protection and preservation of the fur seal in, or habitually resorting to, the waters of Bering Sea." This change of phraseology seems plainly to indicate that the main purpose was to protect the seals by whatever means were found to be necessary. And such must have been the desire; for what object could there have been to regulate the taking of animals unless their existence was to be preserved?

Much stress has been laid upon isolated passages in communications emanating from the State Department of the United States in which it was said, in different forms of language, that the *area of contention* between Great Britain and the United States related only to Bering Sea. That statement was, in a certain sense, strictly accurate, for the dispute between the two Governments arose out of seizures made in that sea. The legality of those seizures was the principal and vital matter then in controversy. No seizures had then been made in the North Pacific Ocean. And these statements, as to the area of contention, were made quite naturally in view of the fact, plainly disclosed by the evidence, that Mr. Blaine, at one time and before the facts in connection with seal life in Bering Sea were fully developed, was of opinion that a zone of 20 marine leagues around the Pribilof Islands, within which pelagic sealing should be prohibited, would be all that was necessary in order to preserve these fur seals from extermination.

Some stress is also laid on the fact that the *modus vivendi* for 1891 and that for 1892 only related to Bering Sea; and, consequently, it is argued, the two governments did not contemplate regulations applicable to the Northern Pacific Ocean. Those who so argue forget that the *modus vivendi* for 1891 was not signed until June 15, 1891, by which time the sealing vessels had all left for the sealing grounds, and a large number, if not the greater part, of the fur seals had then passed from the North Pacific Ocean into Bering Sea, and probably reached their breeding grounds on the Pribilof Islands. In respect to the *modus vivendi* for 1892 it need only be said that Mr. Blaine endeavored to have it extended to the North Pacific Ocean as well as to Bering Sea. He was, no doubt, moved to this course by the fact that the two Governments, as early as December 18, 1891, had signed the text of the articles that were to go into the treaty, thereafter to be put in form, and by one of which articles it was required that the regulations prescribed by the arbitrators should look to the proper protection and preservation, not simply of the fur seals in Bering Sea, but such as habitually resorted to that sea.

He was also aware of the fact that as early as June 11, 1891, in giving assurance that he would unite in the appointment of a Joint Commission to ascertain what measures were necessary for the preservation of these fur seals, the President had distinctly informed the British Minister that adequate measures to that end "should embrace the whole of Bering Sea and portions of the North Pacific Ocean." So, in his letter to Sir Julian Pauncefote of February 24, 1892, before the treaty was signed, Mr. Blaine, referring to the proposed *modus vivendi* for 1892, said: "If Her Majesty's Government would make her efforts most effective, the sealing in the North Pacific Ocean should be forbidden; for there the slaughter of the mothers heavy with young is greatest. This would require a notice to the large number of sealers who are preparing to go forth from British Columbia. The number is said to be greater than ever before, and without any law to regulate the killing of seals the destruction will be immense. All this suggests the need of an effective *modus*. Holding an arbitration in regard to the rightful mode of taking seals, while their destruction goes forward, would be as if, while an arbitration to the title of land were in progress, one party should remove all the timber." Mr. Blaine would not have suggested that, pending the arbitration, the *modus* for 1892 be made applicable both to Bering Sea and the North Pacific Ocean, if he had not supposed that the treaty which he was about formally to conclude on behalf of his Government, invested the Arbitrators with authority to establish regulations applicable to all the waters traversed by these seals in their migration routes from and to the Pribilof Islands. Two days after writing the letter last referred to, Mr. Blaine communicated to Sir Julian Pauncefote a copy of a telegram, that day received by him from the United States consul at Victoria, in relation to the large number of sealing vessels about to sail, and said: "I think from this you will see that if we do not come to an understanding soon, there will be no need of our agreement relating to seals in the North Pacific or in the Bering Sea." *U. S. Case, Vol. 1, App. 353–4.*

Sir Julian Pauncefote replying, under date of February 28, 1892, to Mr. Blaine's note of February 24, referred to the statement of the latter that "if Her Majesty's Government would make their efforts most effective the sealing in the North Pacific Ocean should be forbidden." If, as is now contended, the treaty then about to be signed, and which was signed the next day, did not contemplate regulations for the preservation of these fur seals while they were in the North Pacific Ocean on their migration routes, it would have been easy for the British Minister to state that fact as a conclusive reason why the *modus vivendi* for 1892 should only apply to Bering Sea. But no such reason was assigned for the refusal of the British Government to extend the *modus* for that year to the North Pacific Ocean. The United States Government was, unfortunately, in such condition at that time, in respect to the arbitration, that it was compelled to accept a *modus* for 1892, applicable only to Bering Sea, or leave both that sea and the North Pacific Ocean entirely open to pelagic sealing pending the arbitration.

Notwithstanding the distinct declaration made to the United States by the British Government, through its representative at Washington, that "the sole object of the negotiation is the preservation of the fur seal species for the benefit of mankind, and that no considerations of advantage to any particular nation, or of benefit to any private interest, should enter into the question;" notwithstanding the explicit assurance, given by the Marquis of Salisbury, that Her Majesty's Government "always have been, and are still, anxious for the arrangement of a convention which shall provide whatever close time in whatever localities is necessary for the preservation of the fur seal species;" and, notwithstanding the express injunction of the treaty that the Arbitrators, upon finding the concurrence of Great Britain necessary to the establishment of regulations "for the proper protection and preservation of the fur seal in, or habitually resorting to, the Bering Sea," shall "determine what concurrent regulations outside the jurisdictional limits of the respective governments are necessary, and over what waters such regulations should extend," the contention now by Her Majesty's Attorney General and his learned associates, is that the Tribunal is without authority or jurisdiction, under the treaty, to prescribe regulations applicable to the North Pacific Ocean, or any regulations which in terms, or by their necessary operation, will result in the prohibition of pelagic sealing. It is contended that no such power can be exerted by this Tribunal, even if the Arbitrators find from the evidence that this race of animals can only be properly protected and preserved by the absolute cessation, during the sealing season, of the hunting and taking of these fur-seals in the waters both of Bering Sea and the North Pacific Ocean traversed by them outside the jurisdictional limits of the respective governments.

These two contentions are opposed by the United States, which insists that, according to the evidence, the continuance of pelagic sealing in the open waters either of Bering Sea or of the Northern Pacific Ocean, during the months of the year when these seals may be taken, is absolutely certain to bring about the extermination of the race in the course of a few years; and that under the power to determine the rights of the citizens or subjects of the two governments, as regards the taking of fur seal in, or habitually resorting to, Bering Sea, and to prescribe concurrent regulations for the proper protection and preservation of such seals, and to declare over what waters such regulations should extend, it is competent for this Tribunal, and is its plain duty, under the treaty, to prescribe regulations looking to a prohibition of pelagic sealing in any waters outside the jurisdictional limits of the respective governments which are traversed by these seals in their regular semiannual migration from and to the Pribilof Islands.

In harmony with the views upon regulations which the counsel for Great Britain present, regulations have been submitted in behalf of Her Britannic Majesty, which, if approved, would establish a zone of 20 miles around the Pribilof Islands within which no seal hunting shall be permitted at any time, nor rifles nor nets used by sealers, and a closed season from the 15th September to the 1st July for Bering Sea. Under such regulations pelagic sealing could be carried on without restraint, and with shotguns—confessedly a destructive, if not the most destructive mode of taking seals—not only in the North Pacific Ocean during the entire season, when seals can be taken in that ocean, but in Bering Sea outside the proposed zone of 20 miles around Pribilof Islands between July 1 and September 15.

The regulations suggested, in behalf of the United States, call for a prohibition, during the entire year, of pelagic sealing in all the waters of Bering Sea and of the North Pacific Ocean, outside the jurisdictional limits of the two Governments, north of the thirty-fifth degree of north latitude, and east of the one hundred and eightieth meridian of longitude from Greenwich. These regulations, it is admitted, cover all the waters habitually traversed by these fur seals in their migration routes from and to the Pribilof Islands, and, if approved, would result in the prohibition practically of all hunting and taking of these seals outside of territorial waters.

Much was said, in argument, as to the authority of the Tribunal to prescribe regulations that would entirely prohibit pelagic sealing during the months in each year when, by reason of the weather and the condition of the seas, the hunting and taking of seals is impracticable. The British counsel contended that it is beyond the power of the Arbitrators to prescribe regulations of that character. They argued that the Tribunal could not do indirectly what they could not do directly; that prohibition, in terms, or by the necessary operation of regulations, is not regulation; that the power to regulate is not a power to prohibit. This view, it may be observed, would place it beyond the power of this Tribunal to prescribe such regulations as those decided upon, provisionally, in 1888, between the diplomatic representatives of Great Britain, the United States, and Russia, as a basis of negotiation, namely (to use the words of Lord Salisbury), " that the space to be covered by the proposed convention should be the sea between America and Russia, north of the forty-seventh degree of latitude; that the close time should extend from the 15th April to the 1st November; that during that time the slaughter of all seals should be forbidden."

When enforcing the view last stated, counsel asked us whether a power given by the legislative department to a municipal corporation to regulate, within its limits, the sale of ardent spirits would give to such corporation authority to prohibit all sales of such spirits. Perhaps not. But the case put does not meet the one before the Tribunal. A legislative enactment of the kind referred to would show upon its face an intention to permit some sales of ardent spirits, under regulations to be prescribed by the municipal corporation. It might well be that a prohibition of all sales, by refusing all licenses to sell, would in the case supposed, defeat the intention of the legislature. The rule of interpretation which has been invoked has no application to the present case. If the treaty empowered this Tribunal to *regulate* pelagic sealing it could, not unreasonably, be contended that the two Governments had no purpose to prohibit altogether and under all circumstances, the hunting of fur seals in the open seas, but only to authorize the regulation of that particular mode of taking these animals. The power given is to prescribe such concurrent regulations " outside the jurisdictional limits of the respective Governments" as may be necessary "for the proper protection and preservation of the fur seal in, or habitually resorting to, the Bering Sea," and to declare "over what waters such regulations should extend." The end to be accomplished is the proper protection and preservation of the seals which habitually resort to that sea. Clearly a regulation which did not look to that end would fall short of what the treaty contemplated. The plain duty, therefore, of this Tribunal is to provide by concurrent regulations for the preservation of these animals, if regulations of that character are necessary to accomplish such a result. And that duty can be performed by means of regulations, which the two Governments are under solemn obligation to respect and to enforce against their respective citizens or subjects.

. I will add that if this Tribunal is without power to prescribe such regulations as are necessary for the proper protection and preservation of this race of animals, then the result of its proceedings can not possibly be, as both countries intended it should be, "a full, perfect, and final settlement of all the questions referred to the Arbitrators." It is mere play upon words to say, in respect to this treaty, that prohibition is not regulation, and that regulations or rules, calling in express words or by their operation for a prohibition of pelagic sealing, are beyond the powers given to this Tribunal, even if it appeared that regulations of that character are absolutely necessary to prevent the extermination of the fur seals frequenting the Pribilof Islands. The manifest result of this interpretation of the treaty is that while the Tribunal may prescribe regulations for the proper protection and preservation of these animals, the business of taking them in the high seas may still be carried on even though it should involve the destruction of the species. Can anyone believe that Great Britain would have asked the United States to so stultify itself as to sign a treaty which, either in words or by necessary implication, would have admitted of such a result? Does anyone believe that a treaty rendering such a result possible would have been signed by any diplomatic representative of the United States, or would have been approved by its President or by any member of the Senate of the United States?

I express at this time no opinion as to what regulations are in fact, and upon a view of all the evidence, necessary to the proper protection and preservation of those fur seals. Nor do I ask the Tribunal now to make any declaration upon the weight of the evidence touching that or any other issue. I am without knowledge of the views of the Arbitrators upon the various questions of right or issues of fact to be determined by them, and I ask no expression of opinion touching any of those questions in advance of their being reached in the regular course of our proceedings in conference. But as indicating the grounds upon which a declaration is asked at this time, as to the powers of this Tribunal under the treaty, I may say that there is a large amount of evidence in the record tending to show that the hunting and taking of these fur seals, according to the methods now practiced by pelagic sealers in the open waters either of the Bering Sea or of the North Pacific Ocean, if continued, will certainly result at no distant day in the complete extermination of the race. My purpose is only to show that the power to prescribe regulations, which expressly or by their practical operation will prohibit pelagic sealing, was intended to be conferred and has been conferred by the treaty, with respect to the waters both of Bering Sea and of the North Pacific Ocean, traversed by these fur seals in their going from and returning to the Pribilof Islands.

This Tribunal, I insist, has not been constituted for the purpose of conserving the interests of the Canadian and American sealers who, within the past ten years, have devised a mode of taking these fur seals in the open seas, by means which, all concede, are destructive, because not admitting of any discrimination as to sex, nor, still less, of any discrimination between females that are heavy with young and those that have not been impregnated. We are not here with authority to make an award, simply by way of compromise, so that each side in this dispute may have an opportunity to say that it has not been entirely unsuccessful in its contentions before this Tribunal. Our authority has a much wider field of operation. If the repeated avowals of the two nations, who seek an amicable settlement of their differences by means of arbitration, are not to be wholly discredited, we are here, in their names, and by their joint authority, to protect and preserve this race of animals from extermination if we find that concurrent regulations to that end are necessary. A failure or refusal to exercise the power, plainly given, to prescribe such regulations as are necessary to prevent the extermination of this race of useful animals, will, in my judgment, wholly defeat the principal object for which this Tribunal was created.

Matters involving the jurisdiction and power of the Tribunal to deal with every aspect of this case, as it may affect the supreme object of

11492——3

the protection and preservation of these fur seals, should, I submit, be passed upon before the Arbitrators enter upon the consideration of the several questions of right submitted for determination.

The duty of this Tribunal to prescribe regulations arises when the determination of the questions submitted to us, "as to the exclusive jurisdiction of the United States," leaves the subject in such position "that the concurrence of Great Britain is necessary to the establishment of regulations for the proper protection and preservation of the fur seal in, or habitually resorting to, the Bering Sea." Such are the express words of Article VII. If the United States has not such exclusive jurisdiction—that is, such sovereign power—as enables it to enact *laws*, binding upon all, whether citizens of the United States or subjects of other countries, for the protection and preservation of these seals, in all the waters both of Bering Sea and of the North Pacific Ocean traversed by them—and no such claim has been preferred before us—then we know, at this time, that the concurrence of Great Britain is necessary to the establishment of regulations, whatever conclusion may be reached upon the issue as to property and protection presented by the fifth question of Article VI.

If it be held that the United States has no right of property in these seals, and no right to protect them when found outside the ordinary three-mile limit, then the duty to prescribe concurrent regulations becomes manifest. But regulations of that character are, in my judgment, necessary though, perhaps, not equally so, for the proper protection and preservation of the seals, if the Tribunal holds that such right of property or protection does appertain to the United States; for, in that case, the only means which the Government of that country could employ would be those which the law permits to individual owners of property for its protection. But that would be inadequate protection, without the concurrence of Great Britain, manifested by such legislation as would bind its subjects wherever they may be, and compel them, under proper penalties, to respect any right of property or protection accorded to the United States by the award or decision of this Tribunal. So that it is certain that we must come to the subject of regulations for the proper protection and preservation of this race of animals.

If the Arbitrators believe that the race will be soon exterminated unless pelagic sealing is prohibited, in both Bering Sea and the North Pacific Ocean, during all the months when they may be taken in the open waters, but that the Tribunal is without power, under the treaty, to prescribe regulations of that character, is it not, as I have heretofore suggested, our duty to suspend further action for a time, in order that the two Governments may have an opportunity to so amend the treaty, under which we are proceeding, as to enable us to preserve this race from extermination? Shall we ignore the fact that both Governments have protested, in every form of language, that they desired the preservation of these animals without reference to considerations of profit or advantage to any nation or to individuals of any nation? Shall it be assumed that either of the great nations before us wish the Tribunal to conclude its labors and adjourn without prescribing concurrent regulations that are, in fact, necessary for the preservation of these seals? As these questions touching the competency of the Tribunal to deal with the subject of the preservation of these animals have been distinctly raised by Great Britain and must be decided, I submit that they should be examined and decided, at the threshold of our proceedings in conference.

Senator Morgan authorizes me to say that he concurs in this opinion.

[At the close of the discussion Senator Morgan offered, as a substitute for the motion of Mr. Justice Harlan, the following: "'This Tribunal of Arbitration is empowered by the Treaty of February 29, 1892, between the United States and Great Britain, to determine what concurrent regulations are proper to be adopted and enforced by the action of the respective governments, applicable to their respective citizens or subjects, outside of their respective territorial limits and outside of Bering Sea, for the protection and preservation of fur seals in, or habitually resorting to, Bering Sea." This substitute was accepted by Mr. Justice Harlan, and was adopted, one Arbitrator voting in the negative. It was agreed that the consideration of the subject embraced in the second branch of the original motion of Mr. Justice Harlan be postponed until the Tribunal should reach the subject of regulations in order, and should determine that regulations were made necessary by the conclusions reached upon other questions named in the treaty.]

PART II

THE MERITS OF THE VARIOUS QUESTIONS SUBMITTED TO THE TRIBUNAL FOR DETERMINATION.

1.

GENERAL STATEMENT OF THE FACTS OUT OF WHICH THE PRESENT CONTROVERSY BETWEEN THE TWO NATIONS AROSE, AND THE HISTORY OF THE NEGOTIATIONS RESULTING IN THE TREATY OF FEBRUARY 29, 1892.

Before entering upon the examination of the important questions submitted for determination, it will be well to recall the general course of the negotiations that preceded the making of the treaty under which we are proceeding, and the principal facts out of which the present controversy between the two governments originated. Some of these facts have already been stated by me when considering, at a former session of this Tribunal, the question of its competency to make regulations applicable to the North Pacific Ocean, and which also, in terms, or by their necessary operation, would put an end to pelagic sealing in the waters traversed by the Pribilof seals. But it is well, even at the risk of repetition, to restate them in this connection.

The controversy had its origin in certain seizures of vessels, alleged to belong to, or to be in the possession or under the control of, British subjects who were engaged, at the time, in the waters of Bering Sea outside of the ordinary limits of territorial jurisdiction, in hunting and taking fur-seals which had their breeding grounds on the islands of St. Paul and St. George, two of the four islands in Bering Sea constituting the Pribilof group.

The seizures referred to were made in 1886, 1887, and 1889 by public armed vessels acting under instructions from the Executive Department of the Government of the United States.

The Pribilof Islands are situated in Bering Sea, latitude 57° north, longitude 170° west from Greenwich, about 300 miles from Cape Newenham, on the mainland of Alaska Territory, and about 200 miles north of the Aleutian Islands, the latter islands extending several hundred miles westwardly and southwesterly from the peninsula of Alaska into the Pacific Ocean. They were discovered in 1786 and 1787 by Gerassim Pribilof, a Russian navigator, while he was endeavoring to ascertain upon what shores the herd of fur seals habitually landed, which had been observed to pass once a year northwardly, and once a year southwardly, through the channels between the Aleutian Islands.

Those islands, after their discovery, remained continuously in the possession of Russia until 1867. In that year the Emperor, by treaty, ceded to the United States "all the territory and dominion" then possessed by him "on the continent of America and in the adjacent islands," and contained within certain defined geographical limits. The eastern limit of the territory and dominion so conveyed was declared to be the line of demarcation between the Russian and British possessions in North America, as established by articles III and IV of the treaty, which will be hereafter referred to, between Russia and Great Britain of February (28) 16, 1825.

The western limit is thus defined by the treaty of 1867:

"The western limit within which the territories and dominion conveyed are contained passes through a point in Bering's Straits on the parallel of 65° 30' north latitude, at its intersection by the meridian which passes midway between the Islands of Kruzenstern or Ignalook, and the Island of Ratmanoff or Noonarbook, and proceeds due north, without limitation, into the same Frozen Ocean. The same western limit, beginning at the same initial point, proceeds thence in a course nearly southwest, through Bering's Straits and Bering's Sea so as to pass midway between the northwest point of the Island of St. Lawrence and the southeast point of Cape Choukotski, to the meridian of 172, west longitude; thence, from the intersection of that meridian, in a southwesterly direction, so as to pass midway between the Island of Attu and Copper Island of the Komandorski couplet, a group in the North Pacific Ocean, to the meridian of 193° west longitude, so as to include in the territory conveyed the whole of the Aleutian Islands east of that meridian."

That treaty further provided: "The cession of territory and dominion herein made is hereby declared to be free and unencumbered by any reservations, privileges, franchises, grants, or possessions by any associated companies, whether corporate or incorporate, Russian or any other, or by any parties, except merely private individual property holders; and the session hereby made conveys all the rights, franchises, and privileges now belonging to Russia in the said territory or dominion and appurtenances thereto." (15 U. S. Stat., 539.)

The Pribilof Islands are east of the line thus defined as the western limit within which are the territory and dominion conveyed by Russia to the United States.

By an act of the Congress of the United States approved March 3, 1869, the islands of St. Paul and St. George in Alaska were declared "a special reservation for Government purposes," and it was made unlawful for any person to land or remain on either of them, except by authority of the Secretary of the Treasury. This statute was followed by an act approved July 1, 1870, the expressed object of which was to prevent the extermination of fur-bearing animals in Alaska. The provisions of the acts of 1869 and 1870 are reproduced in the Revised Statutes of the United States of 1873. Those sections* show the extent of authority and jurisdiction, which has been asserted by the United

*SEC. 1954. The laws of the United States relating to customs, commerce, and navigation are extended to and over all the mainlands, islands, and waters of the territory ceded to the United States by the Emperor of Russia by treaty concluded at Washington on the thirtieth day of March, anno Domini one thousand eight hundred and sixty-seven, so far as the same may be applicable thereto.

SEC. 1956. No person shall kill any otter, mink, marten, sable, or fur-seal, or other fur-bearing animal within the limits of Alaska Territory, or in the waters thereof; and every person guilty thereof shall, for each offense, be fined not less than two hundred nor more than one thousand dollars or imprisoned not more than six months, or both; and all vessels, their tackle, apparel, furniture and cargo, found engaged in violation of this section shall be forfeited. But the Secretary of the Treasury shall have power to authorize the killing of any such mink, marten, sable, or other fur-bearing animal, except fur-seals, under such regulations as he may prescribe; and it shall be the duty of the Secretary to prevent the killing of any fur-seal, and to provide for the execution of the provisions of this section until it is otherwise provided by law; nor shall he grant any special privileges under this section.

SEC. 1959. The islands of Saint Paul and Saint George in Alaska, are declared a special reservation for Government purposes; and until otherwise provided by law it shall be unlawful for any person to land or remain on either of those islands, except by the authority of the Secretary of the Treasury; and any person found on either of those islands contrary to the provisions hereof shall be summarily removed; and it shall be the duty of the Secretary of War to carry this section into effect.

SEC. 1960. It shall be unlawful to kill any fur-seal upon the islands of Saint Paul and Saint George, or in the waters adjacent thereto, except during the months of June, July, September, and October in each year; and it shall be unlawful to kill such seals at any time by the use of firearms, or by other means tending to drive the seals away from those islands; but the natives of the islands shall have the privilege of killing such young seal as may be necessary for their own food and

States, over the territory and waters within the limits referred to in the treaty of 1867.

By a subsequent act, passed March 2, 1889, section 1956 of the Revised Statutes, forbidding the killing of "any otter, mink, marten, sable or fur seal, or other fur-bearing animals within the limits of Alaska Territory, or in the waters thereof," was declared "to include and apply to all the dominion of the United States in the waters of Bering Sea;" and it was made the duty of the President, at a timely season in each year, to issue his proclamation warning all persons against entering said waters for the purpose of violating the provisions of said section, and to cause one or more vessels of the United States to diligently cruise said waters and arrest all persons, and seize all vessels found to be, or to have been, engaged in any violation of the laws of the United States therein.

In execution of the above statutory provisions, the Secretary of the

---

clothing during other months, and also such old seals as may be required for their own clothing, and for the manufacture of boats for their own use; and the killing in such cases shall be limited and controlled by such regulations as may be prescribed by the Secretary of the Treasury.

SEC. 1961. It shall be unlawful to kill any female seal, or any seal less than one year old, at any season of the year, except as above provided; and it shall also be unlawful to kill any seal in the waters adjacent to the islands of Saint Paul and Saint George, or on the beaches, cliffs or rocks where they haul up from the sea to remain; and every person who violates the provisions of this or the preceding section shall be punished for each offense by a fine of not less than two hundred dollars nor more than one thousand dollars, or by imprisonment not more than six months, or by both such fine and imprisonment; and all vessels, their tackle, apparel, and furniture, whose crews are found engaged in the violation of either this or the preceding section, shall be forfeited to the United States.

SEC. 1962. For the period of twenty years from the first of July, eighteen hundred and seventy, the number of fur-seals which may be killed for their skins upon the Island of Saint Paul is limited to seventy-five thousand per annum, and the number of fur-seal which may be killed for their skin upon the Island of Saint George is limited to twenty-five thousand; but the Secretary of the Treasury may limit the right of killing, if it becomes necessary for the preservation of such seals, with such proportionate reduction of the rents reserved to the Government as may be proper; and every person who knowingly violates either of the provisions of this section shall be punished as provided in the preceding section.

SEC. 1963. When the lease heretofore made by the Secretary of the Treasury to the Alaska Commercial Company of the right to engage in taking fur-seals on the islands of Saint Paul and Saint George, pursuant to the act of the first July, 1870, chapter one hundred and eighty-nine, or when any future similar lease expires, or is surrendered, forfeited or terminated, the Secretary shall lease to proper and responsible

Treasury has, from time to time, leased to an incorporated company the right to engage in the business of taking fur seals on the islands of St. Paul and St. George, under regulations prescribed by that officer.

It was under this state of the law, so far as the statutes of the United States were concerned, that seizures of vessels were made. The British Government protested against those seizures as an unauthorized interference with the rights of its subjects on the high seas. Its Minister at Washington, Sir Lionel Sackville West, in a letter dated January 9, 1887, and addressed to Mr. Bayard, the American Secretary of State, said : "It is unnecessary for me to allude further to the information with which Her Majesty's Government have been furnished respecting these seizures of British vessels in the open seas, and which for some time past has been in the possession of the United States Gov-

parties, for the best advantage of the United States, having due regard to the interest of the Government, the native inhabitants, their comfort, maintenance and education, as well as to the interest of the parties heretofore engaged in trade, and the protection of the fisheries, the right of taking fur-seals on the islands herein named, and of sending a vessel or vessels to the islands for the skins of such seals, for the term of twenty years, at an annual rental of not less than fifty thousand dollars, to be reserved in such lease and secured by a deposit of United States bonds to that amount; and every such lease shall be duly executed in duplicate, and shall not be transferable.

SEC. 1964. The Secretary of the Treasury shall take from the lessees of such islands in all cases a bond, with securities, in a sum not less than five hundred thousand dollars, conditioned for the faithful observance of all the laws and requirements of Congress and the regulations of the Secretary of the Treasury touching the taking of fur-seals and the disposing of the same, and for the payment of all taxes and dues accruing to the United States connected therewith.

SEC. 1965. No persons other than American citizens shall be permitted, by lease or otherwise, to occupy the islands of Saint Paul and Saint George, or either of them, for the purpose of taking the skins of fur-seals therefrom, nor shall any foreign vessel be engaged in taking such skins; and the Secretary of the Treasury shall vacate and declare any lease forfeited if the same be held or operated for the use, benefit, or advantage, directly or indirectly, of any persons other than American citizens.

SEC. 1967. Every person who kills any fur-seal on either of these islands, or in the waters adjacent thereto, without authority of the lessees thereof; and every person who molests, disturbs, or interferes with the lessees, or either of them, or their agents or employés, in the lawful prosecution of their business, under the provisions of this chapter, shall for each offense be punished as described in section 1961; and all vessels, their tackle, apparel, appurtenances, and cargo, whose crews are found engaged in any violation of the provisions of sections 1965 to 1968, inclusive, shall be forfeited to the United States.

SEC. 1968. If any person or company, under any lease herein authorized, know-

ernment, because Her Majesty's Government do not doubt that if, on inquiry, it should prove to be correct, the Government of the United States will, with their well-known sense of justice, admit the illegality of the proceedings resorted to against the British vessels and the British subjects above mentioned, and will cause reasonable reparation to be made for the wrongs to which they have been subjected and for the losses which they have sustained." *U. S. Case, Vol. 1, App., 156.*

Under date of April 12, 1887, Mr. Bayard, writing to the British minister, said: "The remoteness of the scene of the fur-seal fisheries and the special peculiarities of that industry have unavoidably delayed the Treasury officials in framing appropriate regulations and issuing orders to United States vessels to police the Alaskan waters for the protection of the fur seals from indiscriminate slaughter and conse-

ingly kills, or permits to be killed, any number of seals exceeding the number for each island in this chapter prescribed, such person or company shall, in addition to the penalties and forfeitures herein provided, forfeit the whole number of skins of seals killed in that year, or, in case the same have been disposed of, then such person or company shall forfeit the value of the same.

SEC. 1969. In addition to the annual rental required to be reserved in every lease, as provided in section nineteen hundred and sixty-three, a revenue tax or duty of two dollars is laid upon each fur-seal skin taken and shipped from the islands of Saint Paul and Saint George during the continuance of any lease, to be paid into the Treasury of the United States; and the Secretary of the Treasury is empowered to make all needful regulations for the collection and payment of the same, and to secure the comfort, maintenance, education, and protection of the natives of those islands, and also to carry into full effect all the provisions of this chapter except as otherwise prescribed.

SEC. 1970. The Secretary of the Treasury may terminate any lease given to any person, company, or corporation on full and satisfactory proof of the violation of any of the provisions of this chapter or the regulations established by him.

SEC. 1971. The lessees shall furnish to the several masters of vessels employed by them certified copies of the lease held by them respectively, which shall be presented to the Government revenue officer for the time being who may be in charge at the islands as the authority of the party for landing and taking skins.

SEC. 1972. Congress may at any time hereafter alter, amend or repeal sections from 1960 to 1971, both inclusive, of this chapter.

SEC. 1973. The Secretary of the Treasury is authorized to appoint one agent and three assistant agents, who shall be charged with the management of the seal fisheries in Alaska, and the performance of such other duties as may be assigned to them by the Secretary of the Treasury.

SEC. 1975. Such agents shall never be interested, directly or indirectly, in any lease of the right to take seals, nor in any proceeds or profits thereof, either as owner, agent, partner, or otherwise.

quent speedy extermination. The laws of the United States in this behalf are contained in the Revised Statutes relating to Alaska, in sections 1956–1971, and have been in force for upwards of seventeen years; and prior to the seizures of last summer but a single infraction is known to have occurred, and that was promptly punished. The question of instructions to Government vessels in regard to preventing the indiscriminate killing of fur seals is now being considered, and I will inform you at the earliest day possible what has been decided, so that British and other vessels visiting the waters in question can govern themselves accordingly." *U. S. Case, Vol. 1, App., 160.* Subsequently, August 19, 1887, Mr. Bayard addressed communications to the United States ministers in France, Germany, Great Britain, Japan, Russia, and Sweden and Norway, in which he said: "Recent occurrences have drawn the attention of this Department to the necessity of taking steps for the better protection of the fur seal fisheries in Bering Sea. Without raising any question as to the exceptional measures which the peculiar character of the property in question might justify this Government in taking, and without reference to any exceptional marine jurisdiction that might properly be claimed for that end, it is deemed advisable, and I am instructed by the President to so inform you, to attain the desired ends by international coöperation. It is well known that the unregulated and indiscriminate killing of seals in many parts of the world has driven them from place to place, and, by breaking up their habitual resorts, has greatly reduced their number. Under these circumstances, and in view of the common interest of all nations in preventing the indiscriminate destruction and consequent extermination of an animal which contributes so importantly to the commercial wealth and general use of mankind, you are hereby instructed to draw the attention of the Government to which you are accredited to the subject, and to invite it to enter into such an arrangement with the Government of the United States as will prevent the citizens of either country from killing seal in Bering Sea at such times and places, and by such methods as at present are pursued, and which threaten the speedy extermination of those animals and consequent serious loss to mankind. The ministers of the United States to Germany, Sweden and Norway, Russia, Japan, and Great Britain have been each similarly addressed on the subject referred to in this instruction." *U. S. Case, Vol. 1, App., 168.*

A copy of this communication having been received by Mr. Phelps,

United States minister at London, he had an interview with Lord Salisbury, the British Secretary of State for Foreign Affairs, and proposed that the two governments should adopt a code of regulations for the preservation of the seals in Bering Sea from destruction at improper times and by improper means by the citizens of either country—such agreement to be entirely irrespective of any questions of conflicting jurisdiction in those waters. This proposal, Mr. Phelps reported, was acquiesced in by Lord Salisbury, who suggested that the American Minister obtain from his Government and submit a sketch of a system of regulations that would be adequate for the purpose. *U. S. Case, Vol. 1, App., 171.*

Under date of February 7, 1888, Mr. Bayard wrote to Mr. Phelps disclosing, in some detail, the reasons why prompt action was necessary in order to prevent the entire destruction of the fur seals frequenting the islands of the United States in Bering Sea, as well as those found on the islands belonging to Russia. Responding to the suggestion in respect to code of regulations, he said:

"The only way of obviating the lamentable result above predicted appears to be by the United States, Great Britian, and other interested powers taking concerted action to prevent their citizens or subjects from killing fur seals with firearms or other destructive weapons north of 50 degrees of north latitude, and between 160 degrees of longitude west and 170 degrees of longitude east from Greenwich, during the period intervening between April 15 and November 1. To prevent the killing within a marine belt of 40 or 50 miles during that period would be ineffectual as a preservative measure. This would clearly be so during the approach of the seals to the islands. And after their arrival there such a limit of protection would also be insufficient, since the rapid progress of the seals through the water enables them to go great distances from the islands in so short a time that it has been calculated that an ordinary seal could go to the Aleutian Islands and back, in all a distance of 300 or 400 miles, in less than two days." What would take place unless steps were taken to preserve this race Mr. Bayard proceeded to show: "That the extermination of the fur seals must soon take place unless they are protected from destruction in Bering Sea is shown by the fate of the animal in other parts of the world, in the absence of concerted action among the nations interested for its preservation. Formerly, many thousands of seals were obtained annually from the South Pacific Islands and from the coasts of Chile and South

Africa. They were also common in the Falkland Islands and the adjacent seas. But in those islands, where hundreds of thousands of skins were formerly obtained, there have been taken, according to the best statistics, since 1880, less than 1,500 skins. In some cases the indiscriminate slaughter, especially by use of firearms, has in a few years resulted in completely breaking up extensive rookeries. * * * It is manifestly for the interests of all nations that so deplorable a thing should not be allowed to occur. As has already been stated, on the Pribilof Islands this Government strictly limits the number of seals that may be killed under its own lease to an American company, and citizens of the United States have, during the past year, been arrested, and ten American vessels seized for killing fur seals in Bering Sea." He further observed that Great Britain, in coöperating with the United States to prevent the destruction of fur seals in Bering Sea would aid in perpetuating an extensive and valuable industry in which her own citizens have the most lucrative share. *U. S. Case, Vol. 1, p. 172.*

Mr. Phelps, upon receiving this communication, held an interview, in London, with both Lord Salisbury and the Russian Ambassador, M. de Staal, and reported, under date of February 25, 1888, that his lordship assented to the proposition of Mr. Bayard, and that he would also join the United States Government in any preventive measures it may be thought best to adopt, by orders issued to the naval vessels in that region of the respective governments. *U. S. Case, Vol. 1, App., 173.* The Russian ambassador concurred, so far as his personal opinion was concerned, in the propriety of the proposed measures for the protection of the seals, and promised to communicate at once with his Government.

In reply to the last letter Mr. Bayard wrote to Mr. Phelps: "It is hoped that Lord Salisbury will give it favorable consideration, as there can be no doubt of the importance of preserving the seal fisheries in Bering Sea, and it is also desirable that this should be done by an arrangement between the governments interested without the United States being called upon to consider what special measures of its own the exceptional character of the property in question might require it to take in case of the refusal of foreign powers to give their coöperation. Whether legislation would be necessary to enable the United States and Great Britain to carry out measures for the protection of the seals would depend much upon the character of the regulation; but it is probable that legislation would be required. The manner of protecting the seals would depend upon the kind of arrangement which Great Britain would be willing to make with the United States for the policing of the seas and for the trial of British subjects violating the regulations which the two governments may agree upon for such protection." *U. S. Case, Vol. 1, App., 175.*

During a temporary absence of Mr. Phelps from London, Mr. White, the United States Chargé d'Affaires, had an interview with Lord Salisbury and the Russian ambassador, and reported that M. de Staal expressed a desire, on behalf of his government, to include in the area to be protected by the convention the Sea of Okhotsk, or at least that portion of it in which Robben Island is situated, there being, he said, in that region large numbers of seals whose destruction is threatened in the same way as those in Bering Sea; and that Lord Salisbury, in order to meet the Russian Government's wishes respecting the waters surrounding Robben Island, suggested that, besides the whole of Bering Sea, those portions of the sea of Okhotsk and of the Pacific Ocean north of latitude 47 degrees should be included in the proposed arrangement. His lordship intimated, furthermore, that the period proposed by the United States for a close time, April 15 to November 1, might interfere with the trade longer than absolutely necessary for the protection of the seals, and he suggested October 1, instead of a month later, as the termination of the period of seal protection. *U. S. Case, Vol., 1, App., 179.*

Mr. Bayard, in reply, said that he did object to the inclusion of the Sea of Okhotsk, or so much of it as was necessary for the protection of the seals; nor did he deem it absolutely necessary to insist on the extension of the close season till the 1st of November. Only such a period was desired as was requisite for the end in view. But that success may be assured in the efforts of the various governments interested in the protection of the seals, it seemed advisable to take the 15th of October instead of the 1st as the date of the close time, although, the 1st of November would be safer. *U. S. Case, Vol. 1, App., 180.*

At the argument there was some controversy between counsel as to whether Lord Salisbury had, in fact, *agreed* to any particular mode of protecting these fur seals from destruction. It is quite sufficient, in any view of this case, to accept the account Lord Salisbury himself gave of the meeting between himself and the representatives of the United States and Russia, on which occasion was considered the question of the preservation of the furseal species. The principal interview on this subject was held on the 16th of April, 1888, and its result was stated the same day in an official communication from Lord Salisbury to the British Minister at Washington. Lord Salisbury said: "At this preliminary discussion it was decided provisionally, in order to furnish a basis for negotiation, and without definitely pledging our governments, that the space to be covered by the proposed convention should be the sea between America and Russia north of the 47th degree of latitude; that the close time should extend from the 15th of April to the 1st of November; that during that time the slaughter of all seals should be forbidden, and vessels engaged in it should be liable to seizure by the cruisers of any of the three powers and should be taken to the port of their own nationality for condemnation; that the traffic in arms, alcohol, and powder, should be prohibited in all the islands of those seas; and that, as soon as the three powers had concluded a convention, they should join in submitting it for the assent of the other maritime powers of the northern seas. The United States chargé d'affaires was exceedingly earnest in pressing on us the importance of dispatch, on account of the inconceivable slaughter that had been and was still going on in those seas. He stated that, in addition to the vast quantity brought to market, it was a common practice for those engaged in the trade to shoot all seals they might meet in the open sea, and that of these a great number sank, so that their skins could not be recovered." *British Case, Vol. 3, App., 196; U. S. Case, Vol. 1, App., 238.*

A similar communication was sent to Sir R. Morier, the British Ambassador at St. Petersburg.

These negotiations resulted in nothing of a practical nature because of the objections raised by the Canadian Government to any such plan as that to which the representatives of Great Britain, the United States and Russia, "provisionally, in order to furnish a basis for negotiation," assented at the meeting of April 16, 1888.

Mr. Phelps, had a conversation with Lord Salisbury on the 13th of August, 1888, and again pressed for the completion of the convention, as the proposed extermination of the seals by Canadian vessels was understood to be rapidly proceeding. His lordship did not question the propriety or importance of taking measures to prevent the wanton destruction of so valuable an industry, in which, as he remarked, England had a large interests of its own. But he said that the Canadian Government objected to any such restrictions, and that until its consent could be obtained, Her Majesty's Government was not willing to enter into the convention; that time would be requisite to bring about that; and that meanwhile the convention must wait. It then became apparent to Mr. Phelps that the British Government would not execute the desired convention without the concurrence of Canada. Writing to Mr. Bayard, September 12, 1888, Mr. Phelps, in giving an account of his interview with Lord Salisbury, said: "Certain Canadian vessels are making a profit out of the destruction of the seal in the breeding season in the waters in question, inhuman and wasteful as it is. That it leads to the speedy extermination of the animal is no loss to Canada, because no part of these seal fisheries belong to that country; and the only profit open to it in connection with them is by destroying the seal in the open sea during the breeding time, although many of the animals killed in that way are lost, and those saved are worth much less than when killed at the proper time. Under these circumstances, the Government of the United States must, in my opinion, either submit to have these valuable fisheries destroyed or must take measures to prevent their destruction by capturing the vessels employed in it. Between these alternatives it does not appear to me there should be the slightest hesitation." *U. S. Case, Vol. 1, pp. 181, 182.*

Upon the accession of Mr. Harrison to the office of President, the matters in dispute between the two Governments being unsettled, again became the subject of diplomatic correspondence. That correspondence is too voluminous to be reproduced in this opinion. But a reference to an interview between Mr. Blaine and the British minister at Washington, which took place October 24, 1889, together with extracts from some of the communications emanating from the State Department, will suffice to show the general grounds upon which the position then taken by the United States was based.

In the report which Sir Julian Pauncefote made to Lord Salisbury of the above interview, it is said:

"We had a great deal of friendly discussion, in the course of which he stated that the seizures of the Canadian seal fishing vessels had been effected by the Treasury Department, which is charged with the protection and collection of the revenue (including that derived from the Alaska Company), and the measure had been resorted to under the belief that it was warranted by the act of Congress and the proclamation of the President. In this view the Department had been confirmed by the judgment of the district court of Alaska. I observed that this appeared like an assertion of the *mare clausum* doctrine, which I could hardly believe would be revived at the present day by his Government or any other, to which he replied that his Government had not officially asserted such a claim, and therefore it was unnecessary to discuss it. As a matter of fact there had been no interference with any Canadian vessels in Bering Sea except such as were found engaged in the capture and destruction of fur seals. But his Government claimed the exclusive right of seal fishery, which the United States, and Russia before them, had practically enjoyed for generations without any attempt at interference from any other country. The fur seal was a species most valuable to mankind and the Bering Sea was its last stronghold. The United States had bought the islands in that sea to which these creatures periodically resort to lay their young, and now Canadian fishermen step in and slaughter the seals on their passage to the islands, without taking heed of the warnings given, by Canadian officials themselves, that the result must inevitably be the extermination of the species. This was an abuse, not only reprehensible in itself, and opposed to the interests of mankind, but an infraction of the rights of the United States. It inflicted, moreover, a serious injury on a neighboring and friendly State, by depriving it of the fruits of an industry on which vast sums of money had been expended, and which had long been pursued exclusively and for the general benefit. The case was so strong as to necessitate measures of self-defense for the vindication of the rights of the United States and the protection of this valuable fishery from destruction. I replied that as regarded the question of right I could not admit that the seizure of the Canadian vessels was justified under the terms of the act of Congress or of the proclamation of the President. Municipal legislation could have no operation against foreign vessels beyond territorial waters. A claim of exclusive fishery on the high seas was opposed to international law, and no such right could be acquired by prescription. Mr. Blaine observed that he thought Great Britain enjoyed such a right in relation to pearl fisheries in some parts of the world. I said I was not aware of any such case. As regarded the question of fact, namely, the extermination of the fur seal species and the necessity for a 'close season,' there was unfortunately a conflict of opinion. But if, upon a further and more complete examination of the evidence, Her Majesty's Government should come to the conclusion that a 'close season' is really necessary, and if an agreement should be arrived at on the subject, all differences on questions of legal right would *ipso facto* disappear. Mr. Blaine expressed his readiness to proceed to such an inquiry, adding that he would be prepared to establish from Canadian evidence alone the absolute necessity for a 'close season,' but he strongly insisted that the inquiry should take place here and be entirely of a diplomatic character. * * * As regards compensation, if an agreement should be arrived at, he felt sure that his Government would not wish that private individuals who had acted *bona fide* in the belief that they were exercising their lawful rights should be the victims of a grave dispute between two great countries, which had happily been adjusted. He was not without hope, therefore, that the wishes I had expressed might be met, and that all might be arranged in a manner which should involve no humiliation on either side. His tone was friendly throughout, and he manifested a strong desire to let all questions of legal right and international law disappear in an agreement for a 'close season,' which he believes to be urgently called for in the common interest. It only now remains for me to solicit your lordship's instructions in regard to the suggestion of resuming in Washington the tripartite negotiation, with a view to arriving, if possible, at such a solution as is proposed by Mr. Blaine." *British Case, Vol. 3, App. 350–351.*

After this interview the British Government made complaints of other seizures of British vessels in the open waters of Bering Sea. Those complaints were met by Mr. Blaine in his letter of January 22, 1890, addressed to Sir Julian Pauncefote. As that letter contains a fuller statement of the position of the United States than had been made up to that time, nearly the whole of it is given, as follows:

"In the opinion of the President, the Canadian vessels arrested and detained in the Bering Sea were engaged in a pursuit that was in itself *contra bonos mores*, a pursuit which of necessity involves a serious and permanent injury to the rights of the Government and people of the United States. To establish this ground it is not necessary to argue the question of the extent and nature of the sovereignty of this Government over the waters of Bering Sea; it is not necessary to explain, certainly not to define, the powers and privileges ceded by His Imperial Majesty, the Emperor of Russia, in the treaty by which the Alaskan Territory was transferred to the United States. The weighty considerations growing out of the acquisition of that territory, with all the rights on land and sea inseparably connected therewith, may be safely left out of view, while the grounds are set forth upon

11492——4

which this Government rests its justification for the action complained
of by Her Majesty's Government. It cannot be unknown to Her
Majesty's Government that one of the most valuable sources of revenue
from the Alaskan possessions is the fur seal fisheries of the Bering
Sea. These fisheries had been exclusively controlled by the Government of Russia, without interference or without question, from their
original discovery until the cession of Alaska to the United States in
1867. From 1867 to 1886 the possession in which Russia had been
undisturbed was enjoyed by this Government also. There was no
interruption and no intrusion from any source. Vessels from other
nations passing from time to time through Bering Sea to the Arctic
Ocean in pursuit of whales had always abstained from taking part in
the capture of seals.

"This uniform avoidance of all attempts to take fur seal in those
waters had been a constant recognition of the right held and exercised
first by Russia and subsequently by this Government. It has also been
the recognition of a fact now held beyond denial or doubt that the taking of seals in the open sea rapidly leads to their extinction. This is
not only the well-known opinion of experts, both British and American,
based upon prolonged observation and investigation, but the fact has
also been demonstrated in a wide sense by the well nigh total destruction of all seal fisheries except the one in Bering Sea, which the Government of the United States is now striving to preserve, not altogether
for the use of the American people, but for the use of the world at large.

"The killing of seals in the open sea involves the destruction of the
female in common with the male. The slaughter of the female seal is
reckoned as an immediate loss of three seals, besides the future loss of
the whole number which the bearing seal may produce in the successive years of life. The destruction which results from killing seals in
the open sea proceeds, therefore, by a ratio which constantly and rapidly increases, and insures the total extermination of the species within
a very brief period. It has thus become known that the only proper
time for the slaughter of seals is at the season when they betake themselves to the land, because the land is the only place where the necessary discrimination can be made as to the age and sex of the seal. It
would seem, then, by fair reasoning, that nations not possessing the
territory upon which seals can increase their numbers by natural growth,
and thus afford an annual supply of skins for the use of mankind, should
refrain from the slaughter in open sea, where the destruction of the
species is sure and swift.

"After the acquisition of Alaska the Government of the United States, through competent agents working under the direction of the best experts, gave careful attention to the improvement of the seal fisheries. Proceeding by a close obedience to the laws of nature, and rigidly limiting the number to be annually slaughtered, the Government succeeded in increasing the total number of seals and adding correspondingly and largely to the value of the fisheries. In the course of a few years of intelligent and interesting experiment the number that could be safely slaughtered was fixed at 100,000 annually. The company to which the administration of the fisheries was intrusted, by a lease from this Government, has paid a rental of $50,000 per annum. and in addition thereto $2.62½ per skin for the total number taken. The skins were regularly transported to London to be dressed and prepared for the markets of the world, and the business had grown so large that the earnings of English laborers, since Alaska was transferred to the United States, amount in the aggregate to more than $12,000,000. The entire business was then conducted peacefully, lawfully, and profitably—profitably to the United States, for the rental was yielding a moderate interest on the large sum which this Government had paid for Alaska, including the rights now at issue; profitably to the Alaskan Company, which, under governmental direction and restriction, had given unwearied pains to the care and development of the fisheries; profitably to the Aleuts, who were receiving a fair pecuniary reward for their labors, and were elevated from semi-savagery to civilization and to the enjoyment of schools and churches provided for their benefit by the Government of the United States, and, last of all, profitably to a large body of English laborers, who had constant employment and received good wages.

"This, in brief, was the condition of the Alaska fur seal fisheries down to the year 1886. The precedents, customs, and rights had been established and enjoyed either by Russia or the United States for nearly a century. The two nations were the only powers that owned a foot of land on the continents that bordered, or on the islands included within, the Bering waters where the seals resort to breed. Into this peaceful and secluded field of labor, whose benefits were so equitably shared by the native Aleuts of the Pribilof Islands, by the United States, and by England, certain Canadian vessels in 1886 asserted their right to enter and by their ruthless course to destroy the fisheries, and with them to destroy also the resulting industries which are so valuable. The

Government of the United States at once proceeded to check this movement, which, unchecked, was sure to do great and irreparabl harm. It was cause of unfeigned surprise to the United States that Her Majesty's Government should immediately interfere to defend and encourage (surely to encourage by defending) the course of the Canadians in disturbing an industry which had been carefully developed for more than ninety years under the flags of Russia and the United States— developed in such a manner as not to interfere with the public rights or the private industries of any other people or any other person.

" Whence did the ships of Canada derive the right to do in 1886 that which they had refrained from doing for more than ninety years ? Upon what grounds did Her Majesty's Government defend in the year 1886 a course of conduct in the Bering Sea which she had carefully avoided ever since the discovery of that sea ? By what reasoning did Her Majesty's Government conclude that an act may be committed with impunity against the rights of the United States which had never been attempted against the same rights when held by the Russian Empire ?

"So great has been the injury to the fisheries from the irregular and destructive slaughter of seals in the open waters of the Bering Sea by Canadian vessels that, whereas the Government had allowed 100,000 to be taken annually for a series of years, it is now compelled to reduce the number to 60,000. If four years of this violation of natural law and neighbor's rights has reduced the annual slaughter of seal by 40 per cent, it is easy to see how short a period will be required to work the total destruction of the fisheries.

"The ground upon which Her Majesty's Government justifies, or at least defends, the course of the Canadian vessels rests upon the fact that they are committing their acts of destruction on the high seas, viz, more than 3 marine miles from the shore line. It is doubtful whether Her Majesty's Government would abide by this rule if the attempt were made to interfere with the pearl fisheries of Ceylon, which extend more than 20 miles from the shore line and have been enjoyed by England without molestation ever since their acquisition. So well recognized is the British ownership of those fisheries, regardless of the limit of the 3-mile line, that Her Majesty's Government feels authorized to sell the pearl-fishing right from year to year to the highest bidder. Nor is it credible that modes of fishing on the Grand Banks, altogether practicable, but highly destructive, would be justified or even permitted by Great Britain on the plea that the vicious acts were committed more than 3 miles from the shore.

"There are, according to scientific authority, "great colonies of fish" on the "Newfoundland Banks." These colonies resemble the seats of great populations on land. They remain stationary, having a limited range of water in which they live and die. In these great "colonies" it is, according to expert judgment, comparatively easy to explode dynamite or giant powder in such manner as to kill vast quantities of fish and at the same time destroy countless numbers of eggs. Stringent laws have been necessary to prevent the taking of fish by the use of dynamite in many of the rivers and lakes of the United States. The same mode of fishing could readily be adopted with effect on the more shallow parts of the banks, but the destruction of fish in proportion to the catch, says a high authority, might be as great as 10,000 to 1. Would Her Majesty's Government think that so wicked an act could not be prevented and its perpetrators punished simply because it had been committed outside of the 3-mile line?

"Why are not the two cases parallel? The Canadian vessels are engaged in the taking of fur seals in a manner that destroys the power of reproduction and insures the extermination of the species. In exterminating the species an article useful to mankind is totally destroyed in order that temporary and immoral gain may be acquired by a few persons. By the employment of dynamite on the banks it is not probable that the total destruction of fish could be accomplished, but a serious diminution of a valuable food for man might assuredly result. Does Her Majesty's Government seriously maintain that the law of nations is powerless to prevent such violation of the common rights of man? Are the supporters of justice in all nations to be declared incompetent to prevent wrongs so odious and so destructive?

"In the judgment of this Government, the law of the sea is not lawlessness. Nor can the law of the sea and the liberty which it confers and which it protects be perverted to justify acts which are immoral in themselves, which inevitably tend to results against the interests and against the welfare of mankind. One step beyond that which Her Majesty's Government has taken in this contention, and piracy finds its justification. The President does not conceive it possible that Her Majesty's Government could, in fact, be less indifferent to these evil results than is the Government of the United States. But he hopes that Her Majesty's Government will, after this frank expression of views, more readily comprehend the position of the Government of the United States touching this serious question. This Government has been ready to concede much in order to adjust all differences of view, and has, in the judgment of the President, already proposed a solution, not only equitable, but generous. Thus far Her Majesty's Government has declined to accept the proposal of the United States. The President now awaits with deep interest, not unmixed with solicitude, any proposition for reasonable adjustment which Her Majesty's Government may submit. The forcible resistance to which this Government is constrained in the Bering Sea is, in the President's judgment, demanded not only by the necessity of defending the traditional and long-established rights of the United States, but also the rights of good government and of good morals the world over.

"In this contention the Government of the United States has no occasion and no desire to withdraw or modify the positions which it has at any time maintained against the claims of the Imperial Government of Russia. The United States will not withhold from any nation the privileges which it demanded for itself when Alaska was part of the Russian Empire. Nor is the Government of the United States disposed to exercise in those possessions any less power or authority than it was willing to concede to the Imperial Government of Russia when its sovereignty extended over them. The President is persuaded that all friendly nations will concede to the United States the same rights and privileges on the lands and in the waters of Alaska which the same friendly nations have always conceded to the Empire of Russia." *U. S. Case, Vol. I, App., 200.*

In his letter of December 17, 1890, in reply to Lord Salisbury's letter of August 2, 1890, Mr. Blaine discusses with much elaboration and with signal ability all the questions then in dispute between the two governments. In that letter he says:

"I am directed by the President to say that, on behalf of the United States, he is willing to adopt the text used in the act of Parliament to exclude ships from hovering nearer to the island of St. Helena than 8 marine leagues, or he will take the example cited by Sir George Baden-Powell, where, by permission of Her Majesty's Government, control over a part of the ocean 600 miles wide is to-day authorized by Australian law. The President will ask the Government of Great Britain to agree to the distance of 20 marine leagues—within which no ship shall hover around the islands of St. Paul and St. George from the 15th of May to the 15th of October of each year. This will prove an effective mode of preserving the seal fisheries for the use of the civilized world—

a mode which in view of Great Britain's assumption of power over the open ocean she can not with consistency decline. Great Britain prescribed 8 leagues at St. Helena; but the obvious necessities in the Bering Sea will, on the basis of this precedent, justify 20 leagues for the protection of the American seal fisheries.

"The United States desires only such control over a limited extent of the waters in the Bering Sea, for a part of each year, as will be sufficient to insure the protection of the fur seal fisheries, already injured, possibly, to an irreparable extent by the intrusion of Canadian vessels, sailing with the encouragement of Great Britain and protected by her flag. The gravest wrong is committed when (as in many instances is the case) American citizens, refusing obedience to the laws of their own country, have gone into partnership with the British flag and engaged in the destruction of the seal fisheries which belong to the United States. So general, so notorious, and so shamelessly avowed has this practice become that last season, according to the report of the American consul at Victoria, when the intruders assembled at Unalaska on the 4th of July, previous to entering Bering Sea, the day was celebrated in a patriotic and spirited manner by the American citizens, who at the time were protected by the British flag in their violation of the laws of their own country.

"With such agencies as these, devised by the Dominion of Canada, and protected by the flag of Great Britain, American rights and interests have, within the past four years, been damaged to the extent of millions of dollars, with no corresponding gain to those who caused the loss. * * *

"The repeated assertions that the Government of the United States demands that the Bering Sea be pronounced *mare clausum* are without foundation. The Government has never claimed it and never desired it. It expressly disavows it. At the same time the United States does not lack abundant authority, according to the ablest exponents of international law, for holding a small section of the Bering Sea for the protection of the fur seals. Controlling a comparatively restricted area of water for that one specific purpose is by no means the equivalent of declaring the sea, or any part thereof, *mare clausum*. Nor is it by any means so serious an obstruction as Great Britain assumed to make it in the South Atlantic, nor so groundless an interference with the common law of the sea as is maintained by British authority to-day in the Indian Ocean." *U. S. Case, Vol. I, App., 263, 284, 286.*

In the same letter he observes that the President, not desiring the long postponement which an examination of the legal authorities from Ulpian to Phillimore and Kent would involve, refers to the following passages in the letter of Mr. Phelps of September 12, 1888, as fully expressing his own views:

"Much learning has been expended upon the discussion of the abstract question of the right of *mare clausum*. I do not conceive it to be applicable to the present case. Here is a valuable fishery and a large, and, if properly managed, permanent industry, the property of the nations on whose shores it is carried on. It is proposed by the colony of a foreign nation, in defiance of the joint remonstrance of all the countries interested, to destroy this business by the indiscriminate slaughter and extermination of the animals in question in the open neighboring sea during the period of gestation, when the common dictates of humanity ought to protect them were there no interest at all involved. And it is suggested that we are prevented from defending ourselves against such depredations because the sea at a certain distance from the coast is free. The same line of argument would take under its protection piracy and the slave trade, when prosecuted in the open sea, or would justify one nation in destroying the commerce of another by placing dangerous obstructions and derelicts in the open sea near its coasts. There are many things which can not be allowed to be done on the open sea with impunity, and against which every sea is *mare clausum*; and the right of self-defense as to person and property prevails there as fully as elsewhere. If the fish upon Canadian coasts could be destroyed by scattering poison in the open sea adjacent with some small profit to those engaged in it, would Canada, upon the just principles of international law, be held defenceless in such a case? Yet that process would be no more destructive, inhuman, and wanton than this. If precedents are wanting for a defense so necessary and proper it is because precedents for such a course of conduct are likewise unknown. The best international law has arisen from precedents that have been established when the just occasion for them arose, undeterred by the discussion of abstract and inadequate rules." *U. S. Case, Vol. 1, App., 263, 287.*

At a later date, in his letter of June 14, 1891, to Sir Julian Pauncefote, Mr. Blaine said:

"In the opinion of the President Lord Salisbury is wholly and strangely in error in making the following statement: 'Nor do they (the advisers of the President) reply, as a justification for the seizure of British ships in the open sea, upon the contention that the interests of the seal fisheries give to the United States Government any right for that purpose which, according to international law, it would not otherwise possess.' The Government of the United States has steadily held just the reverse of the position which Lord Salisbury has imputed to it. It holds that the ownership of the islands upon which the seals breed, that the habit of the seals in regularly resorting thither and rearing their young thereon, that their going out from the islands in search of food and regularly returning thereto, and all the facts and incidents of their relation to the island, give the United States a property interest therein; that this property interest was claimed and exercised by Russia during the whole period of its sovereignty over the land and waters of Alaska; that England recognized this property interest so far as recognition is implied by abstaining from all interference with it during the whole period of Russia's ownership of Alaska and during the first nineteen years of the sovereignty of the United States. It is yet to be determined whether the lawless intrusion of Canadian vessels in 1886 and subsequent years has changed the law and equity of the case theretofore prevailing." *U. S. Case, Vol. 1, App., 295, 298.*

The general contention of the British Government, during the negotiations, so far as the questions of right and jurisdiction were concerned, was that Russia neither asserted nor exercised, and could never have rightfully asserted or exercised, exclusive jurisdiction or exclusive rights in the open waters of Bering Sea, except that by the Ukase of 1821 she forbade foreign vessels from approaching nearer than 100 Italian miles from the coast of the North American continent between Bering Strait and the fifty-first degree of north latitude, or the coasts of the Asiatic continent from the same strait to the forty-fifth degree of north latitude, or the intervening islands belonging to her; that against this prohibition both Great Britain and the United States earnestly protested, and it was withdrawn or abandoned by Russia when she made the treaty of 1824 with the United States, and that of 1825 with Great Britain; that the pursuit of fur seals in the open seas could not of itself be regarded as *contra bonos mores* unless and until, for special reasons, it has been agreed by international arrangement to forbid it; that Great Britain has always claimed the freedom of navigation and fishing in the waters of Bering Sea outside the usual territorial limit of

one marine league from the coast; that the public right to fish, catch
seals, or pursue any other lawful occupation on the high seas can not
be held to be abandoned by a nation from the mere fact that for a certain number of years it has not suited the subjects of that nation to
exercise it; that fur seals were animals *feræ naturæ*, and were *res
nullius* until caught; that no person could have property in them
until he had actually reduced them into possession by capture, and
that any interference by the United States with the hunting and
taking of these fur seals, in the open waters of the ocean, by the
citizens or subjects of Great Britain, was a violation of rights secured
to them by the law of nations.

The result of the negotiations was the treaty of February 29, 1892,
under which this Tribunal is proceeding.

2.

JURISDICTION AND RIGHTS ASSERTED AND EXERCISED BY RUS-
SIA IN BERING SEA, AND IN RESPECT TO THE SEAL FISHERIES
IN THAT SEA, PRIOR TO THE CESSION OF 1867 OF ALASKA TO
THE UNITED STATES.
EFFECT OF THE TREATY CONCLUDED IN 1825 BETWEEN RUSSIA
AND GREAT BRITAIN.
THE RIGHTS THAT PASSED TO THE UNITED STATES BY THE
TREATY OF CESSION OF 1867.

With the knowledge of the origin and history of the controversy
between the two Governments which the above statement furnishes we
are the better prepared to consider the particular questions which
this treaty requires this Tribunal to determine.

By Article VI of the treaty of February 29, 1892, it was provided
that

"In deciding the matters submitted to the Arbitrators it is agreed
that the following five points shall be submitted to them in order that
their award shall embrace a distinct decision upon each of said five
points, to wit:

"1. What exclusive jurisdiction in the sea now known as the Bering
Sea, and what exclusive rights in the seal fisheries therein, did Russia
assert and exercise prior and up to the time of the cession of Alaska to
the United States?

"2. How far were these claims of jurisdiction as to the seal fisheries
recognized and conceded by Great Britain?

"3. Was the body of water now known as the Bering Sea included in the phrase 'Pacific Ocean,' as used in the treaty of 1825 between Great Britain and Russia, and what rights, if any, in the Bering Sea were held and exclusively exercised by Russia after said treaty?

"4. Did not all the rights of Russia as to jurisdiction and as to the seal fisheries in Bering Sea east of the water boundary in the treaty between the United States and Russia of the 30th March, 1867, pass unimpaired to the United States under that treaty?

"5. Has the United States any right, and, if so, what right, of protection or property in the fur seals frequenting the islands of the United States in Bering Sea when such seals are found outside the ordinary three-mile limit?"

All of the points specified in this article of the treaty are, in my judgment, embraced in the general questions for the amicable settlement of which this Tribunal has been constituted, and which are described in Article I of the treaty as questions "concerning the jurisdictional rights of the United States in the waters of Bering Sea, and concerning also the preservation of the fur seal in, or habitually resorting to, said sea, and the rights of the citizens or subjects of either country as regards the taking of fur seal in, or habitually resorting to, the said waters." These general questions may properly be met by the answers the Tribunal makes to the points particularly named in Article VI. If they are not so met, then it will be the duty of Arbitrators to make such additional answers as will cover all the matters embraced in Article I. An award that does not dispose of those points, as well as of the several matters generally named in Article I, might be disregarded as not such a decision as the treaty requires. It was not within the contemplation of the two governments that any matter embraced in either article should be left undetermined by the Tribunal. In the belief that the entire controversy in respect to the questions and points enumerated in those articles would be concluded by the award, the two governments engaged, in Article XIV, "to consider the result of the proceedings of the Tribunal of Arbitration, as a full, perfect, and final settlement of all questions referred to the Arbitrators," and to coöperate in securing the adhesion of other powers to such regulations as might be prescribed.

The first point in Article VI of the Treaty involves an inquiry as to—
What exclusive jurisdiction in the sea now known as the Bering Sea,

and what exclusive rights in the seal fisheries therein, did Russia assert and exercise prior and up to the time of the cession of Alaska to the United States?

The relations held by Russia to Bering Sea and to the fisheries therein, largely involve the interpretation to be given to what are called the Ukases of 1799 and 1821, to the treaty of 1824 between Russia and the United States, and the treaty of 1825 between Russia and Great Britain. Those treaties were the result of negotiations that followed the vigorous protests made by the United States and Great Britain against the Ukase of 1821. I will later on consider their effect upon any claims of jurisdiction and authority asserted by Russia.

The Ukase of 1799, as it is commonly called, was little more than a charter granted to the Russian American Company. The material portions of it are in these words:

"By the grace of a merciful God, we, Paul the First, Emporor and Autocrat of all the Russias, etc. To the Russian American Company under our highest protection. The benefits and advantages resulting to our empire from the hunting and trading carried on by our loyal subjects in the northeastern seas and along the coasts of America have attracted our imperial attention and consideration; therefore, having taken under our immediate protection a company organized for the above-named purpose of carrying on hunting and trading, we allow it to assume the appellation of "Russian American Company, operating under our Highest Protection;" and for the purpose of aiding the company in its enterprises, we allow the commanders of our land and sea forces to employ said forces in the company's aid, if occasion requires it, while for further relief and assistance of said company, and having examined their rules and regulations, we hereby declare it to be our highest Imperial will to grant to this company for a period of twenty years the following rights and privileges:

"I. By the right of discovery in past times by Russian navigators of the northeastern part of America, beginning from the fifty-fifth degree of north latitude and of the chain of islands extending from Kamchatka to the north to America, and southward to Japan, and by right of possession of the same by Russia, we most graciously permit the company to have the use of all hunting grounds and establishments now existing on the northeastern coast of America, from the above-mentioned fifty-fifth degree to Bering Strait, and also on the Aleutian, Kurile, and other islands situated in the Northeastern Ocean.

"II. To make new discoveries not only north of the fifty-fifth degree of north latitude but farther to the south, and to occupy the new lands discovered as Russian possessions, according to prescribed rules, if they have not been previously occupied by or been dependent on any other nation.

"III. To use and profit by everything that has been or shall be discovered in those localities, on the surface and in the interior of the earth, without competition from others.

"IV. We most graciously permit this company to establish settlements in future times wherever they are wanted, according to its best knowledge and belief, and fortify them to insure the safety of the inhabitants, and to send ships to those shores with goods and hunters, without any obstacles on the part of the Government.

"V. To extend their navigation to all adjoining nations and hold business intercourse with all surrounding powers, upon obtaining their free consent for the purpose, and under our highest protection to enable them to prosecute their enterprises with greater force and advantage.

"VI. To employ for navigation, hunting, and all other business, free and unsuspected people, having no illegal views or intentions.   *   *   *

"X. The exclusive right is most graciously granted to the company for a period of twenty years, to use and enjoy, in the above extent of country and islands, all profits and advantages derived from hunting, trade, industries, and discovery of new lands, prohibiting the enjoyment of these profits and advantages not only to those who would wish to sail to those countries on their own account, but to all former hunters and trappers who have been engaged in this trade and have their vessels and furs at those places; and other companies which may have been formed will not be allowed to continue their business unless they unite with the present company with their free consent; but such private companies or traders as have their vessels in those regions can either sell their property, or, with the company's consent, remain until they have obtained a cargo, but no longer than is required for the loading and return of the vessel; and after that nobody will have any privileges but this one company, which will be protected in the enjoyment of all the rights mentioned.

"XI. Under our highest protection the Russian-American Company will have full control over all above-mentioned localities, and exercise judicial powers in minor cases. The company will also be permitted to use all local facilities for fortifications in the defense of the country under their control against foreign attacks. Only partners of the company shall be employed in the administration of the new possessions in charge of the company." *U. S. Case, Vol. 1, App., 14.*

This is the translation of the Ukase of 1799 as given in the original Cases of both governments. It is also identical with that found in Bancroft's History of Alaska, the author stating that the translation adopted by him is based on the full text of the charter from Golovnin in Materialui I. 77–80. *Bancroft's Works, Vol. 33, History of Alaska, p. 379.*

In the British Counter Case it is said that the above translation is inaccurate, and what is now claimed to be a correct rendering of the original Russian document, as given by Golovnin and Tikhmenic, is produced. But at the oral argument it was admitted that the differences between these translations did not materially affect any questions depending upon the construction of the Ukase of 1799. For that reason the latter translation is not embodied in this opinion.

Did this Ukase assert an exclusive jurisdiction upon the part of Russia over any part of Bering Sea beyond ordinary territorial waters?

It is quite true that at the time the Ukase of 1799 was issued all the islands in Bering Sea had become a part of the territory of Russia by right of discovery and occupancy, within the rules announced by the Supreme Court of the United States in *Johnson vs. McItosh, 8 Wheat., 543, 572.* In that case Chief Justice Marshall, speaking for the court, said: "On the discovery of this immense continent, the great nations of Europe were eager to appropriate to themselves so much of it as they could respectively require. Its vast extent afforded an ample field to the ambition and enterprise of all; and the character and religion of its inhabitants afforded an apology for considering them as a people over whom the superior genius of Europe might claim an ascendancy. The potentates of the old world found no difficulty in convincing themselves that they made ample compensation to the inhabitants of the new by bestowing upon them civilization and Christianity in exchange for unlimited independence. But as they were all in pursuit of nearly the same object it was necessary, in order to avoid conflicting settlements and consequent war with each other, to establish a principle, which all should acknowledge as the law, by which the right of acquisition, which they all asserted, should be regulated as between themselves. This principle was that discovery gave title to the government by whose subjects, or by whose authority, it was made, against all other European governments, which title might be consummated by possession. The exclusion of all other Europeans necessarily gave to the nation making the discovery the sole right of acquiring the soil from the natives, and establishing settlements upon it. It was a right with which no Europeans could interfere. It was a right which all asserted for themselves, and to the assertion of which by others all assented."

In my judgment there is nothing in the Ukase of 1799 which either expressly or by necessary implication indicates the purpose of Russia to assert such sovereign authority over the open waters of Bering Sea as would enable it to exclude the vessels of other powers from that sea, or even to prohibit hunting or fishing in its waters, beyond the ordinary territorial limits prescribed by the law of nations.

Prior to 1799 numerous rival companies or associations, maintained by Russian capital, were engaged in trading with the native inhabitants residing on the coasts or islands of Bering Sea. Many com plaints were made to the Emperor of cruelty and wrong practices by those associations toward the natives. The "promyshleniki," it was said, "could easily take by force what they had not the means to buy, or what the natives did not care to sell." "Thus," says Bancroft, "for many years matters were allowed to take their course; but toward the end of the eighteenth century the threatened exhaustion of the known sources of supply caused much uneasiness among the Siberian mer chants engaged in the fur trade, and some of them endeavored to rem edy the evil by soliciting special privileges from the Government for the exclusive right to certain islands, with the understanding that a fixed percentage of the gross yield—usually one-tenth—was to be paid into the public treasury. Such privileges were granted freely enough, but it was another matter to make the numerous half-piratical traders respect or even pay the least attention to them." *History of Alaska*, *375-6*. And we have the authority of a report made by a committee, under royal permission, for saying that out of this condition of affairs arose the necessity recognized by the Russian Government of one strong company which "would serve on the one hand to perpetuate Russian supremacy there, and on the other would prevent many dis orders and preserve the fur trade, the principal wealth of the country, affording protection to the natives against violence and abuse, and tending toward a general improvement of their condition." Hence the creation of the Russian-American Company by the Ukase of 1799, to which, according to the same report, "was granted full privileges, for a period of twenty years, *on the coast* of Northwestern America, beginning from latitude 55° north and including *the chain of islands* extending from Kamschatka northward to America and southward to Japan; the exclusive right to all enterprises, whether hunting, trading, or building, and to new discoveries, with strict prohibition from profiting by any of these pursuits not only to all parties who might engage in them on their own responsibility, but also to those who formerly had ships and establishments there, except those who have united with the new company." *Bancroft's History of Alaska,* *379; Report on Russ. Amer. Colonies, MS. vi, 13.*

Undoubtedly it was intended that the Russian-American Company should enjoy these rights and privileges without competition—that is, exclusively, against all, whether Russian subjects or the subjects of other countries. But the rights and privileges so granted were only such as related to business carried on within the territorial dominion or authority of Russia. If the translation of this Ukase, as given in the original Cases of the two governments be the correct one, the exclusive right granted to the Russian-American Company for twenty years was only to use and enjoy "in the above *extent of country and islands* all profits and advantages derived from hunting, trade, industries, and discovery of new lands." If the translation embodied in the British Counter Case be the correct one, then the grant was of an "exclusive right to all acquisitions, industries, trade, establishments, and discovery of new countries" throughout the "entire extent of the *lands and islands* described." Neither translation supports the suggestion that the Emperor of Russia intended to assert sovereign power over any part of Bering Sea outside of territorial waters, and thereby interfere with the freedom of navigation in the open waters of that sea, or with any such use of those waters by the citizens or subjects of other countries as was sanctioned by the law of nations. He intended only to assert an exclusive right to control, for the benefit of a particular company taken under his protection, all the profits and advantages to be derived from the business, trading, and industries conducted *within territorial waters and on the coasts and islands of* *Russia.* When the Ukase of 1799 was issued, the hunting of fur seals in the open waters of the ocean, beyond territorial jurisdiction, was unknown.

The only part of the Ukase of 1799 that seems to give any support whatever to the opposite view are the words in the first paragraph referring to the benefits and advantages that resulted to the Empire from the hunting and trading carried on by the Emperor's loyal subjects "*in the northeastern seas* and along the coasts of America." But that was merely a recital—in what may, not unreasonably, be called the preamble of the company's charter—of the fact that Russians had been engaged in hunting and trading, not only "along the coasts of America," but "in the northeastern seas;" not that they had been so engaged in those waters, to the exclusion of the citizens or subjects of other countries rightfully engaged in commerce and navigation on the high seas.

This is made clear by the granting clause of the company's charter, which, referring to the discovery by Russian navigators of the northeastern [northwestern] part of America, and of certain islands, and of the possession held in those localities by Russia, permits the company to have the use, (not of the northeastern seas, but) of all hunting grounds and establishments then existing "on the northeastern [northwestern] *coast* of America," from the fifty-fifth degree of latitude to Bering Strait, "and also *on* the Aleutian, Kurile, and other *islands*, situated in the Northeastern Ocean." And, as already stated, the exclusive right, granted to the company, as declared in section 10, was "to use and enjoy, in the above-described *extent of country and islands*, all profits and advantages derived from hunting, trade, industries, and discovery of new lands."

In my judgment there is nothing in the record which even remotely sustains the theory that Russia intended, by the Ukase of 1799, to assert exclusive jurisdiction over, or any sovereign control of, the northeastern sea outside of territorial waters. The only purpose was to give to a favored company exclusive privileges within the territory and dominion of that nation. In respect to that Ukase, Mr. Middleton, the United States Minister at St. Petersburg, who negotiated the Treaty of 1824 with Russia, said, in a letter to Mr. Adams that it "is, in its *form*, an act purely domestic, and was never notified to any foreign state with injunction to respect its provisions." *American State Papers, Foreign Relations, vol. 5, p. 461.*

Nor, in my judgment, is there any document or fact in the public history of Russia, as disclosed in the record before us, which justifies the contention that that country asserted or exercised, prior to 1821, exclusive jurisdiction over the waters of Bering Sea or any exclusive rights in the seal fisheries in that sea, outside of territorial waters.

This brings us to an examination of the Ukase of 1821, the provisions of which, as well as the negotiations that arose from its promulgation, were the subject of extended comment by counsel.

Between 1799 and 1821 the waters of Bering Sea were visited by vessels from various countries in charge of persons engaged in the hunting of whales, and who also carried on illicit and forbidden trade of different kinds with the native inhabitants of Russian territories, in violation of the established policy of the Russian Government. For the purpose of breaking up that trade and enforcing the policy of his Government, the Emperor of Russia issued the following Edict, called the Ukase of 1821:

"Observing from reports submitted to us that the trade of our subjects on the Aleutian Islands and on the northwest coast of America, appertaining unto Russia, is subjected, because of secret and illicit traffic, to oppression and impediments; and finding that the principal cause of these difficulties is the want of rules establishing the boundary for navigation along these coasts, and the order of naval communication as well in these places as on the whole of the eastern coast of Siberia and the Kurile Islands, WE have deemed it necessary to determine these communications by specific regulations which are hereto attached.

In forwarding these regulations to the directing senate, we command that the same be published for universal information, and that the proper measures be taken to carry them into execution."

Those regulations are entitled "*Rules established for the limits of navigation and order of communication along the coast of eastern Siberia, the northwest coast of America, and the Aleutian, Kurile, and other islands.*" As given in the Cases of both Governments, they contain among other provisions, the following:

"SEC. 1. The pursuits of commerce, whaling, and fishery, and of all other industries, on all islands, ports, and gulfs, including the whole of the northwest coast of America, beginning from the Bering Straits, to the fifty first degree of northern latitude, also from the Aleutian Islands to the eastern coast of Siberia, as well as along the Kurile Islands, from Bering Straits to the South Cape of the Islands of Urup, viz: to the 45° 50' northern latitude, is exclusively granted to Russian subjects.

"SEC. 2. It is therefore prohibited to all foreign vessels, not only to land on the coasts and islands belonging to Russia, as stated above, but also to approach them within less than 100 Italian miles. The transgressor's vessel is subject to confiscation, along with the whole cargo.

"SEC. 3. An exception to this rule is to be made in favor of vessels carried thither by heavy gales or real want of provisions and unable to make any other shore but such as belongs to Russia. In those cases they are obliged to produce convincing proofs of actual reason for such exception. Ships of friendly governments merely on discoveries are likewise exempt from the foregoing rule. In this case, however, they must previously be provided with passports from the Russian minister of the Navy.

"SEC. 4. Foreign merchant ships which, for reasons stated in the foregoing rule, touch at any of the above-mentioned coasts are obliged to endeavor to choose a place where the Russians are settled, and to act as hereunder stated.

"SEC. 14. It is likewise interdicted to foreign ships to carry on any traffic or barter with the natives of the islands and of the northwest coast of America in the whole extent above mentioned. A ship convicted of any trade shall be confiscated.

"SEC. 25. In case a ship of the Russian Imperial Navy, or one belonging to the Russian-American Company, meet a foreign vessel on the above-stated coasts, in harbors or roads within the before-mentioned limits, and the commander find grounds by the present regulation that the ship be liable to seizure he is to act as follows:

"SEC. 26. The commander of a Russian vessel suspecting a foreign to be liable to confiscation, must inquire and search the same, and, finding her guilty, take possession of her. Should the foreign vessel resist he should employ persuasion, then threats, and at last force, endeavoring, however, at all events, to do this with as much reserve as possible. If the foreign vessel employ force against force, then he shall consider the same as an evident enemy, and force her to surrender according to the naval laws." *U. S. Case*, Vol. I, p. 16.

In Mr. Blaine's letter of June 30, 1890, to Sir Julian Pauncefote, there is a translation of sections 1 and 2 of this Ukase that differs somewhat (though not, in my opinion, materially) from the translation of the same sections given in the Cases of the two Governments. The translation followed by Mr. Blaine is as follows:

"SEC. 1. The transaction of commerce and the pursuit of whaling and fishing, or any other industry on the islands, in the harbors and inlets, and, in general, all along the northwestern coast of America from Bering Strait to the fifty-first parallel of northern latitude, and likewise on the Aleutian Islands and along the eastern coast of Siberia, and on the Kurile Islands; that is, from Bering Straits to the southern promontory of the Island of Urup, viz, as far south as latitude 45° 50' north, are exclusively reserved to subjects of the Russian Government.

"SEC. 2. Accordingly, no foreign vessel shall be allowed either to put to shore at any of the coasts and islands under Russian dominion, as specified in the preceding section, or even to approach the same to within a distance of less than 100 Italian miles. Any vessel contravening this provision shall be subject to confiscation with her whole cargo." *U. S. Case, Vol. 1, App., 221, 226.*

Does the Ukase of 1821—looking first to its words only—import an assertion upon the part of Russia of exclusive jurisdiction over the open waters of Bering Sea, or of exclusive rights in what are called the seal fisheries in those waters? If not, what was the extent and nature of the jurisdiction so asserted?

This Ukase appears, upon its face, to be based upon reports submitted to the Emperor touching the trade of his subjects, not in Bering Sea, but "*on* the Aleutian *Islands* and *on* the northwest *coast* of America." The first regulation has reference to "the pursuits of commerce, whaling, and fishery, and of all other industry on all *islands*, ports, and gulfs, including the whole of the northwest *coast* of America," and "*along* the Kurile Islands." The same regulation according to the translation given in the letter of Secretary Blaine to Sir Julian Pauncefote, refers to "the transaction of commerce and the pursuits of whaling and fishing, or any other industry, on the *islands*, in the harbors and inlets, and, in general, *all along* the northwestern *coast* of America."

Considering next the circumstances under which this Ukase was issued, we find that Russia had numerous colonial establishments and industries on certain coasts and islands. And there were ports, gulfs, harbors, and inlets contiguous to its possessions, and constituting part of its territorial waters, in which foreigners carried on trade to the prejudice of the Russian-American Company and in violation of the established policy of Russia. The Emperor, as his edict shows, claimed that an illicit trade had been illegally carried on by foreigners with those establishments and with the native population. He desired that Russian subjects alone should enjoy the benefits of those establishments, and of the industries under the control of or belonging to Russia. It was "therefore"—that is, to that end—foreign vessels were prohibited, not from entering Bering Sea, but from landing on the coasts and islands of Russia named in the first regulation, or approaching them within less than 100 Italian miles. The transgressor's vessel and cargo would not have been subject to confiscation, under the regulations established, by engaging in whaling or fishing in the open waters outside of the line defined in the second regulation, namely, 100 Italian miles from the particular coasts and islands specified in the Ukase and regulations. Whether, therefore, reference be made to the words of the Ukase or to the circumstances under which it was promulgated, it is quite clear that Russia did not intend by that edict to assert any exclusive authority over the waters of Bering Sea outside of 100 Italian miles from the coasts and islands described in the first regulation.

That we have properly interpreted the Ukase and regulations of 1821 is, in part, shown by the second charter granted to the Russian-American Company, a few days after the above regulations were promulgated. That charter states that the company was established " for carrying on industries and trade *on the mainland* of Northwestern America, *on* the Aleutian *Islands*, and *on* the Kurile *Islands*," and that "it enjoys the privilege of hunting and fishing to the exclusion of all other Russian or foreign subjects," not throughout Bering Sea, but "throughout the *territories* long since in the possession of Russia on the coast of Northwest America, beginning at the northern point of the Island of Vancouver in latitude 51° north, and extending to Bering Strait and beyond, as well as *on all islands* adjoining this coast, and all those situated between that coast and the eastern shore of Siberia, as well as *on* the Kurile *Islands* where the company has engaged in the hunting down to the South Cape of the Island of Urup, in latitude 45° 50'." This clearly indicates that the exclusive privileges granted to the Russian-American Company had no reference to hunting, trading, fishing, and industries in the open seas outside of 100 Italian miles from the coasts defined in the regulations of 1821. That line was established by Russia simply as a means—and it was deemed by the Emperor sufficient for that purpose—of preventing foreigners from coming into contact with its colonial trade and industries, and thereby interfering with the enjoyment by the Russian-American Company of the exclusive rights and privileges granted to it.

Turning to the diplomatic correspondence between Russia and the United States, what do we find? This Ukase, and the regulations promulgated in execution of it, were brought to the attention of the governments of both the United States and of Great Britian; to the former, by M. de Poletica, the Russian minister at Washington, in an official communication dated January 30, 1822, addressed to John Quincy Adams, the American Secretary of State. Mr. Adams replied, under date of February 25, 1822, expressing, by direction of the President, his surprise at this "assertion of a territorial claim on the part of Russia extending to the fifty-first degree of north latitude on this continent, and a regulation interdicting to all commercial vessels other than Russian, under the penalty of seizure and confiscation, to approach upon the high seas within 100 Italian miles of the shore to which that claim is made to apply." After observing that the exclusion of the vessels of citizens of the United States from the shore "beyond the ordinary distance to which territorial jurisdiction extends" had excited still greater surprise, he inquired whether the Russian minister was authorized to give explanation of the grounds of right, upon principles generally recognized by the laws and usages of nations, which could warrant the action of Russia. *U. S. Case, Vol. 1, App., 132.* It is clear that Mr. Adams did not interpret the Ukase as asserting jurisdiction over Bering Sea, except to the extent of 100 Italian miles from the coasts specified. Equally explicit were the declarations of the American Minister at St. Petersburg, who in a confidential memorandum sent to Mr. Adams, said: "The extension of territorial rights to the distance of 100 Italian miles upon two opposite continents, and the prohibition of approaching to the same distance from these coasts, or from those of all the intervening islands, are innovations on the law of nations, and measures unexampled." *American State Papers, Vol. 5, p. 452.*

M. Poletica, February 28, 1822, replied at some length, in justification of the edict promulgated by the Emperor of Russia. He recited numerous facts which, in his judgment, sustained the claims of Russia to the extent specified in the regulations for the Russian-American Company—resting the title of his Government upon first discovery, first occupancy, and peaceable, uncontested possession for more than half a century prior to the independence of the United States. In respect to the territory claimed by Russia, he said that the Imperial Government, in assigning for limits to the Russian possessions on the northwest coast of America, on the one side Bering Strait and on the other the fifty-first degree of north latitude, has only made a moderate use of an incontestable right, "since the Russian navigators, who were the first to explore that part of the American continent in 1741, pushed their discovery as far north as the forty-ninth degree of north latitude." The fifty-first degree, therefore, he said, was no more than a mean point between the Russian establishment of New Archangel, situated under the fifty-seventh degree, and the American colony at the mouth of the Columbia, which is found under the forty-sixth degree of the same latitude.

To what extent the Ukase was intended to interfere with the free use of the waters outside of ordinary territorial limits, will appear in the following extracts from the above letter of M. Poletica:

"I shall be more succinct, sir, in the exposition of the motives which determined the Imperial Government to prohibit foreign vessels from approaching the northwest coast of America, belonging to Russia, within the distance of at least 100 Italian miles. This measure, however severe it may at first view appear, is, after all, but a measure of prevention. It is exclusively directed against the culpable enterprises of foreign adventurers, who, not content with exercising upon the coasts above mentioned an illicit trade very prejudicial to the rights reserved entirely to the Russian-American Company, take upon them besides to furnish arms and ammunition to the natives in the Russian provinces in America, exciting them likewise, in every manner, to resistance and revolt against the authorities there established. The American Government doubtless recollects that the irregular conduct of these adventurers, the majority of whom was composed of American citizens, has been the object of the most pressing remonstrances on the part of Russia to the Federal Government from the time that diplomatic missions were organized between the two countries. These remonstrances, repeated at different times, remain constantly without effect, and the inconveniences to which they ought to bring a remedy continue to increase. * * * Pacific means not having brought any alleviation to the just grievances of the Russian-American Company against foreign navigators in the waters which environ the establishments on the northwest coast of America, the Imperial Government saw itself under the necessity of having recourse to the means of coercion, and of measuring the rigor according to the inveterate character of the evil to which it wished to put a stop. Yet, it is easy to discover, upon examining closely the last regulation of the Russian-American Company, that no spirit of hostility had anything to do with its formation. The most minute precautions have been taken in it to prevent abuses of authority on the part of commanders of Russian cruisers appointed for the execution of said regulation. At the same time it has not been neglected to give all the timely publicity necessary to put those upon their guard against whom the measure is aimed. Its action, therefore, can only reach the foreign vessels which, in spite of the notification, will expose themselves to seizure by infringing *upon the line marked out in the regulation.* The Government flatters itself that these cases will be very rare; if all remain as at present appears, not one.

"I ought, in the last place, to request you to consider, sir, that the Russian possessions in the Pacific Ocean extend, on the northwest coast of America, from Bering Strait to the fifty-first degree of north latitude, and on the opposite side of Asia and the islands adjacent from the same strait to the forty-fifth degree. The extent of sea to which these possessions form the limits, comprehends all the conditions attached to *shut seas* ('mers fermées'), and the Russian Government might consequently judge itself authorized to exercise upon this sea the right of sovereignty, and especially that of entirely interdicting the entrance of foreigners. *But it preferred asserting only its essential rights,* without taking any advantage of localities." *British Case, Vol. 1, App., pp. 28, 30; U. S. Case, Vol. 1, App., 133.*

Equally explicit were the declarations made by the Russian Government, to the British Government, in an official communication, dated November 12, 1821, addressed by Baron Nicolay, the Russian Ambassador at London, to the Marquis of Londonderry, then at the head of the British Foreign Office. After referring to the complaints which the operations of smugglers and adventurers *along the northwest coast* of America belonging to Russia have more than once given rise to, which operations had for their object "a fraudulent commerce in furs and other articles which are exclusively reserved to the Russo-American Company," and betrayed a purpose to excite resistance or revolt, upon the part of the natives, to established authority, Baron Nicolay said:

"It was, therefore, necessary to take severe measures against these intrigues, and to protect the company against the hurtful prejudices that resulted, and it was with that end in view that the annexed regulation has just been published.

"*This new regulation does not forbid foreign vessels to navigate the seas that wash the shores of the Russian Possessions on the northwest coast of America and the northeast coast of Asia.* Such a prohibition— which it would not have been difficult to enforce with a sufficient naval force—would, of a truth, have been the most efficacious means of protecting the interests of the Russo-American Company; and, moreover, it would appear to be based upon incontestable rights. For, on the one hand, to remove all foreign ships, once for all, from the coast above referred to, would be to put an end forever to the illegal operations which it is necessary to prevent. On the other hand—considering the Russian possessions, which extend on the northwest coast of America from the Bering Strait to the fifty-first degree of north latitude, as well as on the coast of Asia opposite and on the adjacent islands, from the same strait to 45°—it can not be denied that the sea of which these possessions form the bounds embraces all the conditions that the most widely known and best accredited publicists have attached to the definition of a closed sea, and that, therefore, the Russian Government has perfect authority to exercise the rights of sovereignty over that sea and particularly that of forbidding the approach of foreigners. Nevertheless, however important the considerations may have been that claimed such a measure, however legitimate such a measure would in itself have been, the Imperial Government did not wish, on this occasion, to exercise a power which is assured to it by the most sacred title of possession, and which is, besides, confirmed by irrefragable authorities. The Government, however, *limited itself*—as can be seen by the newly published regulation—to forbidding all foreign vessels not only to land on the settlements of the American Company, and on the Peninsula of Kamschatka and the coasts of the Okhotsk Sea, but also to sail *along the coast* of these possessions, and, as a rule, *to approach them within 100 Italian miles.*

"Vessels of the Imperial Marine have just been sent to see that this arrangement is carried out. The arrangement appears to us to be as lawful as it is urgent. For, if it is shown that the Imperial Government had strictly the right to close to foreigners that portion of the Pacific Ocean which is bounded by our possessions in America and Asia, *a fortiori* the right in virtue of which it has just adopted *a much less restrictive measure* should not be called in question. This right, in effect, is universally admitted, and all maritime powers have exercised it more or less, in their colonial system." *British Case, Vol. 2, App., p. 1.*

These official declarations of the Russian Government through its accredited representatives are in harmony with the words of the Ukase of 1821. They show: (1) That the object of that Ukase was to prevent foreigners (to use the language of M. de Poletica) "from exercising upon the coasts above mentioned an illicit trade very prejudicial to the rights reserved entirely to the Russian-American Company," and from furnishing "arms and ammunition to the natives in the Russian possessions in America," and (to use the language of Baron Nicolay) from landing "on the settlements of the American Company, and on the Peninsula of Kamschatka and the coasts of Okhotsk Sea, and from sailing along the coasts of those possessions, and, as a rule, from approaching them within 100 Italian miles." (2) That, in order to accomplish those ends, foreign vessels were not to infringe upon "the line marked out in the regulations," and therefore not to approach the coasts within a less distance than that specified. (3) That while Russia claimed that it could justly assert the rights of sovereignty over all the waters between the North American and Asiatic Continents, from Bering Strait to the fifty-first degree of north latitude on the American side, and from the same strait to the forty-fifth degree of north latitude on the Asiatic side, it limited in the Ukase of 1821 its actual assertion of sovereignty over the waters within or inside of a certain line. It consequently declared that the Ukase of 1821 had reference only to the waters within 100 Italian miles from the coasts mentioned.

Additional proof of all this is found in the letter of Mr. Adams, the American Secretary of State, of March 30, 1822, replying to the above communication from M. Poletica, and in the latter of M. Poletica to Mr. Adams, dated April, A. D. 1822. Mr. Adams, in his letter, said : " With regard to the suggestion that the Russian Government might have justified the exercise of sovereignty over the Pacific Ocean as a close sea, because it claims territory both on its American and Asiatic shores, it may suffice to say that the distance from shore to shore on this sea, in the latitude of 51 degrees north, is not less than 90 degrees of longitude or 4,000 miles." To this M. Poletica responded : " In the same manner the great extent of the Pacific Ocean at the fifty-first degree of north latitude can not invalidate the right which Russia may have of considering that part of the ocean as close. But as the Imperial Government has not thought it fit to take advantage of that right, all further discussion on this subject would be idle." *U. S. Case, Vol. 1, App., 134, 135.*

The next point in Article VI to be considered is that involved in the inquiry :

" *How far were these claims of jurisdiction as to the seal fisheries recognized and conceded by Great Britain ?* "

The use here of the word "jurisdiction" creates some doubt as to the precise object of the question. But it must be assumed that the purpose was to ascertain whether, in the judgment of this Tribunal, Great Britain recognized and conceded any claim of jurisdiction, upon the part of Russia, over the waters of Bering Sea, or over any fisheries in that sea, outside of the ordinary limit of territorial waters. So interpreting the question, I have no doubt of the answer which must be made to it. The official correspondence between the governments of Great Britain and Russia shows that throughout the whole of the negotiations following the Ukase of 1821, and resulting in the treaty of 1825, Great Britain stood firmly by the position, not only that the territorial jurisdiction asserted by Russia on the northwest coast was in excess of what it was entitled to claim, but that the prohibition by that Ukase of the approach of foreign vessels nearer than 100 Italian miles to those coasts was an assertion of sovereignty over the open waters of the Sea, which was forbidden by the established principles of international law.

Let us see what was recognized and conceded by Great Britain during her negotiations with Russia.

In his communication of January 18, 1822, addressed to Count Lieven, the Russian Ambassador at London, in reply to the letter of Baron Nicolay, covering a copy of the Ukase of 1821, the Marquis of Londonderry, then at the head of the British Foreign Office, said: "Upon the subject of this Ukase generally, and especially upon the two main principles of claim laid down therein, viz, an exclusive sovereignty alleged to belong to Russia over the territories therein described, as also the exclusive right of navigating and trading *within the maritime limits therein set forth*, His Britannic Majesty must be understood as hereby reserving all his rights, not being prepared to admit that the intercourse which is allowed on the face of this instrument to have hitherto subsisted on those coasts, and in those seas, can be deemed to be illicit, or that the ships of friendly powers, even supposing an unqualified sovereignty was proved to appertain to the Imperial Crown in the vast and very imperfectly occupied territories, could, by the acknowledged laws of nations, be excluded from navigating within the distance of 100 Italian miles as therein laid down, from the coast, the exclusive dominion of which is assumed (but, as His Majesty's Government conceive, in error) to belong to His Imperial Majesty, the Emperor of all the Russias." *British Case, Vol. 2, App., 14.*

Subsequently, September 27, 1822, Mr. George Canning, the successor of Lord Londonderry, in the British Foreign Office, writing to the Duke of Wellington, who had been commissioned to acquaint the Russian Government with the views held by the British Government said that with respect to the points in the Ukase which had the effect of extending the territorial rights of Russia over the adjacent seas to the " unprecedented " distance of 100 miles from the line of coast, and of closing a hitherto unobstructed passage (through Bering Straits), at that time the object of important discoveries for the promotion of general commerce and navigation, those pretensions were considered by the best legal authorities as positive innovations on the right of navigation, and as such, could receive no explanation from further discussion, nor by any possibility be justified. Common usage, he said, which has obtained the force of law, had indeed assigned to coasts and shores an accessorial boundary to a short limited distance for purposes of protection and general convenience, in no manner interfering with the rights of others, and not obstructing the freedom of general commerce and navigation. But that important qualification, he observed, the extent of Russia's claim entirely excluded, and when such a prohibition was applied to a long line of coasts, and also to intermediate islands in remote seas, where navigation was beset with innumerable and unforeseen difficulties, and where the principal employment of the fisheries must be pursued under circumstances that were incompatible with the prescribed courses, " all particular considerations concur, in an especial manner; with the general principle, in repelling such a pretension as an encroachment on the freedom of navigation, and the inalienable rights of all nations." He expressed satisfaction in believing from a conference which he had had with Count Lieven that upon these two points—"the attempt to shut up the passage altogether, and the claim of exclusive dominion to so enormous a distance from the coast—the Russian Government are prepared entirely to waive their pretensions." *British Case, Vol. II, App., 22.*

After receiving this letter, the Duke of Wellington, November 28, 1822, delivered to Count Nesselrode, at the head of the Russian ministry, a confidential memorandum, in which he objected first, to the claim of sovereignty set forth in the Ukase; and, secondly, to the mode in which it is exercised. "The best writers on the laws of nations," he observed, "do not attribute exclusive sovereignty, particularly of continents, to those who have first discovered them, and although we might on good grounds dispute with Russia the priority of discovery of these continents, we contend that the much more easily proved, more conclusive, and more certain title of occupation and use ought to decide the claim of sovereignty." He explicitly declared that Great Britain could not admit the right of any power possessing the sovereignty of a country to exclude the vessels of others from the seas on its coasts *to the distance of 100 Italian miles.* *British Case, Vol. II, p. 23.*

The Duke of Wellington, writing on the same day to Count Lieven and repeating the objection of the British Government to the Ukase, so far as it assumed for Russia an exclusive sovereignty in the continent of North America, observed: "The second ground on which we object to the Ukase is that His Imperial Majesty thereby excludes from *a certain considerable extent of the open sea* vessels of other nations. We contend that the assumption of this power is contrary to the law of nations, and we cannot found a negotiation upon a paper in which it is again broadly asserted. We contend that no power whatever can exclude another from the use of the open sea. A power can exclude itself from the navigation of a certain coast, sea, etc., by its own act or engagement, but it cannot by right be excluded by another." *British Case, Vol. II, App. 25.*

I am unable to find a single sentence in all the diplomatic correspondence that took place between Russia and Great Britain, touching the Ukase of 1821, showing, or tending to show, that Great Britain modified, in the slightest degree the position taken by its representatives from the very outset, namely, that the maritime jurisdiction or authority claimed by Russia, upon whatever ground rested, to the extent of 100 Italian miles from its coasts, was inconsistent with the law of nations. On the contrary, after the expiration of more than two years without an agreement being reached as to the disputed questions of maritime supremacy and territorial sovereignty, and when serious apprehensions were felt that no satisfactory solution of those questions would be reached, Mr. Stratford Canning was sent by the British Government to St. Petersburg as Plenipotentiary to effect, if possible, a settlement of the pending dispute. He received a letter of instructions from Mr. George Canning, in which will be found an extended review of all previous efforts to accommodate the differences between the two countries, and a full statement of the grounds upon which Great Britain stood in respect to this Ukase.

If any doubt could arise from previous correspondence as to whether Great Britain recognized and conceded any jurisdiction upon the part of Russia in the waters of Bering Sea, outside of ordinary territorial limits, as those limits are defined by international law, that doubt will be removed by the examination of the letter of Mr. George Canning to Mr. Stratford Canning, of December 8, 1824, which was after the Treaty of 1824 between the United States and Russia was signed. That letter, inclosing a *projet* of settlement, is too lengthy to be inserted in full here, and the following extract from it must suffice:

"The whole negotiation grows out of the Ukase of 1821. So entirely and absolutely true is this proposition that the settlement of the limits of the respective possessions of Great Britain and Russia on the Northwest coast of America was proposed by us only as a mode of facilitating the adjustment of the difference arising from the Ukase by enabling the Court of Russia, under the cover of a more comprehensive arrangement, to withdraw, with less appearance of concession, the offensive pretensions of that edict. It is comparatively indifferent to us whether we hasten or postpone all questions respecting the limits of territorial possession on the continent of America, but the pretensions of the Russian Ukase of 1821 to exclusive dominion over the Pacific could not continue longer unrepealed without compelling us to take some measure of public and effectual remonstrance against it. * *

"That this Ukase is not acted upon, and that instructions have been long ago sent by the Russian Government to their cruisers in the Pacific to suspend the execution of its provisions, is true; but a private disavowal of a published claim is no security against the revival of that claim. The suspension of the execution of a principle may be perfectly compatible with the continued maintenance of the principle itself, and when we have seen in the course of this negotiation that the Russian claim to the possession of the coast of America down to latitude 59° rests in fact on no other ground than the presumed acquiescence of the nations of Europe in the provisions of the Ukase published by the Emperor Paul in the year 1800 [1799], against which it is affirmed that no public remonstrance was made, it becomes us to be exceedingly careful that we do not, by a similar neglect, on the present occasion allow a similar presumption to be raised as to an acquiescence in the Ukase of 1821. The right of the subjects of His Majesty to navigate freely in the Pacific can not be held as a matter of indulgence from any power. Having once been publicly questioned it must be publicly acknowledged. * * *

"It will, of course, strike the Russian plenipotentiaries that by the adoption of the American article respecting navigation, etc., the provision for an exclusive fishery of two leagues from the coasts of our respective possessions falls to the ground. But the omission is, in truth, immaterial. The law of nations assigns the exclusive sovereignty of one league to each power on its own coasts, without any specific stipulation, and though Sir Charles Bagot was authorized to sign the convention with the specific stipulation of two leagues, in ignorance of what had been decided in the American convention at the time, yet, after that convention has been some months before the world, and after the opportunity of consideration has been forced upon us by the act of Russia herself, we can not now consent in negotiating *de novo* to a stipulation which, while it is absolutely unimportant to any practical good, would appear to establish a contrast between the United States and us to our disadvantage. Count Nesselrode himself has frankly admitted that it was natural that we should expect, and reasonable that we should receive, at the hands of Russia, equal measure in all respects, with the United States of America.

"It remains only, in recapitulation, to remind you of the origin and principles of the whole negotiation. It is *not* on our part essentially a negotiation about limits. It is the demand of the repeal of an offensive and unjustifiable arrogation of exclusive jurisdiction over an ocean of unmeasured extent, but a demand qualified and mitigated in its manner in order that its justice may be acknowledged and satisfied without soreness or humiliation on the part of Russia. We negotiate about territory to cover the remonstrance upon principle. But any attempt to take undue advantage of this voluntary facility we must oppose. If the present '*projet*' is agreeable to Russia, we are ready to conclude and sign the treaty. If the territorial arrangements are not satisfactory, we are ready to postpone them; and to conclude and sign the essential part, that which relates to navigation alone, adding an article, stipulating to negotiate about territorial limits hereafter. But we are not prepared to defer any longer the settlement of that essential part of the question, and if Russia will neither sign the whole convention nor that essential part of it, she must not take it amiss that we resort to some mode of recording in the face of the world our protest against the pretensions of the Ukase of 1821, and of effectually securing our own interests against the possibility of its future operation." *British Case, Vol. 2, App., 73.*

The opposition of Great Britain to Russia's claim of maritime supremacy within 100 Italian miles from the coasts mentioned in the Ukase of 1821 was not more decided or persistent than that of the United States. The action taken by the United States is not irrelevant to the present discussion, because; as will presently appear, its counsel insists that Russia's treaty of 1825 with Great Britain is to be interpreted to mean just what the treaty of 1824 with the United States was understood by Russia, with the knowledge of the United States, to mean.

Referring to the reasons assigned by M. Poletica upon which Russia based the territorial and maritime claims asserted in that Ukase, Mr. Adams, the American Secretary of State, said, in reply: "This pretension is to be considered not only with reference to the question of territorial right, but also to that prohibition to the vessels of other nations, including those of the United States, to approach within 100 Italian miles of the coasts. From the period of the existence of the United States as an independent nation, their vessels have freely navigated those seas, and the right to navigate them is a part of that independence." Again: "As little can the United States accede to the justice of the reason assigned for the prohibition above mentioned. The right of the citizens of the United States to hold commerce with the aboriginal natives of the northwest coast of America, without the territorial jurisdiction of other nations, even in arms and munitions of war, is as clear and indisputable as that of navigating the seas. That right has never been exercised in a spirit unfriendly to Russia; and, although general complaints have occasionally been made on the subject of this commerce by some of your predecessors, no specific ground of charge has ever been alleged by them of any transaction in it by which the United States were, by the ordinary laws and usages of nations, bound either to restrain or punish. Had any such charge been made, it would have received the most pointed attention of this Government, with the sincerest and firmest disposition to perform every act and obligation of justice to yours which could have been required. I am commanded by the President of the United States to assure you that this disposition will continue to be entertained, together with the earnest desire that the harmonious relations between the two countries may be preserved.

Relying upon the assurance in your note of similar dispositions reciprocally entertained by His Imperial Majesty towards the United
States, the President is persuaded that the citizens of this Union will
remain unmolested in the prosecution of their lawful commerce, and
that no effect will be given to an interdiction manifestly incompatible
with their rights." *U. S. Case, Vol. 1, App., 131.*

Mr. Middleton, the American minister at St. Petersburg, writing to
Mr. Adams under date of August 8, 1822, said: "To Mr. Speransky,
Governor-General of Siberia, who had been one of the committee origi-
nating this measure, I stated my objections at length. He informed
me that the first intention had been (as M. Poletica afterward wrote
you) to declare the northern portion of the Pacific Ocean as *mare
clausum*, but *that idea being abandoned*, probably on account of its
extravagance, they determined to adopt the more moderate measure *of
establishing limits* to the maritime jurisdiction on their coasts, such as
should secure to the Russian American Fur Company the monopoly of
the very lucrative traffic they carry on. In order to do this they
sought a precedent and found the distance of 30 leagues named in the
treaty of Utrecht, and which may be calculated at about 100 Italian
miles, sufficient for all purposes. I replied ironically that a still better
precedent might have been pointed out to them in the papal bull of
1493, which established as a line of demarcation between the Spaniards
and Portuguese a meridian to be drawn at the distance of 100 miles
west of the Azores, and that the expression 'Italian miles' used in the
Ukase, very naturally might lead to the conclusion that this was actually
the precedent looked to. He took my remarks in good part, and I am
disposed to think that this conversation led him to make reflections
which did not tend to confirm his first impressions, for I found him
afterward at different times speaking confidentially upon the subject.
For some time past I began to perceive that the provisions of the Ukase
would not be persisted in. It appears to have been signed by the
Emperor without sufficient examination, and may be fairly considered
as having been surreptitiously obtained. There can be little doubt,
therefore, that with a little patience and management it will be molded
into a less objectionable shape." *U. S. Case, Vol. 1, App. 136.*

But this is not at all. Mr. Adams, writing to Mr. Middleton, under
date of July 22, 1823, said: "From the tenor of the Ukase the pretensions of the Imperial Government extend to an exclusive territorial

11492——6

jurisdiction from the forty-fifth degree of north latitude, on the Asiastic coast, to the latitude of fifty-one north on the western coast of the American continent; and they assume the right of interdicting the navigation and the fishery of all other nations *to the extent of 100 miles from the whole of the coast.* The United States can admit no part of these claims. Their right of navigation and of fishing is per- fect, and has been in constant exercise from the earliest times, after the peace of 1783, throughout the whole extent of the Southern Ocean, subject only to the ordinary exceptions and exclusions of the territorial jurisdictions, which, so far as Russian rights are concerned, are con- fined to certain islands north of the fifty-fifth degree of latitude, and have no existence in the continent of America." *U. S. Case, Vol. 1, App., 141.*

As tending further to show the construction placed by the United States upon the Ukase of 1821, and its decided opposition to the pre- tensions of Russia, reference may be made to the letter of Mr. Adams, written under date of July 23, 1823, to Mr. Rush, the American minister at London. In that letter Mr. Adams said: "By the Ukase of the Emperor Alexander of the 4th (16th) of September, 1821, an exclusive territorial right on the northwest coast of America is asserted as be- longing to Russia, and as extending *from the northwest extremity of the continent* to latitude 51°, and the navigation and fishing of all other nations are interdicted by the same Ukase *to the extent of 100 Italian miles from the coast.* When M. Poletica, the late Russian minister here, was called upon to set forth the grounds of right conformable to the laws of nations which authorized the issuing of this decree, he answered in his letters of February 28 and April 2, 1822, by alleging first discovery, occupancy, and uninterrupted possession. · It appears upon examina- tion that these claims have no foundation in fact."

In the same letter, after combating these claims and referring to the peculiar relations held by the United States to the question of colonial establishments on the North American continent, Mr. Adams said: "A necessary consequence of this state of things will be that the American continents henceforth will no longer be subjects of coloniza- tion. Occupied by civilized independent nations, they will be accessible to Europeans and to each other on that footing alone, and the Pacific Ocean *in every part of it* will remain open to the navigation of all nations in like manner with the Atlantic. Incidental to the condition of National independence and sovereignty, the rights of anterior navigation of their rivers will belong to each of the American nations within its own territories. The application of colonial principles of exclusion, therefore, can not be admitted by the United States as lawful on any part of the northwest coast of America, or as belonging to any European nation. Their own settlements there, when organized as territorial governments, will be adapted to the freedom of their own institutions, and, as constituent parts of the Union, be subject to the principles and provisions of their constitution. The right of carrying on trade with the natives throughout the northwest coast they (the United States) can not renounce. With the Russian settlements at Kodiak, or at New Archangel, they may fairly claim the advantage of a free trade, having so long enjoyed it unmolested, and because it has been and would continue to be as advantageous at least to those settlements as to them. But they will not contest the right of Russia to prohibit the traffic, as strictly confined to the Russian settlement itself and not extending to the original natives of the coast." *U. S. Case, Vol. 1, App., 145, 146, 148.*

Further reference to the diplomatic correspondence relating to the the Ukase of 1821 would seem to be unnecessary. The evidence is overwhelming that the positions taken by the United States and Great Britain were substantially alike, namely, that Russia claimed more territory on the northwest coast of America than it had title to, either by discovery or occupancy, and that its interdict of the approach of foreign vessels nearer to its coasts than 100 Italian miles was contrary to the principles of international law and in violation of the rights of the citizens and subjects of other countries engaged in lawful business on the waters covered by that regulation.

The negotiations between Russia and the United States resulted in the treaty of 1824, the material parts of which are as follows:

"ART. 1. It is agreed that in any part of the Great Ocean, commonly called the Pacific Ocean or South Sea, the respective citizens or subjects of the High Contracting Powers shall be neither disturbed nor restrained either in navigation or in fishing, or in the power of resorting to the coasts, upon points which may not already have been occupied for the purpose of trading with the natives, saving always, the restrictions and conditions determined by the following articles.

" ART. 2. With a view of preventing the rights of navigation and of fishing exercised upon the Great Ocean by the citizens and subjects of the High Contracting Powers from becoming the pretext for an illicit

84

trade, it is agreed that the citizens of the United States shall not resort to any point where there is a Russian establishment, without the permission of the Governor or Commander; and that, reciprocally, the subjects of Russia shall not resort, without permission to any establishment of the United States upon the Northwest Coast.

"ART. 3. It is moreover agreed that, hereafter, there shall not be formed by the citizens of the United States, or under the authority of the said States, any establishment upon the Northwest Coast of America, nor in any of the islands adjacent, to the north of 54° 40' north latitude; and that, in the same manner, there shall be none formed by Russian subjects, or under the authority of Russia, south of the same parallel.

"ART. 4. It is, nevertheless, understood that during a term of ten years, counting from the signature of the present convention, the ships of both powers or which may belong to their citizens or subjects respectively, may reciprocally frequent, without any hindrance whatever, the interior seas, gulfs, harbors and creeks, upon the coast mentioned in the preceding Article, for the purpose of fishing and trading with the natives of the country." *U. S. Stat. vol. 8, p. 302.*

The negotiations between Russia and Great Britain resulted in the treaty of 1825, as follows:

"I. It is agreed that the respective subjects of the high contracting Parties shall not be troubled or molested, in any part of the Great Ocean, commonly called the Pacific Ocean, either in navigating the same, in fishing therein, or in landing at such parts of the coast as shall not have been already occupied, in order to trade with the natives, under the restrictions and conditions specified in the following articles.

"II. In order to prevent the right of navigating and fishing, exercised upon the ocean by the subjects of the high contracting Parties, from becoming the pretext of an illicit commerce, it is agreed that the subjects of His Britannic Majesty shall not land at any place where there may be a Russian establishment, without the permission of the Governor or Commandant; and on that other hand, that Russian subjects shall not land, without permission, at any British establishment of the Northwest coast.

"III. The line of demarkation between the possessions of the high contracting Parties, upon the coast of the continent and the Islands of America to the Northwest, shall be drawn in the manner following:

Commencing from the southernmost point of the island called Prince of Wales Island, which point lies in the parallel of 54 degrees forty minutes, north latitude, and between the one hundred and thirty-first, and the one hundred and thirty-third degree of west longitude (Meridian of Greenwich), the said line shall ascend to the north along the channel called Portland Channel, as far as the point of the continent where it strikes the fifty-sixth degree of north latitude; from this last mentioned point the line of demarkation shall follow the summit of the mountains situated parallel to the coast, as far as the point of intersection of the one hundred and forty-first degree, of west longitude (of the same meridian) and, finally, from the said point of intersection, the said meridian line of the one hundred and forty-first degree, in its prolongation as far as the Frozen Ocean, shall form the limit between the Russian and British possessions on the continent of America to the Northwest.

"IV. With reference to the line of demarkation laid down in the preceding article it is understood:

First. That the Island called Prince of Wales Island shall belong wholly to Russia.

Second. That wherever the summit of the mountains which extend in a direction parallel to the coast, from the fifty-sixth degree of north latitude to the point of intersection of the one hundred and forty-first degree of west longitude, shall prove to be at the distance of more than ten marine leagues from the ocean, the limit between the British possessions and the line of coast which is to belong to Russia, as above mentioned, shall be formed by a line parallel to the windings of the coast, and which shall never exceed the distance of ten marine leagues therefrom.

" V. It is moreover agreed, that no establishment shall be formed by either of the two parties within the limits assigned by the two preceding articles to the possessions of the other; consequently, British subjects shall not form any establishment either upon the coast, or upon the border of the continent comprised within the limits of the Russian possessions, as designated in the two preceding articles; and, in like manner, no establishment shall be formed by Russian subjects beyond the said limits.

" VI. It is understood that the subjects of His Britannic Majesty, from whatever quarter they may arrive, whether from the ocean, or from the interior of the continent, shall forever enjoy the right of navigating freely, and without any hindrance whatever, all the rivers and streams which, in their course towards the Pacific Ocean, may cross the line of demarkation upon the line of coast described in article three of the present Convention.

" VII. It is also understood that for the space of ten years from the signature of the present convention, the vessels of the two Powers, or those belonging to their respective subjects, shall mutually be at liberty to frequent, without any hindrance whatever, all the inland seas, the gulfs, havens, and creeks on the coast mentioned in article three for the purposes of fishing and trading with the natives.

"VIII. The port of Sitka, or Nova Archangelsk, shall be open to the commerce and vessels of British subjects for the space of ten years from the date of the exchange of the ratifications of the present convention. In the event of an extention of this term of ten years being granted to any other power, the like extention shall be granted also to Great Britain.

" IX. The above-mentioned liberty of commerce shall not apply to the trade in spirituous liquors, in fire-arms, or other arms, gunpowder or other warlike stores; the high contracting Parties reciprocally engaging not to permit the above-mentioned articles to be sold or delivered, in any manner whatever, to the natives of the country.

" X. Every British or Russian vessel navigating the Pacific Ocean, which may be compelled by storms or by accident, to take shelter in the ports of the respective Parties, shall be at liberty to refit therein, to provide itself with all necessary stores, and to put to sea again, without paying any other port and lighthouse dues, which shall be the same as those paid by national vessels. In case, however, the master of such vessel should be under the necessity of disposing of a part of his merchandise in order to defray his expenses, he shall conform himself to the regulations and tariffs of the place where he may have landed."

From these treaties it will be seen that the respective subjects or citizens of the High Contracting Parties were not to be molested or disturbed in navigating, or in fishing in, any part of the Pacific Ocean, or in landing on the coasts of either country, not then occupied, in order to trade with the natives, except under certain specified conditions which have no bearing upon the present controversy.

We now come to the third point in Article VI of the Treaty—

Was the body of water now known as the Bering Sea included in the phrase "Pacific Ocean," as used in the treaty of 1825 between Great Britain and Russia; and what rights, if any, in the Bering Sea were held and exclusively exercised by Russia after said treaty?

An affirmative answer to this question would sustain the position taken by Mr. Blaine, to the effect that the treaty of 1825, as between Russia and Great Britain, had reference only to the dispute in respect to the boundary line between those countries on the northwest coast of America, south of the 60th degree of north latitude, and to the waters of the Pacific Ocean south of the Alaskan Peninsula, and in no way to the waters of Bering Sea, or to the Ukase of 1821 in its application to the waters of that Sea. If that position was well taken, it might be fairly contended that Great Britain by signing the treaty of 1825, impliedly recognized, or determined not to further question, the validity of the Ukase of 1821 in its application to the waters of Bering Sea, for the distance of 100 Italian miles from its shores and islands in that sea. But if "Pacific Ocean" in the treaty of 1825 embraced Bering Sea, it would follow that that treaty had the effect to annul or withdraw that Ukase, so far as it asserted authority in Russia to molest or disturb the subjects of Great Britain in navigating, or fishing in, any of the open waters of Bering Sea or of the north Pacific Ocean.

It will be observed that there is no substantial difference between the treaties of 1824 and 1825, in respect to the description given of the waters in which the citizens or subjects of the High Contracting Parties were to enjoy freedom of navigation and fishing. The words in the treaty of 1824, "the Great Ocean, commonly called the Pacific Ocean or South Sea," evidently describe the same waters as the words, "the Great Ocean, commonly called the Pacific Ocean," in the treaty of 1825.

Before the latter treaty was negotiated the British Government had in its possession a copy of the treaty between Russia and the United States. Mr. George Canning, in his letter of December 8th, 1824, referring to a *projet* proposed by Great Britain, and which Russia rejected, and to a counter *projet* proposed by Russia which Great Britain had rejected, said that the stipulation for free navigation in the Pacific stood in the front of the Convention concluded between Russia and the United States of America; that no reason existed why upon similar claims Great Britain should not obtain exactly the like satisfaction; that for reasons of the same nature Great Britain could not consent that the liberty of navigation through Bering Straits be stated in the treaty as a boon from Russia; that the tendency of such a statement would be to give countenance to those claims of exclusive jurisdiction against which Great Britain on its own behalf, and on that of the whole civilized world, protested. No specification of this sort, he said, was found in the Convention with the United States of America, and yet it could not be doubted that the Americans considered themselves as secured in the right of navigating Bering Straits and the sea beyond them. "It can not be expected," he said, "that England should receive as a boon that which the United States hold as a right so unquestionable as not to be worth recording. Perhaps the simplest course after all will be to substitute, for all that part of the 'projet' and 'counter projet' which relates to maritime rights and to navigation, the first two articles of the convention already concluded by the court of St. Petersburg with the United States of America in the order in which they stand in that convention. Russia can not mean to give to the United States of America what she withholds from us; nor to withhold from us anything that she has consented to give to the United States. The uniformity of stipulations *in pari materia* gives clearness and force to both arrangements, and will establish that footing of equality between the several contracting parties which it is most desirable should exist between three powers whose interests come so nearly in contact with each other in a part of the globe in which no other power is concerned." *British Case, Vol. 2, App., 73.*

In view of these and similar declarations by British representatives, made before the negotiation of the treaty of 1825, it is earnestly contended that that treaty must receive the same interpretation that would be given to the treaty of 1824 as construed by Russia and the United States. And it is said that Russia and the United States, before the ratification of the treaty of 1824, substantially agreed that that treaty did not refer to the waters of Bering Sea, and, consequently, it is argued, "Pacific Ocean," as used in both treaties, must be held not to include that Sea.

The facts upon which these contentions, in respect to the treaty of 1824, are based, may be thus summarized:

The treaty of 1824 was signed at St. Petersburg April 5 (17), 1824.

Shortly thereafter the Russian-American Company represented to the Russian Government that consequences injurious to its rights might result from its ratification. The subject was referred by the Emperor to a committee, at the head of which was Count Nesselrode. That committee, July 21, 1824, made a report, which received the approval of the Emperor. After enumerating the advantages that would accrue to Russia from carrying out the treaty, the report proceeds: "7. That as the sovereignty of Russia over the coasts of Siberia and the Aleutian Islands has long been admitted by all the powers, it follows that the said coasts and islands can not be alluded to in the articles of the said treaty, which refers only to the disputed territory on the northwest coast of America and to the adjacent islands; that, even supposing the contrary, Russia has established permanent settlements, not only on the coast of Siberia but also on the Aleutian group of islands; hence, American subjects could not, by virtue of the second article of the treaty of April 5-17 land at the maritime places there, nor carry on sealing and fishing without the permission of our commandants or governors. Moreover, the coasts of Siberia and the Aleutian Islands are not washed by the Southern Sea, of which alone mention is made in the first article of the treaty, but by the Northern Ocean and the seas of Kamchatka and Ohkotsk, which form no part of the Southern Sea on any known map or in any geography. 8. Lastly, we must not lose sight of the fact that, by the treaty of April 5-17 all the disputes to which the regulations of September 4 (16), 1821, gave rise, are terminated, which regulations were issued at the formal and reiterated request of the Russian-American Company; that those disputes had already assumed important proportions, and would certainly be renewed if Russia did not ratify the treaty, in which case it would be impossible to foresee the end of them or their consequences. These weighty reasons impel the majority of the members of the committee to state as their opinion:

"That the treaty of April 5-17 must be ratified, and that, for the prevention of any incorrect interpretation of that act, Gen. Baron Tuyll may be instructed at the proper time to make the declaration mentioned in the draft of the communication read by Count Nesselrode. The Minister of Finance and Acting State Counselor Drushinin, while admitting the necessity of ratifying the treaty of April 5-17, express and place on record the special opinion hereto annexed in the proctocol, to the effect that Baron Tuyll should be instructed at the exchange of

the ratification of that treaty to stipulate that the right of free hunting
and fishing granted by the twelfth article of the said treaty shall extend
only from 54° 40′ to the latitude of Cross Sound." *U. S. Counter
Case, 156, 157.*

This report was communicated by the Russian Minister of Finance
to the Russian-American Company, in a communication which closed
with these words: "From these documents the board will see that, for
the avoidance of all misunderstandings in the execution of the above
mentioned convention, and in conformity with the desire of the company, the necessary instructions have already been given to Baron
Tuyll, our minister at Washington, to the effect that the northwestern
coast of America, along the extent of which, by the provisions of the
convention, free trading and fishing are permitted subjects of the North
American States, extends from 54° 40′ northwards to Yakutat (Bering)
Bay." *U. S. Counter Case, 155.*

The instructions received by Baron Tuyll from his Government were
communicated by him informally to Mr. Adams, the American Secretary of State. This appears from the Diary of Mr. Adams, under date
of December 5, 1824, at which time the treaty of 1824 had not been
approved by the United States Senate. The account which Mr. Adams
gives in his Diary of Baron Tuyll's interview with him, is as follows:

"*6th, Monday.*—Baron Tuyll, the Russian Minister, wrote me a note
requesting an immediate interview, in consequence of instructions
received yesterday from his court. He came, and after intimating that
he was under some embarrassment in executing his instructions, said
that the Russian American Company, upon learning the purport of the
northwest coast convention, concluded last June by Mr. Middleton, were
extremely dissatisfied ("a jeté des hauts cris"), and by means of their
influence had prevailed upon his Government to send him these instructions upon two points. One was, that he should deliver, upon
the exchange of the ratifications of the convention, an explanatory
note, purporting that the Russian Government did not understand that
the convention would give liberty to the citizens of the United States
to trade on the coasts of Siberia and the Aleutian Islands. The other
was, to propose a modification of the convention by which our vessels
should be prohibited from trading on the northwest coast north of
latitude 57. With regard to the former of these points he left with
me a minute in writing.

"I told him that we should be disposed to do everything to accommodate the views of his Government that was in our power, but that a modification of the convention could be made no otherwise than by a new convention, and *that the construction of the convention as concluded belonged to other departments of the Government, for which the Executive had no authority to stipulate; that if on the exchange of the ratifications he should deliver to me a note of the purport of that which he now informally gave me, I should give him an answer of that import, namely, that the construction of treaties depending here upon the judiciary tribunals, the Executive Government, even if disposed to acquiesce in that of the Russian Government as announced by him, could not be binding upon the courts nor upon this nation.* I added that the convention would be submitted immediately to the Senate; that if anything affecting its construction, or, still more, modifying its meaning, were to be presented on the part of the Russian Government before or at the exchange of ratifications, it must be laid before the Senate, and could have no other possible effect than of starting doubts and perhaps hesitation in that body, and of favoring the views of those, if such there were, who might wish to defeat the ratification itself of the convention. This was an object of great solicitude to both Governments, not only for the adjustment of a difficult question which had arisen between them, but for the promotion of that harmony which was so much in the policy of the two countries, which might emphatically be termed natural friends to each other. If, therefore, he would permit me to suggest to him what I thought would be his best course, it would be to wait for the exchange of the ratifications and make it purely and simply; that afterwards, if the instructions of his Government were imperative, he might present the note, *to which I now informed him what would be in substance my answer.* It necessarily could not be otherwise. But if his instructions left it discretionary with him, he would do still better to inform his government of the state of things here, of the purport of our conference, and of what my answer must be if he should present the note. I believed his court would then deem it best that he should not present the note at all. Their apprehensions had been excited by an interest not very friendly to the good understanding between the United States and Russia. Our merchants would not go to trouble the Russians on the coast of Siberia or north of the fifty-seventh degree of latitude, and it was wisest not to put such fancies into their heads. At least, the Imperial Government might wait to see the operation of the convention before taking any further step, and I was confident they would hear no complaint resulting from it. If they should, then would be the time for adjusting the construction or negotiating a modification of the convention; and whoever might be at the head of the administration of the United States, he might be assured that every disposition would be cherished to remove all causes of dissatisfaction and to accommodate the wishes and the just policy of the Emperor.

"The Baron said that these ideas had occurred to himself; that he had made this application in pursuance of his instructions, *but he was aware of the distribution of powers in our Constitution and of the incompetency of the Executive to adjust questions.* He would, therefore, wait for the exchange of the ratifications without presenting his note, and reserve for future consideration whether to present it shortly afterwards or to inform his court of what he had done and ask their further instructions as to what he shall definitively do on the subject. He therefore requested me to consider what had now passed between us as if it had not taken place ("non a venu"), to which I readily assented, assuring him, as I had done heretofore, that the President had the highest personal confidence in him and in his exertions to foster the harmony between the two countries. I reported immediately to the President the substance of this conversation, and he concurred in the propriety of the baron's final determination." *Memoirs of John Quincy Adams, Vol. 6, p. 485.*

In conformity (it may be assumed) with Mr. Adams' advice or intimations Baron Tuyll forebore to file any official note upon the subject prior to the ratification of the treaty by the United States. The treaty having been ratified January 15, 1825, and January 25, 1825, Baron Tuyll, under instructions from his Government, filed in the Department of State, the following Explanatory Note:

"Explanatory note to be presented to the Government of the United States at the time of the exchange of ratifications, with a view to removing with more certainty all occasion for future discussions, by means of which it will be seen that the Aleutian Islands, the coast of Siberia, and the Russian possessions in general on the northwest coast of America to 59° 30' of north latitude are positively excepted from the liberty of hunting, fishing, and commerce stipulated in favor of citizens of the United States for ten years.

"This seems to be only a natural consequence of the stipulations agreed upon, for the coasts of Siberia are washed by the Sea of Okhotsk, the Sea of Kamschatka, and the Icy Sea, and not by the South Sea mentioned in the first article of the convention of April 5 (17), 1824. The Aleutian Islands are also washed by the Sea of Kamschatka, or Northern Ocean.

"It is not the intention of Russia to impede the free navigation of the Pacific Ocean. She would be satisfied with causing to be recognized, as well as understood and placed beyond all manner of doubt, the principle that beyond 59° 30′ no foreign vessel can approach her coasts and her islands, nor fish nor hunt within the distance of two marine leagues. This will not prevent the reception of foreign vessels which have been damaged or beaten by storm." *U. S. Case, Vol. 1, App., 275; Memoirs of John Quincy Adams, Vol. 6, p. 435.*

In respect to these matters Mr. Blaine observed: "Of course his (Baron Tuyll's) act at that time did not affect the text of the treaty, but it placed in the hands of the Government of the United States an unofficial note which significantly told what Russia's construction of the treaty would be if, unhappily, any difference as to its meaning should arise between the two governments. But Mr. Adams' friendly intimation removed all danger of dispute, for it conveyed to Russia the assurance that the treaty as negotiated contained, in effect, the provisions which the Russian note was designed to supply. From that time until Alaska, with all its rights of land and water, was transferred to the United States—a period of forty-three years—no act or word on the part of either government ever impeached the full validity of the treaty as it was understood both by Mr. Adams and Baron Tuyll at the time it was formally proclaimed. While these important matters were transpiring in Washington negotiations between Russia and England (ending in the treaty of 1825) were in progress in St. Petersburg. The instructions to Baron Tuyll concerning the Russian-American treaty were fully reflected in the care with which the Anglo-Russian treaty was constructed—a fact to which I have already adverted in full. There was, indeed, a possibility that the true meaning of the treaty with the United States might be misunderstood, and it was, therefore, the evident purpose of the Russian Government to make the treaty with England so plain and so clear as to leave no room for doubt and to baffle all attempts at misconstruction. The Government of the United States finds the full advantage to it in the caution taken by Russia in

1825, and can, therefore, quote the Anglo-Russian treaty with the utmost confidence that its meaning can not be changed from that clear, unmistakable text which throughout all the articles sustains the American contention. The Explanatory Note filed with this Government by Baron Tuyll is so plain in its text that after the lapse of sixty-six years the exact meaning can neither be misapprehended nor misrepresented. It draws the distinction between the Pacific Ocean and the waters now known as the Bering Sea so particularly and so perspicuously that no answer can be made to it. It will bear the closest analysis in every particular. It is not the intention of Russia to impede the free navigation of the Pacific Ocean. This frank and explicit statement shows with what entire good faith Russia had withdrawn in both treaties the offensive Ukase of Alexander so far as the Pacific Ocean was made subject to it. Another avowal is equally explicit, viz, that the coast of Siberia, the northwest coast of America to 59° 30′ north latitude—that is, down to 59° 30′, the explanatory note reckoned from north to south—and the Aleutian Islands are positively excepted from the liberty of hunting, fishing, and commerce, stipulated in favor of citizens of the United States for ten years." *U. S. Case, Vol. I, App., 277, 278.*

It seems to me that the interview between Baron Tuyll and Mr. Adams is of far less consequence than that attached to it by Mr. Blaine. Nor, in my judgment, are the inferences which he draws from it justified by the facts as disclosed by the Russian documents and by the Diary of Mr. Adams.

Recurring to the treaty of 1824, it will be remembered that Article 1 secured to the respective citizens and subjects of the contracting powers freedom of navigation and fishing in every part of the Great Ocean commonly called the Pacific Ocean, or South Sea, and also the right to resort to coasts upon points not then occupied for the purpose of trading with the natives, subject to or saving the restrictions and conditions prescribed in the succeeding articles. Among those conditions were: 1. By Article II, citizens of the United States should not resort to any point where there was a Russian establishment without the permission of the Government or commander, and the subjects of Russia should not resort, without permission, to any establishment of the United States upon the northwest coast. 2. By Article III, neither the United States nor its citizens should form any establishment upon the northwest coast of America, nor in the islands adjacent, to the north of fifty-four degrees and forty minutes of north latitude, and that, in the same manner, there shall be none formed by Russian subjects or under the authority of Russia south of the same parallel. But by Article IV it was provided that for a period of ten years the ships of either country might frequent the interior seas, gulfs, harbors, and creeks, upon the coast mentioned in the preceding article, for the purpose of fishing and trading with the natives of the country.

Now it is apparent from the proceedings of the Nesselrode conference of July 21, 1824, the Diary of Mr. Adams, and the Explanatory Note of Baron Tuyll, that the Russian-American Company were not at all disturbed by the broad recognition in Article I of freedom of navigation and fishing throughout the whole of the Great Ocean. Their uneasiness had reference to the possibility that the treaty could be construed as giving the right for ten years to trade *on the coast of Siberia and the Aleutian Islands.* The substance of the answer made by the Russian Government to the Russian-American Company was that the article of the treaty reserving the right to resort for ten years to certain "interior seas, gulfs, harbors, and creeks" referred to the waters that washed the coast mentioned in Article III, which was the coast most in dispute between the two countries, and, therefore, did not authorize citizens of the United States to trade on the coasts of Siberia and the Aleutian Islands which were never in dispute, and over which Russia for a long time, and without question, had exercised sovereign authority; in other words, that the privilege of trading for ten years did not extend to the coast of Siberia, or to the Aleutian Islands, or to the Russian possessions *in general* on the entire northwest coast of America, but only to the coasts, embracing the territory in dispute between the two countries, south of 59° 30′ north latitude. Nowhere in the documents referred to is there a suggestion that Russia understood the treaty of 1824 as reserving to itself any peculiar or paramount authority over the waters of the Pacific Ocean outside of the ordinary limit of territorial jurisdiction. The only part of any document implying that, in the judgment of the Russian authorities, the treaty had no reference to Bering Sea, is the statement incidentally in the proceedings of the Nesselrode Conference and in the Explanatory Note of Baron Tuyll, to the effect that the coasts of Siberia and the Aleutian Islands were not washed "by the Southern Sea" mentioned in Article II. But there is no evidence in Mr. Adams's Diary that he assented to this view. He waived any discussion of the question.

It was impossible for him to have assented to the views of Baron Tuyll except upon the theory that he recognized the treaty of 1824 as having no reference at all to the waters of the Bering Sea as part of the Great Ocean commonly called the Pacific Ocean or South Sea, a conclusion at variance with all that he contended for throughout the negotiations arising from the Ukase of 1821. In my opinion, Mr. Blaine was mistaken in saying that Mr. Adams expressed his concurrence in Baron Tuyll's interpretation of the treaty of 1824. It is, I think, quite clear that Mr. Adams prudently withheld any expression of his opinion, disclaiming authority in himself or in the President of the United States to change or give any binding interpretation of the treaty. He frankly stated to Baron Tuyll that the treaty as made must, when ratified, be carried out according to its proper interpretation and meaning. He warned him that if, on the exchange of the ratifications, he should deliver a note of the purport of that informally delivered, he, Mr. Adams, should tell him "that the construction of treaties depending here upon the judiciary tribunals, the Executive Government, even if disposed to acquiesce in that of the Russian Government as announced by him, could not be binding upon the courts nor upon this nation." Baron Tuyll distinctly said that he understood the relations subsisting in America between the executive and judicial departments of Government. So that the utmost that can be said is, that the United States had notice, before the ratification of the treaty of 1824, of the interpretation which Russia, possibly, at some future time, would place upon the treaty, so far as it embraced the subject to which Baron Tuyll referred in his Explanatory Note.

The material inquiry, however, is whether Great Britain had any notice of what took place in the interview between Baron Tuyll and Mr. Adams. This question must be answered in the negative. It is not claimed that the Explanatory Note of Baron Tuyll was ever published or brought to light from the files of the State Department of the United States until it was produced in this case. Nor is it pretended that a copy of it was ever sent to Great Britain. The only document relied upon to show knowledge upon the part of Great Britain of the interpretation placed by the United States upon the treaty of 1824 is the letter of Mr. Addington, the British representative at Washington, written August 2, 1824, to Mr. George Canning. Mr. Addington said: "A convention concluded between this Government and that of Russia for the settlement of the respective claims of the two nations to the intercourse with the northwestern coast of America reached the Department of State a few days since. The main points determined by this instrument are, as far as I can collect from the American Secretary of State, (1) the enjoyment of a free and unrestricted intercourse by each nation with all the settlements of the other on the northwest coast of America, and (2) a stipulation that no new settlements shall be formed by Russia south, or by the United States north, of latitude 51° 40'. The question of the *mare clausum*, the sovereignty over which was asserted by the Emperor of Russia in his celebrated Ukase of 1821, but virtually, if not expressly, renounced by a subsequent declaration of that sovereign, has, Mr. Adams assures me, not been touched upon in the above-mentioned treaty. Mr. Adams seemed to consider any formal stipulation recording that renunciation as unnecessary and supererogatory." *British Case, App. Vol. 2, p. 66.*

It is to be observed, in reference to this letter, that it was written many months prior to the interview with Baron Tuyll, and only a few days after the treaty of 1824 had reached the United States Department of State. Besides, if the writer of that letter understood Mr. Adams to say that the question of free navigation and fishing by the citizens and subjects of Russia and the United States in the Pacific Ocean had "not been touched upon in the treaty" of 1824, it is clear that he must have wholly misapprehended the observations of the American Secretary of State. The treaty, upon its face, shows just the contrary. M. de Poletica, it will be remembered, at the very outset of the negotiations between Russia and the United States, expressly waived the question of the right of Russia to regard the whole sea between the North American and Asiatic continents north of 51° north latitude on one side and 45° north latitude on the other side, as a "shut sea," and only insisted upon Russia's right, as a means of protecting its colonial industries and trade, to prevent foreign vessels from coming nearer to her coasts that 100 Italian miles. If Mr. Adams said to Mr. Addington that the question of *mare clausum* had not been touched upon in the treaty of 1824 he meant only that the question of *mare clausum*, or "shut sea," as stated in its broadest aspect, but expressly waived, by M. Poletica, had not been specifically disposed of by that treaty. He could not have said that the right of the subjects and citizens of the two countries to freely navigate and fish in the open waters of the sea was left untouched by the treaty of 1824.

11492——7

That Great Britain signed the treaty of 1825 without any knowledge that the treaty of 1824 would be interpreted otherwise than by its words, according to their natural signification, is shown by the letter of Mr. Stratford Canning (who negotiated the treaty of 1825) to Mr. George Canning, under date of April 3–15, 1825, in which he said: "Referring to the American treaty, I am assured as well by Count Nesselrode as by Mr. Middleton [the American minister at St. Petersburg] that the ratification of that instrument was not accompanied by any explanations calculated to modify or affect in any way the force and meaning of its articles. But I understand that at the close of the negotiation of that treaty a protocol, intended by the Russians to fix more specifically the limitations of the right of trading with their possessions, and understood by the American envoy as having no such effect, was drawn up and signed by both parties. No reference whatever was made to this paper by the Russian plenipotentiaries in the course of my negotiations with them; and you are aware, sir, that the articles of the convention which I concluded depend for their force entirely on the general acceptation of the terms in which they are expressed." It does not appear that any such protocol was ever, in fact, executed; at any rate, we have no evidence that it was executed.

If this were a case between the United States and Russia, involving the question as to whether the treaty of 1824, in using the words "Pacific Ocean," covered the waters of Bering Sea, other considerations might possibly arise than those which must determine that question under the treaty of 1825 with Great Britain. Here the inquiry is whether Great Britain and Russia in that treaty referred to "Pacific Ocean" as including Bering Sea. And that inquiry can only be determined, apart from the words of the treaty itself, by what passed between the representatives of those two countries during the negotiations resulting in the treaty between them, of which the only evidence is found in the letters and official documents having reference to those negotiations.

Did Russia and Great Britain intend that Article I of the treaty of 1825, by which those powers agreed that their respective subjects "shall not be troubled or molested in any part of the Great Ocean commonly called the Pacific Ocean, either in navigating the same or in fishing therein," should be applicable to Bering Sea? Did either Government at the time the negotiations were opened, or when the treaty was concluded, regard Bering Sea as outside of the ocean "commonly called the Pacific Ocean"? In view of the grounds upon which Great Britain, during negotiations extending over three years, steadily rested its objections to the Ukase of 1821, can it be presumed or supposed that she intended to leave that Ukase in force as to the waters of Bering Sea and thereby recognize the right of Russia to prohibit British vessels from approaching any of the coasts of that sea nearer than 100 Italian miles?

It seems to me that these questions must all be answered in the negative. What waters, according to the understanding of *Russia*, at the date of the treaty, were in fact embraced in the Pacific Ocean? Upon this point there is scarcely room for doubt. In the letter of Baron Nicolay, dated November 12, 1821, in which he gave notice to the British Government of the Ukase of 1821, he states that the possessions of Russia "extend on the northwest coast of America from the Bering Strait to the fifty-first degree of north latitude, as well as on the coast of Asia opposite and on the adjacent islands, from the same strait to forty-five degrees," and that if " the Imperial Government had strictly the right to close to foreigners that portion of the Pacific Ocean which is bounded by our possessions in America and Asia, *a fortiori*, the right in virtue of which it has just adopted a much less restrictive measure should not be called in question." In the letter, already referred to, of February 28, 1822, in which M. Poletica stated fully the grounds upon which Russia based the Ukase of 1821, he stated that the first discoveries of Russia on the northwest coast of America went back to the time of Peter I, and belonged to the attempt made towards the end of his reign " to find a passage from the Icy Sea into the Pacific Ocean"; implying that the Icy Sea, which is now known as the Arctic Ocean, was connected with the Pacific Ocean. In the same letter, in which he describes the limits assigned to Russian possessions by the Ukase of 1821, M. Poletica states that " the Russian possessions in the Pacific Ocean extend on the northwest coast of America from Bering Strait to the fifty-first degree of north latitude, and on the opposite side of Asia and the islands adjacent from the same strait to the forty-fifth degree." It thus appears that Russia, by its representatives, in language too clear to admit of doubt as to its meaning, regarded all of its possessions on the northwest coast of America, extending from Bering Strait to the fifty-first degree of north latitude, as being on the Pacific Ocean.

It is equally clear that Great Britain so understood the matter. In no dispatch emanating from the British Foreign Office is there anything indicating that, in its judgment, Bering Sea was not a part of the Great Ocean commonly called the Pacific Ocean, or that its Government was concerned simply about navigation and fishing in the waters south of the Alaskan Peninsula, which washed the shores of the particular territory, limited in extent, and then in dispute between that country and Russia. On the contrary, in the *projet* of a convention which Mr. George Canning, on the 12th of July, 1824, prepared for the consideration of Russia, it distinctly appears that Great Britain contemplated a treaty covering all the coasts and waters on the North American coast from Bering Strait southward. Article I in that draft provided: "It is agreed between the high contracting parties that their respective subjects shall enjoy the right of free navigation along *the whole extent of the Pacific Ocean, comprehending the sea within Bering Straits*, and shall be neither troubled nor molested in carrying on their trade and fisheries, *in all parts of the said ocean, either to the northward or southward thereof;* it being well understood that the said right of fishery shall not be exercised by the subjects of either of the two powers nearer than two marine leagues from the respective possessions of the other."

In his letter inclosing this *projet* to Sir Charles Bagot, the British minister at St. Petersburg, Mr. Canning said: "Your Excellency will observe that there are but two points which have struck Count Lieven as susceptible of any question. The first is the assumption of the base of the mountains, instead of the summit, as the line of boundary; the second, the extension of the right of the navigation *of the Pacific to the sea beyond Bering Straits*. As to the second point, it is, perhaps, as Count Lieven remarks, new. But it is to be remarked, in return, that the circumstances under which this additional security is required will be new also. By the territorial demarcation agreed to in this '*projet*', Russia will become possessed, in acknowledged sovereignty, of both sides of Bering's Straits. The power which could think of making the Pacific a *mare clausum* may not unnaturally be supposed capable of a disposition to apply the same character to a strait comprehended between two shores of which it becomes the undisputed owner; but the shutting up of Bering Straits, or the power to shut them up hereafter, would be a thing not to be tolerated by England. Nor could we submit to be excluded, either positively or constructively, from a sea in which the skill and science of our seamen has been and is still employed in enterprises interesting not to this country alone, but to the whole civilized world. The protection given by the convention to the American coasts of each power may (if it is thought necessary) be extended in terms to the coasts of the Russian Asiatic territory; but in some way or other, if not in the form now prescribed, the free navigation of Bering's Straits and of the seas beyond them must be secured to us." *British Case, Vol. 2, App. 65.*

Of course Mr. Canning, when he framed the above draft of a convention regarded the waters immediately south of "the sea within Bering Strait" as part of the Pacific Ocean. The same draft shows that he contemplated the settlement of the rights of the two nations on the entire coasts and in all the waters south of Bering Strait. And such evidently was the purpose of Russia, which offered a counter-*projet* of a convention, to settle, "according to the principle of mutual accommodation, the boundary between their possessions and settlements on the northwest coast of America, as well as divers questions relating to commerce, navigation, and fishing by their respective subjects in the Pacific Ocean." After defining the line of demarcation between the possessions of the two high contracting parties on the northwest coast of America and the adjacent islands, and according to the vessels and the subjects of the two powers the right in the possessions of the two powers, as defined, for ten years " to freely frequent the gulfs, harbors, and creeks in those parts of the islands and of the coast which are not occupied by either Russian or English settlements, and there to engage in fishing and commerce with the natives of the country," the Russian counter-projet proceeds: "Art. IV. In future no settlement shall be formed by His Britannic Majesty's subjects within the limits of Russian possessions set out in Articles I and II, and, in like manner, none shall be formed by the subjects of His Majesty the Emperor of all the Russias outside of the said limits. Art. V. The High Contracting Parties stipulate moreover, that their respective subjects will have the right to freely navigate *the whole extent of the Pacific Ocean, both towards the north and south,* without any hindrance whatever, and that they will enjoy the right of fishery in the high seas, but that this latter right shall never be exercised within a distance of two marine leagues from the coast or possessions—whether Russian or British. Art. VI. His Majesty the Emperor of all the Russias, being anxious to give a special proof of his regard for the interests of His Britannic Majesty's subjects, and to render more useful the success of the enterprises which will eventually result in the discovery of a passage on the north of the American continent, consents that the freedom of navigation mentioned in the preceding article shall apply, under the same conditions, to Bering Strait, *and to the sea situated to the northward of said strait.* Art. VII. Any Russian or British ships navigating *the Pacific Ocean and the sea above mentioned* that may be obliged, by storms or by damages, to take refuge in the respective ports of the High Contracting Parties, shall be allowed to refit therein, and to take aboard everything necessary, and to sail away again freely, without paying any other charges than port and lighthouse dues, which shall be the same as those paid by national vessels." *British Case, Vol. 2, App., 68, 69.*

Is it not apparent from this counter-*projet* that Russia regarded the "sea situated to the northward" of Bering Strait, that is, the Arctic Sea, as being separated from the Pacific Ocean only by the waters of that Strait, and therefore that what is now called Bering Sea was regarded by the Government of that country as part of the Pacific Ocean? If Russia did not then regard Bering Sea as a part of the Pacific Ocean, it would follow that the privilege given by Article VII of the counter-*projet* to "Russian or British ships navigating the Pacific Ocean *and the sea above mentioned*" (the sea north of Bering Strait) to take temporary refuge, in case of storms or damage, in the respective ports of the two countries, could not be exercised by a British vessel navigating Bering Sea. A purpose to make such a distinction ought not to be imputed to Russia. It ought not to be supposed that Russia intended to assent to the navigation by British vessels of Bering Strait and the sea to the northward of it, and yet restrict the right of navigation in the waters immediately south of Bering Strait. This supposition is entirely inconsistent with the declaration in the counter-*projet* that the treaty which the two governments were seeking to negotiate had in view the settlement of questions relating to commerce, navigation, and fishing by their respective subjects "in the Pacific Ocean."

The documentary evidence to which we have referred all tends to show that Great Britain was chiefly concerned about the assumption by Russia, in the Ukase of 1821, of exclusive dominion over the Pacific Ocean, and that it regarded the question of territorial limits on the continent of America as subordinate and relatively unimportant. It earnestly sought the repeal of an edict that asserted "exclusive jurisdiction over an ocean of unmeasured extent." It withdrew its offer to establish "an exclusive fishery of two leagues from the coasts" of the respective countries, and suggested that one league to each power on its own coasts, as recognized by the law of nations, would suffice and was all that she would admit.

Not long after this letter of December 8, 1824, the treaty between Russia and Great Britain, in the form above given, was signed. Mr. Stratford Canning, in the letter informing Mr. George Canning of that fact, said, among other things: "With respect to Bering Straits I am happy to have it in my power to assure you, on the joint authority of the Russian plenipotentiaries, that the Emperor of Russia has no intention whatever of maintaining any exclusive claim to the navigation of those straits, or of the seas north of them." Is it to be supposed that the British plenipotentiary understood Russia as asserting or reserving exclusive rights in the sea south of those straits?

In view of this array of documentary evidence the Tribunal is asked to find that the treaty of 1825 used the words "Pacific Ocean" as embracing only the waters of Bering Sea. If we so declare, then our finding will, in effect, be a declaration that although Great Britian, during negotiations covering several years, persistently demanded the abrogation of an edict asserting for Russia the right to establish a line 100 Italian miles from its shores, washed by seas too vast in extent and too immediately connected with the great oceans of the world to come under the exclusive jurisdiction of any nation, she finally agreed to withdraw her opposition to that assumption of jurisdiction so far as it related to Bering Sea, more than 1,000 miles in length and more than 1,200 miles in width; and this notwithstanding in no part of the voluminous correspondence preceding the treaty of 1825 is there one word that expressly, or by necessary implication, indicates any purpose on the part of Russia to demand, or upon the part of Great Britian to concede, that the Ukase of 1821 should remain in force as to Bering Sea, as distinguished from the North Pacific Ocean.

I have been unable to reach that conclusion. Nor can that position be sustained consistently with the position taken by Russia itself after 1825 as to the scope and effect of the treaties of 1824 and 1825. The evidence is conclusive that Russia—whatever may have been embodied in the proceedings of the Nessdrode conference after the treaty of 1824 was signed—understood both treaties to have annulled the Ukase of 1821 in its application to foreign vessels, so far as to secure to the citizens of Great Britain and America entire freedom of navigation and rights of fishing throughout the whole of Bering Sea, outside of territorial waters.

In Tickmenief's "Historical Review of the formation of the Russian American Company and their proceedings to the present time", published at St. Petersburg in 1863 (*Part I, pp. 130–139*), it is said: "In 1842 Etolin, governor of the colony, informed the company that in the course of his tour of inspection he had come across several American ships. Although circumstances had prevented his communicating with them at the time, he had reason to believe that they were whalers. In corroboration of this he stated that for some time he had been receiving reports from various parts of the colony of the appearance of American whalers in the neighborhood of the harbors and shores of the colony. Amongst these reports the most noteworthy was that of Captain Kadnikoff, the commander of the company's ship Naslicdnik Alexander, who stated that, on a voyage from Sitka to Okhotsk, he had hailed a whaler flying the American flag. The master informed him that he had come from the Sandwich Islands in company with thirty other ships to whale on both sides of the western extremity of the peninsula of Alaska and the eastern islands of the Aleutian group belonging to that peninsula, and that as many as 200 whalers were coming from the United States the same year. Captain Kadnikoff also ascertained from the master that in 1841 he had whaled in the same waters in company with fifty other ships, and that his ship secured thirteen whales, from which 1,000 barrels of oil were obtained." *British Case, Vol. 1, App. 40.*

In reply to an application by the Russian American Company to prevent the Americans from fishing in the waters of the colony, the Russian foreign office, in 1842, said: "The claim to a *mare clausum*, if we wished to advance such a claim in respect to *the northern part of the Pacific Ocean*, could not be theoretically justified. Under Article I of the convention of 1824 between Russia and the United States, which is still in force, American citizens have a right to fish *in all parts of the Pacific Ocean*. But under Article IV of the same convention, the ten years' period mentioned in that article having expired, we have power to forbid American vessels to visit *inland* seas, gulfs, harbors, and bays, for the purposes of fishing and trading with the natives. *That is the limit of our rights*, and we have no power to prevent American ships from taking whales *in the open sea*." *Letter from the Department of Manufactures and Internal Trade, December 11, 1842, No. 5191, Dielo. Arkh. Kom., 1842, goda, No. 11, str. 7. British Case, Vol. 1, App. 40.*

Again, in 1843, the question was presented to the Russian Foreign Office whether the claim of foreigners to take whales in Russian waters ought not to be limited by a line drawn at a distance of at least three leagues, or nine Italian miles, from the shores of the colony. The Russian Foreign Office, in 1843, said: "The fixing of a line at sea within which foreign vessels should be prohibited from whaling off our shores would not be in accordance with the spirit of the convention of 1824, and *would be contrary to the provisions of our convention of 1825 with Great Britain.* Moreover, the adoption of such a measure, without preliminary negotiation and arrangement with the other powers, might lead to protests, since no clear and uniform agreement has yet been arrived at among nations in regard to the limit of jurisdiction at sea." *British Case, Vol. 1, App. 41.*

Subsequently, in 1846, the governor-general of Siberia, in consequence of what were regarded as new aggressions on the part of whalers, expressed the opinion that, in order to limit the whaling operations of foreigners, it would be fair to forbid them to come within 40 Italian miles of the Russian shores, the ports of Petropavlosk and Okhotsh to be excluded, and a payment of 100 silver roubles to be demanded at those ports from any vessel for the right of whaling. He recommended the employment of a cruiser to watch foreign vessels. But the Russian Foreign Office, in 1847, said: "*We have no right* to exclude foreign ships *from that part of the Great Ocean which separates the eastern shore of Siberia from the northwestern shore of America,* or to make the payment of a sum of money a condition to allowing them to take whales." *British Case, Vol. 1, App. 41.*

Of course, the waters here referred to included the whole of Bering Sea, and the language used by the Russian Foreign Office leaves no room to doubt that Russia regarded Bering Sea as part of the "Great Ocean." Nor can we suppose that Russia, after the treaty of 1825, regarded the prohibition in the Ukase of 1821 against foreign vessels approaching its shores nearer than 100 Italian miles as in force against the subjects of Great Britain, or against the people of any nation at the time of the cession of 1867 to America.

It may be said that the official declarations of the Russian Foreign Office as to the spirit and meaning of the treaties of 1824 and 1825 had reference to the hunting of whales and not to the hunting of fur seals. But there is no ground to suppose that foreign vessels employed in hunting whales in Bering Sea had, in the judgment of the high contracting parties, any less rights than those employed in the hunting of fur seals in the same waters. There is no trace in the record of any purpose upon the part of Russia to claim larger rights in the open waters of Bering Sea in respect to the hunting of fur seals than in respect to the hunting of whales. In fact, prior to 1867, there was no such thing known as the hunting of these fur seals in the high seas, except, perhaps, a few were taken by the natives along the coasts with spears and harpoons.

There is one argument, in support of the contention that "Pacific Ocean" in the treaties of 1824 and 1825 do not include Bering Sea, which deserves examination. It is, that upon a vast number of maps published prior to 1825 the waters north of the Aleutian Islands and between Alaska and Siberia were designated separately from the waters south of those islands, and that if Russia and Great Britain intended that the treaty of 1825 should embrace the waters of Bering Sea some reference would have been made to that sea in the form of words used on maps designating it as a separate body of water. To Mr. Blaine's letter of December 17, 1890, is attached a list of 105 maps, covering the period from 1743 to 1829, showing that on those maps the waters south of Bering Sea are variously designated as the Pacific Ocean, Océan Pacifique, Stilles Meer, the Great Ocean, Grand Mer, Grosser Ocean, the Great South Sea, Grosser Sud-Sea, North Pacific, Mer du Sud, etc. On those maps the waters north of the Aleutian Islands are as a general rule designated specially, sometimes by the words "Sea of Kamschatka," and at other times by the name of "Bering Sea."

But, upon examining those and other maps, it appears that, in most instances, the words "Sea of Kamschatka" and "Bering Sea" are often in letters so small as compared with the words "Pacific Ocean," "Great Ocean," "Great South Sea," etc., lower down on the map, as to justify the conclusion that the former body of water was regarded as a part of the latter. This view is supported by the fact that on many charts, and in many geographies, encyclopedias, and other publications prior to and since 1825 (references to some of which are given in the margin*) Bering

---

*Morse's American Geography, London, 1794, p. 650: "Russian Empire. This immense empire stretches from the Baltic Sea and Sweden on the west to Kamschatka and the Pacific Ocean on the east, and from the Frozen Ocean on the north to about the forty-fourth degree of latitude on the south."

Malham's Naval Gazeteer, London, 1795, Vol. 2, p. 4: "Kamschatka Sea is a large branch of the Oriental or North Pacific Ocean."

Sea was often referred to as constituting a part of the Pacific Ocean or South Sea, or the North Pacific Ocean. These facts explain how it was that the treaty of 1824 described the Great Ocean, on which there should be freedom of navigation and fishing, as the body of waters commonly called the Pacific Ocean or South Sea. This description was first suggested in the *projet* presented to the Russian Government by Mr. Middleton, the American minister at St. Petersburg, the words of which were, "in any part of the Great Ocean, vulgarly called the Pacific or South Sea." *American State Papers, Vol. 5, p. 464.*

Ibid, Vol. 1, p. 42: "Bering's Straits, which is the passage from the North Pacific Ocean to the Arctic Sea."

Brooke's General Gazeteer, 1803: "Bering's Island—An island in the Pacific Ocean."

Montefiore's Commercial Dictionary, 1803: "Kamschatka—Bounded on the east and south by the North Pacific Ocean."

Cruttwell's New Universal Gazeteer, 1808: "Kamschatka—Peninsula, bounded on the east and south by the North Pacific Ocean.

Rees's Cyclopædia, Vol. 2d, London, 1819.—"Pacific Ocean, or South Sea, in geography, that vast ocean which separates Asia from America. It is called Pacific from the moderate weather which the first mariners who sailed in it met with between the tropics; and it was called the South Sea because the Spaniards crossed the isthmus of Darien from north to south. It is properly the western ocean with regard to America. Geographers call the South Sea *Mare Pacificum*, the *Pacific Ocean* as being less infested with storms than the Atlantic. * * * This ocean is divided into two great parts. That lying east from Kamschatka, between Siberia and America, is eminently styled the Eastern or the Pacific Ocean; that on the west side from Kamschatka, between Siberia, the Chinese Mongoley, and the Kwielly Islands is called the Sea of Okhotsk. From the different places it touches it assumes different names, e. g, from the place where the river Anadyr falls into it, it is called the Sea of Anadyr, about Kamschatka, the Sea of Kamschatka; and the bay between the districts of Okhotsk and Kamschatka is called the Sea of Okhotsk."

Encyclopédie Méthodique Géographie, Paris, Vol. 2, p. 591: "2d. L'Océan pacifique, la mer du sud, ou la grand mer, qui est située entre les côtes orientales d'Asie, et occidentales d'Amérique."

(The Pacific Ocean, the South Sea, or the Great Sea, which is situated between the coasts of Asia and the western coasts of America.)

Encyclopédie du Dix-Neuvième Siècle (Encyclopedia of the 19th Century), Paris, Vol. 17, p. 429; Océan Pacifique ou mer du sud, appelée aussi grande Mer entre l'Amérique et l'Asie, entre le cercle polaire du nord et celui du sud. (The Pacific Ocean, or the South Sea, called also the Great Sea, between America and Asia, and between the northern polar circle and the southern.)

Edinburgh Gazeteer, 1822. Vol. 1, p. 432: "Behring's Island—an island in the North Pacific Ocean."

I am of opinion in view of all the evidence—which includes many documents that do not appear to have been brought to the attention of Mr. Blaine during his correspondence with Lord Salisbury—that the words Pacific Ocean in the treaty of 1825 included, and were intended by Russia and Great Britain to include, the waters of Bering Sea as part of "the Great Ocean commonly called the Pacific Ocean."

Respecting the seal fisheries in Bering Sea, named in the first and second points of Article VI of the treaty—if the reference be to the fur-seal industries conducted under the license or authority of Russia *on the islands* situated in that sea—it is clear, from the records in our hands, that Russia, from a date prior to the beginning of the present century down to the cession in 1867 of Alaska to the United States, had the exclusive right to such fisheries, and that her rights, in that regard, were

---

General Gazeteer, London, 1825: "Beering's Island—in the North Pacific Ocean."

New London Gazeteer, 1823: "Beering's Island—in the Pacific."

Edinburgh Gazeteer, London, 1827, Vol. 1, p. 412: "Kamschatka (Peninsula). On the east it has the North Pacific Ocean, and on the west that large gulf of it called the Sea of Okhotsk."

Arrowsmith's Grammar of Modern Geography, 1832: "Bhering's Strait connects the Frozen Ocean with the Pacific. The Anadir flows into the Pacific Ocean."

Penny Encyclopedia, London, 1843, p. 116: "Pacific Ocean extends between America on the east and Asia and Australia on the west. * * * It is called the South Sea, because vessels sailing from Europe can only enter it after a long southerly course. The name of South Sea has been limited in later times to the southern portion of the Pacific. The Pacific is the greatest expanse of water on the globe, of which it covers more than one-half of the surface. * * * Behring's Strait, which may be considered as its most northern boundary, lies between East Cape in Asia and Cape Prince of Wales near 66° north latitude, and is less than 40 miles wide."

London Encyclopedia, 1845, Vol. 16, p. 102: Following Malte Brown's Précis de la Geographie Universelle, this book describes the Eastern or Great Pacific Ocean as embracing among other waters "the Northeastern Ocean between Asia and North America," the "seas of Japan, Kamschatka, and Beering's Strait," making "a part of it."

Encyclopedia Americana, Philadelphia, 1845, Vol. 9, p. 476: "Pacific Ocean; the great mass of waters extending from Beering's Straits to the Antarctic Circle, a distance of 3,200 leagues, and from Asia and New Holland to America. * * * It was at first called the South Sea by the European navigators, who entered it from the north. Magellan gave it the name of Pacific," etc.

New American Cyclopedia, by Ripley and Dana, 1851: "Pacific Ocean: Between longitude 70° west and 110° east; that is, for the space of 180°, or over one entire half of the globe. It covers the greater part of the earth's surface from Behring's Straits to the Polar Circle, that separates it from the Antarctic Ocean."

Harper's Statistical Gazeteer of the World. By Smith. New York: 1855. "Rus-

recognized and conceded by Great Britain, in the sense that that country never, in any form, disputed such right, although neither Great Britain nor the United States ever recognized or conceded even the qualified jurisdiction asserted by Russia, in the Ukase of 1821, to forbid foreign vessels from approaching nearer than 100 Italian miles from her coasts or islands. In respect to seal fisheries, if any, conducted in the open waters of Bering Sea outside of territorial waters, Russia neither held nor exclusively exercised any right not possessed, in such open waters, by all other nations.

In respect to the fourth point of Article VI, it was not disputed in argument (as of course it could not be) that whatever *rights*—that is, whatever legal rights—Russia had, as to jurisdiction and as to

sian America comprises the whole of the continent of northwest America west of longitude 144° west and a strip on the coast extending south to latitude 55° north, bounded on the east by British America, south and west by the Pacific Ocean, and north by the Arctic Ocean," etc.

Cyclopedia of Geography, by Knight, 1856: "Behring's Strait, which connects the Pacific with the Arctic Ocean, is formed by the approach of the continents of America and Asia."

McCulloch's Geographical Dictionary, by Martin, 1866: "Pacific Ocean: Its extreme southern limit is the Antarctic Circle, from which it stretches northward through 132° of latitude to Behring Strait, which separates it from the Arctic Ocean."

Blackie's Imperial Gazeteer, London, 1874, Vol. 2, p. 558: "In the north the Pacific gradually contracts in width; the continents of America and Asia, stretching out and approximating, so as to leave the comparatively narrow channel of Behring's Strait as the only communication between the Pacific and the Arctic Oceans."

American Cyclopedia, New York, 1875, Vol. 1, p. 480: "Behring Sea. That part of the Pacific Ocean which lies immediately south of Behring Strait."

Encyclopedia Britannica, Edinburgh. Ninth Ed., 1875-1889, Vol. 18, p. 115: "The Pacific Ocean is bounded on the north by Behring's Strait and the coasts of Russia and Alaska. * * * It extends through 132° of latitude; in other words, it measures 9,000 miles from north to south. From east to west its breadth varies from about 40 miles at Behring's Strait," etc. In the English edition it is stated in a footnote that the Pacific Ocean was formerly called the South Sea.

Worcester's Dictionary of the English Language, Philadelphia, 1887: "Behring Sea: A part of the Pacific Ocean north of the Aleutian Islands."

Chambers's Cyclopædia, 1888: "Behring Strait connects the Pacific Ocean with the Arctic Ocean. Behring Sea: A part of the Pacific Ocean commonly known as the Sea of Kamchatka."

seal fisheries in Bering Sea east of the water boundary defined in the treaty of March 30, 1867, between Russia and the United States, passed unimpaired to the United States. She conveyed all her territory and dominion, and all the rights, franchises, and privileges which she possessed in such territory and dominion, within the limits defined by that treaty, free and unincumbered by any reservations, privileges, grants, or possession, by any company or individuals. The deed of cession of 1867 necessarily embraced all of Russia's *rights*, whatever they were, in the fur seals frequenting the Pribilof Islands, and in the industries carried on there for more than three-quarters of a century prior to 1867.

If I am correct in the views above expressed, the answers to the first four points of Article VI should be, substantially, as follows:

To the first.—Prior to and up to the time of the cession of Alaska to the United States, Russia did not assert nor exercise any exclusive jurisdiction in Bering Sea, or any exclusive rights in the fur seal fisheries in that sea, *outside of ordinary territorial waters*, except that in the Ukase of 1821 she did assert the right to prevent foreign vessels from approaching nearer than 100 Italian miles the coasts and islands named in that Ukase. But, pending the negotiations to which that Ukase gave rise, Russia voluntarily suspended its execution, so far as to direct its officers to restrict their surveillance of foreign vessels to the distance of cannon shot from the shores mentioned, and by the treaty of 1824 with the United States, as well as by that of 1825 with Great Britain, the above Ukase was withdrawn, and the claim of authority or the power to prohibit foreign vessels from approaching the coasts nearer than 100 Italian miles was abandoned, by the agreement embodied in those treaties to the effect that the respective citizens and subjects of the high contracting parties should not be troubled or molested, in any part of the Great Ocean commonly called the Pacific Ocean, either in navigating the same or in fishing therein, or in landing at such parts of the coast as shall not have been already occupied, in order to trade with the natives, under the restrictions and conditions specified in other articles of those treaties.

To the second.—Great Britain never recognized nor conceded any claim by Russia of exclusive jurisdiction in Bering Sea, nor of exclusive rights as to the seal fisheries therein, outside of ordinary territorial waters; although she did recognize and concede Russia's exclusive jurisdiction within her own territory and such jurisdiction inside of territorial waters as was consistent with the law of nations.

To the third.—The body of water now known as Bering Sea was included in the phrase "Pacific Ocean" as used in the treaty of 1825 between Great Britain and Russia, and, after that treaty, Russia neither held nor exercised any rights in the waters of Bering Sea, outside of ordinary territorial waters, that did not belong in the same waters to other countries.

To the fourth.—All the rights of Russia as to jurisdiction, and as to the seal fisheries in Bering Sea, east of the water boundary in the treaty between the United States and Russia of March 30, 1867, passed, under that treaty, unimpaired to the United States.

3.

THE RIGHT OF PROPERTY ASSERTED BY THE UNITED STATES IN THE PRIBILOF HERD OF SEALS, AND ITS RIGHT, WHETHER AS OWNER OF THE HERD, OR SIMPLY AS OWNER OF THE FUR SEAL INDUSTRY ON THE PRIBILOF ISLANDS, TO PROTECT THE SEALS AGAINST PELAGIC SEALING.

I come now to the most important and interesting question presented for determination, namely, that involved in the fifth point of Article VI of the Treaty:

"*Has the United States any right, and if so, what right of protection or property in the fur-seals frequenting the islands of the United States in Bering Sea when such seals are found outside the ordinary three-mile limit?*"

It is necessary to a proper understanding of this question, in its bearing upon the general subject of the preservation of this race of animals, that we recall the facts (never before so fully developed as in the evidence now adduced) touching their history, nature, and habits as well as the results that necessarily follow from hunting and killing them in the high seas. These facts should be clearly apprehended before we enter upon the consideration of the principles of law and justice applicable to the case. They should be brought together here, even at the risk of some repetition.

These facts—stating only such as are admitted or are established by overwhelming evidence—are as follows:

1. The animals in question belong to the species commonly designated by naturalists as the Northern Fur Seal, and are valuable for purposes

of raiment and food. The race has only four breeding places: Commander Islands, in the western part of Bering Sea, near the coast of Asia; Robben Reef, in the Sea of Okhotsk ; the Kurile Islands, on the west side of the Pacific Ocean, near the coasts of Japan and Asia ; and the islands of St. Paul and St. George, part of the Pribilof group in Bering Sea. The Pribilof seals so far differ from others of the Northern Fur Seal species that their pelage can readily be distinguished by experts from that of the seals of other herds.

2. The taking or killing of fur seals, for commercial purposes, at the islands of St. Paul and St. George, during the eighty years of Russia's ownership of the Pribilof Islands, was conducted under the license or authority of that nation. And the exclusive right of Russia, during that period, to control that business, so conducted, for its exclusive benefit or for the advantage of its subjects, was not disputed by any other country.

3. By a joint resolution of the Congress of the United States, approved March 3, 1869, providing for the more effective protection of the fur seal in Alaska, the islands of St. Paul and St. George—which, with other islands in Bering Sea, became the property of the United States by virtue of the cession from Russia of March 30, 1867—were declared to be "a special Reservation for Government purposes;" and it was made unlawful for any person to land or remain on either of the two islands named, except by the authority of the Secretary of the Treasury; any person found on either island without such authority being liable to be summarily removed.

Subsequently, by an act of Congress, entitled "An act to prevent the extermination of the fur-bearing animals in Alaska," approved July 1, 1870, it was made unlawful to kill any fur seal upon the islands of St. Paul and St. George, or in the waters adjacent thereto (except during certain named months), or to kill such seals at any time with firearms, or to use any means that tended to drive the seals from the islands; the natives on the islands being, however, allowed the privilege (subject to regulations prescribed by the Secretary of the Treasury) of killing, during other months, such young or old seals as were necessary for food and clothing. By the same statute it was made unlawful to kill any female seal, or any seal less than one year old, at any season of the year (except as provided in the case of natives), or to kill any seal in the waters adjacent to the islands, or on the beaches, cliffs, or rocks where they hauled up from the sea to remain; any person violating the above provisions or either of them being made liable to a fine of not less than \$200 nor more than \$1,000, or to imprisonment not exceeding six months, or both to such fine and imprisonment at the discretion of the court having cognizance of the offense; all vessels, their tackle, apparel, and furniture, whose crew were found engaged in violating the provisions of the act, to be forfeited to the United States.

The same act provided that, for the period of twenty years, the number of seals killed for their skins should be limited to 75,000 per annum upon the island of St. Paul, and 25,000 upon the island of St. George; subject, however, to the power of the Secretary of the Treasury to limit the right of killing, if that should become necessary for the preservation of the seals, with such proportionate reduction of the rents reserved to the Government, as was right and proper. The Secretary was required to lease for the term of twenty years, to proper and responsible parties, for the best advantage of the Government, the native inhabitants, their comfort, maintenance, and education, as well as to the interest of the parties previously engaged in the trade, and the protection of the fur seals, the right to engage in the business of taking fur seals on the islands of St. Paul and St. George, and to send a vessel or vessels to those islands for the skins of the seals; taking from the lessee or lessees bond with sufficient sureties in the sum of not less than \$500,000, conditioned for the faithful observance of all the laws of Congress and of the regulations of the Secretary of the Treasury, touching the subject matter of taking fur seals, and disposing of the same, and for the payment of all taxes and dues. It was further provided, that at the end of the lease, other like leases could be made; but no persons other than American citizens were permitted to occupy the islands or either of them, for the purpose of taking the skins of fur seals, nor any vessel allowed to engage in taking such skins; any lease made by the Secretary of the Treasury being subject to forfeiture if it was held or operated, directly or indirectly, for the use, benefit, or advantage of any person other than American citizens.

These and other provisions having for their object the utilization of these animals for purposes of revenue and commerce, and their protection against indiscriminate slaughter on the islands, or in the adjacent waters, were preserved in the Revised Statutes of the United States of 1873, §§. 1954 to 1976, inclusive.

11492——8

By another act of Congress, approved March 2, 1889, it was provided that section 1956 of the Revised Statutes, prohibiting the killing of any otter, mink, marten, sable or seal, or other fur-bearing animal, within the limits of Alaska Territory or in the waters thereof was declared to include and apply to all the dominion of the United States in the waters of Bering Sea; and it was made the duty of the President, at a timely season in each year, to issue his proclamation and cause the same to be published at each United States port of entry on the Pacific coast, warning all persons against entering those waters for the purpose of violating the provisions of that section.

4. The Pribilof herd is found, *en masse*, every year on the islands of St. Paul and St. George. They remain there about four or five months. Much longer time intervenes between the first arrival of some, and the departure from the islands of those who last leave them for the season. The period during which the herd abides on those islands, is called the breeding season. They return there regularly for the purpose of breeding and rearing their young, and of shedding and renewing their coats of fur.

5. The breeding males, called bulls, arrive in the early part of May or by the middle of that month. Each bull, immediately after coming from the sea, establishes himself upon the rocky beach, appropriating as much space as will be needed for his female companions after they arrive. The non-breeding males, or bachelors, arrive during the same month, and take position, substantially in a body, and, as a general rule, in the rear of the spaces occupied by the bulls. Sometimes the bachelors occupy spaces near the water, but separate from those occupied by the bulls and their female companions. Early in June the female seals, called cows, begin to emerge in bodies or droves from the sea, and to enter the spaces provided for them by the bulls. By the 10th of July substantially the entire herd is established on the islands. Each bull appropriates for the season at least fifteen or twenty female seals.

Within a few hours, it may be, always within a few days, after reaching the islands, the mother seal, impregnated during the breeding season of the previous year, gives birth to a single pup, the period of gestation being eleven or twelve months, the pups born being about equally divided between the sexes. The pups are conceived on the islands during the breeding season. Cohabitation, for any effective purpose, in the water, is impossible. The females appear to have an unerring instinct as to the time when the period of gestation will end. The cows, after being delivered of their pups, remain for a few weeks with the bulls by whom they have been appropriated. They go from the islands into the sea as often as nature suggests to be necessary for the purpose of obtaining fish for food by which they are nourished while suckling their young. A cow, while nursing its pup, often goes long distances from the islands in search of fish. Capt. Shepard, of the United States Marine service, who examined the skins taken from sealing vessels seized in 1887 and 1889, over 12,000 in number, two thirds or three-fourths being the skins of females, says: "Of the females taken in the Pacific Ocean, and early in the season in Bering Sea, nearly all are heavy with young, and the death of the female necessarily causes the death of the unborn pup seal; in fact, I have seen on nearly every vessel seized the pelts of unborn pups which had been taken from their mothers. Of the females taken in Bering Sea nearly all are in milk, and I have seen the milk come from the carcases of dead females lying on the decks of sealing vessels which were more than 100 miles from the Pribilof Islands. From this fact, and from the further fact that I have seen seals in the water over 150 miles from the islands during the summer, I am convinced that the female, after giving birth to her young on the rookeries, goes at least 150 miles, in many cases, from the islands in search of food." Robert H. McManus, a journalist of Victoria, who had devoted some attention to the sealing industry, referring to a catch of seals in Bering Sea when he was present, says that over three-fourths of that catch were cows in milk. This, he says, at a distance of 200 miles from the rookeries, shows that the nursing cows ramble all over the Bering Sea in search of their chief food, the codfish, though these are chiefly found on the banks along the coast of the Aleutian Islands. In the Canadian Fisheries Report of 1886, it is stated that of the seals taken that year, "the greatest number were killed in Bering Sea, and were nearly all cows or female seals;" and in the report of 1888, that "over 60 per cent of the entire catch of Bering Sea is made up of female seals." The record is full of similar evidence.

6. Upon returning from her search for food the mother seal hunts up her pup, and will refuse her milk to the pup of any other cow. An intelligent witness thus describes the general habits of the mother seal and its pup: "The cows appear to go to and come from the water quite frequently, and usually return to the spot or its neighborhood, where they leave their pups crying out for them and recognizing their individual

cries, though ten thousand around all together should bleat at once. They quickly single out their own and attend them. It would be a very unfortunate matter if the mothers could not identify their young by sound, since their pups get together like a great swarm of bees, spread out upon the ground in 'pods' or groups, while they are young and not very large, but by the middle and end of September until they leave in November they cluster together, sleeping and frolicking by tens of thousands. A mother comes up from the water where she has been to wash, and perhaps to feed for the last day or two, about where she thinks her pup should be, but misses it, and finds instead a swarm of pups in which it has been incorporated, owing to its great fondness for society. The mother, without at first entering into the crowd of thousands, calls out just as a sheep does for her lambs, listens, and out of all the din she—if not at first, at the end of a few trials—recognizes the voice of her offspring and then advances, striking out right and left, and over the crowd toward the position from which it replies; but if the pup at this time happens to be asleep she hears nothing from it, even though it were close by, and in this case the cow, after calling for a time without being answered, curls herself up and takes a nap, or lazily basks, and is most likely more successful when she calls again." Another witness of large experience says: "As already stated, the females now mostly spend their time in the water, returning on shore only to suckle their young as they require food. On landing the mother calls out to her young with a plaintive bleat like that of a sheep calling to her lamb. As she approaches the mass several of the young ones answer and start to meet her, responding to her call as a young lamb answers its parent. As she meets them she looks at them, touches them with her nose as if smelling them, and passes hurriedly on until she meets her own, which she at once recognizes. After caressing him she lies down and allows him to suck and often falls into a sound sleep very quickly after."

If the mother seal is killed while out at sea in search of fish for food, her pup, left behind on the islands, and requiring the milk of its mother for eight weeks or more after its birth, will die from starvation. This fact is placed beyond dispute by the evidence, and is not, I think, seriously questioned.

The pups do not take to swimming naturally. They are enticed or forced by their mother, from time to time, into the water and taught to swim. If a pup, by accident, is born in the sea, it will immediately sink and be drowned. As already stated, the race is both conceived and comes into existence on land, and from the necessities of its physical nature must abide upon land during several months of the year.

7. In the latter part of September or early in October, the breeding season having closed, the pups having learned to swim, and the ice around the islands increasing the difficulty of going into the sea for fish food, the herd begins to leave the islands, in squads or bands of different sizes, proceeding in a southerly and southeasterly direction through the middle passes of the Aleutian Islands into the North Pacific Ocean south of those islands, where they get into the warmer water of the Japanese current. During the winter months many of the seals are seen off the coasts of California and Oregon. The bulls do not go so far south, and do not accompany the herd in its general migrations, usually remaining in the Gulf of Alaska until they return to the breeding grounds. In the beginning of the year the seals turn their faces towards their land home, moving leisurely in small schools or bands, but substantially as a herd, northwardly and opposite to the coasts of Oregon, Washington, British Columbia, and Alaska, thence westwardly, through the eastern passes of the Aleutian Islands, back into Bering Sea, to their breeding grounds on the islands of St. Paul and St. George. They occupy year after year substantially the same places on the islands.

Their general migration route each year from the Pribilof Islands through the passes of the Aleutian Islands into the Pacific Ocean and back to their land home on those islands, is well known to sealers and navigators.

8. While on the islands they are subject to the control, for every practical or commercial purpose, of those who are there by the authority or license of the United States. Credible witnesses, familiar with the habits of these animals, state that the young seals, before being weaned, could be easily handled and branded with the mark of the United States. So complete is the subjection of these animals, old and young, to control, while on the islands during the breeding season, *that such of them as it may be desirable to take for commercial purposes, can be readily separated from all the others.* Indeed, if pelagic sealing continues to such an extent as to imperil the existence of the race, and if the United States should find it to be unprofitable to hold the islands of St. Paul and St. George as a Government Reservation, to be used exclusively by these animals as their breeding grounds, it could take substantially

tho entire herd, in any one breeding season, and put the proceeds of the sale of their skins into its treasury.

9. Neither in Bering Sea, nor in the North Pacific Ocean, does the Pribilof herd intermingle, to any appreciable extent, with the herds of northern fur seals frequenting the islands on the Asiatic coast. The migration routes of the latter are altogether in the waters on the western side of the Pacific Ocean, while the Pribilof herd never have gone west of the one hundred and eightieth degree of longitude from Greenwich, and very few have ever been seen so far west. This fact is conclusively established by the evidence, and is recognized in the separate reports made by the commissioners who were appointed by the two governments (two by each government) to investigate and make report upon the facts having relation to seal life and the measures necessary for its proper protection and preservation.

The American Commissioners, Profs. Merriam and Mendenhall, in their separate report made under the authority of the treaty between the two governments, say:

"The fur seals of the Pribilof Islands *do not mix with those of the Commander and Kurile Islands at any time of the year.* In summer the two herds remain *entirely distinct,* separated by a water interval of several hundred miles; and in their winter migrations those from the Pribilof Islands follow the American coast in a southeasterly direction, while those from the Commander and Kurile Islands follow the Siberian and Japan coasts in a southwesterly direction, the two herds being separated in winter by a water interval of several thousand miles. This regularity in the movements of the different herds is in obedience to the well-known law that *migratory animals follow definite routes in migration and return year after year to the same place to breed.* Were it not for this law there would be no such thing as stability of species, for interbreeding and existence under diverse physiographic conditions would destroy all specific characters." *U. S. Case, 323.*

The British Commissioners, Prof. Dawson, and Sir George Baden-Powell, in their separate report, under the same authority, say:

"Respecting the migration range of the fur seals which resort to Commander Islands, to Robben Island, and in smaller numbers to several places in the Kurile Islands, as more fully noted in subsequent pages, comparatively little has been recorded; but the result of inquiries made in various directions, when brought together, are sufficient to enable its general character and the area which it covers to be outlined. The deficiency in information for the Asiatic coast depends upon the fact that pelagic sealing, as understood on the coast of America, is there practically unknown, while the people inhabiting the coast and its adjacent islands do not, like the Indians and Aleuts of the opposite side of the North Pacific, naturally venture far to sea for hunting purposes. The facts already cited in connection with the migration of the seals on the east side of the Pacific show that these animals enter and leave Bering Sea almost entirely by the eastern passes through the Aleutian chain, and that only under exceptional circumstances, and under stress of weather, are some young seals, while on their way south, driven as far to the west as Atka Island. No large bodies of migrating seals are known to pass near Attu Island, the westernmost of the Aleutians, and *no young seals have ever within memory been seen there.* These circumstances, with others which it is not necessary to detail here, are sufficient to demonstrate that *the main migration routes of the seals frequenting the Commander Islands do not touch the Aleutian chain*, and there is every reason to believe that although the seals become more or less commingled in Bering Sea, during the summer, *the migration routes of the two sides of the North Pacific are essentially distinct.* The inquiries and observations now made, however, enable it to be shown that the fur seals of the two sides of the North Pacific belong *in the main to practically distinct migration tracts*, both of which are elsewhere traced out and described, and it is believed that while to a certain extent transfers of individual seals or of small groups occur, probably every year, between the Pribilof and Commander tribes, that this is exceptional rather than normal. *It is not believed that any voluntary or systematic movement of fur seals takes place from one group of breeding islands to the other*, but it is probable that a continual harassing of the seals upon one group might result, in a course of years, in a corresponding gradual accession to the other group.

"There is no evidence whatever to show that any considerable branch of the seal tribe which has its winter home off the coast of British Columbia resorts in summer to the Commander Islands, whether voluntarily or led thither in pursuit of food fishes; and inquiries along the Aleutian chain show that no regular migration route follows its direc- tion, whether to the north or south of the islands. It is certain that the young seals, in going southward from the Pribilof Islands, only rarely get drifted westward as far as the one hundred and seventy-second meridian of west longitude, while Attu Island, on the one hundred and seventy-third meridian east is never visited by young seals, and therefore lies between the regular autumn migration routes of the seals going from the Pribilof and Commander Islands respectively." *Secs. 197, 198, 453, 454.*

10. The herd habitually resorting to the islands of St. Paul and St. George is the same that has resorted there in the spring, summer, and fall of every year for the past century and more without any change whatever in their habits or in their migration routes. Since the discovery of the islands, the seals frequenting them have never resorted, for any purpose whatever, to other coasts or lands. This, no doubt, is due to the fact that they find on the Pribilof Islands, and nowhere else, the isolation required for the breeding season, as well as the climatic and physical conditions necessary to their life wants, among which conditions are an uniformly low temperature and an overcast sky and foggy atmosphere that serves to protect them against the sun's rays while they remain at the rookeries during the long summer season. Whatever may be the reason for their never having landed upon any other shores, it is indisputably shown that they have regularly resorted to those islands as their breeding grounds for a period so long that the memory of man runneth not to the contrary. And the contrary is not asserted.

11. Prior to 1883 or 1885 the taking of these fur seals at sea was exclusively by Indians or natives inside territorial waters, at any rate, quite near the coasts. They employed for that purpose only small canoes and harpoons or spears. Their catch, however, has never been large in any year, and has not materially affected the industry conducted at the islands of St. Paul and St. George, nor apparently diminished the number of the herd.

But in 1883 a schooner manned by hunters skilled in taking seals entered Bering Sea and returned with more than 2,000 seals. This stimulated the business of taking these animals in the open waters beyond the territorial jurisdiction of the respective governments. In 1885 firearms were first used in hunting seals. Large schooners or vessels now go out into the ocean in the route traversed by the seals and send out small boats manned by hunters with rifles or shotguns. Ordinarily, only the head of the seal can be seen as it moves through, or lies asleep, in the water; those thus asleep being, as a general rule, mother seals heavy with young, who, being disabled by their condition from making rapid movements, are easily approached and killed. It is indisputably shown by the evidence that at least 75 per cent of all seals shot by pelagic sealers and actually secured are female seals, the larger part of whom are far advanced in pregnancy when so taken. As soon as the mother seal is taken by pelagic sealers, her body is opened and the unborn pup thrown into the sea. It is also shown that large numbers of seals, that are shot at and wounded or killed, sink and are entirely lost before the hunter can reach them with his small boat. The number so lost varies according to the skill of the hunter in using fire arms and the implements carried for the purpose of securing the seal that has been wounded or killed, before it sinks. But, making a fair average of the per cent given by witnesses on both sides, it is certain that, in addition to the seals actually taken by hunters using fire arms, not less than 25 to 40 per cent of all seals wounded sink before they are reached by the hunter, and are entirely lost. *In pelagic sealing there can be no selective killing so far as sex is concerned, for it is agreed that a hunter can not tell whether the seal at which he shoots in the water is of the male or female sex.* Such an attack upon the breeding females, if continued for a few years, will, of course, result in the extermination of this polygamous race. The slaughter of the female seal not only involves the loss of the mother and its unborn pup, but, as Mr. Blaine well said, "the future loss of the whole number which the bearing seal may produce in the successive years of life. The destruction which results from killing seals in the open sea proceeds, therefore, by a ratio which constantly and rapidly increases, and insures the total extermination of the species within a very brief period." Besides, in the long run, the killing of a female which has not yet borne young, or which is too young to have borne many pups, is more destructive than to kill one somewhat advanced in years.

The largest number of vessels engaged in hunting these fur seals on the high seas outside of territorial waters in any year previous to 1886 was 16. The number increased in 1886 to 34, in 1887 to 47, in 1889 to 68, in 1890 to 91, in 1891 to 115, in 1892 to 122. The catch, in the open sea by pelagic hunters of seals belonging to the Pribilof herd has steadily increased for ten years past, so that in the North Pacific Ocean, south of the Aleutian Islands, it amounted to 68,000 in 1891 and at least 70,000 in 1892, the *modus vivendi* for those years excluding pelagic sealers only from Bering Sea.

During the breeding season of 1868, before the United States had established regulations for the taking of fur seals at the Pribilof Islands, and before its authorities had acquired any knowledge as to the necessity of imposing restrictions upon the number to be killed for commercial purposes, seal hunters took on those islands alone about 268,000 of all ages and sexes. The evil was, of course, remedied as soon as the act of 1868 was passed. From 1869 to 1871, inclusive, the average number killed annually on the islands for commercial purposes (taking for this estimate the report of the British commissioners) was 69,258, and from 1872 to 1889, inclusive, 98,211, exclusive, in each period, of the pups killed by natives for food and raiment. In 1890, when the disastrous effects of pelagic sealing began to be more distinctly felt, only 20,995 young males suitable for taking could be found on the islands, and in 1891 only 12,071, including the 7,500 allowed by the *modus vivendi* of that year. By the *modus vivendi* of 1892 only 7,500 were allowed to be taken on the islands. In the present year, under the operation of the latter arrangement, only 7,500 can be taken by the United States or its licensees on the islands, while pelagic sealers are at liberty to take all they can in the North Pacific Ocean. It is not doubted that they will take at least 80,000 this season in those waters.

12. The Commissioners appointed by the United States and Great Britain agree that "since the Alaska purchase a marked diminution of the seals on, and habitually resorting to, the Pribilof Islands, has taken place; that it has been cumulative in effect, and that it is the result of excessive killing by man." They also agree that "for industrial as well as for other obvious reasons, it is incumbent upon all nations, and particularly those having direct commercial interests in fur seals, to provide for their proper protection and preservation."

13. But for the protection given to these seals while on the islands of St. Paul and St. George, first by Russia, and, subsequently, by the United States, the entire herd, frequenting the Islands of St. Paul and St. George since the discovery of those islands (how much longer can not be now known), would long ago have been destroyed by raiders and seal hunters. If the care, supervision, and self-denial practiced by the United States on the islands were withdrawn, the race would be swept out of existence within a very few years.

It is common knowledge that at the close of the last century fur seals of a somewhat different species from the Northern Fur Seals, but having most of the same characteristics, could be seen in numbers almost incredible on numerous coasts and islands in the Southern Ocean, off the coasts of South America. According to the concurrent testimony of navigators and naturalists, all these herds in the southern seas have been annihilated, or so reduced in numbers that it is no longer worth while to visit them, "owing," to use the language of Sir William H. Flower, the distinguished head of the British Natural History Museum, "to the ruthless and indiscriminate slaughter carried on by ignorant and lawless sealers, regardless of everything but immediate profit." We have the authority of the same eminent naturalist for saying: "The only spot in the world where the fur seals are now found in their original, or even increased, numbers, is the Pribilof group, a circumstance entirely owing to the rigid enforcement of the wise regulations of the Alaska Commercial Company. But for this the fur seal before now would have been added to the long list of animals exterminated from the earth by the hand of man." *Fifty-second Congress United States, First session, Senate Ex. Doc. No. 55, pp, 96–97.*

Dr. Philip Lutley Sclater, of the Zoölogical Society of London, in a recent article to which our attention has been called, says, substantially in conformity with the evidence before us: "In former days South Africa, Australia, and South America all supplied seal skins for the market, derived either from the shores of the continents themselves, or from the adjoining islands, to which the fur seals resorted for the purpose of breeding and bringing up their young. But the Antarctic fur seal trade is now practically extinct, owing to the indiscriminate slaughter of these animals, which commenced at the end of the last century and was continued until the reduction in their numbers rendered the trade altogether unprofitable. In a single year, it is said that 300,000 seal skins were taken from the South Shetland Islands, and upward of 3,000,000 are stated to have been carried off from the island of Mas-a-fuero, near Juan Fernandez, in the short space of seven years. In fact, the breeding places, or rookeries, as they are called, of the fur seals in the Antarctic seas have been entirely destroyed. The myriads of seals which formerly resorted to them have been either swept away or reduced to a few individuals, which seek the land in scattered bands and rush to the sea on the approach of man. There can be little question, we see, of the fate that will overtake these animals in other parts of the world unless effective measures are instituted for their protection. Although, therefore, a few lots of seal skins may still be received from the South Seas, the furseal of the North Pacific (*Otaria ursina*) is, in fact, the only source of the present supply of fur seal skins that can be relied upon. At the present epoch only two remaining breeding places of this animal exist. These are in Pribilof islands or Bering Sea, within the territory of Alaska (ceded by Russia to the United States in 1867) and the Commander Islands in the southwest corner of the same sea, which still remain under Russian jurisdiction. Two great herds of fur seals resort to these islands respectively during the summer months for the purpose of breeding and rearing their young."

Again the same scientist: "If there were no other reasons to the contrary it would be quite as fair that the pelagic sealers should catch sixty thousand seals in the open Pacific, as that the American officials should slaughter the same number on the Pribilof Islands. But, *in the former case there is, of course, no possibility of making a selection of age or sex. The pelagic hunter kills every seal he can come across, whether male, female, or young.* According to the American Commissioners, at least 80 per cent of the seals thus taken are females. Worse than this, according to the same authorities, they are principally females heavy with young. Thus, for every seal of this kind taken, two lives are sacrificed. Moreover, as the seal, if shot dead, sinks quickly below the surface, many of the bodies are altogether lost, and another considerable element of wastefulness is thus attached to pelagic sealing. Now, let me ask, what owner of a deer forest in Scotland would consent to his hinds being killed, especially during the breeding season? Is it not likewise on a grouse moor forbidden to shoot grey hens at any time? In these, and in numerous other instances which might be mentioned, *the sanctity of female life* is universally recognized. On the other hand, the fur seal being polygamous, *males* may be killed to a large extent *without fear of injury to the herd,* for, although nearly equal numbers of both sexes appear to be born, one adult male is sufficient for twenty or thirty females. But the selection of males from females, and especially of males of the age required to make the best skins, *can only be effected on land,* where the assembling together of the younger male fur seals on particular spots presents the necessary opportunity. I think, therefore, *that if the fur seal is to be preserved for the use of posterity* every true naturalist will agree with the American Commissioners *that pelagic sealing ought to be altogether suppressed*—in the first place, because it necessarily involves the de-

struction of female life; and in the second place, because of its wastefulness through the frequent failure to recover seals shot at sea.

* * * The fur seal of Alaska (practically now the only remaining
member of the group of fur seals) should be declared to be, to all
intents and purposes, a domestic animal, and its capture absolutely
prohibited except in its home on the Pribilof Islands." *Nineteenth
Century, June, 1893, p. 1038.*

Sir George Baden-Powell, one of the British Commissioners, publicly declared before his appointment as a commissioner, that "as a
matter of fact, the Canadian sealers take very few, if any, seals close to
these (the Pribilof) islands. The main catch is made far out at sea,
and *is almost entirely composed of females.*"

Dr. A. Milne Edwards, director of the Museum of Natural History at
Paris, alluding to the fur seals frequenting Bering Sea, says:

"What has happened in the Southern Ocean may serve as a warning
to us. Less than a century ago these amphibia [fur seals] existed there
in countless herds. In 1808, when Fanning visited the islands of
South Georgia, one ship left those shores carrying away 14,000 sealskins belonging to the species *Arctocephalus Australis.* He himself
obtained 57,000 of them and he estimated at 112,000 the number of
these animals killed during the few weeks the sailors spent there that
year. In 1822 Weddel visited the islands and he estimated at 1,200,000
the number of skins obtained in that locality. The same year 320,000
fur seals were killed in the South Shetlands. The inevitable consequences of this slaughter were a rapid decrease in the number of these
animals. So, in spite of the measures of protection taken during the
last few years by the governor of the Falkland Islands, the seals are
still very rare, and the naturalists of the French expedition of the
Romanche remained for nearly a year at Terra del Fuego and the
Falkland Islands without being able to catch a single specimen. It is
a source of wealth which is now exhausted. It will be thus with the
Callorhinus ursinus in the North Pacific Ocean, and it is time to insure
to these animals a security which may allow them regular reproduction.
I have followed with much attention the investigations which have
been made by the Government of the United States on this subject.
The reports of the Commissioners sent to the Pribilof Islands have
made known to naturalists a very large number of facts of great
scientific interest, and have demonstrated that a regulated system of
killing may be safely applied in the case of these herds of seals when

there is a superfluity of males. What might be called a tax on celi-
bacy was applied in this way in the most satisfactory manner, and the
indefinite preservation of the species would have been assured *if the
emigrants, on their way back to their breeding places, had not been
attacked and pursued in every way.*" *U. S. Case, Vol. 1, App. 119.*

The record contains the opinions of other scientific gentlemen of high
repute, in answer to written inquiries on this subject made by Prof.
Merriam, of the United States Department of Agriculture, and based
upon a full and accurate account of seal life.

Dr. Nehring, Professor of Zoölogy in the Royal Agricultural College
of Berlin: "I am like yourself of the opinion that the remarkable
decrease of fur seals on the rookeries of the Pribilof Islands which has,
of late years, become more and more evident, is to be attributed mainly,
or perhaps exclusively, to the unreasonable destruction caused by the
seal-hunters who ply their avocation in the open sea. The only rational
method of taking the fur seal, and the only one that is not likely to
result in the extermination of this valuable animal, is the one which
has hitherto been employed on the Pribilof Islands under the supervision of the Government." *U. S. Case, Vol. 1, App. 120.*

Prof. Salvadori, of the Museo Zoologico, Turin, Italy: "No doubt
free pelagic sealing is a cause which will act to the destruction of the
seal herds, and to that a stop must be put as soon as possible." *U. S.
Case, Vol. 1, App. 122.*

Prof. Von Schrenck, of the Imperial Academy of Sciences, St.
Petersburg: "I am also persuaded that pelagic sealing, if pursued in
the same manner in future, will necessarily end with the extermination
of the fur seal." *U. S. Case, Vol. 1, App. 122.*

Prof. Giglioli, director of the Zoological Museum, Royal Superior
Institute, Florence, Italy: "In any case, all who are competent in the
matter will admit that no method of capture could be more uselessly
destructive in the case of Pinnipedia than that called pelagic sealing;
not only any kind of selection of the victims is impossible, but it is
admitting much to assert that out of three destroyed one is secured and
utilized, and this for obvious and well-known reasons. In the case
of the North Pacific fur-seal, this mode of capture and destruction
is doubly to be condemned, because the destruction falls nearly exclusively on those, the nursing and pregnant females, which ought on no
account to be killed. * * * I quite agree with you in maintaining
that unless the malpractice of pelagic sealing be prevented or greatly

checked, both in the North Pacific and in the Bering Sea, the economic extermination of *Callorhinus ursinus is merely the matter of a few years.*" *U. S. Case, Vol. 1, App. 423.*

Prof. Blanchard, of the Medical Faculty of Paris, and general secretary of the Zoological Society of France: "By reason of the massacres of which it is the victim, this species is advancing rapidly to its total and final destruction, following the fatal road on which the *Rhytina Stelleri*, the *Monarchus trophicalis*, and the *Macrorhinus angustirostris* have preceded it, to cite only the great mammifers which but recently abounded in the American seas. Now, the irremediable destruction of an eminently useful animal species, such as this one, is, to speak plainly, a *crime* of which we are rendering ourselves guilty towards our descendants. To satisfy our instincts of cupidity we voluntarily exhaust, and that forever, a source of wealth, which properly regulated, ought, on the contrary, to contribute to the prosperity of our own generation and of those which will succeed it. * * * With his harpoons, his firearms, and his machines of every kind, man with whom the instinct of destruction attains its highest point, is the worst enemy of nature and of mankind itself. Happily, while yet in time, the savants sound the alarm. In this century, when we believe in science, we must hope that their voice will not be lost in the desert."

Profs. Lilljeborg and Nordenskiöld, of the Academy of Sciences, Sweden unite in declaring: "As to the former question, the killing of the seals on the rookeries, it seems at present regulated in a suitable manner to effectually prevent the gradual diminishing of the stock. If a wider experience should require some modifications in these regulations, there is no danger but that such modifications will be adopted. It is evidently in the interest of the owners of the rookeries to take care that this source of wealth shall not be lessened by excessive exploitation. Nor will there be any difficulty for studying the conditions of health and thriving of the animals during the rookery season. As to pelagic sealing, it is evident that a systematic hunting of the seals in the open sea on the way to and from or around the rookeries, will very soon cause the complete extinction of this valuable, and, from a scientific point of view, so extremely interesting and important animal, especially as a great number of the animals killed in this manner are pregnant cows, or cows temporarily separated from their pups while seeking food in the vicinity of the rookery. Everyone having some experience in seal hunting can also attest that only a relatively small part of the seals killed or seriously wounded in the open sea can in this manner be caught. We are therefore persuaded that *a prohibition of pelagic sealing is a necessary condition for the prevention of the total extermination of the fur seal.*" *U. S. Case, Vol. 1, App. 428.*

Prof. Middendorf, an eminent scientist of Russia: "The method of treating these animals which was originally adopted by the Russian-American Company at their home on the Pribilof Islands is still continued in the same rational manner, and has, for more than half a century, been found to be excellent, both on account of the large number of seals taken and because they are not exterminated. So long as superfluous young males are killed, not only the existence but even the increase of the herd is assured." *U. S. Case, Vol. 1, App. 430.*

Prof. Hohnb, of Prague. Austria-Hungary: "If the pelagic sealing of the fur seal is carried on still longer, as it has been executed during the last years, the pelagic sealing as a business matter and a 'living' will soon cease by the full extermination of this useful animal." *U. S. Case, Vol. 1, App. 133.*

The abundance of fur seals at the Island of Juan Fernandez two hundred years ago is shown by Dampier, who visited that island in 1683. In his *Voyage Around the World, 5th ed., 1713, Vol. 1, pp. 88, 90,* it is said:

"Seals swarm as thick about this island (of John Fernando, as he terms it) as if they had no other place in the world to live in; for there is not a bay nor rock that one can get ashore on but is full of them. *   *   *   Those at *John Fernando's* have fine, thick, short fur; the like I have not taken notice of anywhere but in these seas. Here are always thousands, I might say possibly millions of them, either sitting on the bays or going and coming in the sea around the island, which is covered with them (as they lie at the top of the water playing and sunning themselves) for a mile or two from the shore. When they come out of the sea they bleat like sheep for their young, and though they pass through hundreds of other young ones before they come to their own, yet they will not suffer any of them to suck. The young ones are like puppies, and lie much ashore, but when beaten by any of us they, as well as the old ones, will make towards the sea, and swim very swift and nimble, tho' on shore they lie very sluggishly, and will not go out of our way unless we beat them, but snap at us. A blow on the nose soon kills them. Large ships might here load themselves with sealskins and trancoyl; for they are extraordinarily fat."

Another writer, referring to the destruction of fur seals in the southern seas, says: "These valuable creatures have often been found frequenting some sterile islands in innumerable multitudes. By way of
illustration we shall refer only to the fur seal, as occurring in South
Shetland. On this barren spot their numbers were such that it has
been estimated that it could have continued permanently to furnish a
return of 100,000 furs a year; which, to say nothing of the public benefit, would have yielded annually, from this spot alone, a very handsome
sum to the adventurers. But what do these men do? In two short
years, 1821–2, so great is the rush, that they destroy 320,000. They
killed all and spared none. The moment an animal landed, though
big with young, it was destroyed. Those on shore were likewise immediately despatched, though the cubs were but a day old. These, of
course, all died, their number, at the lowest calculation, exceeding
100,000. No wonder, then, at the end of the second year the animals in this locality were nearly extinct. So it is, we add, in other
localities, and so with other seals; so with the oil-seals and so with the
whale itself, every addition only making bad worse. And all this
might easily be prevented by a little less barbarous and revolting
cruelty, and a little more enlightened selfishness. Fishermen are by
law restrained as to the size of the meshes of their net in taking many
of our valuable fish; and in the Island of Lobos, in the River Plata,
where, as we have seen, there are quantities of seals, their extermination is prevented by the governor of Montevideo, who farms out the
trade under the restriction that the hunters shall not take them but at
stated periods, ages, etc." *Naturalist's Library*, 95.

Giving due weight to all the evidence adduced by the respective
Governments, including the opinions of eminent naturalists in various
countries, it is absolutely certain —

That this race has been conceived, and has come into existence, upon
the islands of the United States in Bering Sea, which, by formal legislative enactment, have been set apart as a land home for these animals,
where they can breed, and rear their young, and renew their coats of
fur, and to which they may return, and for more than a century have
regularly returned, from their annual migration into the high seas;

That these animals, from the necessities of the race, must come into
existence, and for a large part of each year must abide, upon land;

That the United States, in every form in which it could be done,
consistently with the nature and habits of these animals, has taken
possession of, and appropriated, this race as its property;

11492——9

That the taking of fur seals for commercial purposes at their breeding grounds on the St. Paul and St. George, where alone there can be a discrimination between the sexes, will not itself endanger the existence of the herd if—as was done by Russia and has been done by the United States—the killing is restricted to such proportion of available *males* as will leave a sufficient number for purposes of reproduction;

That the killing of these animals in large numbers at any other place than their land home or breeding grounds will speedily result in the loss of the race to the world;

That unrestrained pelagic sealing in Bering Sea or in the North Pacific Ocean, *even if no seals be taken on the islands by the United States or its lessees,* will result in the extermination, within a very few years, of the entire race frequenting those islands;

That but for the care, supervision, and protection bestowed upon these animals at their land home by the United States, the race would long ago have become extinct;

That if such care, supervision, or protection be withdrawn, the race would be destroyed; and,

That the United States, by its ownership of the breeding grounds of these animals is alone, of all the nations of the earth, in a position to take or control the taking of these animals, so that their increase may be regularly obtained for use without at all impairing the stock.

In the light of the above facts, which can not be disputed by anyone familiar with the record, let us inquire as to the principles of law and justice applicable to the case.

The particular question now under consideration involves two propositions, to be separately examined:

First, as to the right of property which is asserted by the United States in the Pribilof herd of seals;

Second, as to the protection of the herd by the United States while the seals are outside of the ordinary three-mile limit.

Much was said in the course of the argument as to the classification of these fur seals among animals. One theory is, that while not strictly domestic animals, they are so nearly like animals of that class that, in determining whether under any circumstances they can become the subject of property, and if so, under what circumstances, they should be classed as domestic animals, or, at least, as domesticated animals. Another theory is, that they are animals *feræ naturæ*, and not subject to exclusive appropriation as property, except in conformity to the principles of law applicable to animals of that class. The first theory has been carefully and elaborately examined and enforced by Senator Morgan. Nothing can be added to what the learned Senator has said upon that subject. I propose to consider the subjects of property and protection in the other aspect named, and will, therefore, inquire whether the claim of the United States to own these seals is supported by any principles of law universally recognized as controlling upon the question of property in animals commonly classed as wild, rather than domestic animals.

The main contentions of the United States, in support of its claim of property, are these:

That while the general rule is that no one can have an absolute property in things *feræ naturæ*, there are animals so near the boundary drawn by the terms wild, tame, and reclaimed, that the question must be determined by a consideration of their nature and habits in connection with the grounds upon which the institution of property stands;

That, according to the established rules of law prevailing in all civilized countries, the essential facts that render useful animals, classed as wild animals, the subjects of property, when in the custody or control of, as well as while temporarily absent from, their masters, are the care, industry, and supervision of man so acting on the natural disposition of the animals as to encourage their habitual return to a particular place and to his custody and power at that place, whereby he is enabled to deal with them *as a whole*, in a similar manner, and so as to obtain from them similar benefits, as in the case of domestic animals; that for all purposes of property, animals so acted upon and dealt with may be assimilated to domestic animals, even if they be not strictly of that class;

That to this class the Pribilof fur seals belong, because at the same season in every year they return to the same place, the islands of St. Paul and St. George, where they become so far subject to the power of the United States that its agents or licensees can treat them in many ways as if they were domestic animals; that all that is needed to ensure their return to and remaining upon those islands from year to year, whereby the benefits of an increase of their numbers can be obtained, is that such agents and lessees shall abstain from repelling them as they approach the land, defend them after they have arrived against pursuit by hunters, disturb them as little as possible when making selections for commercial purposes, and take males only for purposes of commerce; and

That the United States, its agents and lessees, do all that is necessary to secure their return each year to, and their remaining at, the Pribilof Islands for all the purposes for which they must come to, and for a time abide, upon land.

These considerations, it is contended—assuming that these fur seals are of the class commonly called animals *feræ naturæ*—rest upon a principle fundamental in the institution of property, that principle being that whenever any useful wild animals, the supply of which may be exhausted by indiscriminate slaughter, or by reckless handling, "so far submit themselves to the control or dominion of particular men as to enable them *exclusively* to cultivate such animals and to obtain the annual increase for the supply of human wants, and, at the same time, to preserve the stock, they have a property in them; or, in other words, whatever may be justly regarded as the product of human art, industry, and self-denial, must be assigned to those who make these exertions, as their merited reward."

In opposition to this claim of property by the United States, Great Britain contends that these seals are strictly animals *feræ naturæ;* that the only property in them known to the law is dependent on actual, physical possession; that the United States or its licensees have the exclusive right to take possession of them only while they are on the islands of St. Paul and St. George, but that such right is lost when they leave the Islands and go into the high seas, for the purpose of obtaining fish for food, even if they have, when so leaving, the intention to return to their breeding grounds; that the citizens or subjects of all nations have equally the right to kill or take possession of them in the high seas; that while on the Islands neither the United States nor their lessees take manual possession of the seals other than of those actually killed; that, even if it be true that the care, industry, self-denial, and protection bestowed upon these animals while on their breeding grounds has secured, does now secure, and will alone secure, this race from extermination by pelagic sealing, that fact can not give a right of property to the United States; and that the right of pelagic sealers to capture and kill these seals in the open seas, for profit, by any methods they choose to employ, even by such as will certainly or soon destroy the entire race, is supported by the established principles of international law.

While, in a sense, all property has its root in municipal law, I agree that the question as to the ownership of these animals when they are in the open waters of the ocean, the highway of all peoples, is to be determined ultimately by the public law of nations—that is, by those principles common to, and recognized as binding by, all civilized countries in their intercourse and relations with each other. No other law can be appealed to for the settlement of a dispute between sovereign nations as to the ownership of animals when found on the seas beyond their respective territorial limits. But by what considerations are we to be governed in ascertaining what the law of nations recognizes, allows, or forbids?

The counsel for the United States contended, in argument, that in determining what rights are recognized by the law of nations, the Tribunal is not to ignore, but must give effect to, those principles of right reason, justice, humanity, and morality which have their foundation in the law of nature as applied to the institution of property. This view was earnestly combated by the counsel of Great Britain, and it was, in effect, said that the teachings and precepts of the law of nature were of no importance in the present inquiry; that the rights of these two nations could not be made to depend, in any degree, upon abstract principles founded only on reason, justice, humanity, or morality, but must be determined upon grounds of positive law, resting in the affirmative assent of the nations, independently of ethical considerations arising out of distinctions which the conscience of the world makes between what is morally right and what is morally wrong, or between what is supported by sound reason and justice and what is not so supported.

Of course, if there be any settled, recognized rules of the law of nations governing the particular question under consideration, they must control our decision whatever may be our view of their justice. The two nations interested are bound by such rules and the Tribunal may not disregard them, or refuse to give effect to them. But if the precise case before it is not covered by some positive rule, decision or precedent, founded on the conventions or established usages of the civilized nations of the earth, and expressly set forth in the writings of public jurists, we are not, for that reason, to hold that it is not provided for by the law of nations. As a court sitting under municipal authority would be bound, in the absence of precedent, to give judgment according to the principles of right derived from the whole body of the law to which it may properly refer, so this Tribunal, constituted for the determination of questions depending upon the law of nations, may, and if it fulfills the objects for which it was constituted, must, look into the recognized sources of that law and seek in the domain of general jurisprudence for the rule of decision in the case before it. One of the recognized sources of the law of nations are the principles of natural reason and justice applicable to the relations and intercourse of independent political societies. Those principles may be said to have their origin in the Law of Nature, or in what is sometimes called the Natural Law of Equity, because approved by the moral sense of mankind. No earthly tribunal, administering justice between individuals, or between nations, if unfettered by statute, or by binding precedent, may rightfully disregard the rules of reason, morality, humanity, and justice derived from that law. Those rules are not the less binding because not formulated in some book, ordinance, or treaty. Certainly, this Tribunal of Arbitration must regard the rules of international morality and justice, applicable to the subject, and fairly to be deduced from the rights and duties of States and from the nature of moral obligations, as an integral part of the law of nations by which the matters submitted to it are to be determined. The institution of property is ordained by society for its improvement and preservation. And there are certain rules, arising out of the very necessities of that institution, which are common to the jurisprudence of all civilized nations. While these rules may be more frequently found recognized in municipal law, they are so grounded in the well-being of man, and so thoroughly supported by right reason, and natural justice, as to have become universally recognized, and, therefore, must be regarded as part of the common law of civilized countries. Nations, no more than individuals, may disregard those rules, for upon their observance depends the existence of organized society and the security of government among civilized peoples.

That I am not in error in supposing that these views have been generally accepted and are enforced where action is not controlled by statutes or by the provisions of treaties, will appear from the decisions of courts and from the works of writers upon international law.

Chief Justice Marshall, delivering the judgment of the Supreme Court of the United States, after observing that the law of nations is in part unwritten and in part conventional, said that "to ascertain that which is unwritten we resort to the great principles of reason and justice; but as these principles will be differently understood by different nations under different circumstances, we consider them as being, in some degree, fixed and rendered stable by a series of judicial decisions." *Thirty Hhds. of Sugar* vs. *Boyle, etc., 9 Cranch's Reports, 191, 197.*

In the case of *The Helena*, Lord Stowell, considering the principles of international law, observed "that some people have foolishly imagined that there is no other law of nations but that which is derived from positive compact and convention." *4 Robinson's Admiralty, Rep. 7.*

Bacon, in his Dissertation on the Advancement of Learning, says that "there are in nature certain fountains of justice, whence all civil laws are derived but as streams; and like as waters do take tinctures and tastes from the soils through which they run, so do civil laws vary according to the regions and governments where they are planted, though they proceed from the same fountain." *Bk. 2, chap. 23, sec. 14.*

Blackstone declares that the law of nature being coeval with mankind, and dictated by God himself, "is binding all over the globe in all countries, and at all times," and that "no human laws are of any validity if contrary to this, and such of them as are valid derive all their force and all their authority, mediately or immediately, from this original." And he also says: "As it is impossible for the whole race of mankind to be united in one great society, they must necessarily divide into many, and form separate states, commonwealths, and nations, entirely independent of each other and yet liable to mutual intercourse. Hence arises a third kind of law to regulate this mutual intercourse, called the 'law of nations,' which, as none of these states will acknowledge a superiority in the other, can not be dictated by any, but depends entirely upon *the rules of natural law*, or upon mutual compacts, treaties, leagues, and agreements between those several communities; in the construction, also, of which compacts we have no other rule to resort to but *the law of nature*, being the only one to which all the communities are equally subject, and therefore, the civil law very justly observes that *quod naturalis ratio inter omnes homines constituit vocatur jus gentium.*" *Bk. 1, p. 41, 43.*

In his Commentaries on International Law Sir Robert Phillimore says: "Grotius enumerates these sources [of international law] as being '*ipsa natura, leges divinæ, mores, et pacta.*' In 1753 the British Government made an answer to a memorial of the Prussian Government, which was termed by Montesquieu *reponse sans réplique*, and which has been generally recognized as one of the ablest expositions of international law ever embodied in a state paper. In this memorable document the law of nations is said to be founded upon justice, equity, convenience, and the reason of the thing, and confirmed by long usage." *1 Phillimore, ch. 3, sec. 20.* In the judgment delivered by him in *Queen vs.*

Keyn, Law Rep., 2 Exch. Dir. 211, Dr. Phillimore states that this answer was framed by Lord Mansfield and Sir George Lee. The same learned author declares that the sources from which international jurisprudence is derived embrace not only the universal consent of nations, as expressed by positive compact, and as implied by usage, custom, and practice, as disclosed by precedents, treaties, public documents, marine ordinances, the decisions of international tribunals, and the works of eminent writers upon international jurisprudence. but, also, "the Divine law, embodying the principles of eternal justice. implanted by God on all moral and social creatures, of which nations are the aggregates and of which governments are the international organs," as well as "the Revealed Will of God, enforcing and extending these principles of natural justice," and "Reason which governs the application of these principles to particular cases." *1 Phillimore, p. 67, c. 8, § 58*. In the above case of *Queen vs. Keyn*, Sir William Baliol Brett. now Lord Esher, Master of the Rolls, after observing that the authorities made it clear that the consent of nations was requisite to make any proposition a part of the law of nations, well said: "Their consent is to be assumed to the logical application to given facts of the ethical axioms of right and wrong. Such an application is the foundation of every system of law, including necessarily the law of nations." *L. R., 2 Exch. Dir, 131*.

Chancellor Kent, whose writings are known to the jurists of all nations, states in his Commentaries, that the most useful and practical part of the law of nations is. no doubt, instituted or positive law, founded on usage, consent, and agreement, and that it would be improper to separate this law entirely from natural jurisprudence and not to consider it as deriving much of its force and dignity from the same principles of right reason, the same views of the nature and constitution of man, and the same sanction of Divine revelation, as those from which the science of morality is deduced, and he says: "There is a natural and a positive law of nations. By the former every state, in its relations with other states, is bound to conduct itself with justice, good faith. and benevolence; and this application of the law of nature has been called by Vattel the necessary law of nations. because nations are bound by the law of nature to observe it; and it is termed by others the internal law of nations, because it is obligatory upon them in point of conscience." "We ought not. therefore," that great jurist continues, " to separate the science of public law from that of ethics, nor encourage the dangerous suggestion that governments are not so strictly bound by the obligations of truth, justice, and humanity, in relation to

other powers, as they are in the management of their own local con-
cerns." States or bodies politic, he observes, "are to be considered as
moral persons, having a public will, capable and free to do right and
wrong, inasmuch as they are collections of individuals, each of whom
carries with him into the service of the community the same binding
law of morality and religion which ought to control his conduct in private
life. The law of nations is a complex system, composed of various
ingredients. It consists of general principles of right and justice,
equally suitable to the government of individuals in a state of natural
equality and to the relations and conduct of nations; of a collection
of usages and customs, the growth of civilization and commerce
and a code of conventional or positive law." His conclusions upon
this subject are thus stated: "In the absence of these latter regulations, the intercourse and conduct of nations are to be governed by
principles fairly to be deduced from the rights and duties of nations
and the nature of moral obligation; and we have the authority of the
lawyers of antiquity, and of some of the first masters in the modern
school of public law, for placing the moral obligations of nations and
of individuals on similar grounds, and for considering individual and
national morality as parts of one and the same science. The law of
nations, so far as it is founded on the principles of natural law, is
equally binding in every age and upon all mankind." *Kent's Commentaries, Part 1, Lect. 1, pp. 2–1.* These views of Chancellor Kent seem
to be approved by the instructed judgment of Sir Travers Twiss, the
eminent publicist of Great Britain, who has himself divided the Law
of Nations into Natural or Necessary Law, and Positive or Instituted
Law. *The Law of Nations, ch. vi, secs. 82 and 105, ed. 1884, pp. 145, 176.*

Ortolan, in his work on International Rules and Diplomacy of the
Sea, thus states his views: "It is apparent that nations not having
any common legislator over them have frequently no other recourse for
determining their respective rights but to that reasonable sentiment of
right and wrong, to those moral truths already brought to light, and to
those which are still to be demonstrated. This is what is meant when
it is said that natural law is the first basis of international law." *Vol.
1, bk. 1, ch. iv., p. 71.*

Vattel, in the preface of his celebrated work, states that the moderns
are generally agreed in restricting the appellation of the law of nations
to that system of right and justice which ought to prevail between
nations or sovereign states. And in the body of his work he says:
"As men are subject to the law of nature, and as their union in civil

society can not have exempted them from the obligation to observe those laws, since by that union they do not cease to be men, the entire nation, whose common will is but the result of the united wills of the citizens, remains subject to the *law of nature*, and is bound to respect them in all her proceedings." We must, therefore, he says, apply to nations the rules of the law of nature, where they can be applied in a manner suitable to the subject. "in order to discover what their obligations are, and what their rights; consequently, the *law of nations* is originally no other than the *law of nature* applied to nations." *Ch. 56, secs. 5, 6.*

Wheaton, whose authority is recognized by all publicists, says: "International law, as understood among civilized nations, may be defined as consisting of those rules of conduct which reason deduces, as consonant to justice, from the nature of the society existing among independent nations, with such definitions and modifications as may be established by general consent." *International Law, Pt. 1, ch. 1, sec. 14.* Pomeroy, an American writer of distinction, observes: "What is called international law in its general sense, I would call international morality. It consists of those rules founded upon justice and equity, and deduced by right reason, according to which independent states are accustomed to regulate their mutual intercourse, and to which they conform their mutual relations." *International Law, ed. 1886, C. 1, S. 29.* Woolsey, another American writer, cited by both sides in argument, says: "It would be strange if the state, that power which defines rights and makes them real, which creates moral persons or associations with rights and obligations, should have no such relations of its own—should be a physical and not a moral entity. In fact, to take the opposite ground would be to maintain that there is no right and wrong in the intercourse of states, and to leave their conduct to the sway of mere convenience." *Ed. of 1892.*

Burlamaqui, in his Principles of Natural and Politic Law, (p. 14), after quoting with approval the observation of Hobbes that natural law is divided into the natural law of man and the natural law of states, and that the latter is what is called the law of nations, presents the same general view: "Thus natural law and the law of nations are in reality one and the same thing, and differ only by an external denomination. We must, therefore, say that the law of nations, properly so called, and considered as a law proceeding from a superior, is nothing else but the law of nature itself, not applied to men, considered simply as such, but to nations, states, or their chiefs, in the relations they have together, and the several interests they have to manage between each other." *Ed. 1823, Pt. II, c. 6, pp. 135, 6.* In this view Puffendorf expressed his concurrence, observing that he recognized "no other kind of voluntary or positive international law, at least none having force of law, properly so called, and binding upon nations as emanating from a superior." *Vol. 1, book 2, c. 3, § 23, p. 213, 5th. ed.; ed. 1729, English, 119.*

Heinnecius: "The law of nations is the law of nature itself respecting or applied to social life and the affairs of societies and independent states. * * * Hence, we may infer that the law of nature doth not differ from the law of nations, neither in respect of its foundation and first principles nor of its rules, but solely with respect to its object, Wherefore their opinion is groundless who speak of, I know not what, law of nations distinct from the law of nature." *Vol. I, Ed. 1763, Sec. 21, p. 14.*

Hautefeuille: "What is true, and in my opinion, incontestable, is that notions of what is just and right, and what is unjust are found in all men; it is that all individuals of the human race that are in the enjoyment of reason have these notions graven upon their hearts, and that they bring with them into the world when they are born. These notions do not extend to all the details of law as do civil laws, but they have reference to all the most prominent points of law. It cannot be denied that the idea of property is a natural and innate idea. * * The natural or divine law is the only one that can be applied among nations—among beings free from every bond and having no interest in common. * * International law is, therefore, based upon the divine and primitive law; it is all derived from this source." *Vol. 1, p. 46, 1818.*

Martens: "Each nation being considered as a moral being, living in a state of nature, the obligations of one nation towards another are no more than those of individuals, modified and applied to nations; and this is what is called the natural law of nations. It is universal and necessary, because all nations are governed by it, even against their will." *Law of Nations, German, 4th ed. 1829, p. 2 of Introduction.*

Ferguson: "International law, being based on international morality, depends upon the state of progress made in civilization. * * * Investigating thus this spirit of law, we find the definition of International Law to consist of certain rules of conduct which reason, prompted by conscience, deduces as consonant to justice, with such limitations and modifications as may be established by general consent, to meet the exigencies of the present state of society as existing among nations and which modern civilized states regard as binding on them in their relations with one another, with a force comparable in nature and degree to that binding the conscientious person to obey the laws of his country." *Manual of International Law, Dutch, 1881, Vol. 1, Pt. II, chap. 3, sec. 21, p. 66.*

Carlos Testa: "This application of the precepts of natural law, which obliges nations to practice the same duties that it prescribes for individuals, constitutes the law of nations, which, when considered according to its origin (which is based upon natural law), is also called the primitive or necessary law of nations. * * * The origins of international law are therefore three in number: (1) The reason and the conscience of what is just and unjust, independent of any prescription; (2) custom; (3) public treaties. The principles, practices, and usages of the law of nations, in accordance with these limits, regulate the conduct of nations, and it is for this reason that in their generality they constitute international law. Conventional law may abrogate the law of custom, but it loses its character as a law if it establishes provisions at variance with natural law." *Le Droit International Maritime (Portuguese), translated by H. Boutirón, 1886, Pt. 1, ch. 1, p. 46.*

Looking, then, to the reason of the thing, and to the concurrence of views upon this point, among jurists and publicists, I must withhold my assent from the proposition that this Tribunal, in ascertaining whether the law of nations sanctions and supports the claim of property made by the United States, may not consider—the question not being concluded by treaties or precedents—what is demanded in respect to the subject of controversy by the law of nature, that is, by the principles of justice, sound reason, morality, and equity, as recognized and approved by civilized peoples.

The question was propounded in argument whether any precedent precisely in point was recorded in the writings of publicists, or in the judgments of the courts, or in the statutes or ordinances of maritime nations, that supports the claim of the United States to own these seals and protect them when they are in the seas, beyond territorial jurisdiction. This question must, of course, be answered in the negative, because, so far as is known, the case has never before arisen. And it would not now be a practical one but for the intervention of pelagic sealing, the prosecution of which involves the very existence of this race of animals. It has not heretofore been asserted in behalf of any nation that the doctrine of the freedom of the seas recognized it as a *right*, in individuals, even by methods barbarous and cruel, to *exterminate* a race of useful animals, found by them in the high seas, and thereby deprive the world of all benefit to be derived from them. It is more pertinent to inquire whether this claim of property is supported by principles of morality, reason, equity, and justice every where recognized as vital in organized society. It is still more pertinent to inquire whether the law of nations furnishes any precedent opposed or hostile to the claim made by the United States of property in these animals, which are conceived, and, if the race is to exist at all, must be born and reared, on land, and which, although passing much time on the high seas, periodically return to, and, for a time, abide upon the territory of the United States. And they return to and abide upon that territory, under such circumstances, that the United States, the sovereign and owner of the land, and it alone, of all other nations, can, by the exercise of care, industry, and self-denial take the increase for the benefit of the world, without, in any degree, diminishing or impairing the stock. If there is no recorded precedent based upon actual dispute between nations, which would determine such a case, we may properly inquire whether there is such an agreement among civilized nations, in respect to the institution of property and the rules governing the acquisition of property, as will justify us in adjudging that the present claim of the United States rests upon principles universally recognized. If the rules embodied in the concurring municipal law of the different countries of the earth, and founded in reason, justice, and the necessities of organized society, will sustain this claim, our judgment to that effect will be in accordance with the law of nations; for nothing to the contrary appearing in positive enactments, binding upon this Tribunal, it must be assumed when dealing with a question of property, that the nations assent to such rules in the law of property as are common to the jurisprudence of civilized countries. It has been well observed by Sir James Mackintosh, in his famous Discourse on the Law of Nature and Nations, that the two institutions of property and marriage constitute, preserve and improve society; that upon their gradual development depends the progressive civilization of mankind; that on them rests the whole order of civil life; that the duties of men, subjects, princes, lawgivers, and States are all parts of one system of universal morality; and that " the principle of justice, deeply rooted in the nature and interest of man, pervades the whole system, and is discoverable in every part of it, even to its minutest ramification in a legal formality, or in the construction of an article in a treaty." When, therefore, a Tribunal, administering the Law of Nations, is required to consider a question of property, it may not disregard what the principles of justice, right reason, and the necessities of society, evidenced by the concurring municipal law of the world, demand at its hands.

Any other view is, I submit, inadmissible. The law of self-defense is a part of the law of nations, not so much because it is declared to be so by legislation or treaty, but because it is founded in principles of justice and right that are recognized among all peoples. Murder and theft are crimes against society, whether so declared by statute or not, and they would be so regarded by any Tribunal administering the law of nations, if its judgment depended upon its estimate of those acts, not because they are made crimes by any statute or convention binding upon the world, but because all mankind, in recognition of the principles of eternal and natural justice, implanted in man by the Creator, regard them in that light. It is said that even if there be grounds of reason and justice, that is of natural law, why it might be proper and desirable that these fur seals should be held to be the subject of property, such considerations are of no weight whatever in the absence of the general assent of nations that they may be so regarded. Such an argument leads to this strange conclusion: That in the absence of any affirmative assent of nations to a right decision, that is, to a decision conformable to the principles of sound reason, justice, and the necessities of mankind, we must, for the want of such assent, make a wrong decision, that is, one forbidden by sound reason and justice and hostile to the best interests of society. Thus, according to the argument presented, a Tribunal administering international law must, in the absence of the express assent of the nations, reject every new affirmative proposition, however strongly supported by reason, justice, and morality, and thereby establish the contrary as the rule that should govern the conduct of nations. True wisdom, indeed, the Treaty and public law, I submit, require that this Tribunal accept the doctrine that whatever is demanded by right reason, justice, and morality has the sanction of the law of nations, unless it has been otherwise determined by the general assent of mankind. This was the principle declared by Mr. Justice Story, when he said: "I think it may be unequivocally affirmed that every doctrine that may be fairly deduced by correct reasoning from the rights and duties of nations and the nature of moral obligations, may theoretically be said to exist in the law of nations; and unless it be relaxed or waived by the consent of nations, which may be evidenced by their general practice and custom, it may be enforced by a court of justice wherever it arises in judgment." *La Jeune Eugénie, 2 Mason's Reports,* 449.

There are rules governing the acquisition of property, not always sanctioned by legislation, but yet common to the jurisprudence of all countries, and which we may not ignore or refuse to recognize. I cannot conceive it to be possible that the Tribunal, in deciding a question of property in animals, found in the high seas, may disregard the rules of property which are imbedded in the concurring municipal law of civilized nations. That must be deemed the law of all to which all have assented. And so if the Tribunal should hold that these fur seals are the property of the United States when found in the high seas, it would thereby recognize the right of that country to protect them against pelagic sealing, not because that right is secured by statute or treaty, but because by the universal judgment of nations, the owner of property may employ for its protection and preservation such means, not forbidden by law, as may be necessary to that end. It is true, in fact, that the recognized doctrines as to possession, detention, right of possession, and right of property, as they have been applied in cases which have arisen between independent states, are derived from the principles of natural law as understood and as expounded by statesmen and public jurists.

While there are wild animals whose nature and habits preclude the possibility of their being appropriated as property, except when they are confined or are otherwise in actual custody, there are others, valuable to mankind and usually assigned to that class, which, by the common law of the world, may, under given circumstances, become the property of man, without being held in continuous, actual possession.

Attention will first be given to the Roman law, because Reason, which governs the application of the principles of justice to particular cases, is itself "guided and fortified by a constant reference to analogous cases and to the written reason embodied in the text of the Roman law, and in the works of commentators thereupon." *1 Phillimore, c. 8, sec. 58.* The same author observes that "the Roman law may, in truth, be said to be the most valuable of all aids to a correct and full knowledge of international jurisprudence, of which it is indeed, historically speaking, the actual basis." Again : "Independently of the historical value of the Roman law as explanatory of the terms and sense of treaties and of the language of jurists, its importance as a repository of decisions, the spirit of which almost always, and the letter of which very frequently, is applicable to the controversies of independent States, can scarcely be overstated. From this rich treasury of the principles of universal jurisprudence, it will generally be found that the deficiencies

of precedent, usage, and express international authority may be supplied. Throughout the greater portion of Christendom it presents to
each State what may be fairly termed their own consent, bound up in
the municipal jurisprudence of their own country; and this not merely
to the nations of Europe, whose codes are built on the civil law, but to
the numerous colonies and to the independent States which have sprung
from those colonies, and which cover the globe." *1 Phillimore secs. 56
and 37.* Lord Stowell said that a great part of the law of nations was
founded on the civil law. *The Maria, 1 Robinson's Adm. Rep., 363.*
"A great part, then, of international law," Henry Sumner Maine says,
"is Roman law spread over Europe by a process exceedingly like that
which a few centuries earlier had caused other portions of Roman law
to filter into the interstices of every European legal system. * * *
In a book published some years ago on Ancient Law, I made this remark:
'Setting aside the Treaty Law of Nations, it is surprising how large a
part of the system is made up of pure Roman law. Wherever there is
a doctrine of the Roman jurisconsults, affirmed by them to be in harmony with the *jus gentium* [natural law], the Publicists have found a
reason for borrowing it, however plainly it may bear the mark of a
distinctive Roman origin.' * * * The greatest function of the law
of nature was discharged in giving birth to modern international law.
* * * The impression that the Roman law sustained a system of
what would now be called international law, and that this system was
identical with the law of nature, had undoubtedly much influence in
causing the rules of what the Romans called natural law to be engrafted
on and identified with the modern law of nations." *Maine's International Law, pp. 13, 17, 28.* Van Leeuwen: "The Roman law is at the
present day almost everywhere, and by every nation upheld as a common law of nations, and adopted in cases where particular laws or
customs fail." *Roman-Dutch Law, Vol. 1, Bk. 1, Ch. 1, sec. 11, p. 3,
Ed. 1881, Kotze's Translation.* And, "it will generally be found," says
Halleck, "that the deficiencies of precedent, usage, and express international authority may be supplied from the rich treasury of the Roman
civil law. Indeed, the greater number of controversies between States
would find a just solution in this comprehensive system of practical
equity, which furnishes principles of universal jurisprudence applicable
alike to individuals and to States." *1 Halleck's International Law, c.
2, sec. 21.*

These authorities justify recourse to the Roman law, as expounded
by jurists and commentators, for those principles of equity, right,
and justice that constitute a part of the law of nations.

It is said in the Institutes of Justinian:

"11. Things become the property of individuals in many ways; for we obtain the ownership of some by the natural law, which, as we have said, is styled *jus gentium;* and of some by the civil law. It is most convenient, then, to commence with the more ancient law, and it is clear that the more ancient is the natural law, since the nature of things brought it into existence simultaneously with the human race itself; whilst civil laws began to exist when states were first founded, magistrates appointed, and laws written. 12. Wild beasts, therefore, and birds and fishes, that is to say, all animals that live on the earth, in in the sea or in the air, as soon as they are caught by any one, become his at once by virtue of the law of nations. For whatever has previously belonged to no one is granted by natural reason to the first taker. Nor does it matter whether the man catches the wild beast or bird on his own ground or on another's; although a person purposing to enter on another's land for the purpose of hunting or fowling may, of course, be prohibited from entering by the owner if he perceive him. Whatever, then, you have caught of this kind is regarded as yours, so long as it is kept in your custody; but when it has escaped from your custody and reverted to its natural freedom it ceases to be yours, and again belongs to the first taker. And it is considered to have recovered its natural freedom when it has either escaped out of your sight, or is still in sight, but so situated that its pursuit is difficult. 13. It has been debated whether a wild beast is to be considered yours at once, if wounded in such a manner as to be capable of capture; and some have held that it is yours at once, and is to be regarded as yours so long as you are pursuing it; but that if you desist from pursuit it ceases to be yours and again belongs to the first taker. Others have thought that it is not yours until you have actually caught it. And we indorse the latter opinion, because many things may happen to prevent your catching it. 14. Bees, too, are naturally wild. Therefore, any bees which settle upon your tree are no more considered yours, until you have hived them, than birds which have made their nest in that tree of yours; if, therefore, any one else hives them he will be their owner. The honeycomb, too, which they have made, anyone may take away. But undoubtedly if you see a person entering upon your land before anything has been removed (*in integra re*) you may legally forbid him to enter. A swarm which has flown from your hive is considered to be yours, so long as it is in your sight and its pursuit not

11492——10

difficult; otherwise it belongs to the first taker. 15. Peacocks and pigeons are naturally wild, and it is not material that they get into a habit of flying away and coming back; for bees do the same, and their nature is admitted to be wild. Some people, too, have deer so tamed that they habitually go into the woods and come home again, and yet no one denies that these animals also are naturally wild. Still, with regard to animals of this sort, *which go and come regularly, the rule has been. adopted, that they are regarded· as being yours so long as they have the intent of returning;* for if they cease to have that intent they also cease to be yours and become the property of the first taker. And they are held to have lost the intent of returning when they cease from the habit of returning." *Book II, Title I, Abdy & Walker's ed., pp. 82, 83, 84.*

To the same effect is Gaius, who, in his Commentaries, says:

"66. But not only those things which become ours by delivery are acquired by us on natural principles, but also those which we acquire by occupation, on the ground that they previously belonged to no one; of which class are all things caught on land, in the sea, or in the air. 67. If, therefore, we have caught a wild beast, or a bird, or a fish, anything we have so caught at once becomes ours, and is regarded as being ours so long as it is kept in our custody. But when it has escaped from our custody and returned into its natural liberty, it again becomes the property of the first taker, because it ceases to be ours. And it is considered to recover its natural liberty when it has either gone out of our sight or, although it be still in our sight, yet its pursuit is difficult. 68. With regard to those animals which *are accustomed to go and return habitually,* as doves, and bees, and deer, which are in the habit of going into the woods and coming back again, we have this rule handed down: that if they cease to have the intent of returning they also cease to be ours, and become the property of the first taker, and they are considered to cease to have the intent of returning when they have abandoned the habit of returning." *Bk. II, Secs. 66, 67, and 68. Abdy & Walker's ed. p. 98.* See, also, *Hunter's Roman Law, 2d ed., p. 346.*

Van Leeuwen, in his Commentaries on Roman–Dutch Law, enumerates among *res nullius* those which, " although not belonging to anybody, may yet be brought under the dominion or possession of another;" and while stating that there are some wild animals, " as birds, fish, and beasts *inhabiting* the sea or other waters, the air, or the earth," which " may, according to the original institution of laws, be captured and owned by everyone without distinction," he says, in respect to others: " For the animals *that are accustomed to go out and return*, as bees, pigeons, ducks, geese, and the like, although wild by nature, and frequently roaming very far, *are considered to remain our property*, and may not be acquired by anybody unless they have *continued absent, and have been abandoned by us without hope of their returning.*" *Bk. 2, chap. 3.*

Bowyer, in his treatise on Modern Civil Law, while stating the general rule to be that wild animals, birds, and fish, and all animals that are produced in the sea, the heavens, and the earth become the property, by natural law, of whoever takes possession of them, the reason being that whatever is the property of no man becomes, by natural reason, the property of whoever occupies it, says: " Bees, also, are of a wild nature, and therefore they no more become the property of the owner of the soil by swarming in his trees than do the birds which build in them; and they are not his unless he inclose them in a hive. Consequently, whoever hives them makes them his own. And while they are wild anyone may cut off the honeycombs, though the owner of the land may prevent this by warning off trespassers. And a swarm flying from a hive belong to the owner of the hive so long as it is within his sight, but otherwise it is the property of whoever takes possession of it. *With regard to creatures which have the habit of going and returning,* such as pigeons, they remain the property of those to whom they belong *so long as they retain the animus revertendi, or disposition to return.* But when they lose that disposition they become the property of whomsoever secures them. And they must be held to have lost the *animus revertendi* as soon as they have lost the habit of returning," *p. 72.*

It will not be questioned that these authorities show that, according to the Roman law, and under certain circumstances, property may exist in some animals admittedly *feræ naturæ.* What those circumstances are will be presently considered.

The law common to both of the nations here represented, except where some statute has intervened and established a different rule, is in harmony with the rules established in the Roman law. Bracton, after showing that dominion over things by natural right or by the right of nations may be acquired, or lost, in various ways, says: " Occupation also includes shutting up, as in the case of bees, which are wild by nature, for if they should have settled on my tree they would not be any the more mine, until I have shut them up in a hive, than birds which

have made a nest in my tree, and therefore if another person shall shut
them up, he will have the dominion over them. A swarm, also, which
has flown away out of my hive, is so long understood to be mine as
long as it is in my sight, and the overtaking of it is not impossible,
otherwise they belong to the first taker; but if a person shall
capture them, he does not make them his own if he shall know
that they are another's, but he commits a theft unless he has the
intention to restore them. And these things are true, unless sometimes from custom in some parts the practice is otherwise. What
has been said above applies to animals which have remained at all
times wild; and if wild animals have been tamed, and they *by habit
go out and return, fly away, and fly back, such as deer, swan, sea
fowls, and doves, and such like,* another rule has been approved, that
they are so long considered as ours *as long as they have the disposition
to return;* for if they have no disposition to return they cease to be
ours. But they seem to cease to have the disposition to return
when they have abandoned the habit of returning; and the same is
said of fowls and geese which have become wild after being tamed."
Bracton, bk. 2, ch. 1.

Comyn observes that although in things *feræ naturæ,* no one can
have an absolute property, as in deer and conies, in hawks, doves,
herons, pheasants, partridges or other fowls at large and not
reclaimed, or in fish at large in the water, yet a man may have "a
qualified or possessory property in them," as in deer, pheasants, partridges, or hawks, tamed or reclaimed, or doves in a dovecot, or young
herons in their nest, or fish in a tank. "But," he says, "if deer, fowls,
etc., tame or reclaimed, attain their natural liberty, and *have no inclination to return,* the property shall be lost," implying that the right
of property is not lost, so long as the animal or fowl reclaimed or
tamed, has, when leaving the premises of the owner, the inclination to
return. *Digest, Tit. Biens, F. Vol. 2, p. 135.*

In Bacon's Abridgment it is said: "The wild animals, such as deer,
hares, foxes, etc., are understood to be those which by reason of their
swiftness or fierceness fly the dominion of man, and in these no person
can have property, unless they be tamed *or* reclaimed by him; and as
property is *the power that a man hath over any other thing for his own
use, and the ability that he has to apply it to the sustentation of his being,*
when the power ceases his property is lost; and by consequence an
animal of this kind, which, after any seizure, escapes into the wild
common of nature and asserts its own liberty by its swiftness, is no

more mine than any creature in the ladies, because I have it no longer in my power or disposal. Hence it appears that by the common law every man has an equal right to such creatures as were not naturally under the power of man, and that the mere capture or seizure created a property in them." But, says the author: "By taking and taming them they belong to the owner, as do all the other tame animals, so long as they continue in this condition; that is, *as long as they can be considered to have the mind of returning to their masters; for while they appear to be in this state they are plainly the owner's and ought not to be violated;* but when they forsake the houses and habitations of men, and betake themselves to the wood, they are then the property of any man." *Bouvier's Ed., Title, Game, Vol. 1, pp. 431, 432.*

Blackstone says:

"II. Other animals that are not of a tame and domestic nature are either not the objects of property at all, or else fall under our other division, namely, that of qualified, limited, or special property, which is such as is not in its nature permanent, but may sometimes subsist and at other times not subsist. In discussing which subject, I shall, in the first place, show how this species of property may subsist in such animals as are *feræ naturæ*, or of a wild nature, and then how it may subsist in any other things when under particular circumstances.

"First, then, a man may be invested with a qualified, but not an absolute property, in all creatures that are *feræ naturæ*, either *per industriam, propter impotentiam,* or *propter privilegium.*

"1. A qualified property may subsist in animals *feræ naturæ, per industriam hominis,* by a man's reclaiming, and making them tame by art, industry, and education, or by so confining them within his own immediate power that they can not escape and use their natural liberty. And under this head some writers have ranked all the former species of animals we have mentioned, apprehending none to be originally and naturally tame, but only made so by art and custom, as horses, swine, and other cattle, which, if originally left to themselves, would have chosen to rove up and down, seeking their food at large, and are only made domestic by use and familiarity, and are, therefore, say they, called *mansueta, quasi manui assueta.* But, however well this notion may be founded, abstractly considered, our law apprehends the most obvious distinctions to be between such animals as we generally see tame, and are, therefore, seldom, if ever, found wandering at large, which it calls *domitæ naturæ,* and such creatures as are usually found at liberty, which are therefore supposed to be more emphatically *feræ naturæ*, though it may happen that the latter shall be sometimes tamed and confined by the art and industry of man—such as are deer in a park, hares or rabbits in an inclosed warren, doves in a dove house, pheasants or partridges in a mew, hawks that are fed and commanded by their owner, and fish in a private pond or in trunks. These are no longer the property of man than while they continue in his keeping or actual possession; but if at any time they regain their natural liberty his property instantly ceases, *unless they have animum revertendi, which is only to be known by their usual custom of returning.* A maxim which is borrowed from the civil law, *revertendi animum videntur desinere habere tunc, cum revertendi consuetudinem deserverint.* The law therefore, extends this possession further than the mere manual occupation; for my tame hawk, that is pursuing his quarry in my presence, though he is at liberty to go where he pleases, is nevertheless my property, for he has *animum revertendi.* So are my pigeons that are flying at a distance from their home (especially of the carrier kind), and likewise the deer that is chased out of my park or forest, and is instantly pursued by the keeper or forester; all which remain still in my possession, and I still preserve my qualified property in them. * * * Bees also are *feræ naturæ,* but when hived and reclaimed, a man may have a qualified property in them by the law of nature, as well as by the civil law. * * * In all these creatures, reclaimed from the wildness of their nature, the property is not absolute, but defeasible; a property that may be destroyed if they resume their ancient wildness, and are found at large." *Bk. 2, p. 391.*

Kent, in his Commentaries, says:

"Animals *feræ naturæ,* so long as they are reclaimed by the art and power of man, are also the subject of a qualified property; but when they are abandoned, or escape, and return to their natural liberty and ferocity, without the *animus revertendi,* the property in them ceases. While this qualified property continues, it is as much-under the protection of law as any other property, and every invasion of it is redressed in the same manner. The difficulty of ascertaining with precision the application of the law arises from the want of some certain determinate standard or rule by which to determine when an animal is *feræ, vel domitæ naturæ.* If an animal belongs to the class of tame animals, as, for instance, to the class of horses, sheep, or cattle, he is then a subject clearly of absolute property; but if he belongs to the class of animals which are wild by nature, and owe all their temporary docility to the discipline of man, such as deer, fish, and several kind of fowl, then the animal is a subject of qualified property, and which continues so long only as the tameness and dominion remain." Referring to the difference of opinion among naturalists and writers, as to whether all animals were originally tame, and owed their wildness or ferocity to the violence of man, the author says: "The common law has wisely avoided all perplexing questions and refinements of this kind, and has adopted the test laid down by Puffendorf (Laws of Nature and Nations, Bk. 4, C. 6, Sec. 5), by referring the question whether the animal be wild or tame to our knowledge of his habits derived from fact and experience." *2 Kent's Comm.*, 348.

Has there been any departure from these principles in the judicial tribunals of Great Britain or the United States? No case was cited in argument showing that animals *feræ naturæ* could not, under any circumstances, become the subject of property. On the contrary, our attention has been called to cases distinctly proceeding upon the ground that the inquiry whether particular animals, naturally wild, were to be regarded as property, depended upon a consideration of their nature and habits, and the extent to which man, by acting upon their natural instincts or disposition, and by care and watchfulness, has established an industry in respect to them, and induced them to remain so far under his control or power, as to permit him, by means of such control or power to obtain the benefit of their increase, without injuring the stock. This is illustrated by *Davies* vs. *Powell*, Willes Rep., 46, where the principal question was whether deer, in a park of 600 acres, which did not confine them so they could be taken at pleasure, were distrainable for rent. They were not in possession, by actual confinement, and could only have been taken by shooting, or with dogs. The case went off upon the pleadings, but Chief Justice Willes, among other things, said: "It is expressly stated in *Bro. Abr.* tit, 'Property,' pl. 44, and agreed in all the books, that if deer or any other things *feræ naturæ* become tame a man may have a property in them. * * * Upon a supposition, therefore, which I do not admit to be the law now, that a man can have no property in any but tame deer, these must be taken to be tame deer, because it is admitted that the plaintiff had a property in them. * * * Fourth. The last argument, drawn *ab inusitato* though generally a very good one, does not hold in the present case. When the nature of things changes, the rules of law must change too.

When it was holden that deer were not distrainable, it was because they were kept principally for pleasure and not for profit, and were not sold and turned into money as they are now. But now they are become as much a sort of husbandry as horses, cows, sheep, or any other cattle. Whenever they are so, and it is universally known, it would be ridiculous to say that when they are kept merely for profit they are not distrainable as other cattle, though it has been holden that they were not so when they were kept only for pleasure. The rules concerning personal estates, which were laid down when personal estates were but small in proportion to lands, are quite varied, both in courts of law and equity, now that personal estates are so much increased and become so considerable a part of the property of this kingdom "

The case of *Morgan, etc., Executors of Abergavenny* vs. *Williams, Earl of Abergavenny* (*8 C. B., 768*), has a distinct bearing on some aspects of the question under consideration. That was an action of trover to recover damages for the conversion of deer, a considerable number of which had the range of a park, consisting of upwards of 1,100 acres of land, and, in many parts, of a very wild and rough description. Some of the deer were described by witnesses as tame, others as wild, meaning thereby, as the court said, that some were less shy and timid than others. The case appeared to have been tried upon the issues, whether the deer were in what was called a legal park, and whether, in view of the state and condition of the animals, the nature of the place where they were kept, and the mode in which they had been treated, they could be regarded as tamed or reclaimed. The jury found that the park had all the incidents of a legal park, and that the animals had been originally wild, but had been reclaimed. Upon the hearing of a rule nisi for a new trial before Lord Chief Justice Wilde and Justices Maule, Coltman, and Cresswell, the court, referring to the objection that the jury had been misdirected, said: "That it was proper to leave the question to the jury in the terms in which the issue is expressly joined can not be disputed, and the direction that that question must be determined *by referring to the place in which the deer were kept, to the nature and habits of the animals, and to the mode in which they were treated,* appears to the court to be a correct direction; and it seems difficult to ascertain by what other means the question should be determined, whether the evidence in the case was such as to warrant a conclusion that the deer were tamed and reclaimed. The court is, therefore, of opinion that the rule can not be supported on the ground of misdirection. It is not contended that there was no evidence fit to be submitted to the jury, and that, therefore, the plaintiff ought to have been nonsuited; but it is said that the weight of evidence was against the verdict. In considering whether the evidence warranted the verdict upon the issue, whether the deer were tamed or reclaimed, the observations made by Lord Chief Justice Willes in the case of *Davies* vs. *Powell*, are deserving of attention. The difference in regard to the mode and object of keeping deer in modern times from that which anciently prevailed, as pointed out by Lord Chief Justice Willes, can not be overlooked. It is truly stated that ornament and profit are the sole objects for which deer are now ordinarily kept, whether in ancient legal parks, or in modern inclosures so called; the instances being very rare in which deer in such places are kept and used for sport; indeed, their whole management differing very little, if at all, from that of sheep, or of any other animals kept for profit. And in this case, the evidence before adverted to was that the deer were regularly fed in the winter, and does with young were watched; the fawns taken as soon as dropped, and marked; selections from the herd made from time to time, fattened in places prepared for them, and afterwards sold or consumed, with no difference of circumstance than what attached, as before stated, to animals kept for profit and food. As to some being wild and some tame, as it is said, individual animals no doubt differed, as individuals in almost every race of animals are found, under any circumstances, to differ in the degree of tameness that belongs to them. Of deer kept in stalls, some would be found tame and gentle, and others quite irreclaimable, in the sense of temper and quietness. Upon a question whether deer are tamed and reclaimed, *each case must depend upon the particular facts of it;* and in this case the court think that the facts were such as were proper to be submitted to the jury; and, as it was a question of fact for the jury, the court can not perceive any sufficient grounds to warrant it in saying that the jury have come to a wrong conclusion upon the evidence, and do not feel authorized to disturb the verdict; and the rule for a new trial must, therefore, be discharged."

In *Blades* vs. *Higgs*, (*13 C. B. N. S., 844*), in Exchequer Chamber, on appeal, which was an action for the conversion of rabbits, with a count for assault, and which, strictly, only involved the question whether game found, killed, and taken by a trespasser upon the land of another became the property of the owner of the soil, *ratione soli*, or was the property of the trespasser, Baron Wilde, an English judge of high authority, Mellor, J., concurring, said: "It has been urged in this case that an animal *feræ naturæ* could not be the subject of individual property. But this is not so; for the common law affirmed a right of property in animals even though they were *feræ naturæ*, if they were restrained *either by habit* or inclosure within the lands of the owner. We have the authority of Lord Coke's reports for this right in respect of wild animals, such as hawks, deer, and game, if reclaimed, or swans or fish, if kept in a private moat or pond, or doves in a dove cote. But the right of property is not absolute; for, if such deer, game, etc., attain their wild condition again, the property in them is said to be lost. The principle of the common law seems, therefore, to be a very reasonable one, for in cases where either *their own induced habits* or the confinement imposed by man have brought about in the existence of wild animals the character of *fixed abode in a particular locality*, the law does not refuse to recognize in the owner of the land which sustained them a property coextensive with that state of things."

In *Amory* vs. *Flynn* (*10 Johns., New York, 102*), which was an action of trover for two geese of the wild kind, but which had become so tame as to eat out of the hand, the court said: "The geese ought to have been considered as reclaimed, so as to be the subject of property. Their identity was ascertained; they were tame and gentle, and had lost the power or disposition to fly away. They had been frightened and chased by the defendant's son, with the knowledge that they belonged to the plaintiff, and the case affords no color for the inference that the geese had retained their natural liberty as wild fowl, and that the property in them had ceased."

So in *Goff* vs. *Kilts* (*15 Wend., 550*), which was trespass for taking and destroying a swarm of bees, and the honey made by them, it appeared that the swarm left the plaintiff's hive, flew off, and went into a tree on the land of another. The plaintiff (according to the report of the case) kept the bees in sight, followed them, and marked the tree into which they entered. Two months afterwards the tree was cut down, the bees killed, and the honey found in the tree taken by the defendant and others. The plaintiff recovered judgment in the court of original jurisdiction. Upon writ of error the higher court, speaking by Mr. Justice Nelson, an eminent jurist who, at a subsequent date, became a justice of the Supreme Court of the United States, said: "Animals *feræ naturæ*, when reclaimed by the art and power of man, are the subject of a qualified property; if they return to their natural liberty and wildness, without the *animus revertendi*, it ceases. During the existence of the qualified property, it is under the protection of the law the same as any other property and every invasion of it is redressed in the same manner. Bees are *feræ naturæ*, but when hived and reclaimed a person may have a qualified property in them by the law of nature, as well as the civil law. Occupation—that is, hiving or inclosing them—gives property in them. They are now a common species of property and an article of trade, and the. wildness of their nature, by experience and practice, has become essentially subjected to the art and power of man. An unreclaimed swarm, like all other wild animals, belongs to the first occupant—in other words, to the person who first hives them; but if the swarm fly from the hive of another, his qualified property continues so long as he can keep them in sight, and possesses the power to pursue them. Under these circumstances, no one else is entitled to take them 2 *Black. Comm.*, 393; 2 *Kent's Comm.*, 391.) The question here is not between the owner of the soil upon which the tree stood that included the swarm, and the owner of the bees; as to him the owner of the bees would not be able to regain his property, or the fruits of it, without being guilty of trespass; but it by no means follows, from this predicament, that the right to the enjoyment of the property is lost; that the bees therefore become again *feræ naturæ* and belong to the first occupant. If a domestic or tame animal of one person should stray to the inclosure of another, the owner could not follow and retake it without being liable for a trespass. The absolute right of property, notwithstanding, would still continue in him. Of this there can be no doubt. So, in respect to the qualified property in the bees. If it continued in the owner after they hived themselves and abode in the hollow tree, as this qualified interest is under the same protection of the law as if absolute, the like remedy existed in the case of an invasion of it. It can not, I think, be doubted that if the property in the swarm continues while within sight of the owner—in other words, while he can distinguish and identify it in the air—that it equally belongs to him if it settles upon a branch or in the trunk of a tree, and remains there under his observation and charge. If a stranger has no right to take the swarm in the former case, and of which there seems no question, he ought not to be permitted to take it in the latter, when it is more confined and within the control of the occupant."

There is nothing to the contrary of this in *Gillett* vs. *Mason (7 Johns.*

16), cited by the learned counsel for Great Britain. In that case a mere finder of bees claimed, as against one interested in the soil, the right to take them, upon the ground alone that he had marked the tree in which the bees were found. But the court decided that he could not acquire ownership by merely marking the tree, observing that "the land was not his, nor was it in his possession."

In Smith's Treatise on Personal Property, a work recently published, the law is thus stated: "Another mode of obtaining title to personal property by original acquisition, through occupancy, is by reclaiming animals wild by nature, *feræ naturæ*. Wild animals belong to nobody in particular; yet they become the qualified property of any one who subjects them to his possession *or power*. The qualified property thus acquired continues in the captor while possession or control is maintained, or until the animal becomes so far domesticated that it will not voluntarily leave without the *animus revertendi*. When this point is reached, the *qualified* has ripened into *absolute* property, the nature of the animal being changed from *feræ naturæ* to *domitæ naturæ*, wild to tame. Until thus changed, and while in the possession or *power* of the captor, his qualified property will be fully under the cognizance and protection of law; but if the animal escape and regain its natural freedom, without the *animus revertendi*, the captor's title is wholly lost, and any other person may rightfully take the fugitive, thereby acquiring the same qualified property possessed by the first captor; and so on indefinitely." After observing that the speculations of writers who attempt to draw the dividing line between the two classes of animals, wild and tame, and referring to animals that are classed as wild, the author proceeds: "Belonging to the latter [wild] class, are, however, some of an exceptionally mild type that frequently become domesticated, and hence absolute property in their owners; among which are deer, horses, rabbits, doves, and others of like character. Honey bees are *feræ naturæ*; but, when reclaimed and hived, they become the subjects of qualified property. * * If bees when hived escape, or a swarm departs from the hive, the owner does not lose his property in them so long as he pursues and is able to identify them. While property in wild animals can be acquired only by occupancy, actual or constructive, an actual taking is not always necessary to create title; it is sufficient if the pursuer bring the animal *within his power or control*." *Sec. 37.*

From the principles thus announced by courts and jurists, this rule, at least, may be fairly deduced as resting in sound reason, in natural justice, and in a wise public policy: That although animals *feræ natura*, however valuable to the world, are not the subjects of property, while in their original condition of wildness, *beyond the control of man for any purpose whatever*, the law will yet recognize a right of property in them in favor of one who, by acting upon their natural instincts, and by care, watchfulness, self-denial, and industry, induces or causes them *to abide* for stated periods in each year, upon his premises, *so that he, and he only, is in a position to deal with the race as a whole, taking its increase regularly for commercial purposes without impairing the stock.* The authorities proceed upon these grounds: That "occupation," as it is called, is the foundation of property in animals *feræ naturæ;* that the right of property is not lost when the animals are away from their accustomed habitation provided for them upon the premises of the owner, as long as their absence is accompanied with the intention to return; and that such intention is deemed to exist while they have the habit of returning. Occupation is a fact to be determined with reference to the nature and habits of each particular race of animals. What is sufficient occupation in respect to some animals may be wholly inadequate to give a right of property in others. While each case must depend upon its own facts, there must be, in every case of animals *feræ naturæ*, in which a right of property is asserted, *such* an occupation as will enable the owner or controller of the premises to which they habitually resort to establish a husbandry in respect to them—an occupation which gives, at least, such certain, continuons control of them that their increase can be regularly taken for man's use without impairing the stock. Of course, without occupation, the *animus revertendi* will not alone, or in itself, avail to give a right of property in wild animals. But the *animus revertendi* will continue a right of property acquired effectively by occupation. The intention or habit of returning to the premises of the occupier must coexist, at all times, with the fact of occupation. If that intention or habit ceases, that is, if the animals permanently depart from the premises of the owner, the rights acquired by occupation are lost, and they will become the property of the first taker. It is this liability to change in ownership resulting from the loss of control by man, to which writers refer when they speak of qualified property in animals *feræ naturæ*, as distingnished from that full, complete, absolute property that may be lost only by the consent, express or implied, of the owner.

Let us see what are the analogies between the case of these fur seals and the case of certain animals, *feræ naturæ*, which, according to universal law, may become the subject of individual property. This mode of reasoning, although pronounced in argument to be unsafe and likely to mislead, has the sanction of experience. A very large proportion of the judicial decisions in both the United States and Great Britain rest upon the application that has been made in cases, new in their circumstances, of the principle of rules announced in prior cases. Parke, J. in *Mirehouse* vs. *Rennell*, 8 *Bingham*, p. 515, declared it to be of importance to keep this principle of decision steadily in view, not merely for the determination of the particular case, but for the interests of the law as a science. And Dr. Phillimore has well said that analogy has great influence on the decisions of international as well as of municipal tribunals. *1 Phillimore*, § 39. Another writer declares analogy to be the instrument of the progress and development of the law. *Bowyer's Readings, p. 88.* If the conditions, which courts and jurists have held to be sufficient to give a right of property in certain useful animals *feræ naturæ*, substantially exist in the cases of other wild animals, valuable to mankind, and in respect to which no ruling has been made, then the principle of the prior cases, so far as applicable, may well be recognized and enforced in subsequent cases.

In what way, according to the authorities, may property be acquired in a swarm of bees? All that need be done by man, as a condition of acquiring property in them, is to provide, on his premises, a place or hive where they may abide, to which they may come and go at will, and at which a proper proportion of their honey can be obtained from time to time. While in some countries bees are fed, as a general rule they gather, here and there, without man's aid, all that is necessary to nourish them. The owner never puts his hand upon the swarm, or upon individual bees, though he might shut them up, from time to time, in their hive. It has never occurred to any writer or court to consider whether ownership of the swarm depended upon the ability of the owner to identify, and prove ownership of, each individual bee. The question of property does not arise as to individual bees, but only in respect to the swarm. All that the owner need do is to provide a place for the swarm, abstain from taking all the honey made by the bees, but leaving enough to sustain them until the next year, and protect them against disturbance while in the hive. That being done, as long as they occupy that hive for their abiding place, when not moving through the air, and as long as they are in the habit of returning to it, or can be pursued and identified when absent from their hive, the law gives to the owner of the premises a right of property in the swarm. Possession, in fact, of the swarm, or of the individual bees, is not otherwise necessary. Possession, in law, exists, if the swarm regularly abides in the hive so that the product can be regularly obtained for man's use. And when the swarm flies abroad the right of property is not lost as long as it can be pursued and identified, and does not establish another habitation. And this right attaches not only to the swarm that has continuously occupied the hive provided for it, but to new swarms which go out from overpopulated hives in search of another home. The latter, equally with the original swarm, remain the property of the owner of the hive, wherever they may go, as long as they can be identified and until all hope of their being recovered is abandoned.

In the case of wild pigeons, what must man do that he may acquire property in them? Nothing more than to provide a place or box in which they can take shelter, and where they can breed and rear their young in safety. There is no possession in the owner other than that coming from his occupancy of the land, and from his ownership and control of the place provided for the use of the flock. There is no handling (as there could not be) of individual pigeons constituting the flock. But the owner holds such relations to the flock that he can regularly take its increase without diminishing the stock, so long as they continue to frequent the place provided for them. While the capacity to do that exists, the original "occupation," the foundation of the right of property, remains in full force.

In the case of deer, naturally wild, all that is essential to the acquisition of property in them by man is that he provide or keep a place for them, to which, by reason of his care, industry, and forbearance they habitually resort, and where they remain with such regularity under his general supervision, control, and protection that he can, without impairing the stock, reap the benefit of the increase. In the cases cited from the English courts, it does not appear that the deer were taken into actual custody. Their owner simply built a fence around a forest of vast extent, in which the deer roamed at will. Their owner could not lay his hands upon the deer at pleasure. They could be actually taken only as other deer of the forest were taken, by shooting, or with dogs. The owners simply protected them and made a husbandry of them.

Similar observations may be made in respect to geese and swans. If by care and industry a place is provided for them, where they can abide in safety for the purposes of breeding, to which they habitually come, and where they are protected from disturbance, so that their increase may be regularly taken for man's use, all is done that is required to give property in them. While these conditions exist, the right of property remains.

The instinct of a wild animal to resort, for the first time, to a particular place is not, in the case of bees, pigeons, deer, wild geese, or swans, the creation of man. But, in a substantial sense, their subsequent return to *and remaining* at that place from time to time, so that a husbandry can be established with respect to them, is due to the self denial, care and industry of the person who provides for them a place which he maintains and protects for their use. They do not, under the circumstances stated, become tame, within the literal meaning of that word, and so as to lose all their original wildness of nature; but, in the eye of the law, they are so far reclaimed from their natural condition of wildness that they do not always fly from the presence of man, or escape from his dominion and control, but, as the result of his art and industry, remain so far in his power, that their product can be utilized with the same regularity, and almost as readily, as the product of domestic animals may be utilized.

It has been said that the coming of these fur seals to the Pribilof Islands, from year to year, for the purposes already indicated, is not to be attributed to anything that the United States, as the owner of the islands, has done, or has refrained from doing. Is this true? Premising that it is not the number of things done, which determines the value of what is done, let me ask, whether the United States has done all that is necessary in order to utilize this race, without destroying it, or imperiling its existence. Would the seals continue to come to Pribilof Islands, from year to year, if, by the direction or with the assent of the United States, they were met, as they might be, at the shore of the islands, and driven back into the water? Would they remain on the islands during the breeding season except for the care taken, under regulations prescribed by the United States, to induce them to do so, and except for the protection afforded them, while on the islands, against the pursuit of seal hunters having in view immediate profit for themselves rather than the preservation of these animals for the benefit of mankind? These questions must receive an answer in the negative. In view of the habits of the seals, and of the absolute necessity of their being upon land, for several months in each year, for purposes, at least, of breeding and of rearing their young, it cannot be doubted that the very existence of the race depends upon their being cared for and protected at the place to which they habitually resort, and to which, when going back into the sea, they will certainly return the succeeding spring and summer. It will not do to say that these animals, if not allowed to occupy the Pribilof Islands, would seek some other breeding grounds; for, if any change of location should ever take place, the same questions would arise between the owner of the new breeding grounds and pelagic sealers that are presented in this case. But the possibility that these seals, if driven to that course, might seek a new location, can not be made the basis of action by this Tribunal or affect the principles involved in the question submitted for determination; for, we know that these seals, with abundant opportunities to select other breeding grounds, have, for more than a century past, occupied Pribilof Islands as their land home. And there is no reason to believe that they will go elsewhere, as long as the United States keeps those islands exclusively as their breeding grounds, and takes care that they are not disturbed by merciless pelagic sealers who kill without regard to sex, and slaughter mother seals about to deliver their young without the slightest concern on that account. The presumption is conclusive that there are no coasts, near or on the migration-route of these animals, which present the same climatic and other conditions as are found by them at Pribilof Islands.

In respect to the fur seals frequenting the Pribilof Islands, what did Russia do, and what has the United States, succeeding to its rights, done, in order to bring them within the rules of property applicable to animals *feræ naturæ* which may be the basis of a permanent husbandry? Neither hive, box, park, nor other enclosure, has been provided for them, as in the case of bees, pigeons, and deer, respectively, because such a provision is forbidden by the nature and habits of the animals, and would be absolutely useless for any practical purpose. But an abiding place for all the purposes for which they must, of necessity, come to and remain upon land, has been provided for them. Upon the discovery by Russia of the Pribilof Islands it was ascertained that this race made it their land home. Russia desired this condition of things to continue in order that these animals might be

11492——11

utilized for public and commercial purposes, and to that end regulations were established restricting the number to be taken annually for such purposes. That system has been perpetuated and improved by the United States, with the result that the return of these seals to the Pribilof Islands, from year to year, in the same months, and their remaining upon the islands for stated periods, and so that a due proportion of males may be taken without at all disturbing the herd in its entirety, is absolutely assured, provided only the extermination of the race by pelagic sealing is prevented.

But this is not all. We have seen that by an act of Congress, passed soon after the United States acquired Pribilof Islands, the islands of St. Paul and St. George were set apart as the land home of these animals. A place was thus provided for them where they could abide while breeding, and rearing their young, and while their coats of fur were undergoing a change. Only a limited number of persons are allowed to go to or remain on the islands. Regulations have been established preventing the herd from being unduly disturbed while there. Enormous expense has been incurred in providing vessels to guard the breeding grounds against marauding parties engaged in seal hunting; and the Government of the United States protects the race against indiscriminate slaughter while on land. The precautions thus taken for the preservation of the herd may sometimes have been evaded, but it is not to be doubted that if raiders were permitted, without restriction, to capture and kill these seals while on the islands, the race would be speedily exterminated as other animals of like kind have been destroyed in the waters of the Southern Ocean. Further, the United States, recognizing the value of this race of animals to itself and to commerce, forbears to impair the stock through indiscriminate killing, and not only forbids, under severe penalties, the killing of female seals, but limits the taking on the islands each year to such a proportion of males as can safely be taken, for commercial purposes, without destroying the race.

If these animals, from their nature and habits, needed an actual shelter over their heads while at the breeding grounds, and such a shelter was, in fact, provided for them by the United States, could human ingenuity distinguish the case, in principle, from that of other valuable animals *feræ naturæ*, in which, by the law everywhere, property may be acquired by the care and industry of man? Instead of such shelter for their protection during storm and rain the United

States provides them with what their natures and necessities require, namely, a land home where, without disturbance, they breed and rear their young, and where the safety of the race from pursuit and destruction, while at that home, is assured. All this has been done at great expense, and by the exercise of care and supervision. To say that the United States, by providing upon its land a hive for a swarm of bees, or a box for a flock of pigeons, or a place for a lot of deer, in which those animals respectively may abide while breeding and rearing their young, or for other purposes required by their nature, will become the owner of such animals as long as they have the habit of returning to the places so provided for them, whereby their product may be regularly taken for man's use, and yet that it cannot become the owner of a herd or family of fur seals born and reared upon its islands, and for which it provides a land home where they breed and rear their young, where they abide in safety, during stated periods, and to which they regularly return, so that the increase may be taken for commercial purposes without impairing the stock, is, I submit, repugnant to sound reason and inconsistent with recognized principles in the law of property.

It is said that these islands, before their discovery by Russian navigators, were the land home of these animals, and, consequently, that the seals were not provided with that home by Russia or by the United States, which succeeded to Russia's rights. The answer is, that after such discovery the islands of St. Paul and St. George have continued, for more than a century, to be the land home of these animals only because Russia, and subsequently the United States, so ordered. If the United States desired to establish a naval post on Pribilof Islands, or to use those islands for any other public purpose different from those for which they have been used since 1867, it could easily drive the seals back into the sea when they attempted to "haul up" on the islands during the breeding season. Such treatment might result in the destruction of the race, as we cannot be sure from any evidence before us that any other islands would be suitable for their purposes. But no such treatment is, in fact, accorded to them. On the contrary, the islands are preserved for their use as a land home. It is as if the United States had said, upon the acquisition of the islands of St. Paul and St. George: "These valuable animals have their breeding grounds here; other animals of like kind have been exterminated by indiscriminate slaughter, or for the want of governmental protection; this race

shall be preserved from destruction so that mankind can get the benefit of them for food and for raiment; to that end these islands shall not,
as is the case in respect to other parts of the public domain, be subject
to settlement, but shall be set apart as the habitation of these animals
exclusively, where they may breed and rear their young; and they shall
be protected from molestation by seal-hunters while on the islands,
and only such portion of males allowed to be taken, annually, as will
not endanger the integrity of the herd as a whole." All this, it is
argued by counsel for the British Government, is not equivalent to
"occupation," as that word is understood in the law regulating the
acquisition of property in animals *feræ naturæ*, and is of less consequence, as a means of acquiring property in these seals, than that
which is done when a hive is provided for bees, or boxes for pigeons,
or a place for deer. The fact is, the case of these seals is made stronger
in consequence of their peculiar nature and habits of life; their home
on American soil is a permanent home, necessary to their existence,
and in respect to which they never lose the *animus revertendi*.

Again, it has been suggested that these animals pass much of their
time in the high seas, which are free to all, for purposes of food. But
that is quite as immaterial as to say, in the case of bees and pigeons,
that they pass the most, or much, of their time in the open air, which is
free to all. The circumstance that these fur seals go great distances
from the Pribilof Islands in search of food can not affect the principle
involved. Suppose they passed each day in the sea, just beyond the
outer line of territorial waters, but returned each night to the islands;
the question of ownership would be precisely the same, in respect to
the principles governing it, as is now presented, because we know that
while these seals go regularly, at stated periods, each year, over the
same route, into the North Pacific Ocean, they return by the same route
substantially, at the same time in each year, to their breeding grounds on
the islands of St. Paul and St. George. The length of time which they
pass in the high seas, in search of food, is wholly immaterial, in view
of the fact that they will return at a particular time to their land home.
They are unlike in their habits any other known animal that passes its
time partly on land and partly in the high seas. They are not products
of the sea. They can not breathe under the water. They are, in every
substantial sense, as much appurtenant to the islands on which they
are born, and where they breed and rear their young, as if they never

passed beyond territorial waters. Notwithstanding they frequent the sea for purposes of food, they are strictly land, rather than marine, animals, because they are conceived and are born and reared on land, could not be conceived nor come into existence in the waters of the ocean, and must, from the necessities of their nature, abide upon land at stated periods.

Next, it is said that some of the seals which have been on the islands of St. Paul are known to have gone the succeeding year to the island of St. George. The proof on that point is too slight and unsatisfactory to be regarded. But if the fact be as suggested, it would be wholly immaterial in the present inquiry; for both islands, taken together, are the property of one nation, and that nation only is in a position to deal with the race as a whole and save it from extermination.

I have not understood learned counsel to dispute the proposition that, according to the jurisprudence of all civilized nations, some animals *feræ naturæ* are susceptible of ownership. Nor do they insist that the principles recognized in the Roman law, and equally in England and the United States, in respect to the acquisition of property in bees, pigeons, deer, etc., do not obtain in all civilized countries. We have not been referred to any instance in which it has been otherwise declared. But it is earnestly contended that the differences between fur seals on one side and bees, pigeons, deer, and the like, on the other side, are such as to preclude the application to the former of the rules determining the acquisition of property in the latter class of animals. That all these animals are unlike in many respects no one will dispute. But this circumstance is not of legal consequence, unless the differences are such as to prevent the application of the general rule prescribing the conditions on which property may be acquired in wild animals. There are no two classes of domestic animals exactly alike in their nature and habits, but there are qualities *common* to all such animals which justify the law not only in declaring them to be the subject of ownership by man, but in declaring that the right of property in them is not lost while they are absent from the owner, even without the intention of returning to his posesssion. Now, upon what ground rests the general rule that animals *feræ naturæ* may not become the subject of property? And why does the law recognize exceptions to that rule in the case of some animals which admittedly belong, in their original condition, to that class?

The general rule that wild animals become the property of the first taker proceeds upon the ground, stated in the Institutes of Justinian, that "natural reason gives to the first occupant that which had no previous owner." But there are exceptions to the general rule that arise from the necessary wants of society. To the end that it may not lose the benefit of valuable animals, exhaustible in quantity, society, in other words, the law speaking for organized society, stimulates the exercise of care, industry, and self-denial, by permitting ownership in such wild animals as can be induced to come and *remain* so far under human control and supervision that their product can be regularly utilized for the use of mankind without injury to the stock. And *this* right of property is under the protection of the law. If the law did not so declare the inevitable result would be the extermination, by waste or consumption, of many animals that the world needs and with which it would not willingly part.

With respect to wild animals which by universal assent come within the exception to the general rule, the law, I repeat, has prescribed certain conditions as essential to the acquisition of property in them. These conditions all point to *such* occupation or control of the animals by man—the result of his care, industry, and self-denial—as indicates his capacity to reap, regularly, their product without materially diminishing the race itself. And as such conditions may all be performed in the case of bees, pigeons, deer, and the like, the law, in the interest of society, that its wants may be supplied, recognizes a right of property in such animals in every case where the conditions have, in fact, been performed and can be maintained. The only quality common to all of these animals is that man by art and industry may acquire *such* possession and control as will enable him to render to society the useful service, necessary to human life, of reaping from them their regular increase without destroying the stock. This benefit society cannot have, unless it rewards the industry and self-denial so practiced with the right of property; and, therefore, it does so reward those qualities. No man would cultivate bees and furnish the market with honey unless he was promised property in both the original and new swarms. No man would furnish a place for and "cultivate" wild geese, swans, and pigeons, unless they were protected as property, while they are temporarily out of his possession. No man would care for wild deer by enclosing the forest, watching the does when they dropped their fawns, making selections for slaughter, unless he was awarded the right of property in respect to such deer. Out of this condition of things arises the rule, to which I have adverted, that whenever, by the art and industry of man, useful wild animals come so far under control that they can be and are so dealt with by him, that he may carry on this species of husbandry with them, take their whole annual product for human consumption and yet preserve the stock, he has, by universal jurisprudence, a property in them, and when he can not, or does not do this, he has no right of property. This is the true teaching of the cases and authorities to which reference has been made. The property which they recognize is that most appropriately described by Blackstone as property *per industriam*. Expressed in its simplest and most general form, the truth, which the authorities cited enforce, is that whenever any useful thing, not already appropriated, is dependent for its existence on the art and industry of man—whenever man can truly say of a particular useful thing that it is the product of his care and labor, or would not exist without his care and labor—then he may claim that thing as his property.

Do not all these conditions exist in the case of the fur-seals frequenting the Pribilof Islands? Are they not met more certainly in respect to these animals than in the case of those wild animals which the authorities uniformly declare may be appropriated by and become the property of man? Are not these fur seals, when on the Pribilof Islands, so completely in the power of the United States that the entire herd could be taken in any one breeding season? Is it not due to the care, self-denial and supervision of the United States that these animals regularly return, at stated times, to those islands, *and remain* there, for such long periods, and under such circumstances, that a proper proportion of their increase can be readily taken for purposes of revenue and commerce without at all endangering the race? Must not the race perish—would it not long since have perished from the earth—except for the care and self-denial practised towards it by the United States? Is it not beyond dispute that pelagic sealing is certainly and rapidly destructive of this race? Can this race be preserved for the world unless it is recognized as the property of that nation which, alone of all the nations, can protect it from extermination? The care and labor which the United States exerts in respect to these animals is to withdraw the Pribilof Islands from all other possible uses and devote them to these seals; to guard them, at enormous expense, from outside depredation; and to refrain from taking any females, and only a due proportion of males, thereby leaving the stock unimpaired. If either one of these forms of care be withdrawn the race would be swept away with a rapidity only commensurate with the neglect. Human society can have no other interest in useful animals, bestowed for the comfort and sustenance of man, except to preserve the race so that its product may be perpetually enjoyed. If it can obtain this service from one nation only it must of necessity employ that nation and decree to it the appropriate reward. The United States is in a position to render that service. Other nations and their subjects can touch these animals on the sea alone; but they can touch them only to destroy, because the animals cannot possibly be taken on the sea, to any material extent, without speedily exterminating the race. The divine law, reason, justice, and the municipal jurisprudence of all civilized nations, and therefore, as I submit, international law, all concur in declaring that the right thus to destroy that which all mankind is interested in preserving does not exist.

The suggestion has been earnestly pressed that there can be no such appropriation or occupation of these animals, as is requisite to give property, except in respect to such of them as are captured and taken into actual, physical possession. The idea underlying this suggestion is, that there cannot be any legal possession of these fur-seals until they are confined or shut up in an inclosure of some kind. But this view entirely ignores all consideration of what, in view of the nature and habits of the particular animals, is essential to be done in order that they may come under such control that their increase may be regularly taken for use, leaving the stock unimpaired. As to some animals *feræ naturæ*, no such result can possibly be attained unless they are effectively restrained in their liberty by actual confinement. In cases of that kind the right of property is of course lost when manual custody ceases, for the obvious reason that the increase of such animals can never be obtained for the use of man in the absence of their actual continuous confinement. When, therefore, the right of property rests, as in the case of some animals it unquestionably does, alone on actual physical custody, such right is lost when the custody ceases. But, when continuous confinement or custody is not essential in order that the product may be regularly and certainly obtained, then such control as is consistent with the nature of the animals and as will suffice to enable man to establish a husbandry in respect to them, whereby the product may be regularly secured, is all that the law requires in order to give property. Hence, in the cases of bees, pigeons, and deer, actual manual custody is not vital, but ownership and legal possession coexist when there is such control that the annual increase, by means of the owner's care and industry, can be readily taken. Whether boxing up, or fencing, or actual confinement in some mode, of animals *feræ naturæ*, is essential, as a foundation of the right of property, must always depend upon the nature of the particular animal. Actual, continuous possession of the entire race is never necessary to accomplish the ends for which society instituted property. The fundamental inquiry, in every case, I repeat, is whether the person claiming a right of property in particular valuable animals *feræ naturæ* has such general custody or control of the race, *such capacity to deal with it as a whole*, that he is capable of regularly taking their increase at the place to which they habitually, regularly resort, and which his care and industry has provided as their habitation. This inquiry is the only one at all consistent with, or that will certainly secure, those beneficial ends for the accomplishment of which the law wisely enables man to acquire, under given conditions, a property in such animals, and protects his rights in that regard, as long as he is capable of utilizing their increase for commercial purposes. Such right of property is qualified only in the sense that it may be lost by the act of the animal in leaving the premises of the owner and never returning.

As illustrating their view of the question of possession, the learned counsel for Great Britain quote this passage from the treatise of Pollock and Wright on Possession in the Common Law: "On the same ground trespass or theft can not at common law be committed of living animals *feræ naturæ* unless they are tamed or confined. They may be in the park or pond of a person who has the exclusive right to take them, but they are not in his possession unless they are so confined or so powerless by reason of immaturity that they can be taken at pleasure with certainty." *p. 231*. But the authors add, in the next succeeding paragraphs, these significant words: "An animal once tamed or reclaimed may continue in a man's possession although it fly or run abroad at will, if it is *in the habit of returning regularly to a place where it is under his comple control*. Such habit is commonly called *animus revertendi*." The same authors say: "To determine what acts will be sufficient in a particular case we must attend to the circumstances, and especially *to the nature of the thing dealt with, and the manner in which things of the same kind are habitually used and enjoyed.* * * * Again, there is another and quite different way in which possession in law may be independent of *de facto* possession. We may find it convenient that a possessor shall not lose his rights merely by losing physical control, and we may so mould the legal incidents of possession once acquired that possession in law shall continue though there be but a shadow of real or apparent physical power, or no such power at all. This the Common Law has boldly and fully done. * * * Legal possession, in our law, may continue even though the object be to common apprehension really lost or abandoned." P. 13, 18.

The whole subject of possession, as distinguished from ownership, is fully examined in Hunter's Roman Law. "Possession," that author says, "is the occupation of anything with the intention of holding it as owner," and "a thing is said to be occupied or held when the occupier is in a position *to deal with it.*" Again, "In acquiring possession of objects not before owned or possessed by others, the question is whether the intending possessor has so far overcome the physical difficulties *as to be able freely to deal with the subject.*" In reference to possession of things not before owned (*res nullius*) or possessed, the author says that "in such cases to acquire possession is, at the same time, to acquire ownership." Among the examples given by him are those given in the institutes of Justinian and in the Commentaries of Gaius, to which reference has already been made, namely, animals *feræ naturæ* which habitually go away and return to the place provided for them. If while they are absent the occupier has not abandoned the intention of dealing with them to the exclusion of all other persons, so as to take their increase regularly at the places provided for them, his possession remains while they have the habit of returning. Under such circumstances, and although the animal is for a time out of the view of the occupier, the law holds that neither "occupation" nor the intention to exclude others —both of which are necessary to constitute possession—have ceased to exist. *Hunter's Roman Law, 2d ed., pp. 311, 311, 315, Title Possession.*

Of course it is not to be disputed in this case that the United States, by what it has done and can do on the islands of St. Paul and St. George, is in a position where it can deal with this entire race of animals so as regularly to take their increase without materially affecting its existence or integrity, nor that it has intended to appropriate or "occupy" this herd to the exclusion of all other nations or peoples.

Speculate as we may about some aspects of this case, or differ as we may about the weight of evidence upon some points, this is absolutely certain: If the United States had actual manual custody of each of these animals, at all times in the year, it could not *properly* deal with them in any other mode than that pursued by it, namely, to take *only such part of the males each year as will leave the race or herd unimpaired in its entirety for the use of man.* And they can not possibly be dealt with *in that manner, and with such results, except by the United States or its licensees, or at any other place than at the breeding grounds on its islands.* All this is so clearly established that no one, having the slightest regard for the evidence, will assert the contrary.

I have referred to the self-denial practiced by the United States in restricting the taking of seals at the Pribilof Islands to males of proper age and in such limited numbers as will not cause a substantial impairment of the stock. The Government of that country, let me repeat, has the power, if it chooses to exercise it, of taking in any one year such an undue proportion of the seals, male and female, which frequent its islands as would give the United States an immediate profit of large amount. Its power over the seals while on the islands is so absolute that, as counsel suggest, it could practically exterminate the race almost at one stroke. But it recognizes a moral obligation resting upon it to preserve, not to destroy, a race of animals useful to the world. In order that the species may be preserved for itself and for mankind it abstains from sacrificing the race for the sake of temporary or present profit. This abstinence is industry under another name. And this principle of abstinence, or saving, is recognized by all writers upon economic questions as a potent agency in the creation of wealth and in the progress of the world.

John Stuart Mill, in his Principles of Economy, has said that "as the wages of the laborer is the remuneration of labor, so the profits of the capitalists are properly the remuneration of abstinence." *Vol. 2, p. 481.*

A recent writer upon the ethics of usury and interest has said: "On the hypothesis that all have equal opportunities of social progress, the social destroyers of its wealth deserve condemnation, while those who have served the cause of progress by saving from personal consumption a part of the earth's produce and devoting it to the improvement of national mechanism have a claim to an award proportioned to their service and to the efforts which they have made in rendering it. These are the conditions of advance in civilization in the arts and sciences, in literature, and religion. For command over nature differentiates the civilized man from the savage. * * * It appears, hence, how accurate is the common phrase which calls thrift 'saving.' Economists favor such other words as 'abstinence,' deferred 'enjoyment,' and the like; but to 'save' expresses the primary idea that something has been saved from the destruction to which mere animal instinct would devote it. In such salvage lies the progress of the human species from savagery to godhead. By how much has been thus saved has the salvation, material, mental, and moral, of the race been achieved." *Bliss-ard's Ethics and Usury, 1892, p. 26 et seq.* "The origin of all capital," says another writer, "is abstinence, and the reward of this abstinence is profit." *Perry's Introduction to Political Economy, p. 115.*

If it be said that a difficulty in the way of awarding to the United States a right of property in these seals is the impossibility of identifying any particular body of seals as frequenting or habitually resorting to the Pribilof Islands, the answer is that no such description of the situation is justified by the evidence before us. It may be that here and there, in the great ocean separating the American and Asiatic coasts may be found stray, scattered fur seals, of which it might be difficult to say, while they are in the water, and not immediately under the eye, that they belong to a particular herd of northern fur seals, just as it would be difficult to identify a wild pigeon as belonging to a particular flock, or individual bees as belonging to a particular swarm hived at a named place. But such facts can not affect the principle involved in such cases. The evidence is overwhelming that the migratory routes of the northern fur seals frequenting the islands on the Asiatic and Japan coasts are separated by more than 800 miles from the migration routes of the fur seals habitually resorting to Bering Sea and frequenting the Pribilof Islands. There is no appreciable intermingling of the Pribilof seals with other fur seals of the same general species. If there are any exceptions to this rule they are so rare and relate to so few seals as to be of no consequence in the inquiry whether the fur seals frequenting or habitually resorting to the Pribilof Islands do not constitute, substantially, a collective body or herd separate and distinct from every other herd of the same species. That they do constitute a separate and distinct herd is so clearly established that a statement to the contrary might well cause surprise to any one at all familiar with the evidence submitted to us, or who is able to consider it without regard to special

interests depending upon the action of this Tribunal. The treaty identi-
fies the herd to which regulations are to apply by the fact of their habitually resorting to the waters and islands of Bering Sea. If the award so
describes them there will be no uncertainty in the decree. National
legislatures and courts will find no difficulty in following the award,
either in making laws or in applying them to the proper seals.

The only possible objection that can be urged against the claim of
ownership of these fur seal animals by the United States is the general
rule that animals *feræ naturæ* are not subject to individual ownership. But we have seen that, according to settled principles of
law, an exception to this rule has been handed down to us, and is
everywhere recognized, which admits of individual ownership of
useful wild animals, the supply of which is limited, and which, by
reason of their nature and habits, and the control or power which
man may acquire over them, are susceptible of ownership, that is, are
capable of exclusive appropriation. All of these conditions are ful-
filled in the case of the Pribilof fur seals. It is not denied that they
are useful animals, or that the supply is limited. The experience of
the past proves that the race can be easily exterminated if man is
allowed to hunt and slaughter them wherever they may be found, on
the land or in the high seas. It is equally beyond dispute that they
may be exclusively appropriated, because they come, at stated periods,
to the islands of the United States, where they remain under such control that the increase can be obtained for the benefit of the world without any injurious diminution of the stock.

The reason why the doctrines to which I have adverted, have been
taught more directly and fully in municipal jurisprudence is that questions of property more frequently arise between individuals. Nations
do not often engage in judicial controversy with each other upon questions of this character. But there are some things which from their
situation are susceptible only of national ownership. These have been
considered by writers upon international law, and where the same
grounds and reasons exist for the recognition of property, as between
nations, that are found in the cases determined by concurring municipal law, they have conceded national ownership. Illustrations of this
rule are the cases of pearl and other oyster beds, coral reefs, etc., situated on the sea outside of territorial waters, in some instances thirty
or more miles. These gifts of nature are exhaustible, and would be
soon exhausted if treated as *res nullius*, and left open to the indiscrimi-

nate enjoyment of the people of all nations. They cannot well be
enjoyed unless they are under particular control, so that the product
may be taken at the right season and in limited amounts. In other
words, they require that sort of care, restraint, and self-denial which
is induced only by a recognition of property in those who bestow such
care, and practice such restraint and self-denial. I am relieved from
the necessity of showing that these things, even when beyond territorial
waters, may be appropriated as property by the nations in whose neighborhood they lie, and who choose to exercise the restraint and control
required for their preservation; for, the opinions of great writers upon
international law are explicit and concurring to that effect. And Great
Britian in its counter case and by its counsel in argument, distinctly
admit that they are the subject of property. Great Britian, in its Counter Case, referring to the legislation affecting the pearl fisheries of Cey- '
lon, says that "the claim of Ceylon is not to an exceptional extent of
water forming part of the high seas as incidental to the territorial
sovereignty of the island, but is a claim to the products of certain sub-
merged portions of the land, which have been treated from time immemorial by the successive rulers of the island as subjects of property and
jurisdiction." The counsel for the British Government, enforcing the
theory that international law recognizes the right of a state to acquire
the soil under the sea, and consequently the products attached to it,
and referring to the Ceylon and other fisheries, say that this claim "may
be legitimately made to oyster beds, pearl fisheries, and coral reefs."

But looking at the grounds upon which property in pearl and other
oyster beds, coral reefs, and the like, rest, it immediately appears that
those things are incapable of occupation or possession in the ordinary
sense of those words. That they are attached to the soil under the sea
is not, it seems to me, at all controlling in the inquiry as to property. No
such reason is assigned by the writers upon international law. What
they do say on the subject has reference to social utility and to the right
of the nation, near whose territory, these things are found, *to enjoy the
advantages of its peculiar relation to them.* Such things are exhaustible; there is not enough for all; if left open to indiscriminate and
unregulated attack they would be destroyed; whereby a particular
nation would be injured.

Puffendorf says: "As for fishing, though it hath much more abundant subject in the sea than in lakes or rivers, yet 'tis manifest that it
may in part be exhausted, and that if all nations should desire such
right and liberty near the coast of any particular country, that country

must be very much prejudiced in this respect; especially since 'tis very usual that some particular kind of fish, or perhaps some more precious commodity, as pearls, coral, amber, or the like, are to be found only in one part of the sea, and that of no considerable extent. In this case, there is no reason why the borderers should not rather challenge to themselves this happiness of a wealthy shore or sea than those who are sealed at a distance from it." *Law of Nature and Nations, Bk. 4, Chap. 5, Sec. 7.*

Vattel, upon the same general subject: "The various uses of the sea near the coasts render it very susceptible of property. It furnishes fish, shells, pearls, amber, etc. Now, in all these respects, its use is not inexhaustible; wherefore the nation to whom the coasts belong may appropriate to themselves, and convert to their own profit, an advantage which nature has so placed within their reach as to enable them conveniently to take possession of it in the same manner as they possessed themselves of the dominion of the land they inhabit. Who can doubt that the pearl fisheries of Bahren and Ceylon may lawfully become property? And, though, where the catching of fish is the only object, the fishery appears less liable to be exhausted; yet, if a nation have on their coast a particular fishery of a profitable nature, and of which they may become masters, shall they not be permitted to appropriate to themselves that bounteous gift of nature, as an appendage to the country they possess, and to reserve to themselves the great advantages which their commerce may thence derive in case there be a sufficient abundance of fish to furnish the neighboring nations?" Again: "A nation may appropriate to herself those things of which the free and common use would be prejudicial or dangerous to her. This is a second reason for which governments extend their dominion over the sea along their coast as far as they are able to protect their right." *Law of Nations, Bk. II, Chap. 23, Secs. 217, 288.* This passage from Vattel is quoted by Sir Travers Twiss, who says: "The *usus* of all parts of the open Sea in respect to navigation is common to all nations, but the *fructus* is distinguishable in law from the *usus*, and in respect of fish, or zoophites, or fossil substances, may belong in certain parts exclusively to an individual nation." *Ch. XI, Sec. 191.*

The essential grounds upon which the doctrine is placed in these extracts is precisely that upon which the similar decisions have been made in the instances from municipal law of bees, pigeons, and the like. It is that these properties would be destroyed and lost unless they were protected by that care, industry, and self-denial which can be called into activity only by the reasons which the institution of property offers. It is because the neighboring nations and none others can exercise these qualities and thus perform the service of preservation. It is because they fall under the general proposition that where any useful thing is dependent for its existence upon the care and self-denial of particular men, those men have a property in the thing.

That the United States, by its ownership of Pribilof Islands, is in a condition to reap the benefit of these animals, and preserve the race, and that no other nation, by any action it may alone take, can accomplish these beneficial results, and that the preservation of the race does not admit of their being taken at any other place than at their breeding grounds, are conclusive reasons why the law should recognize its claim of property.

Blackstone, observing that there are things in which a permanent property may subsist, but which would be found without a proprietor had not the wisdom of the law provided a remedy to obviate this inconvenience, says that "the legislature of England has universally promoted the grand ends of civil society, the peace and security of individuals, by steadily pursuing that wise and orderly maxim *of assigning to everything capable of ownership a legal and determinate owner."* *Chapter on Property.*

Sir Henry Maine, in his *Treatise on Ancient Law, ch. 8, p. 249,* thus states the principle: "It is only when the rights of property gained a sanction from long practical inviolability, and when the vast majority of objects of employment have been subjected to private ownership, that mere possession is allowed to invest the first possessor with dominion over commodities over which no prior proprietorship has been asserted. The sentiment in which this doctrine originated is absolutely irreconcilable with that infrequency and uncertainty of proprietary rights which distinguish the beginning of civilization. The true basis seems to be not a distinctive bias towards the institution of property, but a presumption, arising out of the long continuance of that institution, that *everything ought to have an owner.* When possession is taken of a 'res nullius,' that is, of an object, which is not, or has never been, reduced to dominion, the possessor is permitted to become proprietor from a feeling that all valuable things are naturally subjects of an exclusive enjoyment, and that in the given case there is no one to invest with the rights of property, except the occupant. The occupant, in short, becomes the owner because all things are presumed to be somebody's property, and because no one can be pointed out as having better right than he to the proprietorship of this particular thing." Of course, as we have seen from the authorities cited, the possession of which the learned writer speaks, is not necessarily actual manual possession, continuously held, which in many cases is impracticable, but that possession in law, that general control, which may exist, although the thing possessed is temporarily absent from its owner with the *animus revertendi*.

So, Mr. Bowyer, in his *Commentaries on the Constitutional Law of England, 2d Ed., London, 1846, p. 427:* "III. The third primary right of the citizen is that of property, which consists in the free use, enjoyment, and disposal of all that is his, without any control or diminution, save by the law of the land. The institution of property—that is to say, the appropriation to particular persons and uses of things which were given by God to all mankind—is of *natural law.* The reason of this is not difficult to discover, for the increase of mankind must soon have rendered community of goods exceedingly inconvenient or impossible consistently with the peace of society; and, indeed, by far the greater number of things cannot be made fully subservient to the use of mankind in the most beneficial manner *unless they be governed by the laws of exclusive appropriation.*"

The suggestion has been much pressed that the authorities cited in support of the claims of property by the United States refer to animals *feræ naturæ* that have been either tamed or reclaimed by the art or industry of man. And it was said that these fur seals are neither tamed nor reclaimed. But upon careful attention to the reasons assigned by courts and writers for the recognition of property, under given circumstances, in bees, pigeons, deer, wild geese, and swans, it will become manifest that there was no purpose to declare in respect to any of these animals that they had lost *all* of their original wildness. Some wild animals may be so tamed, or become so subdued by the treatment accorded to them or by the circumstances attending their situation, as to exhibit very little timidity or shyness in the presence of man. Other animals, usually called wild, but not gentle in their nature, are more difficult to approach. Still others retain, under all circumstances, so much of their original wildness, and so much of their innate fear of man, that it is impossible to handle them as can often be done in the case of some strictly domestic animals. When,

11492——12

therefore, the authorities speak of bees, pigeons, deer, wild geese, and swans, as tamed or reclaimed, they mean, and could mean only, that their original wildness had, by the art and power of man become so far diminished, modified, or controlled, that man is able to establish a husbandry in respect to them, and obtain the benefit of their increase without impairing the race. If animals, originally wild, come under the power and control of man to such an extent that they can be thus "cultivated" and utilized; if such power can be acquired over them that man is able, to use the words of Bacon, to apply them " to the sustentation of his being," then they are "reclaimed" within the meaning of the authorities that recognize a right of property, under named conditions, in animals *feræ naturæ*. Are not these fur seals in every substantial sense, so far "reclaimed" from their original wildness that they can be utilized by man, with quite as much ease as if they were strictly domestic animals? They are peculiarly gentle and docile, and easily approached, although they can be so alarmed as to fear the approach of man. While on their breeding grounds, protected against indiscriminate slaughter at the hands of seal hunters, they are as completely within the control and power of the United States as if they were so many horses, cows, or sheep. And they remain there, for several months in every year, under the power and control of man, without any disposition, under ordinary circumstances, to flee from, or even to become disturbed by his presence. There is, consequently, every reason why in the interests of society, that its increasing wants may be supplied, they should be regarded, for all purposes of property, as reclaimed animals.

In the course of the argument the question was often propounded whether a recognition of the claim of the United States to own this herd of seals would not seriously impair the right which, by universal consent, belongs equally to all, to take and appropriate to their own use such wild animals as have not been previously appropriated by actual confinement, or by some other mode that deprives them of their natural liberty. To this it may be answered, that the principle which I have maintained has no application to those useful animals in respect to which the care, industry, and labor of man is ineffectual or unnecessary to utilize their increase, while preserving the stock. Some of them cannot be brought within the reach or efforts of man; some have not the sure instinct of returning to the same place so that they can be identified; and in respect to others, nature has made such liberal provision for the needs of mankind, and for such an enormous increase in the number of the animals, that there is no occasion for a recognition of property, either as a reward of man's industry or for the preservation of the race. A recognition in favor of the United States of property in the Pribilof herd of seals does not by any means place *all* wild animals in the same category. The conditions which exist in the case of those wild animals which are admittedly subjects of appropriation as property do not exist in the case of all animals *feræ naturæ*. And we need only inquire whether those conditions exist in the case of these fur-seals. If they do, our duty is to apply the principle which those conditions suggest, whatever may be the difficulty of applying it in the case of some wild animals to which counsel have referred in argument.

It is scarcely necessary to say that these principles, in the judgment of some courts, have no application to noxious animals, that can subserve no useful purpose and may be dangerous to the community, except, perhaps, when they are actually confined and are kept for amusement or for scientific purposes. An illustration of this distinction is found in *Hannan* vs. *Mockett* decided by the court of King's Bench, and reported in *2 Barn. & Cress., pp.* 934, 937-8, 943-4, 38, 43, 44. The declaration in that case stated that the plaintiff was possessed of a close of land with trees growing thereon, to which rooks had been used to resort and build their nests and rear their young by reason whereof he had been used to kill and take the rooks and the young thereof, from which great profit and advantage had accrued to him; yet the defendant, wrongfully and maliciously, intending to injure the plaintiff and alarm and drive away the rooks, and to cause them to forsake the trees of the plaintiff, wrongfully and injuriously caused guns loaded with gunpowder to be discharged near the plaintiff's close and thereby disturbed and drove away the rooks, in consequence of which the plaintiff was prevented from killing the rooks and taking the young thereof. The plea was not guilty. Bayley, J., said: "The plaintiff does not state any special right in him to have the rooks resort to his trees; he relies upon that general right which all the King's subjects have, and he describes the profit to arise to him, not from the eggs, but from killing the birds and their young. To maintain an action the plaintiff must have had a right, and the defendant must have done a wrong. A man's rights are the rights of personal liberty, personal security, and private property. Private property is either property in possession, property in action, or property that an individual has a special right to acquire. The injury in this case does not affect any right of personal security or personal liberty, nor any property in possession or in action; and the question then is, whether there is any injury to any property the plaintiff had a special right to acquire. A man in trade has a right in his fair chances of profit, and he gives up time and capital to obtain it. It is for the good of the public that he should. But has it ever been held that a man has a right in the chance of obtaining animals *feræ naturæ*, where he is at no expense in enticing them to his premises, and where it may be at least questionable whether they will be of any service to him, and whether, indeed, they will not be a nuisance to the neighborhood? This is not a claim *propter impotentiam*, because they are young, *propter solum*, because they are on the plaintiff's land, or *propter industriam*, because the plaintiff has brought them to the place or reclaimed them, but *propter usum et consuetudinem* of the birds. They, of their own choice, and without any expenditure or trouble on his part, have a predilection for his trees and are disposed to resort to them. But has he a legal right to insist that they shall be permitted to do so? Allow the right as to these birds and how can it be denied as to all others? In considering a claim of this kind the nature and properties of the birds are not immaterial. The law makes a distinction between animals fitted for food and those which are not; between those which are destructive to private property and those which are not; between those which have received protection by common law or by statute and those which have not. It is not alleged in this declaration that these rooks were fit for food; and we know in fact that they are not generally so used. So far from being protected by law they have been looked upon by the legislature as destructive in their nature, and as nuisances to the neighborhood where they are. That being so, surely a party can have no right to have them resort to his lands, to the injury of his neighbors; and, consequently, no action can be maintainable against a person who prevents their so doing. * * * They certainly answer the description of animals *feræ naturæ*. They are not protected by any statute, but on the contrary have been declared by the legislature to be a nuisance to the neighborhood where they are. That being so, it is quite clear no person can claim a right to have them resort to his lands, nor can any person become a wrongdoer by preventing their so doing. *Keeble* v. *Hickeringill* bears a stronger resemblance to the present than any other case, but it is distinguishable. There it was decided that an action on the case lies for discharging guns near the decoy pond of another, with design to damnify the owner by frightening away the wild fowl resorting thereto, by which the wild fowl are frightened away and the owner damnified. But in the first place it is observable that wild fowl are protected by the statute (25 H. 8. cii.); that they constitute a known article of food, and that a person keeping up a decoy expends money and employs skill in taking that which is of use to the public. It is a profitable mode of employing his land, and was considered by Lord Holt as a description of trade. That case, therefore, stands on a different foundation from this. All the other instances which were referred to in the argument on the part of the plaintiff, are cases of animals specially protected by acts of Parliament, or which are clearly the subject of property. Thus hawks, falcons, swans, partridges, pheasants, pigeons, wild ducks, mallards, teals, widgeons, wild geese, black game, red game, bustards, and herons are all recognized by different statutes as entitled to protection, and consequently, in the eye of the law, are fit to be preserved. Bees are property, and are the subject of larceny. Fisheries are totally different. The fish can do no harm to anyone and constitute a well-known article of food. Upon the ground, therefore, that the plaintiff had no property in these rooks, that they are birds *feræ naturæ*, destructive in their habits, and not protected either by common law or by statute, and that the plaintiff is at no expense with regard to them, we are of opinion that the plaintiff had no right to insist upon having them in his neighborhood and that he can not maintain this action."

The case of *Keeble* v. *Hickeringill* (11 *East*, 574), above referred to, illustrates the rule in respect to animals *ferae naturae* that are useful. That was an action on the case. The plaintiff was the owner of a decoy pond to which wild fowl used to resort. At his own costs and charges, he prepared and procured divers decoy ducks, nets, machines, and other appliances for the decoying and taking of wild fowl, and enjoyed the benefits in taking them. The defendant, knowing these facts, and intending to injure the plaintiff in his vivary, and to fright and drive away the wild fowl, used to resort thither, and to deprive him of his profit, frequently discharged loaded guns at the head of the pond and vivary, whereby he drove away the wild fowl then in the pond. There was a verdict for the plaintiff. Chief Justice Holt said: " I am of opinion that this action doth lie. It seems to be new in its instance, but is not new in the reason or principle of it. For, first, this using or making a decoy is lawful; secondly, this employment of his ground to that use is profitable to the plaintiff, as is the skill and management of that employment. As to the first, every man that hath a property may enjoy it for his pleasure and profit, as for alluring and procuring ducks to come to his pond. To learn the trade of seducing other ducks to come there in order to be taken is not prohibited either by the law of the land or the moral law; but it is as lawful to use art to seduce them, to catch them, and destroy them for the use of mankind as to kill and destroy wild fowl or tame cattle. Then, when a man useth his art or his skill to take them to sell and dispose of for his profit, this is his trade; and he that hinders another in his trade or livelihood is liable for an action for so hindering him.

* * * * * * *

"And when we do know that of long time in the Kingdom these artificial contrivances of decoy ponds and decoy ducks have been used for enticing into these ponds wild fowl in order to be taken for the profit of the owner of the pond, who is at the expense of servants, engines, and other management, whereby the markets of the nation may be furnished, there is great reason to give encouragement thereunto, that the people who are so instrumental by their skill and industry so to furnish the markets should reap the benefits and have their action. But, in short, that which is the true reason is that this action is not brought to recover damage for the loss of the fowl, but for the disturbance." In the report of the same case in (*11 Modern, 75*), the Chief Justice says: "Suppose the defendant had shot in his own ground; if he had occasion to shoot it would be one thing, but to shoot on purpose to damage the plaintiff is another thing and a wrong."

The two cases last cited are alike in that in each the plaintiff sought to recover damages for a malicious injury to an alleged industry. In *Hannam* vs. *Mockett*, the alleged industry was based upon what the plaintiff had done to secure the coming of the rooks to his lands. But as these animals were *feræ naturæ* and were held not to be useful, the plaintiff had no property in them which could be the basis of an industry that the law would protect against such acts as those complained of. In *Keeble* vs. *Hickeringill*, although the action was not brought to recover damages for the loss of the ducks frightened away from the plaintiff's land by the defendant, its foundation was necessarily, that the ducks, although *feræ naturæ*, were useful, and could be the basis of an industry which the law could protect against the wrongful acts of others to the injury of the person who owned the place to which, by his care, they habitually resorted.

It was suggested in argument that if the claim of the United States to own the Pribilof fur seals be sustained, the result would be to establish a monopoly in its favor, by excluding the citizens and subjects of other nations from engaging in the business of taking seals in the open waters of the sea. But surely this can not constitute any reason why the claim should not be sustained if it be well founded in law. Such an objection could be made to property in anything; for all property is monopoly. The world has no interest in permitting the destruction of a race of animals bestowed for the well-being and subsistence of mankind. It so happens that the United States, by its ownership of the Pribilof Islands, is in a situation to care for and preserve these seals for the benefit of the world and to furnish the means of government while taking the annual increase, which ultimately goes into commerce. If its claim be denied, and pelagic sealers are unrestrained in the taking of these animals in the open seas in the destructive mode practiced by them, the species will soon be exterminated. It is idle to say that the existence of these fur seals can possibly be secured, if pelagic sealing to any material or profitable extent is permitted in Bering Sea, or in any part of the North Pacific Ocean where they may be found while on their way back to their home on the Pribilof Islands. If, therefore, pelagic sealing is suppressed and the taking of these seals is restricted to their breeding grounds, where alone it is possible to make a discrimination as to the sex of the animals and as to the number killed for use, the result will be the preservation of the race to the world. The object of the treaty under which we are proceeding was, as the learned Attorney-General of Great Britain conceded in argument, to secure these fur seals against extermination, without reference to any special interests possessed either by the United States or by pelagic sealers. And as they may be preserved by the United States, under the regulations it has established for the taking of male seals at their breeding grounds, and *cannot be preserved at all if unrestrained pelagic sealing continues,* that fact is of conclusive weight in determining whether the right of property in them should be awarded to the United States; for, according to all the authorities, a right of property in animals *feræ naturæ* depends upon the capacity of the party asserting such a right, exclusively to take the increase of such animals from time to time without destroying or impairing the stock. If, therefore, an award of property in favor of the United States will give that country, practically, a monopoly in the business of taking these fur seals for use, it will be a monopoly which all civilized nations are interested in fostering. When a monopoly in a particular nation is the only or the best mode of preserving to man a gift of nature, then the world is not interested in breaking it down in order simply that a few, whose methods of utilizing that gift will surely destroy it, may realize slight temporary gain. The nations do not begrudge the enjoyment by Great Britain and some of its colonies of a monopoly in pearl and other fisheries off their respective coasts, far out in the open sea beyond territorial waters. And so of the coral in which France and Italy are interested, and of the fisheries on which the prosperity of Norway so much depends.

This case, then, although new in its special circumstances, because relating to animals which, in many respects, are unlike all other known animals, is not, to use the words of Chief Justice Holt, new in the reason or principles of it.

Bringing together the principal facts, and the conclusions arising from them, the case presented by the United States, and upon which it asks a judgment at the hands of this Tribunal sustaining its claim to own these seals, not only while they are at their breeding grounds, but when temporarily absent therefrom in the high seas in quest of food, is as follows:

(a) This race of animals is exhaustible in number and is valuable for purposes of raiment and food. They are not a product of the sea, for they are conceived on land, can not be conceived in the ocean, and must, of necessity, come into existence, and for a considerable part of each year abide, upon land.

(b) When away from their land home it is for temporary purposes, and with the absolute certainty that, unless waylaid and killed by pelagic sealers, while they are beyond territorial waters, they will return to that home at a particular time, and remain there for several months, in every year, during which a proper proportion of their increase can be readily taken, leaving the herd unimpaired in its integrity.

(c) The land on which they were born—the islands of St. Paul and St. George—became the property of the United States in 1867, and has been maintained for more than a century, first, by Russia, and afterwards by the United States, exclusively as the habitation of this race, to which they could resort, in safety, and to which for a period so long that the memory of man runneth not to the contrary, they have regularly resorted, for the purpose of breeding and rearing their young, and of renewing their coats of fur.

(d) While on the islands, during the breeding season, they are protected at great expense against indiscriminate slaughter by raiders and seal-hunters. In addition, and that they may not be unduly disturbed while on the breeding grounds, the United States excludes all persons from the islands of St. Paul and St. George, except such as are required in connection with the industry there conducted under its authority or license—that industry being the taking, for purposes of revenue and commerce, such proportion of males as can be safely taken without impairing the stock, and forbidding the killing of all female seals.

(e) On the islands of St. Paul and St. George, during the season, and at no other place, nor at any other time, can discrimination be made in respect to the sex of seals taken for use. Such discrimination is impossible when the seals are taken in the ocean.

(f) The taking of these seals in the high seas to any extent that is profitable to those engaged in it involves the very existence of the race, because the killing by pelagic hunters of seals heavy with young, or suckling mothers, or impregnated females, will inevitably result in the speedy extermination of the race.

(g) So that the taking of these animals at the breeding grounds for commercial purposes, under regulations that enable a proper proportion of males to be taken for use, and the killing of them in the open waters of the ocean, where no discrimination as to sex is possible, is the difference between preserving the race for the benefit of the world and its speedy extermination for the benefit of a few Canadian and American sealers prosecuting a business so barbarous in its methods that President Harrison fitly characterized it as a crime against nature.

(h) The coming of these animals from year to year to the Pribilof Islands and their abiding there, so that their increase can be taken for man's use without impairing the stock, being due entirely to the care and supervision of the United States, if that care, industry, and supervision be omitted or withdrawn, the speedy destruction of the race will certainly follow. The same result will inevitably follow if pelagic sealing be recognized as a *right* under international law, to be restrained, if at all, or effectually, only by a convention to which *all* the great maritime nations of the earth are parties—a convention which all know could never be obtained; and which, if possible to be obtained under any circumstances, could not be had until its object, the preservation of these animals for the use of the world had been defeated in the meantime by the extermination of the race.

(i) On the other hand, a recognition of the right of property asserted by the United States in these animals would secure, beyond all question, the preservation of these animals. Natural justice, right reason, and the interests of mankind, demand that this recognition be given by this Tribunal; for the United States, alone of all the nations, holds such relations to these animals, that it can preserve the race from extermination while utilizing it for the purposes for which it was bestowed upon man. No possible harm, but only good, can come from a judgment to that effect. Such a judgment will declare that the law of nations is adequate to preserve valuable animals whose existence is endangered by the acts of a few who seek temporary profit for themselves in the extermination of the race.

For the reasons stated, I am of opinion that these fur seals, conceived, born, and reared on the islands of St. Paul and St. George, belonging to the United States, are, when found in the high seas on their way back to their land home and breeding grounds on those islands, the property of the United States, and that this right of property is qualified only in the sense that it will cease, when, but not before, they cease to have the habit of returning to the Pribilof Islands after their customary migration into the open waters of Bering Sea and the North Pacific Ocean.

If the claim of the United States to own these fur seals rests, in law, upon a sound foundation, the next inquiry is whether it may protect its property? There can be but one answer to this question. Manifestly it would have the same authority to protect its property that an individual has for the protection of his property. The United States may, to that end, employ any means which the law, under the like circumstances, permits to an individual for the protection of his property. No one questions its right to afford protection, to that extent, while the seals are on its islands, and while they are within territorial waters. That right—if the United States *owns* the seals—is not lost while they are temporarilly absent in the high seas, beyond territorial waters; for, they are rightfully in the high seas, and the United States is rightfully present wherever its ships may be in the high seas. It is scarcely necessary to cite authorities in support of this position. The Attorney-General of Great Britain concedes that "if the fur seal is to be treated as an article of property, there is the right to defend it on the high seas if attacked"—"the ordinary right of defense of possession which belongs to an individual owner of property."

But does the right of the United States to protect this race of animals from extermination by pelagic hunters depend upon its ownership of the herd, while the seals are beyond jurisdictional limits in the high seas? Does that country have such *special pecuniary interest* in the preservation of the race that it may, consistently with the law of nations and independently of any right of property in the herd itself, interpose, if need be by force, to prevent their wanton destruction while absent from the Pribilof Islands? I say wanton destruction, because no one can for a moment doubt that pelagic sealing, if it continues to the extent practiced within the past five years, will soon exterminate this race.

The principal facts upon which the United States rests the contention that, independently of property in this herd of seals, it may use such means as are necessary to prevent the destruction of the race by pelagic sealers, are summarized in the following extracts from the printed argument of the counsel of the United States:

" Here is a herd of amphibious animals, half human in their intelligence, valuable to mankind, almost the last of their species, which from time immemorial have established their home with a constant *animus revertendi* on islands once so remote from the footsteps of man that these, their only denizens, might reasonably have been expected to be permitted to exist and to continue the usefulness for which the beneficence of the Creator designed them. Upon these islands their young are begotten, brought forth, nurtured during the early months of their lives, the land being absolutely necessary to these processes and no other land having ever been sought by them, if any other is, in fact, available, which is gravely to be doubted.

"The Russian and United States Governments, successively proprietors of the islands, have by wise and careful supervision cherished and protected this herd, and have built up from its product a permanent business and industry valuable to themselves and to the world, and a large source of public revenue, and which at the same time preserves the animals from extinction or from any interference inconsistent with the dictates of humanity.

"It is now proposed by individual citizens of another country to lie in wait for these animals on the adjacent sea during the season of reproduction, and to destroy the pregnant females on their way to the islands, the nursing mothers after delivery while temporarily off the islands in pursuit of food, and thereby the young left there to starve after the mothers have been slaughtered; the unavoidable result being the extermination of the whole race and the destruction of the valuable interests therein of the United States Government and of mankind; and the only object being the small, uncertain, and temporary profits to be derived while the process of destruction lasts, by the individuals concerned.

"And it is this conduct, inhuman and barbarous beyond the power of description, criminal by the laws of the United States and of every civilized country so far as its municipal jurisdiction extends, in respect to any wild animal useful to man or even ministering to his harmless pleasure, that is insisted upon as a part of the sacred rights of the freedom of the sea, which no nation can repress or defend against, whatever its necessity. Can anything be added to the statement of this proposition that is necessary to its refutation?

"What precedent for it, ever tolerated by any nation of the earth, is produced? From what writer, judge, jurist, or treaty is authority to be derived for the assertion that the high sea is or ever has been free for such conduct as this, or that any such construction was ever before given to the terms 'freedom of the sea' as to throw it open to the destruction, for the profit of individuals, of valuable national interests of any description whatever?"

The general proposition deduced from these statements is, that no individual can be said to have a *right*, under international law, to *exterminate a race* of valuable animals, for the sake simply of the temporary profit realized from such practices while the process of destruction goes on; consequently, it is argued, the United States may, upon the principles of self-protection or self-preservation, employ, even upon the high seas, such force as is necessary to prevent that destruction and thereby protect the industry which is maintained on its islands for purposes of revenue and commerce as well as for the comfort and maintenance of the native inhabitants of those islands—*the existence of which industry depends absolutely upon the existence of this race of animals.*

This proposition is disputed by Her Britannic Majesty, who insists, by counsel, that her subjects, unless forbidden by the laws of Great Britain, or by some treaty or convention to which that country is a party, are entitled under the law of nations to capture and kill for use or profit, any animals, however valuable, found in the high seas; that this right does not depend in the slightest degree upon the inquiry whether the particular methods employed in capturing and killing the animals are or are not barbarous, or whether the prosecution of the business will or will not result in the speedy extermination of the race, or in the destruction of the fur seal industry maintained by, or under the authority of, the United States on its islands; and that any interference whatever by other nations with the exercise of this right by British subjects is forbidden by the doctrine of the freedom of the seas as recognized by international law.

In respect to that branch of the general proposition advanced by the United States which assumes that pelagic sealing, conducted according to the destructive methods and to the extent now practiced, involves the speedy extermination of the race, and, consequently, the destruction of the fur seal industry established on the Pribilof Islands, I do not care to add anything to what has already been said by me; for it can not be disputed, under the evidence, that such results will speedily follow from unrestrained pelagic sealing. But is it not equally clear that the subjects of Her Britannic Majesty are not entitled, of *right*, under the law of nations, thus to *exterminate* a *race* of useful animals? Certainly no such right is recognized in the municipal law of any civilized country, much less in the law of nations which, all writers agree, rests primarily upon those principles of natural justice and morality, and those distinctions between right and wrong which, in the words of Cicero, are "congenial to the feelings of nature, diffused among all men, uniform, eternal, commanding us to our duty, prohibiting every violation of it—one eternal and immortal law, which can neither be repealed nor derogated from, addressing itself to all nations and all ages, deriving its authority from the common Sovereign of the universe, seeking no other lawgiver and interpreter, carrying home its sanctions to every breast, by the inevitable punishment He inflicts on its transgressors."

There is fair room for discussion as to whether the annihilation of this race of useful animals by individuals or associations of individuals, while such animals are in the high seas, can be legally prevented in any other mode than by a treaty or convention that will control equally the citizens or subjects of *all* nations. But the mind instantly recoils from the suggestion that such practices are in the exercise of a *right* protected by the law of nations, and must be submitted to by the United States, however injurious they may be to its material interests. A declaration by this Tribunal, in express words, or by the necessary effect of its award, that the destruction, from *mere wantonness*, of useful animals, is in the exercise of a *right* secured or protected, by the law of nations, would shock the moral sense of mankind. But, in principle, there can be no difference between the destruction from mere wantonness of these useful animals, and their destruction, for temporary gain, by methods that are inhuman and barbarous, and which will surely result in the speedy extermination of the entire race, thereby defeating the beneficent purposes for which they have been bestowed by the Creator upon man.

If it be said that these animals are given to mankind for their use, and that the taking of them in the high seas is only one mode of utilizing them, the answer is, that the obligations arising from the relations which men and states must sustain to each other forbid any mode of taking them that is plainly incompatible with the existence of the race, and, therefore, destructive of such use. Paley says that from reason or revelation, or from both together, " it appears to be God Almighty's intention that the productions of the earth should be applied to the sustentation of human life;" and, "consequently, all waste and misapplication of these productions is contrary to the divine intention and will, and therefore wrong, for the same reasons that any other crime is so." Among the illustrations given by the author of such wrongs or crimes is the "diminishing the breed of animals by wanton or improvident consumption of the young, as of the spawn of shellfish or the fry of salmon, by the use of unlawful nets or at improper seasons." *Paley's Moral Philosophy, c. XI.* Ahrens, in his Course of Natural Law, states, as the result of rational principles to which the right of property and its exercise are subjected, "that property exists for a rational purpose and for a rational use; it is destined to satisfy the various needs of human life; consequently all arbitrary abuse, all arbitrary destruction, are contrary to right." *Vol. 2, ed. 1876, Bk. I, div. 1, 64; ed. 1860, p. 356.* Schouler, in his Treatise on the Law of Personal Property, says: "Nature teaches the lesson, doubly enforced by revelation, that the right of the human race to own and exercise dominion over the things of this earth in successive generations carries with it a corresponding moral obligation to use, enjoy, and transmit in due course for the benefit of the whole human race, not for ourselves only, or for those who preceded us, but for all who are yet to come besides, that the grand purpose of the Creator and Giver may be accomplished."

Thiers, in his Treatise on Property, says that experience demonstrates the absolute necessity of the institution of property, its appropriateness,

.t usefulness; that property is a general, constant, universal fact, as indispensable to the existence of man as liberty is to his welfare; that, in all ages and in all countries, man has instituted property as the necessary reward of labor, and that property has become a law of his species. *Bk. ii, chapters 1, 2, 3, and 4.* But no writer has ever maintained the monstrous proposition that society when instituting property, recognized the wanton, reckless extermination of a race of useful animals as one of the *rights* inherent in man, or as tolerated by the principles of justice, benevolence, and right which constitute the basis of the law of nations. All will concede that one of the great objects, if not the supreme object, which society expected to accomplish by the institution of property, was to preserve and increase those things, animate and inanimate, that are bestowed upon man for his use. Mankind is entitled to participate in the enjoyment of the things thus bestowed upon the world, and that it may do so, society recognizes the right of every one to appropriate to his own use such things as susceptible of ownership, have not been appropriated by others. He is allowed, under given circumstances, to appropriate to himself, exclusively, valuable animals *feræ naturæ*, but he may not, of right, exterminate the race itself.

If, by care, industry, and self-denial, he can bring the race under such control that he, and he alone, is able to deal with it *as a whole*, taking the increase without diminishing the stock, then as I have already endeavored to show, a recognition of a right of property in him is not only a fair and just return for the care, industry, and self-denial bestowed by him, but is consistent with the objects for which property has been instituted. But he cannot, without committing a wrong against society, exterminate the race itself, either from mere wantonness or by the employment of methods that inevitably lead to that result.

With entire truth, therefore, it may be said that the extermination of this race of animals by the destructive methods of pelagic sealing, involving necessarily the killing in vast numbers of female seals heavy with young or nursing their pups, or impregnated, is a crime against the law of nature, and consequently without any sanction whatever in the law of nations. That law, indeed, recognizes the freedom of the seas for the peoples of all nations, and no nations have stood more firmly by that doctrine or are more interested in its enforcement than Great Britain and the United States. But I have not found in any treatise upon international law, or in the judgment of any court, a hint even that this doctrine confers upon individuals or associations a *right* to employ methods for the taking of useful animals found in the high seas which will exterminate the race, when all know, or may easily know, that such animals may be readily taken at their breeding grounds, and not elsewhere, by methods that regularly give their increase for man's use without at all impairing or diminishing the stock. One method results in the extermination of the race, whereby the object of its creation is entirely defeated; the other results in its preservation, whereby that object is secured. It is inconceivable that the law of nations gives or recognizes the right to employ the former.

No civilized nation does or would permit, within its own territory, the destruction or extermination of a race of useful animals by methods at once cruel and revolting. And yet it is said that such conduct, if practiced on the high seas, the common highway of all peoples, is protected by international law which rests, as jurists and courts agree, primarily upon those principles of morality, justice, right, and humanity, by which the conduct of individuals and states are, and ought to be, guided. Thus the law to which *all* civilized nations have assented is made, by the contention in question, to cover and protect acts which *no one of those nations would, for an instant, tolerate within its limits.* It is beyond all comprehension that an act which every civilized man must condemn can be justified and sustained as having been done in the exercise of a right given or secured by a law based upon the assent of nations.

That I am correct in saying that no nation would permit, within its territory, any methods for the taking of useful wild animals that would result in the speedy extermination of the race is shown by reference to the legislative enactments and regulations in different countries for the protection of valuable animals, the basis of important industries, against the reckless conduct of those who consult temporary gain for themselves at the expense of the rights of the general public.

But it is said: "Grant that the taking of these animals in the high seas, by methods destructive of the race, is *not a right* under the law of nations; grant that the employment of such methods is inhuman and injurious to the best interests of mankind; grant that the fur seal industry maintained at the Pribilof Islands depends absolutely upon these animals not being killed while they are temporarily in the high seas in search of food, or while they are on their way back to their breeding grounds; by what authority does the United States interfere with the movements of the subjects of other countries on the high seas, and by the use of force prevent them from taking these animals while they are beyond the jurisdictional limits of that country?"

This question proceeds upon the ground—propounded, not, indeed, in words, but, in effect, by the argument of counsel—that, without support from treaties or conventions between the maritime nations of the world, the United States is powerless, under the law of nations, to preserve the industry established and maintained by it at the Pribilof Islands against the lawless acts of individuals upon the high seas. These acts are so characterized, because the killing of these fur seals in the high seas, as now practiced, where no discrimination as to sex is possible, and when the extermination of the race will be the inevitable result of such killing, is forbidden by every consideration of humanity, reason, and justice. And, in view of the facts disclosed by the record, it is clear that the killing of these animals by pelagic sealers, while they are in the high seas, on their migration-route, is as certainly destructive of the industry maintained by the United States at the Pribilof Islands *as if the pelagic hunters came personally to the islands, during the breeding season, and engaged there in the indiscriminate slaughter of the animals, without regard to their sex or age.*

That the United States can rightfully control the killing of these animals both on the Pribilof Islands and within its territorial waters will not be disputed. This much, all admit, may be done in virtue of its sovereignty over such country and waters. But as the important industry maintained on the islands can be preserved *only* by preventing the destruction of these animals *after they have passed beyond territorial waters into the high seas, with the intention of returning to their breeding grounds the succeeding spring and summer,* does not the right of self-protection or self-preservation, which belongs to every independent nation, entitle it to protect these animals while temporarily absent from their land home? Vattel says: " In vain does nature prescribe to nations, as well as to individuals, the care of self-preservation, and of advancing their own perfection and happiness, if she does not give them a right to preserve themselves from everything that might render this care ineffectual. * * * Every nation, as well as every man, has, therefore, a right to prevent other nations from obstructing her preservation, her perfection, and happiness—that is, to preserve herself from all injuries; and this right is a perfect one, since it is given to satisfy

11492——13

a natural indispensable obligation; for when we can not use constraint in order to cause our rights to be respected their effects are very uncertain. It is this right to preserve itself from all injury that is called the *right of security*." *Bk. 2, c. 1.* Dr. Phillimore, in his Commentaries on International Law, says: "The right of self-preservation is the first law of nations; as it is of individuals. A society which is not in a condition to repel aggression from without is wanting in its principal duty to the members of which it is composed and to the chief end of its institution. All means which do not affect the independence of other nations are lawful for this end. No nation has a right to prescribe to another what these means shall be, or to require any account of her conduct in this respect." Again, the same author: "We have hitherto considered what measures a nation is entitled to take for the preservation of her safety *within* her dominions. It may happen that the same right may warrant her in extending precautionary measures *without* these limits, and even in transgressing the borders of her neighbor's territory. For international law considers the right of self-preservation as prior and paramount to that of territorial inviolability, and, where they conflict, justifies the maintenance of the former at the expense of the latter right." *1 Phillimore, 252–253, c. 10, §§ 211, 214, 2d ed.* Hall says: " In the last resort almost the whole of the duties of states are subordinated to the right of self-protection. * * * There are, however, circumstances falling short of occasions upon which existence is immediately in question, in which through a sort of extension of the idea of self-preservation to include self-protection against serious hurt, states are allowed to disregard certain of the ordinary rules of law, in the same manner as if their existence were involved." *Hall Int. Law, Pt. II, C. 7. 2 ed., p. 214.*

It has been suggested that the doctrine of self-protection, referred to by writers upon international law, has application only where the acts against which the state defends itself involve its existence, independence, or safety, or the inviolability of its territory, and do not justify in time of peace, any exercise of authority or power by a state, beyond its jurisdictional limits, in order merely to prevent the doing of that which, in its direct effects, will work injury to its material interests.

A familiar illustration of the extent to which a State may go in defending its existence or providing for its safety, is that of a blockade which interferes with the commerce of neutral nations. "The greatest liberty," Manning says, "which law should allow in civil government is the power of doing everything that does not injure any other person, and the greatest liberty which justice among nations demands is that every state may do anything that does not injure any other state with which it is at amity. The freedom of commerce and the rights of war, both undoubted *as long as no injustice results from them, become questionable as soon as their exercise is grievously injurious to any independent state,* but the great difference of the interest concerned makes the trivial nature of the restriction that can justly be placed upon neutrals appear inconsiderable when balanced against the magnitude of the national enterprises which unrestricted neutral trade might compromise. That some interference is justifiable will be obvious on the consideration that if a neutral had the power of unrestricted commerce he might carry to a port blockaded and on the point of surrendering, provisions which would enable it to hold out and so change the whole issue of a war; and thus the vital interests of a nation might be sacrificed to augment the riches of a single individual." *Manning's Law of Nations, Bk. 3, c. 3.*

The force of this principle is not lessened by the suggestion that it relates to a time of war, to the rights of belligerents. The right of self-protection or self-preservation is as complete and perfect in time of peace as in time of war. The means employed when war prevails may not always be used in a time of peace. The test, both in war or in peace, is whether the particular means used are *necessary* to be employed for purposes of self-protection against wrong and injury.

Undoubtedly, the general rule that a state may employ such means for its self-preservation as are necessary to that end, is subject to the qualification stated by Mr. Chitty in his notes to the 7th American edition (1849) of Vattel, namely, that a nation has the right, in time of peace or of war, to diminish the commerce or resources of another by fair rivalry and other means *not in themselves unjust,* precisely as one tradesman may by *fair competition* undersell his neighbor and thereby alienate his customers. P. 142. But this qualification is wholly inapplicable to the present case, for the reason that the killing of these animals in the high seas, by seal hunters, is *in itself unjust,* and as I have attempted to show, does not rest upon any *right* secured by the law of nations to those who are engaged in that mode of taking them. It is equally true that the commonest and simplest form in which the doctrine of self-preservation is illustrated is in cases where a nation employs force beyond its own limits, either on the high seas or within the limits of another state, in order to meet a threatened attack upon its existence or a threatened invasion of its territory. But I am aware of no authority for the broad statement that a nation may not use, upon the high seas, in time of peace, such force as is necessary to prevent the commission of acts which have no sanction in the laws of nations, are in themselves wrong, and, if committed, will inevitably destroy important industries established and maintained by that nation within its territory for purposes of revenue and commerce. The nation thus employing force for the protection of its lawful industries does not thereby appropriate to itself any part of the ocean, or extends its dominion, or interfere with an innocent use of the sea for purposes of navigation or fishing. It only prevents the doing of what can not be rightfully done, and thereby preserves what no one has a right to destroy. The doctrine of the freedom of the seas does not authorize or sanction the destruction of the material interests of a nation by means of acts done on the high seas which are in themselves unjust and wrong, because hostile to the interests of mankind, and contrary to those rules of morality, justice, and right reason which govern the conduct of individuals and nations with each other. Mr. Blaine well said: "The law of the sea is not lawlessness. Nor can the law of the sea and the liberty which it confers and which it protects be perverted to justify acts which are immoral in themselves, which inevitably tend to results against the interests an against the welfare of mankind."

As declared by Mr. Justice Story, speaking for the Supreme Court of the United States, in the case of the *Marianna Flora* (*11 Wheaton, 1, 42*): " Upon the ocean, then, in time of peace, all possess an entire equality. It is the common highway of all, appropriated to the use of all; and no one can vindicate to himself a superior or exclusive prerogative there. Every ship sails there with the unquestionable right of pursuing her own *lawful* business without interruption; but, whatever be that business, she is bound to pursue it in such a manner as not to violate the rights of others. The general maxim in such cases is *sic utero tuo, ut non alienum lædas.*" Observe, that the business upon the high seas, the uninterrupted prosecution of which is protected by the doctrine that the free use of the ocean for navigation and fishing is common to all mankind, is that which is "lawful." This doctrine can not be invoked to support the use of the high seas for the perpetration of wrongs or injuries. On the contrary, the principal ground on which that doctrine rests is that the sea is so vast in extent, and so inexhaustible in its products, that its free use for purposes of navigation and fishing can do no harm to any one.

Twiss, in his work upon the Law of Nations, after observing that

the open sea is by nature not capable of being reduced into the possession, or being effectively occupied, or brought under the empire of one
nation, says: "But independently of these insurmountable difficulties,
the use of the open sea, which consists in navigation, is *innocent* and
inexhaustible; he who navigates upon it *does no harm to any one*, and
the sea in this respect is sufficient for all mankind. But nature does
not give to man a right to appropriate to himself things which may be
innocently used by all, and *which are inexhaustible and sufficient for
all*. For since those things, whilst common to all, are sufficient to
supply the wants of each, whoever should attempt to render himself
sole proprietor of them (to the exclusion of all other participants) would
unreasonably wrest the bounteous gifts of nature from the parties excluded. Further, if the free and common use of a thing, which is incapable of being appropriated, was likely to be prejudicial or dangerous
to a nation, the care of its own safety would authorize it to reduce that
thing under its exclusive empire, if possible, in order to restrict the use
of it on the part of others, by such precautions as prudence might dic-
tate. But this is not the case with the open sea, upon which all persons may navigate without the least prejudice to any nation whatever,
and without exposing any nation thereby to danger. It would thus
seem that there is no natural warrant for any nation to seek to take
possession of the open sea or even to restrict the innocent use of it by
other nations." Again, the same author: " The right of fishing in the
open sea or main ocean is common to all nations, on the same principle
which sanctions the common right of navigation, namely, that he who
fishes in the open sea *does no injury to any one, and the products of
the sea are in this respect inexhaustible and sufficient for all.*" *Twiss,
Law of Nations, Title, Right of the Sea C. 11, §§ 172, 185.* So Grotius: "It is certain that he who would take possession of the sea by
occupation could not prevent a peaceful and *innocent* navigation; such
a transit can not be interdicted even on land, though ordinarily it would
be less necessary and more dangerous." *Bk. 2, c. 3, § 12, page
415.* Vattel: "It is manifest that the use of the open sea which
consists in navigation and fishing is innocent and inexhaustible;
that is to say, he who navigates or fishes is sufficient for all mankind." *Chap. 33, Sec. 291.* Azuni, in his work on the Maritime
Law of Europe, well says that the sea is intended by Providence
to be common to the different nations of the world, "to contribute
to the wants, the commerce, the well-being and the prosperity of all who

have the means of navigating its surface"—not that it may be used of right to the injury of mankind in order that a few may reap a temporary profit from the destruction of that which has been bestowed for the benefit of all. *Pt. 1, c. 1, § 11.* In view of these authorities, how can it be said that the doctrine of the freedom of the seas justifies and protects the use of the seas for the purpose or with the inevitable effect of destroying a race of valuable animals, limited in numbers, easily exhaustible by waste, and in the preservation of which all mankind is interested?

If the United States does not own this herd of seals, and if, in order that they may reap temporary profit, British subjects may, of *right*, exterminate it when found in the high seas, and temporarily absent from its land home, and thus destroy an important industry maintained for more than a century within the present territory of the United States, then, I admit, that any interference by the United States with the hunting and killing of these animals in the high seas by British subjects would be a marine trespass of which their country could rightfully complain. But I deny that any use of the seas for the purpose, or with the certainty, of producing that result, is a lawful use of the ocean, or that the right of the United States to preserve its material interests, thus directly attacked, depends upon the consent of other countries to be manifested by treaty or legislation. The nation, whose interests are thus assailed may stand upon its inalienable right of self-protection, and by force, if need be, prevent the commission of such acts, even if it may not in its own courts inflict personal punishment for such wrongs upon the subjects of other countries who commit them. If it employs for its self-protection more force than is reasonably necessary it will be responsible therefor to the country upon whose subjects such force is used. But its inability to inflict such punishment, in its own courts, can not affect its right, by such force as is necessary, to preserve its material interests by repressing the *acts* of wrongdoers *directly injurious to those interests.* When the books speak of the equal rights of all people to use the ocean for purposes of navigation they mean navigation for purposes that are innocent and lawful, and not for purposes which are, in themselves, unjust and injurious to others.

These views are not at all in conflict with the general rule that a state may not exercise sovereign authority or *jurisdiction* beyond the line of territorial waters, whether that line be a marine league from its shores, or at such distance as may be measured by cannon shot. That rule has its origin in the necessity which every state is under to provide for the safety of its own people and interests. But the right of self-protection or self-preservation does not end with the outer line of mar. ginal or territorial waters. In the very nature of things it could not end with that line without rendering the right valueless.

Rutherford, in his Institutes of Natural Law, gives expression to views upon the doctrine of self-protection which are universally accepted. He says: "In short, the true principles upon which our right of defending either our persons or our goods depends is this: The law of nature does not oblige us to give them up when any one has a mind to hurt them, or to take them from us; and that the law of nature does not oblige us thus to give them up, is evident; because our right to them would be unintelligible, or would, in effect, be no right at all if we were obliged to suffer all mankind to treat them as they pleased, without endeavoring to prevent it. If this, then, is the principle upon which the right of defense depends, we can not expect to find that the law of nature has exactly defined how far we may go, or what we may lawfully do, in endeavoring to prevent an injury which any one designs and attempts to do us. The law allows us to defend our persons or our property; and such a general allowance implies that no particular means of defense are prescribed to us. We may, however, be sure that whatever means are necessary must be lawful, because it would be absurd to suppose that the law of nature allows of defense, and yet forbids us at the same time to do what is necessary for this purpose." *Bk. 1, c. 16, 2d American ed.*

An illustration of these principles is furnished by the case in the Supreme Court of the United States of *Church* vs. *Hubbart* (*2 Cranch's Reports, 186, 231*), decided in 1804. That was an action upon policies of insurance upon the cargo of a vessel, which contained provisions exempting the insurance company from liability in case of a seizure of the vessels by the Portuguese for illicit trade. During the life of the policies the vessel was seized by the Portuguese and condemned in one of its municipal tribunals for a violation by it of the laws of Portugal prohibiting commercial intercourse between its colonies and foreign vessels. On behalf of the insured it was contended, among other things, that the policy of insurance did not exempt the company from liability, unless the seizure was justified by the laws of Portugal and by the law of nations. His counsel said: "The sentence does not go on the ground of illicit trade. At most it only expresses a suspicion. The vessel was seized five leagues from the land, at anchor on the high seas. The seizure was not justified by their [Portuguese] laws. She was not within their territorial jurisdiction. By the law of nations territorial jurisdiction can extend only to the distance of cannon shot from the shore. *Vattel, B. I, c. 23, s. 280, 289.* A vessel has a right to hover on the coast. It is no cause of condemnation. It can, at most, justify a seizure for the purpose of obtaining security that she will not violate the laws of the country. The law which is produced forbids the vessel to enter a port, but does not authorize a seizure upon the open sea. Great Britain, the greatest commercial nation in the world, has extended her revenue laws the whole length of the law of nations, to prevent smuggling. But she authorizes seizures of vessels only within the limits of her ports, or within two leagues of the coast; and then only for the purpose of obtaining security". *1 Bac. Abr., 513.* Counsel for the insurance company, referring to the rule cited from **Vattel**, and observing that it had reference only to the rights of a neutral territory in time of war, said: "It is a very indefinite rule indeed, even for the purpose to which it extends, for it makes the extent of a nation's territory depend upon the weight of metal or projectile force of her cannon. It is a right which must resolve itself into power, and comes to this, that territory extends as far as it can be made to be respected. But this principle does not apply to the right of a nation to cause her revenue and colonial laws to be respected. Here all nations do *assume* at least a greater extent than cannon shot; and other passages from Vattel show the distinctions which are acknowledged on this point."

I have given these extracts from the arguments of counsel to show 'that the question was distinctly presented whether the seizure of the vessel by the Portuguese authorities. outside of its territorial waters five leagues from land, was, for that reason merely, illegal under the law of nations. Upon this question the Supreme Court of the United States, speaking by Chief Justice Marshall, said:

"That the law of nations prohibits the exercise of any act of authority over a vessel in the situation of the *Aurora*, and that this seizure is, on that account, a mere marine trespass, not within the exception, cannot be admitted. To reason from the extent of protection a nation will afford to foreigners to the extent of the means it may use for its own security does not seem to be perfectly correct. It is opposed by principles which are universally acknowledged. The authority of a nation within its own territory is absolute and exclusive. The seizure of a vessel within the range of its cannon by a foreign force is an invasion of that territory, and is a hostile act which it is its duty to repel. But its power to secure itself from injury may certainly be exercised beyond the limits of its territory. Upon this principle the right of a belligerent to search a neutral vessel on the high seas for contraband of war is universally admitted, because the belligerent has a right to prevent the injury done to himself by the assistance intended for his enemy; so too a nation has a right to prohibit any commerce with its colonies. Any attempt to violate the laws made to protect this right is an injury to itself which it may prevent, and it has a right to use the means necessary for its prevention. These means do not appear to be limited within any certain marked boundaries, which remain the same at all times and in all situations. If they are such as unnecessarily to vex and harass foreign lawful commerce, foreign nations will resist their exercise. If they are such as are reasonable and necessary to secure their laws from violation, they will be submitted to.

"In different seas, and on different coasts, a wider or more contracted range, in which to exercise the vigilance of the government, will be assented to. Thus in the channel, where a very great part of the commerce to and from all the north of Europe passes through a very narrow sea, the seizure of vessels on suspicion of attempting an illicit trade, must necessarily be restricted to very narrow limits; but on the coast of *South America*, seldom frequented by vessels but for the purpose of illicit trade, the vigilance of the government may be extended somewhat further; and foreign nations submit to such regulations as are reasonable in themselves, and are really necessary to secure that monopoly of colonial commerce which is claimed by all nations holding distant posessions.

"If this right be extended too far, the exercise of it will be resisted. It has occasioned long and frequent contests, which have sometimes ended in open war. The *English*, it will be recollected, complained of the right claimed by *Spain* to search their vessels on the high seas, which was carried so far that the *guarda costas* of that nation seized vessels not in the neighborhood of their coasts. This practice was the subject of long and fruitless negotiations, and at length of open war. The right of the *Spaniards* was supposed to be exercised unreasonably and vexatiously, but it never was contended that it could only be exercised within the range of the cannon from their batteries. Indeed, the right given to our own revenue cutters, to visit vessels four leagues from our coast, is a declaration that in the opinion of the *American* Government no such principle as that contended for has a real existence." *Church vs. Hubbart, 2 Cranch, 187, 231, 235.*

The diligence of learned counsel has not brought to light any adjudged case, either in England or in America, which is in conflict with or modifies to any extent the principles announced in *Church* vs. *Hubbart*. If the judgment in that case is consistent with the settled principles of international law, it must follow that the right of the United States to prevent the extermination of a race of animals upon whose existence depends an important industry maintained within its limits—an industry which is a source of revenue, and is directly connected with the government of the native inhabitants of the Pribilof Islands—is not to be denied upon the ground merely that such force, to be effective to accomplish that end, must be used on the high seas beyond its territorial waters.

It is a fact, not without interest, that the decision in *Church* vs. *Hubbart* was referred to with approval in the opinion of Lord Chief Justice Cockburn (concurred in by Lush and Field, J. J. and Pollock B.) in the great case of *The Queen* vs. *Keyn* (*L. R. 2 Exch. Div., 63, 211*). The principal question in that case was whether an English criminal court had jurisdiction to try a foreigner, charged with the offense of manslaughter committed by him on his vessel, a foreign ship, while it was passing within three miles of the shores of England on a voyage to a foreign port. In the course of his opinion, the Lord Chief Justice said: "I pass on to the statutory enactments relating to foreigners within the three-mile zone. These enactments may be divided, 1st, into those which are intended to protect the interests of the State and those which are not; 2d, into those in which the foreigner is expressly named, and those in which he has been held to be included by implication only. Hitherto legislation, so far as relates to foreigners in foreign ships in this part of the sea, has been confined to the maintenance of neutral rights and obligations, the prevention of breaches of the revenue and fishery laws, and, under particular circumstances, to cases of collision. In the first two, the legislation is altogether irrespective of the three-mile distance, being founded on a totally different principle, namely, *the right of a state to take all necessary measures for the protection of its territory and rights* and the prevention of any breach of its revenue laws. This principle was well explained by Marshall, C. J., in the case of Church vs. Hubbart (2 Cranch, 234)." After quoting what appears in the above extract from the opinion of Chief Justice Marshall, the Lord Chief Justice proceeds: "To this class of enactments belong the acts imposing penalties for the violation of neutrality and the so-called 'Hovering Acts' and acts relating to the customs."

I have not understood counsel to question the validity, under the law of nations, of the statutes of either England or the United States, commonly known as hovering acts, by which those countries assume to exert their authority (if need be, employing force) beyond the line of territorial waters, when that becomes necessary for the protection of her revenue against those who intend to violate their customs laws and regulations. This is done, to repeat the words of Lord Chief Justice Cockburn, in the exercise of "the right of a state to take all necessary measures for the protection of its territory and rights and the prevention of any breach of its revenue laws." Suppose individuals should organize in England a plan for smuggling goods into the United States in violation of its revenue law, and to that end should load a vessel at Liverpool with the goods thus intended to be introduced clandestinely into the United States and sail from one of the ports of that country in direct execution of their illegal scheme. Would any one doubt the right of the United States, if the circumstances made that course necessary, to authorize the seizure of the goods in mid-ocean and confiscate them? Must the United States, in such a case, forbear to take any steps whatever for the protection of its rights and its revenue until the vessel gets near to its coasts? Upon what principle can the right to cause such seizure outside of territorial waters and within the distance from the shore fixed by hovering acts, be any greater than that of seizing, under the circumstances stated, in mid-ocean?

Suppose, again, that a vessel laden with rags infected with yellow fever were on its way to one of the ports of the United States. Can any one doubt that the government of that country would be entitled, under the law of nations, to cause the seizure of the infected rags in mid-ocean and their destruction, if that mode of proceeding were, under all the circumstances, necessary to protect its people against the danger of yellow fever?

It seems to me that the question as to the extent to which a nation may go in protecting its rights depends entirely on the circumstances of each particular case. If the rights assailed are such as the nation may defend and preserve against the wrongful acts of others, then it may employ, *at the place of attack, from which the injury proceeds, certainly, if that place be not within the exclusive jurisdiction of another power,* all the means necessary to prevent the commission of those acts. In the case before us it appears, by overwhelming evidence, that if pelagic sealing continues to any material extent, the important industry which the United States has established and maintains, at great expense, on the Pribilof Islands, for purposes of revenue and commerce, and for the benefit of all countries, must perish by the acts of individuals and associations of individuals committed beyond its jurisdictional limits, on the high seas, where the ships and peoples of all nations are upon an equality—an industry which has never been interfered with until pelagic sealers devised their barbarous methods for slaughtering female seals, some impregnated, some heavy with young, and others suckling mothers in search of food for the sustenance of themselves and their offspring. If, as already suggested, these acts are done in the exercise of a *right* recognized and secured by the law of nations, then they can not be prevented or restrained by the United States, however injurious they may be to any business conducted within the territory of that nation. But if those acts are not recognized and protected by the law of nations; if no one can claim that all the nations have assented to the doing of that on the high seas which no single nation would permit to be done within its own territory; in short, if no one has the *right*, for mere temporary gain, to destroy useful animals by methods that will inevitably and speedily result in the extermination of the race, then the United States, whose revenue and commerce *are directly involved in the preservation of that race*, may, consistently with the law of nations, protect its interests by preventing the commission of those wrongful acts.

If the views which I have expressed are shared by a majority of the Arbitrators, the answer to the fifth question of Article VI of the treaty should be——

That the herd of fur seals frequenting the islands of St. Paul and St. George in Bering Sea, when found in the ocean, beyond the ordinary three-mile limit, are the property of the United States, and as long as these animals have the habit of returning from their migration-routes to, and of abiding upon, those islands, as their breeding grounds, so that their increase may be regularly taken there, and not elsewhere, without endangering the existence of the race, that nation, in virtue of its ownership of such herd and islands, may rightfully employ, for the protection of those animals against pelagic sealing, such means as the law permits to individuals for the protection of their property; and,

That independently of any right of property in the herd itself, the

United States, simply as the owner of the fur seal industry maintained
by its authority on the islands of St. Paul and St. George, and under
the doctrine of self-protection, may employ such means, including force,
as may be necessary to prevent the commission of acts which will
inevitably result in the speedy extermination of this race of animals,
the basis of that industry, while they are in the high seas beyond territorial waters, and temporarily absent from their breeding grounds or
land home on those islands.

4.

CONCURRENT REGULATIONS.

The Tribunal having determined that the Government of the United
States has no authority or jurisdiction in Bering Sea, beyond the ordinary limit of territorial waters, except such as appertains equally to all
nations, and that it has no right of property in, nor any right to protect, the fur seals frequenting its islands in that sea, when they are
found outside of the ordinary three-mile limit, what is our duty in
respect to Concurrent Regulations for the protection and preservation
of these animals?

We have seen that by the Seventh Article of the Treaty, under
which the Tribunal is proceeding, it is provided:

"If the determination of the foregoing questions as to the exclusive
jurisdiction of the United States shall leave the subject in such position
that the concurrence of Great Britain is necessary to the establishment
of Regulations for the proper protection and preservation of the fur
seal in, or habitually resorting to, the Bering Sea, the Arbitrators shall
then determine what concurrent Regulations outside the jurisdictional
limits of the respective Governments are necessary, and over what
waters such Regulations should extend, and to aid them in that determination the report of a Joint Commission to be appointed by the
respective Governments shall be laid before them, with such other
evidence as either Government may submit.

"The High Contracting Parties furthermore agree to coöperate in
securing the adhesion of other powers to such Regulations."

It is unnecessary to determine whether the words "foregoing questions" in this Article refer to the questions specifically mentioned in
Article VI, or to those of a more general character enumerated in
Article I of the Treaty. In either case, we must proceed to consider
the subject of Regulations; for, if the United States has no "exclusive
jurisdiction" over the waters traversed by these seals in their annual
migrations (as clearly it has not); if, as the majority of the Arbitrators

have declared, that Nation does not own this herd of seals when they are in the high seas, beyond jurisdictional limits, and can not, in virtue of any power it possesses, protect them against pelagic sealing; and if, as the same majority hold, British subjects at any time, or by any methods they choose to employ, may, when unrestrained by the laws of their own country, capture and kill these animals, while they are in the open waters of the ocean, and without limit as to the numbers so taken, it is too clear to admit of discussion that the concurrence of Great Britain is necessary in the establishing of regulations applicable to its own subjects and to waters outside the jurisdictional limits of the respective Governments. So that it must now be decided by the Tribunal, whether concurrent regulations are *necessary* for "the proper protection and preservation" of the seals while they are in the high seas, beyond territorial waters? If so, over what waters shall such regulations extend, and to what extent must pelagic sealing be restricted?

If I have not misapprehended what has been said by Arbitrators during this Conference, we are all agreed that regulations of some kind are necessary; indeed, that an adjournment of this Tribunal without its having prescribed regulations "for the proper protection and preservation of the fur seal in, or habitually resorting to, the Bering Sea," would be regarded as a violation of duty upon the part of its members.

It has been suggested that the Tribunal is without power, under the treaty, to establish any regulations that will have the effect to suppress altogether the business of taking these animals, in the high seas, by the citizens of the respective countries here represented; and that the duty of this Tribunal—it having been decided that pelagic sealing is not forbidden by the law of nations—is to prescribe regulations that will not injure, to any material extent, much less destroy, the business of pelagic sealing. I had occasion, at one of the early sessions of this Tribunal, to express my views as to its powers or competency, under the treaty, in respect to regulations. My opinion then was, and is now, that the Tribunal has the power, and is under a duty, from the discharge of which it may not shrink, to prescribe whatever regulations are necessary for the protection and preservation of these seals when in the high seas. If that end can not be accomplished otherwise than by regulations, which either expressly or by their operation, prohibit all pelagic sealing, then it is our duty to prescribe regulations of that character.

But it is said that, as the two governments have agreed "to coöperate in securing the adhesion of other powers to such regulations" as may be established, the Tribunal must do nothing likely to defeat any effort that may be made to obtain this adhesion of other nations. If we find from the evidence—and, in my opinion, the evidence conclusively shows—that this race can not be preserved, but will be entirely destroyed for all commercial purposes if pelagic sealing is permitted to any material extent, then our duty is to make regulations that will protect the race against such an attack. We must assume that civilized nations will approve and make applicable to their peoples any regulations which have for their object, and which plainly will secure, the preservation of this race for the benefit of mankind. Surely, there can not be "proper" protection and preservation of these seals, when in the high seas, if the regulations adopted by the Tribunal admit of pelagic sealing to an extent that will seriously endanger the existence of the race. If that mode of taking these seals for use can be permitted to an extent that does not materially endanger the integrity of the race, then I concede that to *that* extent—the Tribunal having determined the questions of property and protection against the United States—it may be allowed. I protest against any interpretation of the treaty which assumes that other nations will refuse to give their support to any regulations except such as are based upon a mere *compromise*, as)etween Great Britain and the United States, which leaves this race of inimals unprotected against destruction.

In view of the diplomatic correspondence which has been placed in our hands, there is ground for surprise at the earnestness with which it is contended that other nations could not be expected to assent to regulations that would suppress pelagic sealing, and that this Tribunal, when considering the subject of regulations applicable to the peoples of the United States and Great Britain, should permit the inquiry as to what regulations are in fact necessary to be controlled by conjecture as to what might be agreeable to other nations than those who made the Treaty. From that correspondence (some of which is given in the margin *), it will distinctly appear that Lord Salisbury proposed

---

* What is now the seventh article of the Treaty was proposed by President Harrison as early as June 25, 1891. (U. S. Case, Vol. I, App., 319.)

It having been proposed that the two Governments should sign the text of the seven articles to be inserted in the Arbitration Agreement, and of the Joint Commission Article, as settled in the diplomatic correspondence, in order to record the

to sign the articles which the two Governments agreed should be inserted in the Arbitration Agreement, with a reservation that the Regulations would not become obligatory on Great Britain and the United States "until they have been accepted by the other maritime powers." President Harrison refused, through Mr. Blaine, to permit any such reservation. Lord Salisbury, subsequently, stated that his progress made in the negotiations, Sir Julian Pauncefote wrote to Mr. Blaine, under date of November 23, 1891, expressing the assent of Lord Salisbury to that course. But for the purposes of obviating any doubts that might arise as to the meaning of Article VII, Sir Julian said, in that letter:

"His lordship understands, first, that the necessity of any regulations is left to the Arbitrators, as well as the nature of those regulations, if the necessity is in their judgment proved; secondly, that the regulations will not become obligatory on Great Britain and the United States until they have been accepted by the other maritime powers. Otherwise, as his lordship observes, the two Governments would be simply handing over to others the right of exterminating the seals.

"I have no doubt that you will have no difficulty in concurring in the above reservations, and, subject thereto, I shall be prepared to sign the articles as proposed."

To this letter Mr. Blaine, November 27, 1891, replied:

"You inform me now that Lord Salisbury asks to make two reservations in the sixth article. His first reservation is that 'the necessity of any regulations is left to the arbitrators, as well as the matter of those regulations if the necessity is in their judgment proved.'

"What reason has Lord Salisbury for altering the text of the article to which he had agreed? It is to be presumed that if regulations are needed they will be made, if they are not needed the arbitrators will not make them. The agreement leaves the arbitrators free upon that point. The first reservation, therefore, has no special meaning.

"The second reservation which Lord Salisbury makes is that ·the regulations shall not become obligatory on Great Britain and the United States until they shall have been accepted by the other maritime powers.' Does Lord Salisbury mean that the United States and Great Britain shall refrain from taking seals until every maritime power joins in the regulations, or does he mean that sealing shall be resumed the 1st of May next, and that we shall proceed as before the arbitration until the regulations have been accepted by the other 'maritime powers?'

"'Maritime powers' may mean one thing or another. Lord Salisbury did not say the *principal* maritime powers. France, Spain, Portugal, Italy, Austria, Turkey, Russia, Germany, Sweden, Holland, Belgium, are all maritime powers in the sense that they maintain a navy, great or small. In like manner Brazil, the Argentine Confederation, Chile, Peru, Mexico, and Japan are maritime powers. It would require a long time, three years at least, to get the assent of all these powers. Mr. Bayard, on the 19th of August, 1887, addressed Great Britain, Germany, France, Russia, Sweden and Norway, and Japan with a view to securing some regulations in regard to the

Government would retain the right of raising the point suggested "when the question of framing the regulations came before the Arbitrators." He wished it understood that the Arbitrators would have full discretion in the matter, and might attach " such conditions to the regulations as they may *a priori* judge to be necessary and just to the two powers, in view of the difficulty pointed out." But to this suggestion

seals in Bering Sea. France, Japan, and Russia replied with languid indifference; Great Britain never replied in writing; Germany did not reply at all; Sweden and Norway said the matter was of no interest to them. Thus it will be again. Such a proposition will postpone the matter indefinitely.

" The President regards Lord Salisbury's second reservation, therefore, as a material change in the terms of the arbitration agreed upon by this Government; and he instructs me to say that he does not feel willing to take it into consideration. He adheres to every point of agreement which has been made between the two powers, according to the text which you furnished. He will regret if Lord Salisbury shall insist on a substantially new agreement. He sees no objection to submitting the agreement to the principal maritime powers for their assent, but he can not agree that Great Britain and the United States shall make their adjustment dependent on the action of third parties who have no direct interest in the seal fisheries, or that the settlement shall be postponed until those third parties see fit to act."

Sir Julian Pauncefote, December 1, 1891, in acknowledgment of Mr. Blaine's letter, said:

" As regards the first reservation, Lord Salisbury observes that the statement contained in your note that the clause leaves the arbitrators free to decide whether regulations are needed or not, assures the same end as the proposed reservation, which therefore becomes unnecessary and may be put aside.

" With respect to the second reservation, his lordship states that it was not the intention of Her Majesty's Government to defer putting into practical execution any regulations which the arbitrators may prescribe. Its object is to prevent the fur-seal fishery in Bering Sea from being placed at the mercy of some third power. There is nothing to prevent such third power (Russia, for instance, as the most neighboring nation), if unpledged, from stepping in and securing the fishery at the very seasons and in the very places which may be closed to the sealers of Great Britain and the United States by the regulations.

" Great circumspection is called for in this direction, as British and American sealers might recover their freedom and evade all regulations by simply hoisting the flag of a nonadhering power.

" How is this difficulty to be met ? Lord Salisbury suggests that if, after the lapse of one year from the date of the decree of regulations, it shall appear to either Government that serious injury is occasioned to the fishery from the causes above mentioned, the Government complaining may give notice of the suspension of the regulations during the ensuing year, and in such case the regulations shall be suspended until arrangements are made to remedy the complaint.

" Lord Salisbury further proposes that, in case of any dispute arising between the

11492——14

President Harrison refused his assent, and expressly denied the right of the British Government to appeal to the Arbitrators to decide any point not embraced in the articles of Arbitration. Mr. Blaine, speaking for the President, announced his willingness to sign the articles of agreement "without any reservation whatever." And the representative of Great Britain at Washington, by the direction of Lord Salis-

two Governments as to the gravity of the injury caused to the fishery or as to any other fact, the question in controversy shall be referred for decision to a British and an American admiral, who, if they should be unable to agree, may select an umpire.

"Lord Salisbury desires me to ascertain whether some provision of the above nature would not meet the views of your Government."

Mr. Blaine, under date of December 2, 1891, in reply:

"The President is unable to see the danger which Lord Salisbury apprehends of a third nation engaging in taking seals regardless of the agreement between Great Britain and the United States. The dispute between the two nations has now been in progress for more than five years. During all this time, while Great Britain was maintaining that the Bering Sea was open to all comers at any time as of right, not another European nation has engaged in sealing.

"A German vessel once made its appearance in Bering Sea, but did not return, being satisfied, I suppose, that at the great distance they have to sail, the Germans could not successfully engage in sealing. Russia, whose interference Lord Salisbury seems to specially apprehend, will not dissent from the agreement, because such dissent would put to hazard her own sealing property in the Bering Sea. On the contrary, we may confidently look to Russia to sustain and strengthen whatever agreement Great Britain and the United States may conjointly ordain.

"It is the judgment of the President, therefore, that the apprehension of Lord Salisbury is not well grounded. He believes that, however the arbitration between Great Britain and the United States may terminate, it will be wise for the two nations to unite in a note to the principal powers of Europe, advising them in full of what has been done and confidently asking their approval. He does not believe that, with full explanation, any attempt will be made to disturb the agreement. If, contrary to his firm belief, the agreement shall be disturbed by the interference of a third power, Great Britain and the United States can act conjointly, and they can then far better agree upon what measure may be necessary to prevent the destruction of the seals than they can at this time.

"The President hopes that the arbitration between Great Britain and the United States will be allowed to proceed on the agreement regularly and promptly. It is of great consequence to both nations that the dispute be ended, and that no delay be caused by introducing new elements into the agreement to which both nations have given their consent."

Sir Julian Pauncefote, December 8, 1891:

"The Marquis of Salisbury, to whom I telegraphed the contents of your letter of the 2d instant on the subject of the sixth article of the proposed Bering Sea Arbitration agreement, is under the impression that the President has not rightly under-

bury, signed them, distinctly stating that they were signed *as proposed in Mr. Blaine's note*, that is, " *without any reservation whatever*." And, now, it is contended that while this Tribunal may not make the adhesion of other maritime powers to our Regulations a condition precedent to their being obligatory upon the United States and Great Britain, it may, nevertheless, properly refuse to prescribe regulations that will

------

stood his lordship's apprehension with reference to the regulations to be made by the Arbitrators under that article. His fear is not that the other powers will reject the regulations, but that they will refuse to allow the arrest by British and American cruisers of ships under their flag which may engage in the fur seal fishery in violation of the regulations. Such refusal is highly probable in view of the jealousy which exists as to the right of search on the high seas, and the consequence must inevitably be that during the close season sealing will go on under other flags.

"It can not be the intention of the two Governments, in signing the proposed agreement, to arrive at such a result.

"I do not understand you to dispute that should such a state of things arise the agreement must collapse, as the two Governments could not be expected to enforce on their respective national regulations which are violated under foreign flags to the serious injury of the fishery.

"I hope, therefore, that on further consideration the President will recognize the importance of arriving at some understanding of the kind suggested in my note of the 1st instant."

Mr. Blaine, December 10, 1891, in reply:

"In reply to your note of the 8th instant I have the following observations to make:

"First. Ever since the Bering Sea question has been in dispute (now nearly six years) not one ship from France or Germany has ever engaged in sealing. This affords a strong presumption that none will engage in it in the future.

"A still stronger ground against their taking part is that they can not afford it. From France or Germany to Bering Sea by the sailing line is nearly 20,000 miles, and they would have to make the voyage with a larger ship than can be profitably employed in sealing. They would have to start from home the winter preceding the sealing season, and risk an unusually hazardous voyage. When they reach the fishing grounds they have no territory to which they could resort for any purpose.

"Third. If we wait until we get France to agree that her ships shall be searched by American or British cruisers we will wait until the last seal is taken in Bering Sea.

"Thus much for France and Germany. Other European countries have the same disabilities. Russia, cited by Lord Salisbury as likely to embarrass the United States and England by interference, I should regard as an ally and not an enemy. Nor is it probable that any American country will loan its flag to vessels engaged in violating the Bering Sea regulations.

"To stop the arbitration a whole month on a question of this character promises

suppress or materially diminish pelagic sealing, however necessary such regulations may be for the protection and preservation of this race of animals, if, in view of all the probabilities of the situation we conjecture—it can be nothing more than conjecture—that other nations will not approve them. This would enable Great Britain to accomplish precisely what it could have accomplished had it been permitted to sign the Treaty with a reservation of authority for the Arbitrators to make the assent of the maritime powers a condition of our regulations,

---

ill for its success. Some other less important question even than this, if it can be found, may probably be started. The effect can only be to exhaust the time allotted for arbitration. We must act mutually on what is probable, not on what is remotely possible.

"The President suggests again that the proper mode of proceeding is for regulations to be agreed upon between the United States and Great Britain and then submitted to the principal maritime powers. That is an intelligent and intelligible process. To stop now to consider the regulations for outside nations is to indefinitely postpone the whole question. The President, therefore, adheres to his ground first announced, that we must have the arbitration as already agreed to. He suggests to Lord Salisbury that any other process might make the arbitration impracticable within the time specified."

Sir Julian Pauncefote, under date of December 11, 1891:

"I have the honor to inform you that I telegraphed to the Marquis of Salisbury the substance of your note of yesterday respecting the sixth article of the proposed Bering Sea arbitration agreement, and that I have received a reply from his lordship to the following effect: In view of the strong opinion of the President, reiterated in your note of yesterday, that the danger apprehended by Lord Sailsbury, and explained in my note of the 8th instant, is too remote to justify the delay which might be incurred by guarding against it now, his lordship will yield to the President's appeal and not press for further discussion at this stage.

"Her Majesty's Government of course retain the right of raising the point when the question of framing the regulations comes before the arbitrators, and it is understood that the latter will have full discretion in the matter, and may attach such conditions to the regulations as they may a priori judge to be necessary and just to the two powers in view of the difficulty pointed out.

"With the above observations Lord Salisbury has authorized me to sign the text of the seven articles and of the joint commission article referred to in my note of the 23d ultimo, and it will give me much pleasure to wait upon you at the State Department for that purpose at any time you may appoint."

Mr. Blaine, December 14, 1891, in reply:

"I have the honor to advise you that I submitted your note of the 11th instant to the President. After mature deliberation he has instructed me to say that he objects to Lord Salisbury's making any reservation at all, and that he cannot yield to him the right to appeal to the arbitrators to decide any point not embraced in the articles of arbitration. The President does not admit that Lord Salisbury can reserve

whether self-executing or not, becoming obligatory upon Great Britain and the United States. I can not believe that this Tribunal will proceed upon any such ground as that now suggested by the Counsel for Great Britain.

During the argument much was said about the mode in which the business of taking fur seals on the Pribilof Islands had been conducted by the licensees of the United States. It was said then, and the sug-

the right in any way to affect the decision of the arbitrators. We understand that the arbitration is to proceed on the seven points which are contained in the articles which you and I certify were the very points agreed upon by the two Governments.

"For Lord Salisbury to claim the right to submit this new point to the Arbitrators is to entirely change the arbitration. The President might, in like manner, submit several questions to the Arbitrators, and thus enlarge the subject to such an extent that it would not be the same arbitration to which we have agreed. The President claims the right to have the seven points arbitrated, and respectfully insists that Lord Salisbury shall not change their meaning in any particular. The matters to be arbitrated must be distinctly understood before the Arbitrators are chosen. And after an arbitration is agreed to, neither of the parties can enlarge or contract its scope.

"I am prepared now, as I have been heretofore, to sign the articles of agreement without any reservation whatever, and for that purpose I shall be glad to have you call at the State Department on Wednesday the 16th instant, at 11 o'clock a. m."

Sir Julian Pauncefote, December 17, 1891:

"I have the honor to inform you that I conveyed to the Marquis of Salisbury, by telegram, the substance of your note of the 14th instant, respecting the sixth article of the proposed Bering Sea Arbitration agreement, and that I have received a reply from his lordship in the following sense:

"Lord Salisbury is afraid that, owing to the difficulties incident to telegraphic communications, he has been imperfectly understood by the President. He consented, at the President's request, to defer for the present all further discussion as to what course the two Governments should follow in the event of the regulations prescribed by the Arbitrators being evaded by a change of flag. It was necessary that in doing so he should guard himself against the supposition that by such consent he had narrowed the rights of the contending parties or of the Arbitrators under the agreement.

"But in the communication which was embodied in my note of the 11th instant, his lordship made no reservation, as the President seems to think, nor was any such word used. A reservation would not be valid unless assented to by the other side, and no such assent was asked for. Lord Salisbury entirely agrees with the President in his objection to any point being submitted to the Arbitrators which is not embraced in the agreement and, in conclusion, his lordship authorizes me to sign the articles of the arbitration agreement, as proposed at the close of your note under reply, whenever you may be willing to do so." (U. S. Case, vol. 1, App. 339 to 345).

gestion has been repeated here, that the present depleted condition of this race is due largely, if not principally, to unreasonably large drafts made, for many years past, upon *male* seals while they were on the breeding grounds, whereby vast numbers of that sex, competent for service, and which ought to have been preserved for purposes of reproduction, have been killed. This suggestion is unsupported by any fair view of the evidence. What has been said on that subject by some witnesses, notably by Prof. Elliott, is in gross exaggeration of the facts. No complaint can be justly made of the rules that have been prescribed by the United States in regulation of the taking of these seals on the islands. And it must be conceded that those rules, if observed, do not admit of the taking of an undue proportion of males. The killing of female seals on the islands is absolutely prohibited. While in particular years there was mismanagement to some extent on the islands, nothing done or omitted to be done there, at any time within the past fifteen or twenty years, accounts for the recent and extraordinary diminution in the number of seals frequenting those islands during the breeding season. There is, in my judgment, no possible escape from the conclusion that such diminution is the direct result of pelagic sealing.

What has or has not been done or omitted on the islands, or what may hereafter be done there, can not be made an element in the present inquiry. This Tribunal has no authority to deal with the management of the seals while at their breeding grounds on the islands of St. Paul and St. George, any more than with the mode of taking them within the territorial waters of Canada. The United States would never have submitted to this or to any other Tribunal a question involving its complete control over these seals while on its islands or within its territorial waters. It would not brook any interference with the authority which appertains to it within its own territorial limits. Proper respect for the Government of that nation compels us to assume that it has the desire to correct, and will correct, any abuses that have existed, or that may hereafter exist, in the conduct of the fur seal industry on the Pribilof Islands; just as we must assume, that the Governments of Great Britain and of Canada, after this Tribunal has made its award, will properly control the taking of seals within territorial waters.

The two nations here represented took care to exclude from the consideration of this Tribunal all matters affecting their sovereign authority within jurisdictional limits, and therefore restricted inquiry touching the proper protection and preservation of these seals "to concurrent regulations outside the jurisdictional limits of the respective Government." The irrelevancy, when considering the subject of regulations, of any inquiry as to what has been done or omitted to be done on the islands, is apparent in view of one fact clearly established by the evidence, namely: That pelagic sealing to any material extent—that is, to such extent as will be profitable to sealers—will speedily exterminate this race, *even if the taking of seals is entirely suspended on the islands,* and the United States should expend time and money in protecting the seals during the breeding season, in order simply that pelagic sealers may not be disturbed in their occupation of killing suckling females while in the ocean in search of food for the sustenance of themselves and their young, or in their business of capturing and cutting open the bodies of mother seals, heavy with young, and throwing the unborn pups into the ocean.

Our manifest duty is to inquire what, under the evidence, is the effect of pelagic sealing, in and of itself; and, according to the result of that inquiry and without any reference whatever to what has occurred or may occur on the islands in respect of this race of animals, and without regard to the special interests either of the United States or of pelagic sealers, we should establish, or by our award impose upon the two nations here represented the duty of establishing, such regulations, "outside the jurisdictional limits of the respective Governments" as are necessary for the proper protection and preservation of this herd of fur seals. Anything less from this Tribunal will shake the confidence of the world in the efficacy of arbitration as a means of composing differences between nations in respect to matters of great moment and interest.

I now come to the important practical question as to what regulations, in view of all the evidence, are necessary for the proper protection and preservation of this herd of seals.

We have seen that these seals begin to leave the islands in September, and by November substantially all of them are in the North Pacific Ocean, south of the Aleutian Islands. During December they may be found off the coasts of the United States, north of the 35th degree of north latitude. In January they turn their faces northward, and move, generally in small schools or bands, along, but some distance from, the coasts of the United States and British Columbia. Those in advance go through the passes of the Aleutian Islands, on their way back to the Pribilof Islands, early in June. They are moving through those passes during the whole of that month. By the 1st or 10th of July, the entire herd has left the North Pacific and reassembled at their breeding grounds on the islands of St. Paul and St. George. As soon as the mother seals reach the islands, or within a very few days thereafter, they give birth to their pups, and take position with the bulls by whom they have been appropriated. According to the evidence, the pups require sustenance from their mothers for about eight or ten weeks. During that period, say, during July and August, the mother seals, in vast numbers, go out into the sea, in every direction, often to the distance of 100 and 150 miles, in quest of food to sustain themselves and their young. Seals have been taken in the North Pacific in January, February, and March, but not to any great extent. The opportunity for taking them improves as the season advances. The last half of April and the months of May and June are favorable for pelagic sealing, particularly the two months last named. In Bering Sea the months of July and August are also very favorable for seal hunting. While seals may be taken in that sea during September, it is not, as a general rule, profitable to pursue the business there after August, or, at any rate, after the middle of September. The principal mischiefs from pelagic sealing have come from the killing of the seals in May and June, in the North Pacific, while the herd is moving northward to their land home, and from the killing in July and August, in Bering Sea, of breeding females which have left their pups on the islands for a time and gone into the sea in search of food.

Our attention has been called to various schemes of regulations. In 1888 Mr. Bayard proposed a closed season for the period between April 15 and November 1 of every year, during which the citizens or subjects of the United States and Great Britain should be prevented from killing fur-seals with firearms or other destructive weapons, "north of 50° of north latitude, and between 160° of longitude west and 170° of longitude east of Greenwich." But a much better scheme was agreed upon, provisionally, as a basis of negotiations, at the conference subsequently held, in London, April 16, 1888, between the representatives of the United States, Great Britain, and Russia. By that scheme, if it had been put into operation, a closed season, extending from April 15 to November 1 would have been established, during which no seals could be killed in "*the sea between America and Russia, north of the 17° of latitude.*" But this scheme failed of adoption because of the intervention and protest of Canada, which was effectual to prevent Lord Salisbury from adhering to it as a final settlement of the controversy. At a later stage of the negotiations between the United States and Great Britain Mr. Blaine expressed the willingness of the United States to accept a settlement upon the basis of a zone of 20 marine leagues, within which no ship should hover around the islands of St. Paul and St. George from the 15th of May to the 15th of October of each year. *U. S. Case, Vol. I, App.*, 284.

It is said that the scheme of regulations now proposed by the United States is far more stringent than that proposed by Mr. Bayard and Mr. Blaine, on behalf of the United States. That is true. But it should be remembered that at the time the schemes of Mr. Bayard and Mr. Blaine were proposed, the facts of seal life were not so well known as now, so full have been the recent investigations made by the two Governments, with direct reference to the present controversy, and for the purpose of ascertaining what was required in order to preserve this race of animals from extermination. In view of the fuller knowledge all now have on the subject, no one would be so wanting in frankness as to say that this race of useful animals could possibly survive pelagic sealing under the scheme proposed by Mr. Bayard, or under that proposed by Mr. Blaine. While the British Government has contrasted, to the disadvantage of the United States, the scheme now proposed by the latter, with the propositions made by Mr. Bayard and Mr. Blaine, the United States Government contrasts, to the disadvantage of Great Britain, the scheme now proposed by Her Britannic Majesty with that acceded to, provisionally, by Lord Salisbury in 1888. I am of opinion that the determination of the question before us should not depend upon considerations of this kind. It is of no consequence, in the present inquiry, that the respective governments were willing, at one time, to accept regulations different from those now proposed. We must determine the question of regulations in the light of the facts now disclosed. If we prescribe regulations that are inadequate, we will not stand acquitted in our own consciences, or before the world, by the circumstance that that which is done may have been approved by the two Governments or either of them at sometime in the past, when the facts were not fully developed.

At a former meeting of this Tribunal I presented a scheme of regulations which, in the judgment of my colleague, Senator Morgan, and myself, are adequate for the proper protection and preservation of these seals outside the jurisdictional limits of the respective Governments. That scheme provides that no citizen or subject of either country should

kill, capture, or pursue these fur seals anywhere in the waters of
Bering Sea or of the North Pacific Ocean, outside the jurisdictional
limits of the respective governments, north of the 35° of north latitude (south of which this herd have never been known to go in its
migrations) and east of the 180° of longitude from Greenwich. It also
provides that offending vessels may be seized by the naval or duly-
commissioned officers of either Government, and handed over, as soon
as practicable, to the authorities of the nation to which they respectively belong, to be dealt with by that nation—the witnesses and proof
necessary to establish the offense or to disprove the same being also
sent with the vessel seized. It further provides that every person
guilty of violating these regulations should, for each offense, be fined
not less than $200 nor more than $1,000, or imprisoned not more than
six months, or both; such vessels, their tackle, apparel, furniture, and
cargo to be forfeited and condemned.

Only regulations of this character, which prohibit pelagic sealing
altogether, in all the waters traversed by these seals, will, in my
judgment, make the preservation of this race of animals *absolutely
certain*. Of course, a closed season, covering all of such waters and all
the months of the year when the weather admits of pelagic sealing,
will give, practically, the same security as regulations of a prohibitory
character covering the whole year.

(Mr. Justice Harlan here entered upon an examination of the evidence in detail for
the purpose of showing that he had not overstated the effect of pelagic sealing upon
the Pribilof herd of seals. He read, at length, from the depositions, reports, tables
of figures, etc., introduced by the respective Governments, to show the disastrous
results of pelagic sealing. It is unnecessary to encumber this opinion with the
details of the evidence to which he referred.

When the subject of Regulations was under consideration in the Conference, Mr.
Justice Harlan offered the following resolution, as embodying the views of Senator
Morgan and himself on the question of the competency of the Tribunal:

"*Resolved*, That the purpose of Article VII of the Treaty is to secure in any and
all events, the proper protection and preservation of the herd of seals frequenting
the Pribilof Islands; and in the framing of Regulations, under the Treaty, no extent of pelagic sealing should be allowed which will seriously endanger the accomplishment of that end."

He subsequently presented, with the concurrence of Senator Morgan, the following
motion:

"This Tribunal has power, and it is its duty, under the Treaty, to prescribe such
concurrent Regulations, covering the waters, outside the jurisdictional limits of the
two countries, of both Bering Sea and the North Pacific Ocean, traversed by the fur
seals in, or habitually resorting to, Bering Sea, as may be found necessary for the
proper protection and preservation of such seals, even if such Regulations, when

sanctioned by the legislation of the two Governments, should, by reason of their express provisions, or by their practical operation, result in preventing the hunting and taking of these seals during the seasons when the condition of said waters admits of fur seals being taken by pelagic sealers.")

The scheme proposed by myself may be objected to upon the ground that the regulations which it embodies are self-executing, whereas it is argued this Tribunal has only the power to *recommend* the adoption of regulations, leaving it to the two Governments to enforce them by legislation. I do not assent to this view of the competency of this Tribunal. The two Governments contemplated, and we are so informed by the Treaty, that the result of our proceedings should be considered "as a full, perfect, and final settlement of all the questions referred to the Arbitrators." (Article XIV.) Our final decision or award, when made, will become, in legal effect, a part of the Treaty, as much so as if it was embodied in it. But the Treaty, when thus perfected, will not be a full, perfect, and final settlement of the controversy, if the decision or award is so framed as to amount to nothing practically until the two nations shall have had further negotiations and agreed upon such additional concurrent legislation as will be required in order that the award shall become operative for the proper protection and preservation of this race. I find nothing in the Treaty looking to such a condition of things as the result of our proceedings. Under the Constitution of the United States, a treaty, made pursuant to that instrument, and duly ratified, becomes "the supreme law of the land," without the aid of legislation, except that legislation will be required where the treaty provides for the payment of money. This exception arises from the provision in that Constitution that "no money shall be drawn from the Treasury but in consequence of appropriations made by law." Of course, if, under the British Constitution, regulations established by the Tribunal, providing for the seizure of vessels and the punishment of persons offending against such regulations, can not be made applicable to British vessels and British subjects, without legislative sanction, we must rely upon the good faith of the two Governments interested to give effect to our decision by appropriate enactments. But I do not understand the British Constitution to require legislative approval of the regulations prescribed by the Tribunal before they can become operative against British vessels and British subjects. We have been invested by the two Governments with full power, as Senator Morgan has well said, to write into the Treaty of February 29, 1892, such regulations as we find necessary and such as will be immediately effectual for the proper protection and preservation of these fur seals when they are outside the jurisdictional limits of the respective nations. The engagement of the two Governments with respect to regulations was that they would coöperate in securing the adhesion of other powers "to such Regulations" *as this Tribunal* should prescribe. This could have referred only to regulations which by their own force, without further action of the two Governments, would properly protect and preserve this race of animals. The adhesion of other nations to Regulations which did not, in themselves, secure the protection and preservation of this race, would be of no value.

One of the schemes before us is that proposed by Sir John Thompson. I mean no disrespect to its distinguished author, whose good faith is not questioned, when I say that, in view of all the evidence, that scheme may be fairly entitled "A plan for the certain and speedy extermination of the Pribilof herd of fur seals." Under regulations such as are embodied in that plan all the seals, including gravid females, would be exposed to attack by pelagic sealers during the months of May and June in the North Pacific Ocean; and during July, August, and September in Bering Sea, outside of a zone of thirty miles around the Pribilof Islands, nursing female seals could be slaughtered in vast numbers. The use of rifles and nets are prohibited by this scheme, while it saves to pelagic hunters the use of the destructive shotgun now in general use by them. A prohibition of rifles is of no value whatever if the shotgun is allowed. Nor is it of the slightest consequence that this scheme prohibits the killing of seals in *Bering Sea* (east of the line of demarcation adopted in the Treaty of 1867 between Russia and the United States) *before* the 1st of July and *after* October 1 in each year; for, the seals can not be found in Bering Sea in any numbers worth mentioning after October 1 and before July 1. I object to this scheme upon the further ground that it allows either Government upon notice to put an end to our regulations after a named time. Whatever this Tribunal may do in this matter, let that which is done be final and permanent, subject only to such modifications or change of policy as the two governments, in their wisdom, may mutually agree to make. I see no objection to a reëxamination from time to time, by the two governments, of the subject of regulations but there are many reasons against a reservation to each government of the right to set aside the regulations after the lapse of any given time. This whole subject has been a source of disturbance between these nations for so long a period that the controversy should be now settled and forever put aside. That is what these countries had in view when the Treaty of 1892 was concluded. If we put it in the power of each Government, after a named date, to set aside our regulations, the decision we make will not be a "full, perfect, and final settlement" of these questions. The wisdom and patriotism of the two great nations here represented is a sufficient guarantee that all will be done, by mutual agreement, which further investigation and developments show to be necessary.

Without further elaboration, I must say that the scheme of Sir John Thompson can not be approved if we accept, as justified by.the evidence, what Sir Richard Webster said in his very able argument, when he declared that "no gravid female ought to be killed, so far as it can be reasonably avoided," and that "no nursing female upon whose life that of the pup depends ought to be slaughtered or injured in any way." The same eminent counsel also frankly observed: "It seems to me that upon the simple principle that has governed and controlled the game laws of all civilized people, the killing of a female which is about to bring forth its young, or upon whose life the lives of the young are dependent, is a matter which no Tribunal would indorse by recommendation, and that, therefore, the contrary of that would recommend itself to the mind of this Tribunal."

(After the general discussion in conference upon the subject of regulations was concluded—the Arbitrators named by the Governments of Great Britain and the United States having alone participated in that discussion—the matter was taken under advisement by the Arbitrators from France, Italy, and Norway, and they submitted a scheme of regulations for the consideration of the Tribunal. A copy of that scheme is appended to this opinion, and it became the subject of discussion among the Arbitrators.)

I confess some disappointment in finding that the majority of the Tribunal do not favor regulations which, in terms or by their necessary operation, will put an end to all pelagic sealing in the waters traversed by these fur seals. It is very much to be feared that the theory of compromise has had more weight than, as I submit, it ought to have upon the determination of the pending question. A compromise, between conflicting views, which leaves the preservation of this race *in doubt*, as far as their preservation depends upon regulations, ought not be favored. It seems to me that the supreme object of regulations, the protection and preservation of this race of animals, could not be *certainly* accomplished except by regulations of the kind proposed by me, with the concurrence of Senator Morgan.

But, as our views are not accepted by the Tribunal, the question is presented whether the report made by Baron de Courcel, Marquis Visconti-Venosta and His Excellency M. Gram, shall receive our support. Upon mature reflection, we have concluded to vote in favor of the scheme of regulations recommended by those Arbitrators, although it contains some provisions not acceptable to us. It establishes a zone of 60 miles around the Pribilof Islands, inclusive of territorial waters, within which the taking of seals at any time by the citizens or subjects of either country is to be prohibited. It establishes a closed season, between April 15 and July 31, both inclusive, for all the waters, both of the North Pacific Ocean and of Bering Sea, north of the thirty-fifth degree of north latitude. It allows only sailing vessels to take part in fur seal fishing operations. It forbids the use of nets, firearms, and explosives in fur seal fishing, with the exception of the shotgun in the North Pacific Ocean prior to April 15. While it permits a new examination, by the two Governments, every five years, of the proposed regulations, to ascertain whether there is any occasion to modify them, the regulations now proposed, if adopted, are to remain in force until they shall have been, in whole or in part, abolished or modified by "common agreement" between the two nations. The features of this scheme that are chiefly objectionable are these: (1) It permits pelagic sealing with shotguns, in the North Pacific Ocean, prior to April 15; (2) it allows pelagic sealing, after July 31, in Bering Sea, with harpoons and spears. Notwithstanding these defects in the scheme, there is a *hope*, though not a certainty, that this race may under the regulations so proposed, escape destruction at the hands of pelagic sealers. For that reason, and in the interest of peace between the two nations, Senator Morgan and myself have determined to give our votes in support of this scheme, as the best solution likely to be obtained from the Tribunal of the question of regulations.

(Protocol LIV will show the votes in Conference upon the several resolutions, motions, and plans presented by Arbitrators, relating to regulations, and also votes upon different amendments made in the scheme of Regulations proposed by Baron de Courcel, Marquis Visconti-Venosta and His Excellency M. Gram.)

REGULATIONS PROPOSED BY MR. JUSTICE HARLAN, CONCURRED IN BY SENATOR MORGAN.

ARTICLE 1. No citizen or subject of the United States or Great Britain shall in any manner kill, capture, or pursue anywhere upon the seas, within the limits and boundaries next hereinafter prescribed for the operation of this regulation, any of the animals commonly called fur seals.

ART. 2. The foregoing regulation shall apply to and extend over all those waters, outside the jurisdictional limits of the above-mentioned nations, of the North Pacific Ocean and Bering Sea which are North of the thirty-fifth parallel of north latitude and east of the one hundred and eightieth meridian of longitude from Greenwich.

ART. 3. Every vessel or person offending against these regulations may be seized and detained by the naval or duly commissioned officers of either the United States or Great Britain, but they shall be handed over as soon as practicable to the authorities of the nation to which they respectively belong, who alone shall have jurisdiction to try the offense and impose penalties for the same. The witnesses and proof necessary to establish the offense or to disprove the same found on the vessel shall also be sent with them.

ART. 4. Every person guilty of violating these regulations shall, for each offense, be fined not less than $200 nor more than $1,000, or imprisoned not more than six months, or both; and vessels, their tackle, apparel, furniture, and cargo, found engaged in violating these regulations shall be forfeited and condemned.

REGULATIONS PROPOSED BY SIR JOHN THOMPSON.

ARTICLE 1. No sealing except by licenses which are to be issued at two United States and two Canadian ports on the Pacific coast.

These licenses to be granted only to sailing vessels, and not to be granted earlier than a date that would correspond with the 1st of May in the latitude of Victoria, British Columbia.

ART. 2. Each vessel carrying such license to use a distinctive flag and to keep a record in the official log of the number of seals killed or wounded, and the locality in which the hunting takes place, from day to day; all such entries to be filed with the collectors of customs on the return of the vessels.

ART. 3. The use of rifles and nets in seal fishing is prohibited.

ART. 4. The killing of seals to be prohibited within a zone of 30 miles from the Pribylov Islands, and within a zone of 10 miles around the Aleutian Islands.

ART. 5. The killing of seals to be prohibited in Bering Sea (east of the line of demarcation adopted in the treaty of cession from Russia to the United States) before the 1st of July and after the 1st of October in each year.

ART. 6. The foregoing regulations shall be brought into force from and after a day to be agreed upon by Great Britain and the United States, and shall continue in operation for ten years from the above day; and, unless Great Britain or the United States shall, twelve months before the expiration of the said period of ten years, give notice of intention to terminate their operation, shall continue in force one year longer, and so on from year to year.

REGULATIONS PROPOSED BY BARON DE COURCEL, MARQUIS VISCONTI-VENOSTA, AND HIS EXCELLENCY M. GRAM.

ARTICLE 1. The Governments of the United States and of Great Britain shall forbid their citizens and subjects respectively to kill, capture, or pursue at any time and in any manner whatever, the animals commonly called fur seals, within a zone of 60 miles around the Pribylov Islands, inclusive of the territorial waters.

The miles mentioned in the preceding paragraph are geographical miles, of 60 to a degree of latitude.

ART. 2. The two Governments shall forbid their citizens and subjects respectively to kill, capture, or pursue, in any manner whatever, during the season extending each year from the 15th of April to the 31st of July, both inclusive, the fur seals on the high sea in the part of the Pacific Ocean, inclusive of the Bering Sea, which is situated to the north of the thirty-fifth degree of north latitude.

ART. 3. During the period of the time and in the waters in which the fur seal fishing is allowed only sailing vessels shall be permitted to carry on or take part in fur-seal fishing operations. They will, however, be at liberty to avail themselves of the use of canoes or small boats, propelled wholly by oars.

ART. 4. The sailing vessels authorized to fish for fur seals must be provided with a special license issued for that purpose by its Government and shall be required to carry a distinguishing flag to be prescribed by its Government.

ART. 5. The masters of the vessels engaged in fur seal fishing shall enter accurately in their official log book the date and place of each fur seal fishing operation, and also the number and sex of the seals captured, upon each day. These entries shall be communicated by each of the two Governments to the other at the end of each fishing season.

ART. 6. The use of nets, firearms, and explosives shall be forbidden in the fur seal fishing. This restriction shall not apply to shotguns when such fishing takes place outside of Bering Sea.

ART. 7. The two governments shall take measures to control the fitness of the men authorized to engage in fur seal fishing; these men shall have been proved fit to handle with sufficient skill the weapons by means of which this fishing may be carried on.

ART. 8. The regulations contained in the preceding articles shall not apply to Indians dwelling on the coasts of the territory of the United States or of Great Britain, and carrying on in their canoes, at a small distance from the coasts where they dwell, fur seal fishing.

ART. 9. The concurrent regulations hereby determined with a view to the protection and preservation of the fur seals shall remain in force until they have been, in whole or in part, abolished or modified by common agreement between the governments of the United States and of Great Britain.

The said concurrent regulations shall be submitted every five years to a new examination, so as to enable both interested governments to consider whether, in the light of past experience, there is occasion for any modification thereof.

FINAL DECISION.

Now we, the said Arbitrators, having impartially and carefully examined the said questions, do in like manner by this our award decide and determine the said questions in manner following, that is to say, we decide and determine as to the five points mentioned in Article VI, as to which our award is to embrace a distinct decision upon each of them:

As to the first of the said five points, we, the said Baron de Courcel, Mr. Justice Harlan, Lord Hannen, Sir John Thompson, Marquis Visconti Venosta, and Mr. Gregers Gram, being the majority of the said Arbitrators, do decide and determine as follows:

By the Ukase of 1821, Russia claimed jurisdiction in the sea now known as the Bering Sea, to the extent of 100 Italian miles from the coasts and islands belonging to her; but, in the course of the negotiations which led to the conclusion of the treaties of 1824 with the United States, and of 1825 with Great Britain, Russia admitted that her jurisdiction in the said sea should be restricted to the reach of cannon-shot from shore, and it appears that, from that time up to the time of the cession of Alaska to the United States, Russia never asserted in fact or exercised any exclusive jurisdiction in Bering Sea or any exclusive rights in the seal fisheries therein beyond the ordinary limits of territorial waters.

As to the second of the said five points, we, the said Baron de Courcel, Mr. Justice Harlan, Lord Hannen, Sir John Thompson, Marquis Visconti Venosta, and Mr. Gregers Gram, being a majority of the said Arbitrators, decide and determine that Great Britain did not recognize or concede any claim, upon the part of Russia, to exclusive jurisdiction as to the seal fisheries in Bering Sea, outside of ordinary territorial waters.

As to the third of the said five points, as to so much thereof as requires us to decide whether the body of water known as Bering Sea was included in the phrase "Pacific Ocean," as used in the treaty of 1825 between Great Britain and Russia, we, the said Arbitrators, do unanimously decide and determine that the body of water now known as the Bering Sea was included in the phrase "Pacific Ocean," as used in the said treaty.

And as to so much of the said third point as requires us to decide what rights, if any, in the Bering Sea were held and exclusively exercised by Russia after the said Treaty of 1825, we, the said Baron de Courcel, Mr. Justice Harlan, Lord Hannen, Sir John Thompson, Marquis Visconti Venosta and Mr. Gregers Gram, being a majority of the said Arbitrators, do decide and determine that no exclusive rights as to the seal fisheries therein were held or exercised by Russia outside of ordinary territorial waters after the Treaty of 1825.

As to the forth of the said five points, we, the said Arbitrators, do unanimously decide and determine that all the rights of Russia as to jurisdiction and as to the seal fisheries in Bering Sea, east of the water boundary, in the Treaty between the United States and Russia of the 30th of March, 1867, did pass unimpaired to the United States under the said Treaty.

As to the fifth of the said five points, we, the said Baron de Courcel, Lord Hannen, Sir John Thompson, Marquis Visconti Venosta, and Mr. Gregers Gram, being a majority of the said Arbitrators, do decide and determine that the United States has not any right of protection or property in the fur seals frequenting the islands of the United States in Bering Sea, when such seals are found outside the ordinary three-mile limit.

REGULATIONS PROPOSED BY BARON DE COURCEL, MARQUIS VISCONTI VENOSTA, AND HIS EXCELLENCY M. GRAM, AS AMENDED AND ADOPTED BY A MAJORITY OF THE TRIBUNAL.

ARTICLE 1.

The Government of the United States and of Great Britain shall forbid their citizens and subjects respectively to kill, capture, or pursue, at any time and in any manner whatever, the animals commonly called fur seals, within a zone of 60 miles around the Pribilov Islands, inclusive of the territorial waters.

The miles mentioned in the preceding paragraph are geographical miles, of 60 to a degree of latitude.

ARTICLE 2.

The two Governments shall forbid their citizens and subjects respectively to kill, capture, or pursue, in any manner whatever, during the season extending, each year, from the 1st of May to the 31st of July, both inclusive, the fur seals on the high sea, in the part of the Pacific Ocean, inclusive of the Bering Sea, which is situated to the north of the 35th degree of north latitude, and eastward of the 180th degree of longitude from Greenwich till it strikes the water boundary described in Article 1 of the Treaty of 1867 between the United States and Russia, and following that line up to Bering Straits.

ARTICLE 3.

During the period of time and in the waters in which the fur seal fishing is allowed, only sailing vessels shall be permitted to carry on or take part in fur seal fishing operations. They will however be at liberty to avail themselves of the use of such canoes or undecked boats, propelled by paddles, oars, or sails, as are in common use as fishing boats.

ARTICLE 4.

Each sailing vessel authorized to fish for fur seals must be provided with a special license issued for that purpose by its Government, and shall be required to carry a distinguishing flag to be prescribed by its Government.

ARTICLE 5.

The masters of the vessels engaged in fur seal fishing shall enter accurately in their official log book the date and place of each fur seal fishing operation, and also the number and sex of the seals captured upon each day. These entries shall be communicated by each of the two Governments to the other at the end of each fishing season.

ARTICLE 6.

The use of nets, firearms, and explosives shall be forbidden in the fur seal fishing. This restriction shall not apply to shotguns when such fishing takes place outside of Bering's Sea during the season when it may be lawfully carried on.

ARTICLE 7.

The two Governments shall take measures to control the fitness of the men authorized to engage in fur seal fishing; these men shall have been proved fit to handle with sufficient skill the weapons by means of which this fishing may be carried on.

ARTICLE 8.

The regulations contained in the preceding articles shall not apply to Indians dwelling on the coasts of the territory of the United States or of Great Britain, and carrying on fur seal fishing in canoes or undecked boats not transported by or used in connection with other vessels and propelled wholly by paddles, oars or sails, and manned by not more than five persons each in the way hitherto practiced by the Indians, provided such Indians are not in the employment of other persons, and provided that, when so hunting in canoes or undecked boats, they shall not hunt fur seals outside of territorial waters under contract for the delivery of the skins to any person.

This exemption shall not be construed to affect the municipal law of either country, nor shall it extend to the waters of Bering Sea or the waters of the Aleutian Passes.

Nothing herein contained is intended to interfere with the employment of Indians as hunters or otherwise in connection with fur sealing vessels as heretofore.

ARTICLE 9.

The concurrent regulations hereby determined with a view to the protection and preservation of the fur seals, shall remain in force until they have been, in whole or in part, abolished or modified by common agreement between the Governments of the United States and of Great Britain.

The said concurrent regulations shall be submitted every five years to a new examination, so as to enable both interested Governments to consider whether, in the light of past experience, there is occasion for any modification thereof.

DECLARATIONS MADE BY THE TRIBUNAL OF ARBITRATION AND REFERRED TO THE GOVERNMENTS OF THE UNITED STATES AND GREAT BRITAIN FOR THEIR CONSIDERATION.

I.

The Arbitrators declare that the concurrent regulations, as determined upon by the Tribunal of Arbitration, by virtue of Article VII of the treaty of the 29th of February 1892, being applicable to the high sea only, should, in their opinion, be supplemented by other regulations applicable within the limits of the sovereignty of each of the two powers interested and to be settled by their common agreement.

II.

In view of the critical condition to which it appears certain that the race of fur seals is now reduced in consequence of circumstances not fully known, the Arbitrators think fit to recommend both Governments to come to an understanding in order to prohibit any killing of fur seals, either on land or at sea, for a period of two or three years, or at least one year, subject to such exceptions as the two Governments might think proper to admit of.

Such a measure might be recurred to at occasional intervals if found beneficial.

III.

The Arbitrators declare moreover that, in their opinion, the carrying out of the regulations determined upon by the Tribunal of Arbitration, should be assured by a system of stipulations and measures to be enacted by the two powers, and that the Tribunal must, in consequence, leave it to the two powers to decide upon the means for giving effect to the regulations determined upon by it.

www.ingramcontent.com/pod-product-compliance
Lightning Source LLC
Chambersburg PA
CBHW030112030726
47498CB00007B/2347